# FORCE OF
# NATURE

021

# FORCE OF NATURE
# C.J. BOX

CORVUS

First published in the United States of America
in 2012 by Penguin.

This edition first published in Great Britain in 2012
by Corvus, an imprint of Atlantic Books Ltd.

9 8 7 6 5 4 3 2 1

A CIP catalogue record for this book is available from
the British Library.

Paperback ISBN: 978 0 85789 086 3
E-book ISBN: 978 0 85789 661 2

Printed and bound by CPI Group (UK) Ltd, Croydon, CR0 4YY

Corvus
An imprint of Atlantic Books Ltd
Ormond House
26-27 Boswell Street
London WC1N 3JZ

www.corvus-books.co.uk

*For Gordon Crawford, falconer*
*And Laurie, always . . .*

Turning and turning in the widening gyre
The falcon cannot hear the falconer;
Things fall apart; the centre cannot hold;
Mere anarchy is loosed upon the world,
The blood-dimmed tide is loosed, and everywhere
The ceremony of innocence is drowned;
The best lack all conviction, while the worst
Are full of passionate intensity.

—*William Butler Yeats, "The Second Coming"*

# PART ONE

*The essence of falconry is not what happens to
the quarry but what happens to the falconer.*

—Kenn Filkins, "Khan of the Sky"

# THE MORNING AFTER

HIS NAME WAS Dave Farkus, and he'd recently taken up fly-fishing as a way to meet girls. So far, it hadn't worked out very well.

It was late October, one of those wild fall days containing a fifty-five-degree swing from dawn to dusk, and Farkus stood mid-thigh in waders in the Twelve Sleep River that coursed through the town of Saddlestring, Wyoming. River cottonwoods were so drunk with color the leaves hurt his eyes.

Farkus was short and wiry, with muttonchop sideburns and a slack expression on his face. He'd parked his pickup under the bridge and waded out into the river at mid-morning just as a late-fall Trico hatch created clouds of insects that billowed like terrestrial clouds along the surface of the water. A few trout were rising for them, slurping them down, but he hadn't hooked one yet. Trico flies were not only tiny and hard to tie on his line, they were difficult to see on the water.

He was at wits' end since he'd relocated to the Twelve Sleep Valley from southern Wyoming.

He'd landed in Saddlestring with no job, and he didn't intend to look for one, except the damned natural-gas pipeline company was challenging his disability payments, claiming he'd never really been injured. And his ex-wife, Ardith, had contacted a lawyer about several missed alimony payments and was threatening to take him back to court.

FARKUS WAS intently aware of each car that sizzled by on the bridge over his shoulder. When he heard a car slow down to look at him, he made a long useless cast that, he hoped, looked practiced and elegant, as though he was Brad Pitt's double in the movie *A River Runs Through It*. He wondered how long it would be before a pretty doe-eyed twentysomething tourist would come down to the river and ask for a lesson. But he was starting to believe it would never happen.

He tied on a new fly—something puffy and white that he could see on the water—and felt the power of the current push against his legs.

That's when he heard, upriver, the distinctive hollow *pock* sound of a drift boat striking a rock.

He barely looked up, so intent was he on tying the nearly invisible thin tippet through the loop of his fly. Drift boats filled with fishermen were common on the river. There were several commercial guide operations in town, and it seemed like every other home in Saddle-string had a drift boat on a trailer parked in front of it. The river was shallow because it was late fall and water was at a premium, and it wasn't unusual for guides to miscalculate and hit a rock.

But when he heard a series of mishaps—*pock-pock-pock,* rock-rock-rock—he glanced up from his knot.

The white fiberglass drift boat was coming right at him, sidewise, bumping along the river rocks in a shallow current. No one was at the oars. In fact, no one seemed to be in the boat at all.

Farkus squinted and cursed. If the boat continued on its path it would hit him, maybe knock him right off his feet. Farkus couldn't swim, and if his waders filled with water and he was sucked into that deep pool under the bridge . . .

He uneasily shuffled a few steps back. The river rocks were slick and the current pushed steadily at his legs. The boat kept coming and seemed to pick up speed. He looked around at the bank, then at the bridge, hoping someone would be there to help. But no one was there.

At the last second, before the boat hit him from the side, Farkus cursed again and managed to turn toward it and brace himself with both feet. His fly rod dropped into the water at his side as he reached out with both hands—*"Goddammit!"* he cried out—to grasp the gunwales of the oncoming boat and stop its momentum.

The boat thumped heavily against his palms and he felt the soles of his boots slip and he was pushed a few feet backward. Somehow, though, his right boot wedged between two heavy rocks and stopped fast. So did the boat, although he could feel the pressure of it building, wanting to knock him down. He was sick about his lost fly rod, and thought that if nothing else he could wrestle the boat to shore and sell it for three or four grand, because he sure as hell wasn't going to return it to the idiot who let it get away from him in the first place.

As he stood there in the river, straining against the pressure, he realized it was harder work than it should have been. There was real weight inside the boat, but he was at an angle, bent forward with his head down and his arms straining and outstretched, so he couldn't rise up and look inside without losing his balance and his footing.

Over the next ten minutes, muscles trembling, he worked the boat downstream and closer to the bank. Finally, he stepped into a back eddy of calmer water with a sandy bottom and pulled the boat into it as well. Sweat coursed down his neck, and his thigh muscles twitched with pain.

Then he looked over the gunwale into the bottom of the boat and said, "Jesus Christ!"

He'd never seen so much blood.

# 1

## THE EVENING BEFORE

NATE ROMANOWSKI approached the stand of willows from the north with a grim set to his face and a falcon on his fist. Something was going to die.

It was an hour until dusk in the foothills of the Bighorn Mountains, near the North Fork of the Twelve Sleep River. Storm clouds that had scudded across the big sky all day now bunched to the southeast as if they'd been herded, and they squeezed out intermittent waves of snow pellets that rattled across the dry grass and shivered the dead leaves. A slight breeze hung low to the ground and ferried both the scent of sage and the watery smell of the river through the lowland brush.

The peregrine falcon was blinded with a leather hood topped by a stiff white bristle of pronghorn antelope hair. The bird sat still and upright, secured to the falconer's hand by thin leather jesses tied to its talons and looped through his gloved fingers. The falcon, Nate thought, was still and regal and hungry—tightly packed natural explosives encased by feathers, just waiting for a fuse to be lit.

Although slightly less than twenty-four inches tall, the female he held, once released, was the fastest species on the planet, capable of speeds during its hunting dive of more than two hundred miles an hour. When it balled its talons and struck a bird in flight with that velocity, the result was a concussive explosion of blood, bones, and feathers that still took Nate's breath away.

The falcon, like all his raptors over the years, had no name. And every time he released one to hunt there was a chance she would fly away and simply never return.

He slowed his pace and listened as he approached the wall of willows. Through the brush was a shallow, spring-fed pond not more than three acres across. It was hard to see from the ground but was obvious from the air, and it was the only substantial body of water for miles around except for the river itself. Therefore, it attracted passing waterfowl. And when the breeze shifted he could hear them: the rhythmic, almost subsonic clucking of paddling ducks. The peregrine heard them, too, and responded with an instinctive tightening of her talons on his hand.

Nate raised the bird so he could whisper directly into her hood, "They're here."

NATE WAS TALL and ropy, with long limbs and icy blue eyes set in a hawklike wind-burned face. The hair he'd cut and dyed months before was growing back long and blond but hadn't reached its customary ponytail length. He wore stained camo cargo pants, laced outfitter boots, a faded U.S. Air Force Academy hooded sweatshirt, and a thick canvas Carhartt vest. Strapped to his rib cage on his left side, between the sweatshirt and the vest, was a scoped five-shot .500 Wyoming Express revolver. A three-inch braid of jet-black human hair was attached to the thick muzzle by a leather string.

He reached across his body with his right hand and gently untied the falcon's hood and slipped it off. The peregrine cocked her head at him for a moment, then returned to profile. The single eye he could see was black, piercing, and soulless—the amoral eye of a killer.

Nate opened his left hand to free the jesses, and raised her up. Her wings unfurled and stretched out for a moment, then her talons bunched and pushed off his glove. He turned his face away as he was pummeled with thumping blasts of air from her beating wings and brushes of her wingtips. The first moment of flight was ungainly; she dropped slightly and thrashed to the left, the jesses swinging through the air, her feet long and extended, until she found invisible purchase and began to rise. She cleared the tops of the willows ahead by inches.

The falcon climbed in circles that were tight at first and then larger as she rose above the treetops and found a current. Then, as if she'd burned through the first stage of a booster rocket, she catapulted into the sky.

THE PAST MONTH had been spent in a state of training and trepidation, ever since his longtime colleague Large Merle had shown up gutted at his front door. Nate had transported all seven feet and four hundred fifty pounds of Merle toward the town of Saddlestring in his Jeep, with his friend gasping for breath through chattering teeth. The last thing Large Merle had said before he collapsed was: *"The Five. They've deployed."*

Nate knew exactly what that meant. The showdown he'd been anticipating for years was at hand, and Merle was the latest victim. Large Merle had died with a moaning death rattle five miles out of town, and Nate had flipped a U-turn and returned to his stone house on the banks of the North Fork. He'd said a few private words over the body and had it shipped via Freightliner to Merle's only living relative, a sister in North Dakota. Then he began to prepare for visitors.

———————

THE PEREGRINE FALCON was little more than a pinprick in the sky, a tiny black speck set against roiling thunderheads. Nate watched the bird circle in the ellipse of a lazy thermal spiral. The falcon was so high in the air it took a knowing eye to see it. But the ducks knew the falcon was there because none had attempted to fly.

Nate nodded to himself and tugged on the end of an empty burlap sack he'd tucked through his belt. He flipped the sack over his shoulder to keep it out of the way, and approached the willows in silence.

Before he entered the brush, he paused and looked over his shoulder and scanned the terrain. His small house was far below in the river valley, his Jeep parked next to it. The old structure was bordered by massive old river cottonwood trees with gnarled gray bark and skeletal limbs. Because most of the leaves were gone, he could see his clapboard mews for housing falcons, and an upturned flat-bottomed boat on the bank of the river he used for crossing. On the east side of the North Fork, a steep red wall rose sixty feet into the air. The top was flat and dotted with scrub. Beyond the flat the country rose at a gentle pitch in a series of waves and folds until it melded into the multicolor pockets of aspen and then the dark timber fringe of the mountains. Rounded peaks above the timberline were dusted with the fresh first snow of the fall.

To the west was an undulating treeless sagebrush flat that continued for miles. A single two-track road cut through the sagebrush and meandered its way through cuts and draws to the stone house. There was no other way in, and if someone was coming he could see them from miles away. On the sides of the sections of road out of his vision, he'd installed motion-detection sensors and hidden closed-circuit cameras that would broadcast images of visitors into his house well before he could see them with his naked eye or through his binoculars.

From his vantage point on the plateau where the willows hid the pond, Nate noted how the river had risen. Although there had been little rain and only a few bursts of fall snow, the thirst of the river cottonwoods for water had subsided as the trees withdrew their appetite and focused inward, preparing for winter. Without thousands of trees sucking water from the Twelve Sleep, the level of the river rose high enough to be navigable again.

All was quiet and still in every direction.

Nate turned back around, reached out and parted the stiff willow branches, and stepped inside.

AS THE BRUSH closed around him he could no longer see the peregrine, but he knew she was there by the nervous tittering of the ducks ahead. The ducks weren't alarmed because of his presence or the noise he was making as he pushed through the willows, but because of the falcon in the sky.

He sensed an opening through the branches a moment before he was knee-deep in stagnant water. The bottom of the pond was silty beneath his boots but solid underneath, and with a few more steps he was waist-deep in the pond as mallard and teal ducks scattered in his path, motoring across the surface of the water and sending the alarm to the entire population of twenty or twenty-five ducks. The silt he'd disturbed underfoot plumed through the dark pond water and turned it the color of chocolate milk near his legs.

But not one of the ducks took flight. Nate smiled to himself as he beheld one of nature's brilliant secrets.

For ducks, geese, and other waterfowl, the very silhouette of a peregrine falcon in the sky—even if they'd never encountered one before—was deeply imprinted into their collective psyche. They knew somehow the predator thousands of feet in the air would kill them in an instant if they became airborne, just like they somehow knew the falcon would not hit them on the ground or on the surface of the water. So as long as the ducks didn't fly, they were safe. Their instinct was so ingrained that it superseded even his own intrusion into their world.

He waded across the pond with the burlap sack and gathered up four mallard drakes and dropped them inside as if selecting ripe zucchini. As he chose them, the others swam away and bunched against the reeds, practically climbing over one another to get away. Four was enough, he thought, for two good meals and duck soup later. He'd use the wings as lures for falconry exercises and the feathers as stuffing for training dummies.

Knotting the open end of the sack, Nate waded across the pond and grabbed a fat mallard hen from the flock. As he lifted the bird, her bright orange feet windmilled under her belly, as if she was trying to run through the air. Droplets of pond water beaded on her feathers.

He leaned back and looked up into the sky and held the duck out from his body in full view. Peregrines had incredible eyesight, and he could almost sense the falcon locking in on him and the object in his hand.

Nate drew the hen in close and said, "God bless you and thank you," something he always said to wild creatures before he took an action that would result in their death, then hurled the duck into the air, where it had no option but to fly or drop back to the earth like a rock.

He called out: "For my hunting partner."

The duck came alive with a burst of energy, and started to climb. It flew horizontal and fast, skirting the top of the brush in a mad dash toward the far river.

Hundreds of feet above, in a move made silent by its distance, the peregrine deftly shrugged out of the thermal, tucked its wings tight against its body, balled its talons so they resembled twin hammers, and began to drop headfirst through the sky.

Nate could hear it coming as it shot earthward like a missile. The sound was a kind of high-pitched whistle that increased in volume as it built up velocity.

He glanced over toward the retreating duck. The hen had cleared the willows and was aiming for the river valley, its wings beating so fast they were blurs. It didn't fly in a straight line but seemed to know its only chance was to feint and zigzag through the air.

Somehow, while dropping through the sky at incredible speed, the peregrine homed in on the flying duck and was able to make microscopic flight adjustments in its stoop attack so that when the two objects intersected—with an audible *whap* sound and an explosion of feathers that seemed to fill the sky—Nate took a sharp intake of breath and almost fell back into the water from the sheer bloody beauty of it all.


AS HE MADE his way down the slope toward the river with the sack of wriggling mallards, he paused next to the peregrine. The falcon was eating the remains of the dead duck. Flesh, guts, bones, and feathers filled its gullet to the size of a billiard ball, and its hooked beak was shiny with bright red blood. The bird paused and looked up, their eyes locked, something was exchanged, then the falcon resumed eating.

Nate untied the sack and reached in and grasped a drake by its neck and pulled it out. He cinched the top to contain the others and stashed the sack of live ducks beneath a mountain ash tree and weighted it with a rock. He would have the duck for dinner. This completed the circle—hunt, kill, eat—and always reminded him he was of the natural world and not simply striding atop it.


KNEE-DEEP in the cold water, Nate wrung the neck of the duck with a sharp swing of his arm and held it out away from him as its wings beat in death throes. A full gust of wind roared up the river, roiling the surface of the water and shaking the trees. Golden spade-shaped cottonwood leaves fell into the water like upturned palms and bobbed and floated in the current.

He pushed both thumbs through the taut belly skin of the duck and worked them under its breastbone. The blood inside was hot, and the smell was metallic and pungent. With his left hand, he grasped the body of the duck and with his right he broke the entire breast away until it came free. After tossing the carcass toward the bank, he bent and dipped the breast into the water to clean and cool it. Spirals of dark blood snaked between his knees.

The gust of wind played out and silence returned and he thought he heard a sound. Nate looked up at his falcon to see she had stopped eating and was focusing on something upriver. He followed her gaze as the pointed snout of a drift boat emerged from around a grassy bank.

The wind had overridden the distinctive noises of an approaching boat—the slight lapping of the current on the sides of the fiberglass hull, the squeak of oars being dipped through oarlocks, the shuffle of boots on the boat deck, the scrape of a shallow river rock against the flat bottom.

He was caught, he thought. There was no way he could turn and splash toward the shore and find cover before he was seen. Warning jolts fired through his nerves.

His vest was open, and he reached up and slipped the thong loose that secured his .50 caliber weapon in its shoulder holster. Instinctively, he flexed his fingers in and out and stood up tall as the boat made the turn and came into full view. It was a low-profile open McKenzie-style Hyde drift boat, off-white in color, with a green-and-brown horizontal stripe on the side. There were three men in the boat— one standing behind the casting platform in front, one at the oars, and the third seated in the back. The man in back was slumped over and looked to be injured—or sleeping.

"There's somebody," the man standing in front said over his shoulder to his companions. Then: "Hey, mister. We've got a hurt man here. Can we pull over and call for some help?"

Nate didn't answer. They certainly weren't making any effort to sneak up on him. He made several quick determinations. First, the assassins sent for him in the past had been professionals and had come from out of state. These men looked like locals. Second, it *was* hunting season, and therefore not unusual to see hunters about. Third, he'd been spotted and would have to deal with them one way or the other.

*"Hey,"* the man in the front of the boat called out, standing and straining forward over the casting platform. "Did you hear me, mister? *We need help. We've got a hurt man here. . . ."*

Nate could see the boat and the occupants clearly now. The big man in the bow was thick and tall, with a full black beard and hair curling out from beneath an orange cap. Red hands grasped the top of the casting platform so he could lean over it. Dark eyes pierced out from beneath a flat, wide forehead. He wore a camo jacket and black jeans. The orange cap and the tip of the compound bow that jutted above the hull indicated he was a hunter, not a fisherman. Nate thought he'd seen him before and tried to place him.

Seated low in the center of the boat was a hunched younger man with a knob for a head and tiny hands that wrapped around the grips of the oars. He had a couple of fingers missing. Nate guessed the oarsman to be in his mid-twenties, but there was something shrunken and repellent about him. He had a wide nose that had been smashed flat against his face, high cheekbones, and large ears that ended in points: a gargoyle of sorts.

The slumped man in the back wore a thick jacket and a slouch hat, and his head was dropped forward so Nate couldn't see his face.

"Man, you're a sight for sore eyes," the dark man in the front said to Nate, knowing his voice would carry through the quiet valley as if he were standing next to him. "We've been looking for someone—anyone—for a while now. We haven't even seen a house anywhere."

"There aren't any," Nate said.

"No shit," the gargoyle spat, spinning the boat so the front of it faced the other bank. He began to pull the oars to propel the drift boat toward Nate.

Nate assumed the three men had put their boat in at a public access six miles upriver and had planned to float to another access closer to town. The route was used often in the summer fishing months but rarely in the fall or winter, when the level of the river dropped and the locals turned their attention from fishing to hunting. All of the river miles between the put-in and Nate's stone house were through private ranch land owned by an out-of-state mogul. The mogul's house was miles away from the river, tucked in a valley, and it wasn't likely he would have been home, anyway, even if the men in the boat had gone there. Wyoming law allowed the public to float any river, but it was considered trespassing if the boaters got out or even anchored. The landowners were notorious for prosecuting anyone who pulled ashore, even if the reason was an emergency, so most fishermen chose to float much farther downriver toward Saddlestring, where there was more public land and the fishing was better.

"Do you have a phone we can use?" the man in front asked.

Nate had a satellite phone but ignored the question. He asked, "What's the problem, anyway?"

"Old Paul," the dark man said, pointing at the slumping man. "He's got a bad heart and some kind of nerve condition. He just seized up about an hour ago and started jerking. Shit, he was even foaming at the mouth. He needs to see a doctor fast."

"He's my dad," the gargoyle said with a nasal twang, "and I ain't gonna lose him."

Nate noted that Paul still hadn't moved, and even the shift in the boat hadn't caused him to lift his head.

As the gargoyle pulled back on the oars and moved the drift boat across the current toward Nate, the dark man in front said, "We seen a few deer but nothing to get excited about. Them damn things just stand in the river while we float right past 'em. We coulda killed a half dozen of them if we'd wanted to." He laughed. "God, they're stupid."

"No," Nate said, taking a long second look at the big man and seeing a dangerous idiot. "That's just the way they are."

Like ducks that wouldn't fly when a peregrine was above, big-game animals—even during hunting season—didn't perceive that a threat could come from the water. Nate had harvested deer on the banks or in the river from his own boat. He'd also encountered elk, bears, and moose on the river who watched him float silently by with a mixture of curiosity and familiarity.

"Are you the only one hunting?" Nate asked the dark man as the boat drew closer. The gargoyle and his father weren't wearing blaze orange, and Nate couldn't see additional compound bows or hunting rifles in the craft.

"Yeah," the dark man said. "Stumpy 'n Paul wanted to come along to see a master at work."

"Shit," the gargoyle said in response, shaking his head and making a face.

"I know you," Nate said to the dark man, recalling the circumstances.

"I don't think so." The dark man smiled. But his eyes showed sudden caution.

"You're known as the Mad Archer," Nate said. "My friend Joe Pickett put you in jail a few years back for shooting wildlife with your bow and leaving the meat."

The time he'd encountered the Mad Archer, Nate was with the game warden Joe Pickett in northeastern Wyoming. Joe had handcuffed the man to the bumper of his own truck and called another game warden to come out and pick him up. The Mad Archer, Joe had said, was both evil and bloodthirsty. He was suspected of using his arrows to kill dogs and cats as well, and had wounded the dog Joe rescued, a Labrador/corgi mix named Tube. Nate had heard Joe use the Mad Archer's real name, but he couldn't remember it.

The man flushed. "That might have been," he said, "but it was before I went straight. I play by the rules now, man," he said, gesturing toward his orange hat. He patted his back pocket. "I even got my license back if you want to see it."

"Show it to Joe," Nate said as the bow of the boat came within reach. The gargoyle expected Nate to grasp the bow and pull the boat to the bank. Instead, Nate shoved it away and the boat swung back into the current. A redheaded duck had swum out of the reeds with ten little ducklings in tow in a straight line behind her, and she angled to her right to avoid the floating boat.

"Keep moving," Nate said to them.

"Hey, what about my dad?" the gargoyle asked, his face contorted. He did several front-strokes on the oars to pull the boat back into the calm eddy. "You're fuckin' heartless."

"I'll call the clinic and have them send an ambulance to the take-out," Nate said, stepping backward toward the bank, keeping the men and the boat in front of him. "They should be waiting when you get there. You're not saving any time bringing him onshore now and calling them, anyhow. It would take them longer to get here than it will for you to float to the take-out."

Nate didn't want the Mad Archer anywhere near his house. If the man was as unstable as Joe claimed, his friends Paul and Stumpy were suspect as well. Men who hunted together shared certain characteristics and values, and this was guilt by association with the Mad Archer. Nate had never been troubled making judgments of this kind.

Plus, he'd been seen and the men would talk. Which meant the minute they were gone, he'd have to clear out.

The Mad Archer glared, his fists clenched at his side. As Nate neared the shore, his boot slipped off a river rock and he had to wheel and crow-hop to keep standing.

Then before Nate could look back over his shoulder at the boat and the three men to confirm they were floating downriver, he heard a single whispered word: *"Now."*

Nate spun around in the river and reached across his chest for his weapon. The soles of his boots again slipped on the moss-covered rocks, and he stumbled to his left but not far enough. An arrow tipped with a razor broadhead sliced through the air and hit him between his left shoulder and clavicle.

The figures in the boat who had been still just a moment before were now a blur of motion. The gargoyle was sliding a pump shotgun out of a saddle scabbard that had been hidden beneath his boat seat. The old man Paul was awake and standing, and his long coat was open and he was swinging the muzzle of a military-style carbine toward Nate.

The Mad Archer cursed because his shot had been misplaced due to Nate's stumble, and he was frantically fitting a second arrow into the nock of his bow before drawing the bowstring back again. Because both the old man and the Mad Archer were now standing, the boat pitched slightly from side to side.

Although his left shoulder screamed with pain, Nate pulled his big revolver out from its holster and cocked the hammer and leveled it with a single motion and fired.

The first bullet hit the Mad Archer in the right center of his wide forehead and blew his orange hat straight up into the air. His body collapsed forward across the casting platform.

Nate cocked the revolver on the down stroke from its tremendous kick and swung it left and shot the old man through the heart. Old Paul stiffened and sat straight back onto his swivel seat. His rifle fell into the water. Blood, bits of bone, and tissue pattered across the surface of the water behind him. He slumped forward into the same posture he'd assumed before.

Stumpy the Gargoyle nearly had his shotgun clear of the scabbard, and he looked up at Nate and their eyes met for an instant before he was hit under the right armpit with such great impact that it threw his body to the other side of the boat. The bullet exited clean and smacked the surface of the water a few inches from the other bank, nearly taking out the mother duck.

NATE STAGGERED onto the gravel bank. His ears rang from the three explosions, and the hum blocked out any natural sound. The entire left side of his body felt as if he was hooked up to pulsing electric cables. He holstered his weapon and touched the feathered end of the arrow that was buried in his body. He looked over his left shoulder and could see the bloody tip of the razor broadhead poking out. The arrow was stuck fast, but as far as he could tell it hadn't pierced a major artery or broken bone. All that was destroyed was shoulder muscle.

Out on the river the drift boat turned slowly from left to right and rocked slightly from the fallen crashes of the three dead bodies that were crumpled within it. The still air smelled of acrid gunpowder and the metallic odor of pooling blood.

The mother duck and her ducklings continued downriver in an undulating line, speeding up to get as far away as they could from the disturbance.

On trembling legs, Nate approached one of the thick old cotton-woods that hugged the bank of the river. As he neared it he turned so he faced the water and his back was to the trunk. Slowly, he stepped backward until he felt a jolt of pain as the tip of the broadhead bit into the soft gray bark. Reaching up, he grasped the aluminum shaft with both hands to steady it and leaned back with all his weight, burying the arrow as far as he could into the wood and pinning himself to the tree.

Standing as still as possible, Nate stripped the fletching off the back end of the arrow until it was smooth. Then he took a breath, gritted his teeth, and walked forward, letting the arrow slide through his shoulder.

When it was clear, he glanced over his shoulder at the bloody shaft that remained embedded in the tree trunk. Hot blood coursed down his skin in both front and back, and his shirt was stained dark with it.

As he lurched toward his home for his medical kit, he noted that the boat had drifted away a few hundred yards downriver and was spinning slowly in the current.

He cursed himself. Like the deer and elk in the valley, he hadn't anticipated the threat to come from the water. Or from locals.

# 2

THE NEXT MORNING, a Wyoming game warden swung his green Ford pickup and stock trailer into a pull-through site in Crazy Woman Campground in the Bighorns and shut off the motor. He glanced at his wristwatch—0900, a half hour before he was to meet the trainee—and checked for messages on his cell phone. There were none.

It was Monday, October 22, the heart of elk-hunting season in the mountains. Although opening day had been a week before, the lack of heavy snow meant the hunters wouldn't be out in force yet because they couldn't track the herds.

He got out and pulled his gray wool Filson vest over his red uniform shirt and buttoned it up. Over the right breast pocket of the vest was a two-inch brass pin that read JOE PICKETT GAME WARDEN. On his shoulder was a patch embroidered with a pronghorn antelope. His badge, pinned over his heart, indicated he was GF-48—number forty-eight of the fifty-two game wardens in the state, ranked by seniority. He had once been up to number twenty-four before being fired and later rehired. Unfortunately, when they sent him the replacement badge, he was relegated to starting in the numeric system again. He'd thought about contesting it, but when he considered going up against the thoughtless maw of the bureaucracy it didn't seem worth the trouble.

Joe exhaled a small cloud of condensation. The morning had not yet warmed above freezing, and the sun hadn't risen high enough to melt the scrim of frost on the pine tree boughs all around him or the frozen mat of grass. He loved the snap of a fall morning in the mountains.

The stock trailer door moaned as he opened it, and he led both geldings, the older paint Toby and sprightly young sorrel Rojo, out of the trailer and around the side of it and tied their halters to the barred windows. He saddled Rojo and slid his shotgun into the right saddle scabbard and a scoped Winchester .270 into the left. The saddlebags were already packed with maps, permits, gear, and lunch, and he lashed them to the skirt of the saddle. Toby pawed the ground and blew through his nostrils impatiently, wanting to get going.

"Soon," Joe said to his wife's horse. "Just chill."

Joe Pickett was in his mid-forties, lean, and of medium height and build. He wore a battered gray Stetson and faded Wranglers over lace-up outfitter boots. His service weapon that he rarely drew, a .40 Glock 23, was on his hip, along with handcuffs and a long cylinder of bear spray. A citation book jutted from his back pocket.

With the hot engine block ticking behind him, Joe Pickett leaned against the grille of his unit and speed-dialed his daughter Sheridan, a freshman at the University of Wyoming. She'd been at school since late August.

Her phone rang five times before she picked up.

"What's going on?" he asked. "Sleeping in on your birthday?"

"No, Dad. I just got back to my room from the shower. I don't have class until ten on Mondays." Her voice was clear but she sounded tired, he thought. "Mom already called me, but I guess you know that."

He smiled. Since Sheridan had been born at 6:15 a.m. nineteen years before, Marybeth always woke up her daughter at exactly that time on her birthday. It used to mean opening her bedroom door and rousting her. Now it was an early-morning call. He pictured her in her dormitory room in Laramie with wet hair, speaking in a low tone so she wouldn't wake her roommate.

"You guys aren't going to do that forever, are you?" Sheridan said softly but with a slight exasperated edge. "I mean, no one in their right mind is up at that hour here. Some people are just getting *in*."

Joe chuckled. "How are things going, kiddo? Are you settling in? Making some friends?"

"Both, I guess," she said. "The classes are the easy part. You know how that goes. I know a lot of kids here from high school, but everything's different. I miss you guys . . ." she said, then caught herself.

"It's okay," Joe said. "We miss you. *I* miss you."

"April doesn't," Sheridan said with a laugh. April was their sixteen-year-old foster daughter who had taken over Sheridan's vacant room. Previously, she'd had to share it with fourteen-year-old Lucy. Marybeth, Joe's wife, had discovered a bag of marijuana in April's underwear drawer during the move. Battle lines had been drawn. April had been grounded and had one week left before she could go anywhere other than school, and they'd confiscated her cell phone. But having her at home all the time was no picnic for the rest of the family, either, because no one could darken a room like a sullen April. Lucy did her best to avoid April and all the drama by staying late at school for rehearsals and keeping her bedroom door closed at home.

"I just know she's wearing all my clothes and using all my stuff without asking," Sheridan said. Joe thought about it and recalled April wearing one of Sheridan's sweaters just the day before. "She'll stretch everything out with her big . . . chest."

"No comment," Joe said. Then: "What about friends?"

"A couple," Sheridan said. "One girl in particular named Nadia. We've got a couple of classes together and we started hanging out. She's pretty cool."

"Where's she from?"

"Maryland somewhere. She says she really likes Wyoming."

"Wait to see what she says this winter," Joe said. "There's already some snow in the mountains here." Then: "Hey—you're coming home for Thanksgiving, right?"

"At this point, yes," Sheridan said with hesitation.

Joe felt his ears get hot. "What do you mean, 'At this point'?"

"Nadia asked me if I wanted to go east with her. I've never been east before. I'd like to see D.C."

Joe tried to think of what to say.

"Her parents will cover the ticket," Sheridan said quickly.

"It's not that," Joe said. "I think your mom and your sisters would like to see you. In fact, I know they would."

Silence.

"You're making me feel guilty," she said.

"That's my job."

He heard Sheridan chuckle again. "It might be cool coming home without having Grandmother Missy around."

Joe nodded. Marybeth's mother was supposedly on a world cruise, burning through some of the money she'd inherited from her former husband's death. Joe had encouraged her never to come back.

"Talk to your mother about Thanksgiving," Joe said.

"I will."

As they talked, Joe looked up to see a banged-up green Game and

Fish pickup with state plates turning into the campground off Hazelton Road. His trainee had arrived. Joe waved at the pickup, and it turned into the pull-through and swung around the stock trailer.

"Hey!" Joe shouted. *"Watch those horses."*

The driver hit the brakes with his front bumper just eighteen inches from Rojo's hock, then reversed so he could park in back of the trailer. The trainee looked fresh-faced and humiliated already.

"Where are you?" Sheridan asked.

"Up in the mountains. Area thirty-three and thirty-four—Middle Fork and the Upper South Fork Twelve Sleep River areas. It's time I get out and check all the elk-hunting camps up here. Unfortunately, the department assigned me a trainee to tag along. He looks to be about your age but dumb, based on how he drives."

Sheridan said, "You know, Dad, I miss going with you to do stuff like that."

The statement caught him by surprise. "You do?"

"Yeah," she said. "I miss the mountains, and our horses. I even miss Nate, even though he sort of hung me out there as far as our training goes."

Sheridan had been an apprentice to the master falconer. At one point, she'd desperately wanted to fly her own falcon, but circumstances and Nate's situation had prevented it.

"Maybe someday," Joe said, doubting there would be a someday. "Sheridan, I've got to go before this trainee does something stupid. But happy birthday, kid."

"Thanks, Dad."

He closed the phone and dropped it into his vest pocket as the trainee appeared from around the horse trailer. He was short and stocky, with a thatch of brown hair with highlights in it. He had a square jaw and a nose that had been broken and a walk with an athletic spring in it. He seemed easygoing and eager to please, and he didn't look much older than Sheridan. A good-looking kid, though, Joe thought.

"Joe Pickett?" the trainee asked.

Joe nodded.

"I'm Luke Brueggemann. I'm your trainee. Sorry about nearly hitting your horses."

"You'd have had to answer to my wife if you had," Joe said. "And believe me, it wouldn't be pretty."

Brueggemann nodded. He had a large duffel bag thrown over his shoulder. His red uniform shirt was fresh out of the box, as were his denims.

"Can I say, sir," Brueggemann said, "it's a real thrill for me to meet you. I've heard about you over the years."

Joe took Brueggemann's measure. He remembered being a trainee sixteen years before, when he was right out of college. His mentor had been a man named Vern Dunnegan, and it was in the days when game wardens often made their own law within their districts. He'd learned more from Dunnegan than he'd wanted to. But some of the legitimate skills and lessons from those years still stuck with him.

"I hope it was good," Joe said.

"Most of it," Brueggemann said, grinning and looking away.

"Are you from around here?"

The trainee nodded. "I grew up in Sundance," he said. Sundance was located in Wyoming's Black Hills country, in the northeast section of the square state. "Then I worked with my uncle as a commercial fisherman in Alaska to get money for college. When I came back, I did my four in Laramie and graduated with a wildlife biology degree."

"Good for you," Joe said.

"Thank you."

"My daughter's at UW now," Joe said. "I was just talking to her."

"Go, Pokes," Brueggemann said, nodding in recognition.

"That's Toby," Joe said, gesturing toward the paint horse. "Do you know how to put on a saddle?"

By his expression, Joe could tell Brueggemann had never been this close to a horse before.

"Here's what you need to know about horses: the front end bites and the back end kicks and the middle bucks you off," Joe said. "Come on, I'll show you. And after we get Toby saddled, you need to go through that big bag and figure out what you can tie behind the saddle, because that's all the storage you'll have."

WITH BOTH HORSES saddled and ready, Joe spread a topographical map across the hood of his Ford and pointed at the eleven outfitter camps they would try to inspect over the next two days. Brueggemann paid close attention, and stubbed a finger near one of the first camp locations.

"Isn't that a road that goes right to it?" he asked.

Joe nodded.

"Then why don't we drive there?"

Joe looked at him. "Are you nervous about the horses?"

Brueggemann hesitated, but his answer was obvious: "A little."

"I understand," Joe said. "Always be cautious around horses. As soon as you start to count on them, they'll stab you in the back."

"Then why don't we drive to the camps?" Brueggemann asked softly, not wanting to seem obstinate.

Joe said, "We could drive right to most of them. But they'd hear us coming miles away. And even though most of these guys are good hunters, there are a couple I don't want to know we're out there. So instead of driving right up on them and giving them a chance to hide or stash illegal carcasses away where we can't see them, I'd rather approach them in silence. That way we can circle the camps up in the timber from all sides before we decide to ride in."

Brueggemann sighed and nodded.

"If someone's doing something illegal, like too many elk or dead cow elk in an antler-only area, they'll likely hang the carcasses within walking distance of the camp but out of sight from the road. It works better to know what the situation is before we talk to the hunters."

Joe continued, "I know most of these guys. Half of them are local, and three run guide operations, so they'll have clients in the camps. Of the eleven camps, ten are familiar names. There's only one new guy this year, and I want to find out who he is and what he's up to." He tapped his finger on Camp Five, which was four and a half miles away along the old logging road they'd soon be riding on.

Joe's cell phone rang in his pocket. He grimaced as he pulled it out and looked at the display. It read TWELVE SLEEP COUNTY SHERIFF'S OFFICE.

"This is never good," Joe mumbled out loud. Then: "Joe Pickett."

"Joe, this is Sheriff McLanahan."

Joe rolled his eyes. He and McLanahan had a long history, mostly bad.

"Joe," McLanahan said, "a fisherman down in the river in the middle of town just called me in a panic. He saw what he thought was an empty drift boat floating toward him in the current. When he looked inside, he found three dead bodies."

Joe felt his scalp crawl.

"I need you to come in and take a look at these guys," the sheriff said. "I think they're friends of yours."

*"Friends?"*

McLanahan hung up.

Joe looked to Brueggemann. "Now you'll learn how to unsaddle a horse and lead it into the trailer. We've got a hitch in our plans," he said.

# 3

JOE LOCATED the sheriff, the boat, and the bodies in the garage adjacent to the old county building in Saddlestring. On the way into town he'd listened to the chatter over the radio. Word of the triple homicide was rocketing across the state. Although nearly every resident had several guns at home and many carried weapons in public, there were only fifteen to twenty murders a year in Wyoming. So three at once was big news, and Joe understood the magnitude, just as he was puzzled by McLanahan's mention of the victims as his "friends." He had a dark premonition that one of the bodies might belong to Nate Romanowski, although the idea of anyone actually *getting* to Nate seemed incomprehensible.

As he entered town he was greeted with a new REELECT OUR SHERIFF KYLE MCLANAHAN billboard. On it, the sheriff leaned out of his pickup window to offer a carrot to a horse. Joe shook his head.

Sheriff Kyle McLanahan had it in for him, and their professional relationship had gotten worse in the past few months. McLanahan had made it clear to his deputies that they wouldn't be chastised for making Joe's life miserable. They did it in subtle ways, such as not responding to help requests and losing or delaying paperwork Joe filed.

He'd gotten around it somewhat by working directly with County Attorney Dulcie Schalk and bypassing the sheriff's department.

As election day neared, McLanahan had spent a good deal more time than usual out of his office, meeting voters and playing up his persona of a western caricature. Joe had heard from a few residents that the sheriff cited him in particular as one of the biggest reasons why he'd been humiliated during the trial of Missy, Joe's mother-in-law, who'd been accused of murdering her former husband. Up until the trial, McLanahan seemed to be cruising toward reelection. Not anymore.

JOE PARKED next to a sheriff's department SUV outside the garage. Three other departmental vehicles were lined up on the other side of the open garage door, as was an ambulance and Sheriff McLanahan's pickup. Dulcie Schalk's red Subaru wagon was also out front. Dulcie was also stinging from the outcome of the trial and was still cool to Joe, but he thought he sensed a warming. Dulcie was young, tough, professional, and one of Marybeth's friends. Their mutual love of horses and riding was strong enough that the trial hadn't derailed their friendship.

Joe killed his motor and jumped out and took a deep breath before going inside.

"Hey," Luke Brueggemann called out. He'd parked behind Joe's pickup. "Should I tag along, or what?"

After all he'd been thinking and worrying about, Joe had forgotten about his trainee. Joe put his hands on his hips and thought about it.

"Well?" Brueggemann asked, stopping short of reaching Joe.

"Have you ever seen a dead body?" Joe asked.

"Sure," Brueggemann said, hitching up his pants.

"You have?"

The trainee looked above and to the right of Joe. "My grandma. At her funeral."

Joe smiled, despite the situation. "It's up to you, Luke. I won't force you, but I won't keep you away."

With that, Joe turned and headed for the garage. No footsteps sounded behind him.


"RON CONNELLY," Joe said, as he fought to keep his stomach from churning, "He's known as the Mad Archer. I arrested him twice. The other two are Stumpy and Paul Kelly. They have a shady outfitting business outside of Winchester. I've been trying to catch them poaching for years."

The sheriff had arranged to have all of the county vehicles moved out of the big garage to make space. The three victims were laid out next to one another on thick plastic sheeting on the concrete floor. When Joe first saw them, he was reminded of Old West photos of dead outlaws on display. All three were stiffened into the unnatural positions in which they'd been found.

Joe asked, "Why didn't you just pull their wallets to see who they were?"

Before McLanahan could answer, Dulcie Schalk said, "I told the sheriff not to touch the bodies again until the forensics people could get here."

McLanahan made a face, obviously displeased that Schalk had taken over.

Joe looked around.

The boat they'd arrived in was on the concrete next to the bodies. It smelled of blood. Joe imagined there were gallons of it congealing inside, but he didn't look to confirm it. He did note that the Mad

Archer's compound bow and a Savage twelve-gauge pump shotgun with a synthetic stock had been tagged and placed on a tarp.

"See?" Sheriff McLanahan said to Dulcie Schalk, who stood off to the side, holding her hand over her mouth in horror. "I told you he'd know 'em. They're of his ilk."

Joe ignored the comment and spoke directly to Schalk. "Ron Connelly killed dozens of game animals with his bow and arrows over the years. Down in southern Wyoming where I was stationed for a while, he took potshots at cows and horses, too. I *know* he wounded an eagle once, and that time I caught him and threw him in the clink. But the penalties for poaching and injuring animals are so weak he didn't spend much time in jail.

"Our department has—I should say *had*—alerts out on him," Joe said. "All the game wardens in the state kept a good eye out for this guy. He used to be a tweaker, but I'd heard he cleaned up his act. Apparently not well enough," he said, nodding toward the body.

"The Kellys are real backwoods types," Joe said. "Paul Kelly and his wife, Pam, run a few cows and lease out their stud horse, but other than that they survive off welfare payments and some kind of disability pension Paul got from an accident he'd had when he worked for the county road crew. The disability didn't stop him from running illegal guided hunts, though. Both Paul and Stumpy got the boot from the Wyoming Outfitters and Guides Association a few years ago because of client complaints and their general lack of ethics. One client claimed they dropped him off up in the Savage Run country and forgot to come back and pick him up so he had to walk out for two days. I've had my eye on them for years, but they're pretty slippery."

He nodded toward the bodies. "Or they were, anyway. What doesn't work for me is how the three of them got hooked up. The

Mad Archer was too nuts to keep any friends, and the Kellys stayed completely to themselves."

Two of McLanahan's deputies bookended him. Both were young, muscle-bound, and menacing, and both wore large campaign buttons that read REELECT OUR SHERIFF. Deputy Sollis smirked at Joe through heavy-lidded eyes. Sollis wore a uniform shirt that was a size too small, to show off his biceps and pectorals, and a black mock turtleneck underneath that didn't fully hide the acne rash on his neck from steroid use. Behind the sheriff and his men was Deputy Mike Reed, McLanahan's opponent in the election, who was older, rounder, and balding. Joe liked Reed, and tipped his hat brim to say hello. Reed nodded back.

The sheriff hadn't gotten rid of Reed, which had surprised Joe before he learned the strategy behind it. Keeping him in the department showcased the sheriff's good-guy credentials, but the idea had actually come after McLanahan watched *The Godfather II* and heard Michael Corleone say, "Keep your friends close and your enemies closer." Although Reed was the senior investigator, McLanahan steadily undermined him in the eyes of voters and observers by assigning him to the most menial tasks, such as supervising random DUI roadblocks, overseeing county road cleanup crews, and in one case sending his deputy on a meth-house raid to the wrong address.

Joe asked the sheriff, "They were all in the same boat?"

"Literally," McLanahan guffawed.

Joe shook his head. "Did they get into a tussle and start blasting at each other?"

Deputy Reed said, "We can't say for sure, but we doubt it."

The sheriff acted as if Reed hadn't spoken.

Dulcie Schalk parted her fingers to talk. She was clearly nauseated by the scene in front of her, and likely the enormity of the crime itself. When she spoke, she bit off her words in a tight-mouthed way, as if trying to avoid breathing the fetid air. "Coroner Will Speer is on his way here to take them for autopsies, Joe, but from what we can tell they were all shot to death at the same time. It appears each was killed by a single fatal gunshot. From what the sheriff told me, the firearm used was . . . *huge*."

She attempted to continue but had to look away. Joe had an odd impulse to go over and hug her, but he knew she'd be embarrassed by the gesture in front of the sheriff and his men.

Sollis said, "Huge as in fucking massive. There's entry wounds as big as most exit wounds. And the exit wounds, well, look at that Connelly guy. Half his head is just *gone*." He said it with what sounded like twisted admiration, Joe thought. He refused to look closely at Ron Connelly's wound, despite Sollis's prompting. Joe didn't think he could take it.

"Which means," McLanahan said, "we may not recover the slugs because they passed right through. Even Stumpy there with a full body shot. It looks like the slug went in under one arm and out under the other."

Schalk said through her fingers, "That's why I asked Sheriff Mc-Lanahan to call DCI and bring the FBI in. He may not think we need their expertise, but we do need their resources."

Joe looked over to the sheriff. McLanahan's gunfighter mustache was trimmed, but it still obscured his mouth. He wore a battered cowboy hat and suspenders over his uniform shirt. He'd traded his departmental Glock for a low-slung Colt .45. McLanahan was from West Virginia but chose to look, dress, and talk like a frontier rube. Some were fooled. Joe wasn't. The sheriff's response to Dulcie Schalk's suggestion was to roll his eyes.

Joe knew the sheriff well enough to know he hadn't been called there simply to identify the bodies.

McLanahan rocked back on his boot heels and stabbed his thumbs through his belt loops. To Joe, he said, "Who do we know that is rumored to live upriver from time to time and carry a great big gun?"

Joe was thinking the same thing, but he didn't reply.

"Tell me," McLanahan said, "when is the last time you saw your buddy Nate Romanowski? The fugitive?"

Nate was still being sought by the Feds because Joe had arranged a temporary release the year before and Nate had never turned himself back in. Instead, his friend had gone to ground and had managed to elude them. Which is why Joe saw very little of his friend these days and rarely communicated with him. It was protection for the both of them.

Joe felt Schalk's eyes on him as the sheriff talked.

"It's been a while," Joe said.

"What's a while?" McLanahan asked. "I mean, being that you're sworn to uphold the law and all? It's hard to believe you know the location of a wanted man but you don't find it within yourself to turn him in or arrest him."

"It's not that simple," Joe said. He knew he was flushing. And he knew McLanahan had a point and was making it so the county attorney would hear it.

"Rumor is," Sollis said, cutting in, "your buddy Nate has a history of violence. Some even say he had something to do with the disappearance of our former sheriff, although we could never get enough evidence to make that case. You wouldn't know anything about any of this, would you?"

"Not really," Joe said, grateful the sheriff hadn't asked him about things he did know about, like Nate's habit of ripping ears off suspects. In regard to the end of former Sheriff Bud Barnum, Joe had a suspicion about Nate's involvement, but he'd never voiced it with anyone except Marybeth.

"So," McLanahan said to Joe, shooting a glance at Dulcie Schalk to make sure she was fully engaged in the implication, "you probably wouldn't want to go with us in a few minutes when we drive upriver to check out Nate Romanowski's alleged place of residence? To see if he knows anything about these yahoos that lay before us?"

Joe avoided Schalk's eyes. He said, "I'll go."

McLanahan feigned surprise. "You don't need to put yourself out. Besides, you'll probably get in the way. You always do."

"I said I'm going."

Behind Joe, he heard a sudden retching sound. He turned to see Luke Brueggemann covering his mouth. His eyes were bulging and wet. He turned and threw up on the concrete floor.

"For Christ's sake," McLanahan said to Sollis, "call maintenance and get them to clean that up." To Joe he said, "Can't you control your people?"


JOE PUT his hand under Brueggemann's arm and led him outside. "It's okay," he told his trainee. "It happens."

"Has it happened to you?"

"Yup."

"Those guys aren't going to let me forget about this, are they?"

Joe said, "No, they won't."

Brueggemann wiped at his mouth with the back of his sleeve. "I've seen plenty of dead things before. You know, deer and elk. And I'm not squeamish when it comes to things like that."

Joe nodded, walking them toward a strip of grass on the edge of the parking area in case Brueggemann had to get sick again.

"I did a full head mount of an antelope once, and an eight-point buck," Brueggemann continued, "and I like my venison bloody."

"You can stop," Joe said, wondering what it was his trainee had just said that struck an odd note. But before he could follow it up, Deputy Mike Reed called his name.

"Stay here," Joe said to Brueggemann. He met Reed in the middle of the parking lot.

Reed spoke in low tones that likely couldn't be overheard by his colleagues inside. "You know what's going on here, don't you?"

"What's that?"

Reed said, "The sheriff needs a big win right now. He thinks he's slipping with the voters. Bagging a guy like Romanowski and solving a triple murder would put him back on top."

Joe nodded and looked closely at Reed. "Is this the candidate talking?"

Reed looked up sharply. "What do you mean?"

Joe said, "You know how I get along with the sheriff, but this is a *triple* homicide. He's got to do everything he can to close it fast. I understand that."

"Yeah," Reed said, looking down at his boots. "I guess you're right. But with this guy," he said, jabbing a thumb over his shoulder toward the open garage, "there's always an angle. We both know him well enough to know that."

"What's the angle?" Joe asked.

"You mean besides making you look bad in front of the county attorney?" Reed asked.

Joe sighed and conceded the point.

"All I'm saying," Reed whispered, "is watch your back."

Joe thanked him and said, "You, too."

Reed smiled bitterly. "For me, it's a twenty-four/seven operation."

Joe nodded and left Brueggemann and went back inside the county garage.

WHILE THE SHERIFF gathered his deputies around him and issued orders for arming up for the raid, Dulcie Schalk gestured for Joe to follow her outside. Once they were clear of the garage and the odors inside, she said, "Tell me what he was saying isn't true. Tell me you don't know about a fugitive who might be a cop killer."

Joe looked over his shoulder to make sure Brueggemann and Reed were out of earshot. Reed was back inside the garage. He saw the trainee over by his truck, leaning his head against the front bumper. Joe said to Dulcie, "Like I said. It's complicated."

Her eyes flared. "I'm riding out there with you, and you're going to explain everything to me. And if I'm not satisfied, Joe, there will be hell to pay."

He nodded and held her eyes. He said, "I'll tell you the truth. But I want to give you some advice. It's something Marybeth and I agreed to a long time ago when it comes to Nate Romanowski."

"And that is?" she asked, skeptical.

"Don't ask me things you may not want to know. Just think real hard about that before we talk."

She looked at him quizzically. She whispered, "You aren't threatening me, are you, Joe?"

He shook his head quickly. "Not at all, not at all. It's just that sometimes it doesn't help to know everything there is to know about someone else. That's all I'm saying."

"Marybeth knows Romanowski?" she asked.

"Oh, she does," Joe said. *"She does."*


DULCIE SCHALK went to get fitted for body armor, and Joe used the opportunity to speed-dial Marybeth on his cell phone. His wife worked from nine to three at the Twelve Sleep County Library, and he knew she'd likely just dropped off April and Lucy at school and was settling into her desk. Marybeth was blond with green eyes, and she was slim and attractive. Joe was always surprised he'd landed her. So was his mother-in-law.

"I'm surprised you're calling," she said when she picked up. "I didn't think you'd have a signal up there."

"I'm not in the mountains," he said, and quickly recapped the morning. He heard her gasp when he told her the sheriff was preparing to storm Nate's home.

"Should I warn him?"

Joe closed his eyes. Nate had a satellite phone, and he'd given them both the private number. He'd asked them not to call him unless it was a dire emergency.

"No," Joe said after a few beats. "You shouldn't. I don't want you to get involved in this. Who knows if the sheriff or the Feds can trace back a call? It's possible, you know. And if Nate's involved in this, you could go to jail for tipping him off."

"I don't mind taking that chance," she said defiantly. "After what he's done for us . . ."

"Marybeth, we can't risk it. *You* can't risk it. Besides, Nate is smart. If he's involved, he'll expect the sheriff to show up, and he'll take precautions. And if he wasn't involved, he has ways of knowing that we're on the way."

"This feels rotten, Joe."

"It has to be this way."

"I don't have to like it, and I'm not making any promises."

"I don't like it, either," he said. He said he'd call her as soon as he could to let her know what happened.

"Joe," she said, "don't let any of McLanahan's goons get trigger-happy. I could see one of them going over the top."

He agreed. After they'd disconnected, he made sure the coast was clear in all directions—Brueggemann was still recovering, and Schalk wasn't back with her vest—before he stepped behind his pickup and called Nate's number.

There was no answer.

4

"THIS REMINDS ME a lot of the first time I ever met Nate Romanowski," Joe said to Dulcie as they sped down the state highway in the midst of the sheriff's department caravan of SUVs. "Nine years ago, different sheriff, similar situation."

Joe recounted how Nate had been arrested for murder, beaten, and jailed. The former sheriff considered it a slam-dunk case, but Joe was able to prove Nate's innocence, and the outlaw falconer had pledged to protect Joe and his family.

"Over the years," Joe said, "we've been through a lot and he's never broken his word. We've had our disagreements, and I don't want to get into all the details, but he's been there for us. So I hope you understand that it isn't an easy thing to turn him over to the Feds. That's where he comes from, and we're not sure he'd make it out alive."

Dulcie recoiled. "What do you mean, he might not make it out alive? This is our government you're talking about, Joe."

He nodded. Luke Brueggemann was in the caravan as well, his pickup hovering in Joe's rearview mirror.

Joe recalled other incidents over the years, things he'd stored in his memory drawer but never reopened. When they'd first met Nate he mentioned he'd just come from Montana. Because of Nate's sudden violent appearance and the way he'd said it, Marybeth was curious and did some research on the library computers, and keyed on a headline from the *Great Falls Tribune* that read "Two Dead in U.S. 87 Rollover." The story said that a damaged vehicle with out-of-state plates had been called in to the Montana Highway Patrol twenty-one miles north of town near Fort Benton. The identities of the occupants were unknown at the time, but authorities were investigating.

On the next page, a smaller story identified the victims of a multiple-rollover accident as two men, aged thirty-two and thirty-seven, from Arlington, Virginia, and Washington, D.C., respectively. Both were killed on impact. The highway patrol suggested that judging by the skid marks, it was possible that the engine to the late-model SUV had lost power or died as the vehicle approached a sharp grade with several turns, and that the driver was unable to negotiate the sharpest of the turns and blew through a guardrail and rolled to the bottom of the canyon, flipping at least seven times. The passenger was thrown from the vehicle, and the driver was crushed behind the wheel.

"Witness Sought in Rollover Investigation," the third, and smallest, headline read. In the story, the highway patrol reported that they were seeking a potential witness to the rollover on U.S. 87 that killed two men from out of state. Specifically, they were looking for the driver of an older-model Jeep with Montana plates that was seen passing a speed checkpoint near Great Falls. The authorities estimated that the Jeep may have been in the vicinity of the rollover near the time it occurred, and that the driver could have seen the accident happen.

Joe later learned that Nate drove a Jeep, and that his preferred weapon at the time, a five-shot .454 Casull manufactured by Freedom Arms, in Freedom, Wyoming, was the only handgun designated a "car killer" by the U.S. Secret Service because the bullets had the power to penetrate the engine block of a vehicle and render it useless.

Several years later, a man named Randan Bello arrived in Saddlestring from Virginia and started asking around about Nate Romanowski. He found a source in the former sheriff, Bud Barnum, and the two became fast friends. One particular fall morning, a housekeeping employee at the Holiday Inn observed Barnum arriving at the hotel and waiting for Bello to join him in his SUV. The two left together and didn't come back. The sheriff's vehicle was never located, although two years later a couple of elk hunters reported that they'd seen wreckage deep in the bottom of Savage Run Canyon. Joe had investigated, but their directions were poor and he'd never spotted anything.

He remembered Large Merle, a restaurant owner who lived on the road that led to Outlaw Canyon, where Nate had relocated after federal warrants were issued for him, asking Joe, "Did Nate ever tell you about that time in Haiti? When the four drugged-out rebels jumped him?"

"No."

Merle shook his head and chuckled, the fat jiggling under his arms and under his chin. "Quite a story," Merle said. "Especially the part about guts strung through the trees like popcorn strings. Ask him about that one sometime!"

Joe never did. But he'd heard that Merle was missing as well. He'd simply not shown up to open his little restaurant in Kaycee one morning a month before.

JOE SAID, "I've never gotten the whole story from Nate, and I've never wanted to hear it. He's tried to tell me a few times, but I shut him down because I don't want to know. But it involves something he did in Special Forces. It's one of the reasons he moved out here— to get away."

Dulcie asked about Nate's age and background.

"Late thirties, early forties," Joe said. "I don't know his birthday or where he grew up, but I've always been under the impression he was familiar with Wyoming and Montana from his youth because he seems to know his way around. He's also familiar with Idaho." Joe let that just hang there and hoped she wouldn't ask about Idaho in particular.

She didn't, but she asked how Nate supported himself. "From what you say, he seems to have no problem getting weapons and equipment."

Joe shrugged. "I don't think it's criminal, but I wouldn't swear to it. All I know is he's never seemed to be hurting for money. He's tried to tell me some things, but I wouldn't listen."

"You have a strange relationship," she said.

"Yup."

"Do you think he's capable of something like what we saw back there in the garage?"

Joe didn't hesitate. "Nate is capable of anything, but he's not random. That's the thing about him. He has his own code and he can be ruthless and cold, but he doesn't do things like that unless provoked. Unless they drew down on him first. And presuming the sheriff is right, why would three low-rent characters like Connelly and the Kellys even want to tangle with someone like Nate? That's why this doesn't make any sense."

She shrugged. "Maybe they were involved with him in some way? In the way he makes his mysterious money?"

"Not possible," Joe said. "He wouldn't associate with people like that. Not to say he doesn't know some unsavory types—he does. But he operates on a whole different level."

"Maybe they were after his money?"

Joe said, "In that case, they were even stupider than I thought. But as soon as we get clear of this, I'm going to go out to the Kelly place and talk to Paul's wife and Stumpy's mother. Pam is her name, I believe. She might know something, and I don't trust the sheriff to follow up with her."

Dulcie rubbed her chin. "Was there a federal reward out for him?"

"If there was, this is the first I've heard of it," he said, tumbling that idea over in his mind.

She said, "And even if there wasn't, one or all of these three might have trouble with the Feds over something or other. It's possible they went after Nate as a bargaining chip."

"It's a possibility," Joe said. "I never thought of that."

"Let's keep an open mind," she said.

Joe eyed her skeptically and held his tongue.

"I learned a few things in Missy's murder trial," she said defensively. "One is never to fully trust McLanahan's theories or judgment. The other is never to underestimate the depth of depravity of the criminal mind."

"You're being a little rough on yourself, Dulcie," he said after a beat. "You're young. Don't get too hard."

She looked over at him, puzzled.

"When it comes to folks, I always try to err on the side of good-will," Joe said. Then: "It's gotten me in a lot of hot water, but it's better that way."

She laughed, surprised, and asked, "How is that?"

Joe said, "I've never tried to find out what terrible thing Nate was involved in that drove him out here. I just take him at face value.

From what he's shown me and what he's done for my family, that's good enough. That was what I meant earlier about not always needing to know everything. When a man wants a whole new life, I guess I'm okay with that."

A minute later, she said, "And Marybeth—she's okay with you knowing him? From what you've told me I don't think I'd want him around my children, provided I had any."

Joe looked ahead. Deputy Sollis was in the lead, followed by two other deputies, Mike Reed, and Sheriff McLanahan. It was less than four miles to the turnoff to Nate's place on the bank of the river.

"We're both comfortable with him," Joe said. "In fact, he's been the master falconer to my daughter Sheridan, who is his apprentice. Marybeth and Nate, well, let's just say they have a special friendship."

*"Explain."* Her eyes sparkled wickedly, Joe thought.

He tried to think of the right words. He decided on, "Marybeth and I have a marriage based on trust. But if we didn't . . ."

She grinned. "So he's hot."

"So they tell me," Joe sighed.

"I'll have to ask her about him the next time we go riding," she said.

Joe moaned. "He might not even be at his place. Nate has a habit of vanishing for weeks and then suddenly showing up where you don't expect him to be. He might have been gone this whole time, and this entire deal we have going here might be a waste of time and effort."

"I'm looking forward to meeting him," she said, as if she hadn't heard a word Joe said. Dulcie Schalk was attractive and unmarried, and he'd heard the local gossips having coffee at the Burg-O-Pardner restaurant speculate about her sexuality, but Joe had never doubted she liked men. As Marybeth had said, pickings were slim in Twelve Sleep County, Wyoming.

Sollis began to slow down on the highway. The two-track road that led three miles to Nate's had no markings or signs. In the winter, it drifted over and was inaccessible.

Joe looked to the southwest. A lazy curl of black smoke rose from where the river coursed through the valley where Nate's place was located.

"Trouble," Joe said, chinning toward the smoke.

# 5

NATE ROMANOWSKI watched the procession of vehicles stream down the two-track through binoculars. He counted seven of them—four look-alike sheriff's department SUVs, the sheriff's pickup, and two green pickups with decals on the doors bringing up the rear.

*"Joe,"* he said aloud. He glanced down at his satellite phone. An hour before, Joe had tried to call him but he hadn't picked up. Five minutes later, there had been another call from Marybeth Pickett that he declined to answer. But both calls coming so close to each other told him all he needed to know.

Nate was on his belly in a tangle of aspen high on the slope not far from where he'd hunted ducks the day before. His peregrine and prairie falcon were hooded a few feet behind him in the gold carpet of fallen leaves. The birds stood erect like still little sentinels, waiting to be unleashed.

For the hundredth time that day, he cursed his actions the evening before. He'd let himself be taken in by the three men in the boat simply because they were locals, and he hadn't connected their presence with The Five, the Special Forces unit he'd been in. That had been his first mistake. His second was that in the pain from the arrow through his shoulder, he'd let the boat simply float away downriver where it would eventually be found.

The two calls from Joe and Marybeth confirmed that it had.

So he'd been off his game. But an arrow in his flesh and the killing of three men had focused his mind, and he knew he was in the midst of a battle that might turn out to be his last. The rules hadn't changed as much as they'd been adapted to his location and circumstances. And he hadn't seen it coming.

THAT MORNING, he'd made his plan. Through a haze of pain and with the use of only one arm, he'd sunk his boat, burned the mews to the ground, and gathered all his gear and clothing into piles on the floor of his house before torching that, too. He'd smashed his electronic gear into bite-sized pieces and thrown only a few of his possessions into an old military duffel bag, along with the last bricks of cash, to take with him.

On a gravel bar in the river, he'd found the carbine the old man Paul had aimed at him. The rifle was in good shape after he'd dried and cleaned it. It was an all-weather Ruger Mini-14 Ranch rifle chambered in 6.8-millimeter with a thirty-round clip and a scope. He'd decided to keep it because the weapon would be good for precision work and for laying down cover fire, if necessary. The stock was black synthetic. The rifle, along with his .500, would serve his needs, he thought.

NATE HAD KILLED an antelope several days before and packed the carcass in ice in a dug-out icehouse fifty yards downriver. After cleaning his wounds with alcohol and taping on compresses, he'd sliced off the tenderloins and back straps and ate one of the back straps whole after searing it and seasoning it with salt and pepper. The light and flavorful lean meat seemed to help speed the replenishing of his blood supply. It was pure protein from the wild, and he thought it had healing properties.

IN HIS CIRCUMSTANCES, he'd decided to trim his life down to the bone. He'd taken only what he could carry. He'd eat only wild game and fish that he caught. And he'd get rid of his phone now that he'd made three calls on it; one to the Wind River Indian Reservation, the next to colleagues in the Idaho compound, and the third to a man in Colorado Springs.

IT HURT TO SHIFT his position, even to follow the oncoming procession through his field glasses. His shoulder screamed at him, and he'd noticed that his skin was purplish near the entry wound, and the dark wine color was expanding out. He had no painkilling drugs available and had spent most of the previous night fighting back waves of delirium. He'd lost a lot of blood.

As the caravan neared, he removed the satellite phone from its cover and placed it on a rock and smashed it into pieces with the butt of the rifle. In the pile of shards, he located the memory chip and therefore his call record, and flicked it into a mud bog on the edge of the aspens. By doing so, he was eliminating the last object in his possession that would leave a digital trace of his whereabouts.

THE FIRST SUV entered his yard and stopped with a lurch in front of his smoldering house. A strapping sheriff's deputy in full assault gear blasted out of the door with a semiautomatic rifle and aimed it toward the front door. The other SUVs roared in on both sides of it, and the occupants flew out of their vehicles in a similar fashion. They were so far away that he couldn't hear their shouts and warnings but assumed what they were yelling by their gestures and body movements. Nate had done enough assault training that he knew all the moves and objectives. These guys were sloppy and predictable and wouldn't have lasted long if he'd decided to make a stand against them, he thought. They were overgrown boys playing army with real weapons. Considering their leadership, he wasn't surprised.

He shifted his field of view over to the sheriff, who had parked his truck behind the row of SUVs. McLanahan ambled out, shouting instructions to the deputies in front of him and talking on a handheld radio to someone else. The first green pickup continued on through his yard and braked to a stop near the river. Another green pickup stuck close behind it. Nate sharpened his focus a bit.

Joe Pickett and the county attorney climbed out of the first truck. Joe wasn't armored up and didn't carry a long gun of any kind. Nate watched as Joe fitted his gray Stetson on his head. Even from that distance, and through undulating waves of condensation from the still-moist earth, Nate could tell that Joe had a pained expression on his face.

"Sorry, my friend," Nate whispered.


AS THE DEPUTIES cautiously approached the smoldering structure and the sheriff walked around uselessly behind them, Nate kept his binoculars on Joe. He watched as his friend ordered another Game and Fish employee to lead Schalk away from the open to cover behind the SUVs.

Then he shifted back to Joe, as the game warden kicked through the remains of the falcon mews, then walked down to the river and gazed into the water. On the bank, he leaned back and scanned the horizon on top of the high bluff. Apparently, the sheriff shouted something at him—probably for walking around in the open without a long gun in his red uniform shirt—but Joe waved him off.

Joe walked over to the side of the stone walls of the house where Nate parked his Jeep, and bent over to look at the ground. Then he walked a distance downriver, surveying ahead of him in the mud and sand. What was he following? Nate's tracks?

The game warden stopped suddenly near the old river cottonwoods as if jerked on a leash. He stared at the tree trunks, then cautiously looked over his shoulder toward the SUVs and the assault team.

With a feeling like a slight electric shock through his bowels, Nate realized what Joe was looking at. He'd made *three* mistakes.

"Uh-oh," Nate whispered. The arrow he'd been hit with was still embedded in the bark of the tree. An arrow likely covered with dried blood and his DNA. If the arrow was analyzed, the investigators would know that Nate had not only been there, but he'd been wounded. And so would The Five.

Nate said, *"What are you going to do, Joe?"* He felt for his friend. Joe was straight and upright and burdened with ethics, responsibility, and a sense of duty that had gotten him into trouble many times. It was something Nate admired about Joe, and a trait he'd shared many years before it had been destroyed.

He watched as Joe checked again to make sure no one was looking, then reached up quickly and wrenched the arrow from the tree. Then he ambled down to the river with the shaft hidden tight against the length of his leg and he flipped it into the fast current.

Nate closed his eyes for a moment and said, "Thank you."

LATER, after the assault team had finally left and the sun was slipping behind the western mountains, Nate freed the jesses and unhooded both birds. With his good right hand, he raised the prairie falcon and released him to the sky. He lifted the peregrine, and she cocked her head and stared at him with her black eyes.

"Go," he said, prompting her by lifting her up and down. She gripped his hand, and her talons tightened painfully through the glove.

"Really," he said. *"Go."*

Although she was likely hungry and there were ducks and geese cruising the river to find a place to settle for the night, she didn't spread her wings.

"I *mean* it," he said. "It's been good. You were a great hunter, but we both need to be free right now. We'll meet again in this world or the next. Now *go.*"

As he flung her into the air, his wounded shoulder bit him like a jackal and the pain nearly took him to his knees.

The peregrine shot out her wings and beat them until she grasped the air. He watched her climb, but she didn't seem to be concentrating on the river, the ducks, or the geese. She rose almost reluctantly, he thought. It wasn't supposed to be this way, he told himself. When a falconer and falcon parted, it was supposed to be the falcon's idea.

But she was still up there, a dot against the evening clouds, when he hiked down the other side of the rise to where he'd hidden his Jeep in a tangle of junipers.

# PART TWO

*To be a serious falconer a person must be a mixture of predator and St. Francis, with all the masochistic self-discipline of a Zen student. There will never be more than a few such people.*

—Steve Bodio, *A Rage for Falcons*

# 6

IT WAS UNNATURALLY dark on the wide, rutted roads of the Wind River Indian Reservation because, Nate guessed, someone had once again decided to drive around and shoot out all the overhead lights. He confirmed his suspicion when he heard the crunching of broken glass from the shattered bulbs beneath the tires of the Jeep as he slowly cruised down Norkok Street toward Fort Washakie. Despite the chill of the evening, he kept his windows down so all his senses could be engaged. Dried leaves rattled in the canopy of old trees and skittered across the road. The last sigh of the evening sun painted a bold red slash on the square top of Crowheart Butte in his rearview mirror.

In the 1860s, Chief Washakie of the Eastern Shoshone tribe ended a war with the encroaching Crow by fighting one-on-one with Chief Big Robber, the Crow leader. Washakie killed Big Robber and cut his heart out and stuck it on the end of his war lance in tribute to the fallen enemy. Hence the name of the butte. The reservation itself was huge, 2.2 million acres—the same size as Yellowstone Park. It was home to 2,500 Eastern Shoshone and 5,000 Northern Arapaho. In the old cemetery Nate drove past the last shard of sun glinting off rusted metal headboards and footboards that reached up out of the ground. Because the Indians interred their dead on scaffolds and the Jesuits insisted on burial, a compromise was reached: the bodies had been buried in their deathbeds.

Nate felt a sudden dark pang as he looked over the cemetery when he thought of Alisha, his lover. He had left her body on scaffolding of his own construction just two months before. He hadn't been back to the canyon where she'd been killed. He'd never go back.

All that remained of her except for his memories was the braided strand of her hair tied to the barrel of his .500 Wyoming Express revolver.

AS NATE slid down the roads in the dark, he glanced at still-life scenes of the residents through their windows. For some reason, the Indians seldom closed their curtains. He saw families gathered for dinner, people watching television, and in the lit-up opening of a single-car garage, a pair of young men in bloodied camo skinning a mule deer.

Alice Thunder's faded white bungalow was located just off Black Coal Road, and Nate cruised by it without slowing. Muted lights were on inside, and her GMC Envoy was parked under a carport on the side of her house. She lived alone there, and it appeared she didn't have company.

He did a three-point turn in the road and came back and turned onto a weedy two-track behind her house and parked where his Jeep couldn't be seen from the road.

Nate padded up the broken concrete walk to her back entrance and tapped on the metal screen door. Dogs inside yipped and howled, but through the sound he could feel her heavy footfalls approach.

She didn't turn on the porch light but stood behind the storm door and squinted at him. Small mixed-breed dogs boiled around and through her stout legs.

"Is that you, Nate Romanowski?" she asked.

He nodded and leaned his head against the peeling doorframe. His legs felt suddenly weak from his injury.

"If I invite you in this house, am I committing a federal crime?"

"Maybe," Nate said.

She yelled at her dogs to get away from the door, then cracked it open. He smelled a waft of warm air mixed with the smell of baking bread and wet dog hair.

"Get in here before someone sees you," she said. "You're hurt, aren't you?"

"Yes," he said, letting her lead him into the kitchen. Four or five dogs sniffed at his pants and boots. Alice Thunder was not a hugger or a smiler or an open enthusiast.

"Do you want to sit?" she asked, gesturing toward the table. She'd not yet set it for her evening meal.

"I brought you some ducks," he said, handing over the burlap sack.

"I love duck," she said.

"I remember you saying that. Careful, they're live."

"I'll twist their heads off in a minute," she said, ushering him to the table. "We can eat two of them. Do you want to eat duck?"

He sat heavily. His shoulder pounded at him, each pulse of blood brought a stab of pain. "Duck would be good," he said.


ALICE THUNDER was short and heavy, and her face was the shape and size of a hubcap. She had thick short fingers and a flat large nose and warm brown eyes. As the receptionist for the Indian high school for twenty-two years, she knew everyone and everyone knew her. She'd befriended Nate's lost lover Alisha when she'd moved back to the reservation to teach, and after Alisha's grandmother died, Alice Thunder had stepped in. Alisha's high school basketball photo was balanced on the top of her bookcase. Nate knew the two of them were related in some way, but he wasn't sure of the details. It was often the case on the reservation.

Her house was small, simple, and very lived-in. There were few pictures on the walls and a noticeable lack of gewgaws. Unlike some of the other Indian homes Nate had been invited into, there were no romantic portrayals of noble Plains Indians or rugs depicting maidens or warriors. Only the doll made of bent, packed straw and faded leather clothing on a shelf hinted at sentimentality. She'd once told Nate that her grandfather, an important tribal elder, had made it for her when she was a child.

"First I'll kill the ducks," Alice said, "then I'll see what's wrong with you. And I'm telling you now I want to eat most of the duck fat. I hope you don't want any."

"I already know what's wrong with me," Nate said. "I just need some help with the dressing. And you can have all the duck fat."

"So why are you bleeding?"

"I got shot with an arrow."

"Where's the arrow?"

"I pulled it out."

Alice Thunder paused at the back door with the sack of ducks and looked Nate over slowly. He couldn't tell whether she was amused at him or puzzled, or both. She had a way of making her face still while her eyes probed.

"Did you think an Indian woman would be able to help you more than the docs at the clinic because you were shot with an arrow?"

He said, "I can't go to the clinic."

"Ah, yes," she said. "You're an outlaw, I almost forgot." Then she bumped the back door open with her big hip and went outside to kill and clean the birds.

The little dogs gathered at the back door to whine and watch.

HE SAT without saying anything when she came back into the kitchen with three bloody duck breasts. She dipped them into a bowl of buttermilk, dredged them in flour and cornmeal, and dropped them into a cast-iron skillet bubbling with melted lard. She covered bits of bright-yellow fat in the flour as well and dropped them into the lard to create rich cracklings.

"Take off your shirt and let me take a look at your wound," she said over her shoulder. "Was it an Indian who shot you?"

"No," Nate said. "A redneck."

"There are Indian rednecks."

"This wasn't one of them," he said, rising painfully and reaching up with his right hand to unzip his vest.

Alice never said "natives" or "Native Americans." She always said "Indians."

While the duck breasts sizzled, she turned around and put her hands on her hips and closed one eye as she observed the bloody compresses he'd taped on himself.

"Sloppy," she said. "But keep it on until after we eat. Then I'll change it."

NATE LOOKED away as she stripped the old bandage and bathed the wounds with alcohol swabs and taped them.

"Does it sting?" she asked.

"It does," he said, and chinned toward her ticking woodstove. "Make sure to burn the old bandages and everything you're using to clean me up. Don't leave a trace of it in your house."

She paused, then continued cleaning. "You don't want to leave your DNA?"

"That's right."

"But you've been here in the past. I can't get rid of everything you might have touched."

"You don't need to," he said. "Just the blood."

"I don't think there's any infection," she said, shuffling her feet so she could get a good look at the holes in front and back, "but I've got some antibiotics and anti-inflammatory drugs I'll send with you. I'm not a doctor. You may need to go see one."

He grunted his thanks. Finally, he asked, "Don't you want to know what happened?"

She said, "I think I know. I heard about the boat they found in Saddlestring. Everybody's heard about that."

"I suppose so."

"There is one thing I want to know," she said.

He waited.

"Why did you come to me? Why didn't you go to see your friend, the game warden, and his wife?"

"Too risky," Nate said.

"But you don't mind risking me?" she asked. It was a flat statement, and not accusatory.

"I've been meaning to come by for a long time," he said. She stood aside as he got to his feet and pulled his shirt and vest back on. His shoulder ached, but the binding was tight and clean, and he gained a bit more movement in his left arm.

Nate went out the back door and returned with his duffel bag. He unzipped it and gave her a block of cash.

Alice took it from him and put it quickly on the table.

"It's ten thousand dollars," he said. "I wanted you to have it."

She shook her head. "Are you buying my silence?"

"No. I want you to use it however you see fit. But maybe you'd consider using some of it in Alisha's memory. Maybe a scholarship fund for her students, or memorial or something."

Surprisingly, he noted moisture in her dark eyes. "I miss her," she said.

"I miss her, too," he said, and gave her a thin braid of Alisha's hair. It was similar to the strand he'd attached to his gun. She took it from him and sniffed it and worked it through her fingers and held it there.

"It's my fault, I know that," he said. "If it wasn't for me, she wouldn't have been in the wrong place. I know that."

"Tell me what happened," she asked. "I've heard rumors, but no one else was there."

Nate said, "Two intruders breached my security and attacked the place I lived. Alisha was visiting for the weekend. I was outside when it happened. Alisha wasn't. She didn't suffer, at least."

"But you have," she said. It was a statement.

"If my life was more normal . . ."

Alice shook her head as if to discount him. She said, "Don't take all the blame. You're talking to someone who lives in a place that's never been normal. It's not so unusual to me, and it wasn't unusual to her. She would have followed you anywhere, I'm sure."

"I found the men who did it," Nate said. "I put them down."

She looked away.

"I need to go," he said.

She stepped aside. As he neared the door, she said, "A man came by the school last week and asked about Alisha. But I knew he was really asking about you."

NATE PAUSED and turned. "What did you tell him?"

"The truth," she said. "I told him Alisha no longer worked there, that she had left the school and the res."

"But no more than that?"

"No. Then I waited. He acted kind of put-out and asked me where he could contact her. I told him I didn't know. He asked me if I knew anyone who might know of her location. Any friends, for example."

Nate leaned against her kitchen counter, waiting for more.

She continued, "He asked me, doesn't she have a friend who is a falconer? Did I know where he can be reached?"

He arched his eyebrows.

"I told him I didn't know where you were. And I didn't, either. I told him if he wanted to try and find you he should ask the local game warden, Joe Pickett."

Nate felt a chill. "You mentioned Joe?"

"I thought that might make him go away. He seemed like the kind of guy who wouldn't really want to talk to a law enforcement officer."

"Describe him," Nate said.

She closed her eyes, as if conjuring up an image. "Tall, white, maybe six-foot-two or -three. He was older than you by ten years or so, but in good shape. He had light brown hair and blue eyes. His eyes were set close together, and he had a long thin nose. High cheekbones, but Scandinavian, not Indian. His face was angular and his mouth was small. He had a mouth like a pink rose, I thought. Like he wanted to kiss somebody. But he gave me a bad feeling."

She opened her eyes.

Nate nodded. "Did he give you a name?"

She said, "Bob White."

Nate snorted.

"It seemed like a fake name," she said.

"It is. Did you see what he was driving?"

She shook her head. "I didn't look out in the visitor's parking lot. I didn't think of it until later, and by then he was gone."

Nate asked, "How much vacation time do you have?"

She cocked her head to the side, puzzled at the question. "I have a lot," she said. "I never take any days off."

"Alice," he said, "I want you to take some of that money and go someplace you always wanted to go. Take a couple weeks. Just please promise me you'll go away for a while."

"Do you think he'll come back? Do you think he'd hurt me?"

Nate shrugged. "I don't know, but we don't want to take a chance."

She thought about it. "I always wanted to go to Austin and see the bats. You know, the bats that come out every night from under that bridge and fly? I like bats."

"Then go to Austin," he said. "See the bats. And when you get bored with them, go somewhere else and see some other bats. Just get out of this place for a while."

She looked at him for a long time. Her face never moved.

"Start packing tonight," Nate said.

"Who is this man?" she asked.

Nate said, "Someone I used to work with. And believe me, he's not someone you want to see again."

He recalled Large Merle's last words, and it all made sense to him. *They've deployed.*

# 7

AFTER LEAVING Alice Thunder's home, Nate saw lights through the roadside trees and turned in to an alleyway that led behind the small lighted building. The sign in front flickered from ancient fluorescent bulbs inside, but it read BAD BOB's NATIVE AMERICAN OUTLET. It was a convenience store at the junction that sold gasoline, food, and inauthentic Indian trinkets to tourists. Three old pickups were parked at odd angles in front. One, an older model blue Dodge, had its back end aimed to the side and Nate could read the bumper sticker. It showed a graphic of four Apaches holding rifles and it read HOME-LAND SECURITY: FIGHTING TERRORISM SINCE 1492. Another sticker read MY HEROES HAVE ALWAYS KILLED COWBOYS.

Bad Bob, the owner of the pickup, also rented DVDs and computer games to boys on the reservation. The back room was where the men gathered to talk and loiter and Bob held court. On the side of the store was one of the few remaining pay telephone booths still in operation on the res. Nate pulled up next to it and dropped two quarters into the slot and punched numbers.

"Dispatch," answered a woman with a nasally voice.

"Hey," Nate said. "I need to report a game violation. Is this the hotline I'm supposed to call?"

"It can be," she said. "This is the general state dispatch center, but we can take your information and forward it to the proper agency. What is your name, where are you calling from, and what is the nature of the call?"

He hesitated for effect, then said, "My name's not important, but I'm calling from a pay phone in Twelve Sleep County. I just saw a crime, and I want to report it."

Nate described a scenario where someone in a pickup with a spotlight—he used Bad Bob's vehicle for inspiration—was firing indiscriminately at a herd of mule deer just off Hazelton Road near Crazy Woman Creek. He said it was awful, and gave her the location.

"When did this happen?" she asked.

"Just a few minutes ago," he said. "I just got to a phone. You've got to send someone up there."

"Are you sure you can't give me your name?" she asked. "We might need to follow up and contact you for better directions."

"The directions are perfect," he said.

"I'll contact the game warden in the district and relay your report," she said. "I can't promise he'll be there right away, though. It's a huge district, and he may be off duty right now."

"Thank you," Nate said.

"*Thank you* for calling the Stop Poaching Hotline," she said, obviously reading from a screen.


WHEN NATE hung up the phone, he looked up to see Bad Bob coming around the corner of the store holding a lever-action rifle. Bad Bob was shaped like a barrel and had a wide oval face pocked with acne scars. His hair was black, and it glistened from the gel he used to slick the sides down and spike the top. He was wearing a Denver Broncos jersey, baggy trousers, and unlaced Nike high-tops. When he saw Nate, he said, "Jesus!" and jumped back and raised the rifle.

Nate didn't reach up for his weapon. He said, "Bob, it's me. Put the rifle down."

"You fuckin' scared me, man," Bob said. "I heard something and I was going out back to see if them bears were in my Dumpster again. I've been asking the tribe for some bear-proof garbage cans for months, and they keep saying they'll bring some, but here we are and I still got damn bears." He patted the rifle. "I'm gonna smoke one if I catch him and make me a bearskin rug."

Bad Bob was Alisha's brother. Nate hadn't seen him since her death.

"I'm sorry about your sister, Bob," Nate said.

Bad Bob lowered the rifle and lowered his voice. "Yeah, she was always too good to be true, you know."

Nate didn't respond to that. Bob was Alisha's older brother, and they'd had a strained relationship and rarely spoke to each other. Alisha had left the reservation after high school, got a degree, married, and moved comfortably in Denver social circles. After her divorce, she'd returned to the res on a mission to try and help the students move up and out. She believed in entrepreneurship and individualism, and fought against a group mentality. Bob, on the other hand, rarely ventured off the res and gave talks encouraging the tribes to secede from the union. But he never mailed back a government check, either. The convenience store had been passed down from an uncle who died of cancer, and it had become Bob's headquarters. The sign in front lured white tourists into the store so Bob could insult them face-to-face.

Bob said, "I heard that the couple of guys who did it are taking the dirt nap."

"They are," Nate said.

Bad Bob nodded with satisfaction. "So what are you doing here, man? I thought you left the country."

"I'm passing through," Nate said. "Just using your phone before I leave."

"Why don't you come in? I got some coffee on, and there's some wine getting passed around in there."

"No, thanks," Nate said. "I've got to go. But I've got one question for you."

Bob leaned the rifle against the brick wall of his store and walked forward and slumped against Nate's Jeep and looked down at his shoes. "You want to know when you'll be getting some of that loan back, I know. But times have been really tough around here. When there's all that unemployment out there outside the res, you can imagine what it's like inside. Shit, I run credit accounts for all these mooks until government check day and then I just *hope* they'll come in and pay off their tabs."

"It's not that," Nate said. "I was wondering if you or any of your friends have seen a guy." He described "Bob White."

Bad Bob took a long time answering. "I think he might have got gas last week," he said. "At least it sort of sounds like him, man. All you white people look alike to me." Bob grinned.

"Not now," Nate said impatiently. "Was it him?"

"Maybe. I don't know. He pulled out front, gassed up his rig, and left. We didn't have a conversation, really. Oh—he asked how to get to the school."

Nate nodded. It would have been the same day the man met Alice Thunder.

"What was he driving?"

Bob rubbed his chin. "I'm trying to remember. Oh, yeah, It was a nice rig, one of these crossovers; part luxury car and part SUV. An Audi Q7. First one I've seen on the res. It was dark gray or blue."

"Plates?"

"I don't remember, but I think if they was out-of-state I would have noticed. But maybe not."

"Anybody with him?"

"Naw," Bob said. "He was alone. But I do remember he had a bunch of shit piled in the backseat. Gear bags or luggage or something. Nobody could have sat back there because there wasn't room."

Nate asked, "How did he pay?"

"Cash," Bob said. "That I remember. Not many people pay in cash these days, they all use cards. But he peeled some twenties off a roll and I gave him change. That I remember."

Nate nodded. Then, "Bob, we didn't have this talk. You never saw me tonight."

Bob looked over, wanting to hear more.

"That's all. Forget I was here."

"All right," Bob said with hesitation.

"And forget about the loan," Nate said, restarting his Jeep.

"Thanks, man," Bob said, stepping away from the Jeep. It was perfunctory. As far as Nate knew, Bob had *never* repaid a loan, and he didn't expect him to start now.


A FEW HUNDRED YARDS up the reservation road toward the mountains and Hazelton Road, Nate saw a sow black bear in his headlights and swerved to miss it. In the red glow of his taillights he watched her amble down the faded center stripe of the asphalt en route to Bad Bob's Dumpster.

# 8

CRAZY WOMAN CAMPGROUND was empty except for two travel trailers full of elk hunters in the farthest reaches of the campsite. Nate could hear the hunters whoop from time to time, and he hummed along with old country music emanating from one of the closest RVs. Because of the possibility of being seen by any of the hunters if they chose to go for a walk in the dark, he moved his Jeep out to Hazelton Road, drove a mile away from the entrance of the campground, and backed it deep into the trees on an old logging road and waited.

It was nearly midnight when he saw a glimpse of distant headlights coming down the road. Just as suddenly, the lights doused. Joe, he thought, had hit his sneak lights as he got close to where the poacher had been reported. Sneak lights were mounted under the bumper and threw a dim pool of light out directly in front of the vehicle so potential violators couldn't see him coming up the gravel road.

It was a cool, clear night and the stars were brilliant. The only sound was the occasional eerie and high-pitched elk bugle from the wall of thick trees on the rising mountains behind him. Upper Doyle Creek tinkled lightly on the other side of the road, deeply undercutting the grass banks on its circuitous route to the Twelve Sleep River.

Joe was almost upon him before he realized it. Nate saw the dull orb of light from beneath the front of the pickup, got a whiff of exhaust and heard the low rumble of the engine, and there he was, creeping along the gravel road, windows open so he could hear shots.

"Joe," Nate said aloud.

The pickup braked to a stop. "Nate? Where are you?"

Nate fished a mini-Maglite flashlight out of his vest and swept it along the road in front of him until the light reflected from the headlights of his Jeep in the brush.

"This way," he said, stepping aside.

As Joe turned off the gravel road and rumbled by Nate, his friend said, "There are no poachers, are there?"

"No."


NATE USED his flashlight to see ahead as he led Joe deeper into the trees to the edge of a small clearing. He jabbed the beam of light on a fallen tree trunk and said, "Have a seat," while he kicked enough grapefruit-sized rocks free from the soil to make a small fire ring. Nate bunched a handful of dried grass in the center of the ring, lit it with a match, and started feeding the flames with dried pine needles and twigs.

He said, "I couldn't risk calling you or coming to your place because I don't know if you're being watched and I can't afford to leave any physical or digital records of my location or movements. The last thing I want to do is involve you or your family in what's happening."

Joe cleared his throat and sat back. "Good thing I showed up alone, then. The department assigned me a trainee, but when I called the TeePee Motel he wasn't in, so I didn't bring him along. I don't know where he is."

"That would have been unfortunate," Nate said.

Joe leaned forward with his elbows on the tops of his knees and squinted at Nate. "So what *is* happening, Nate?"

Nate continued to feed twigs to the flame and didn't look up. "Those three guys in the boat. They drew on me and I put them down. One of them shot me in the shoulder with an arrow."

"Ron Connelly, the Mad Archer, I'd guess," Joe interjected.

"Yes. They took me by surprise because they were locals. I let my guard down and they took advantage of it, which I think was the strategy all along. It was self-defense, Joe. Two of them were pulling guns as I shot them, and the one in front—the Mad Archer—had already put an arrow into me. I want you to know that even though you can't really help me, because I know how you are. I understand it's too late for that anymore."

Nate took Joe's lack of response as agreement. He said, "When you go off the grid, there are advantages and disadvantages. I always knew that. I'm not accountable for anything except to my own code, which is how I want it, because I trust my code more than any set of laws manipulated by those with their hands on the levers. But that's an old story," he said.

Joe nodded for him to go on.

Nate said, "I'm nonexistent as far as the government is concerned, and that's harder these days than you'd think. But when something like this happens—or what happened to Alisha—I can't respond through normal channels. I can't let anyone know. I smashed my phone and there's no way to find me. But I can't call the cops or get a lawyer to defend me because then I'm back in the system and that's where the bastards want me to be."

Joe nodded, thinking it over, and finally asked, "How are you doing? You said you got hit with an arrow."

Nate tented a half dozen bigger sticks over the fire and watched as the flames licked around them like tongues tasting peppermint sticks before they ignited. "I'm okay," he said. "I can barely use my left arm, but it's healing. I'm okay. I'll be in *yarak* soon."

"*'Yarak'*?"

"Falconry term. Look it up," Nate said, waving the exchange away.

"I can't take you into town, but I could take you to the clinic on the res," Joe said. "We might be able to work something out with them to keep it confidential. You've got lots of friends there."

Nate shook his head. "No—I won't involve anyone else in this. This thing I'm in is mine alone. And anybody who comes near me could get into trouble that's not of their doing. I learned that when I stopped in to see Alice Thunder. I can't risk anybody else, Joe. It's not right."

Joe looked confused.

"Alice promised me she would take a flight out," Nate said. "But I could see her finding an excuse not to leave. The only thing I'll ask you is to tail up and make sure she goes on vacation. Can I ask you that?"

"Done," Joe said.

"What I couldn't figure out," Nate said, nodding, "is *why*. Why would three locals decide to try to rub me out? I didn't even know them very well, and I'd never had any trouble with them. And I'm pretty sure the people I used to work with who want me dead wouldn't associate with rubes like that. The Mad Archer and the Kellys weren't professionals. They were rednecks with guns, and like everybody around here, they knew how to aim and shoot, but that didn't qualify them as anything special."

Joe said, "I might know something about it."

Nate looked up, surprised. There was enough flickering orange light now that he could see Joe's face.

"This afternoon, I went out to the Kelly place," Joe said. "Two of the men you killed were Kellys—Paul the father and his son Ronald, better known as Stumpy."

"The gargoyle," Nate said with derision. "I've done it before, but I don't take any pleasure killing the mentally or physically handicapped, even if they want to kill me."

Joe hesitated, looking Nate over. Then he said haltingly, "No one I've ever known would make a statement like that."

Nate shrugged, and Joe continued, "Yeah, him. Anyway, I talked to Paul's wife and Stumpy's mom, Pam Kelly. She's in a state of rage because you took two of her men away, and it wasn't a very pleasant conversation," Joe said.

Nate asked, "You went and talked to her? Is this after the sheriff interviewed her?"

Joe shook his head. "McLanahan did a cursory call to her saying he was sorry for her loss. But he didn't interview her."

"But you did," Nate said as a statement.

"She's a piece of work, and I wouldn't want to cross her. She's mad at Paul and the world in general. She was literally tearing her hair out. I mean, she had strands of it in her fingers when I showed up."

Nate said, "It didn't have to happen."

"I know," Joe said. "But try telling that to Pam Kelly. The weird thing was I didn't get the impression she was crazy from grieving as much as angry that Paul and Stumpy had let her down. Anyway, I asked her why she thought Paul and Stumpy went out in their boat with the Mad Archer. At first, she acted like she had no idea at all, but I could tell she was lying about part of it."

"Which part?"

"I don't think she knew anything about the boat trip in particular. For all she knew, they were going hunting. It took a while to get to the bottom of why they were with the Mad Archer. Apparently, they'd met him just a couple of weeks ago and he recruited them into some scheme that would make them big money. Pam Kelly didn't know what it was, but she *really* liked the idea of big money and didn't ask a lot of questions."

Joe sighed and said, "It's no secret that all the trouble Stumpy and Paul got into with their illegal guiding operation was all run out of Pam's home office. She wants nice things but she was stuck with a loser. Paul's disability checks didn't go very far, I guess. I've heard it said that she wore the pants in that family, and my talk with her confirmed that."

Nate said, "Someone was going to pay them to kill me?"

"That's what I got out of it," Joe said.

"Did she say who it was? It sure as hell wasn't the Mad Archer, I'm sure."

Joe said, "There are probably fifty-four game wardens across this state who aren't very busted up about what happened to that guy. So at least you've got that going for you."

Nate smiled.

"No, I don't think it was Ron Connelly behind anything. He was a dupe just like the Kellys," Joe said. "I asked Pam Kelly who might have been behind it and she said she saw a man with them a couple of weeks ago. She'd gone to visit her sister in rehab in Riverton and wasn't expected back for a couple of days, but her sister had flown the coop. So she got home before she was expected back and apparently surprised them all—Paul, Stumpy, Ron Connelly, and a mystery man—when she walked into the kitchen and found them sitting at her table. The man she didn't know got up and walked out and drove away and she never saw him again. When she asked her husband who the man was, he said he didn't know his name but he was the one who had the big money. She called him the Game Changer.

She said Paul seemed to be scared of this Game Changer guy and didn't want to talk about him *at all*."

"Did she describe him?" Nate asked.

Joe fished his small spiral notebook out of his breast pocket and flipped it open. "Tall, pale, mid-fifties. Dressed well. Kind of handsome in a scary way, she said. He had 'creepy' eyes and a mouth like a girl model. That's what she said, 'a mouth like a girl model.'"

Nate shook his head in recognition.

"So you know about him?" Joe asked.

"Yes, and now it's starting to make some sense. He also went to the school to ask about Alisha. What I don't know is why he came himself, and why now."

"Does this guy have a name?" Joe asked.

"John Nemecek," Nate said.

Joe repeated the name phonetically, "John *Nemma-check*."

"Yes. He was my master falconer. I was his apprentice. We used to work together. He saved my life more than once, and I saved his."

Joe asked, "So he's a friend?"

"He was once. But that was years ago."

"Not anymore, then?"

Nate paused, then said, "Joe, he's the most dangerous man I've ever met."

Joe simply stared. Then he asked, "Why would he pay the Kellys and the Mad Archer to take you down?"

Nate said, "Because that's one of their tactics: recruit local tribesmen."

Joe sat up straight and asked, *"What?"*

Nate said, "Even with the name, you're not going to find out anything about him. Like me, he's been off the grid for years. But unlike me, he's been hiding in plain sight."

Joe said, "Local tribesmen?"

Nate stirred the fire so the flames erupted and the dry pine lengths popped sparks. He said, "COIN. Counterinsurgency tactics. How much do you want to know? I've tried to tell you before, but you didn't want to hear it."

Joe cocked one eye. "And I'm not sure I want to hear it now. Just tell me: how much trouble are you in?"

Nate sat back on the cool ground and met Joe's eyes. He said, "He'll probably kill me. I'm just being realistic. He's *that* good."

Joe's face fell.

"In a way, I deserve it," Nate said. "In fact, I'm resigned to the fact. Considering what I carry around with me, it may even come as a relief. I'd welcome some kind of conclusion. Except for one thing."

"What's that?" Joe asked, almost in a whisper.

"John Nemecek deserves it even more than I do."


NATE THOUGHT Joe looked like he was in physical pain, the way he kept writhing around while seated on the log. Nate could guess at the source: Joe wanted to know almost as badly as he didn't want to know. And Nate understood. Joe was a sworn officer of the law. He took his oath seriously. He'd managed to stay just over to the right side of the line all these years because he wasn't keeping Nate's secrets—secrets that might lead Joe to turn his friend in or arrest him outright. Not to mention what Joe would think of him if he knew.

Nate said, "I'll let you off the hook for now so you can relax."

Joe looked up with the quizzical Labrador-type expression he sometimes had, even if he didn't know it.

"I'll save it for when you have to know," Nate said. "When there's no choice. It might be sooner than you think, but for now we can move on."

Joe seemed to be okay with that. He asked, "Do you have a game plan for this Nemecek guy?"

Nate shrugged, "I'm still working it out. But what I do know is that something has happened to cause him to come out here for me in person. In the past, as you know, he sent surrogates. I was able to, um, make them go away."

As he said it, he could see Joe withdrawing a little, so Nate brought it back to vagaries.

"Anyway, I need to do some investigating of my own," Nate said. "I'll find out what's happened that made him feel like he had to come out here and take care of things himself. He's secretive and cautious, and he's always been an expert when it comes to getting things done and not leaving any fingerprints of his own on the operations. So for him to leave his lair, well, something is pressing him hard. If I find out what it was, I might have an angle."

Joe said, "Did he send someone out here to take care of Large Merle? Get him out of the way? No one's seen the guy in a month."

Nate was surprised Joe was aware of the disappearance of Large Merle, but he didn't give it away. Joe once again impressed him with his innate ability to dig deep and look at the world through his own eyes.

"Yes," Nate said. "He sent a young woman. He knew Merle well enough to know his soft spot, and that's how he got to him. Merle should have known better. Not many young and attractive women show interest in a giant."

Joe asked, "Is Merle the last one of your friends from the old days?"

Nate shook his head. "Not entirely. I've still got some allies, but there aren't many left. A few of them died of natural causes. A couple went straight and won't even acknowledge our old unit. A couple more are in prison, where they tried to put me. And there is a small group of them . . . in another state. They're off the grid, too."

"Can they help?" Joe asked. Nate wasn't sure Joe knew about the conclave in Idaho, but he'd made references in the past and his friend was probably aware. For one thing, Joe knew Diane Shober, for whom they'd both searched in the Sierra Madre, was in Idaho. But Joe didn't let on anything, and Nate didn't press.

"I'm going to find that out soon," Nate said. "I'm going to go away for a while. Nemecek won't hang around here if he thinks I'm gone."

"Can *I* help?"

"I don't want you any more involved, as I said. The farther you stay away from me, the better."

Joe sighed heavily. "I can keep an eye out, at least," he said. "If this Nemecek is still in the area, I might get a lead on him. It's a small town, Nate. Not much goes on somebody doesn't talk about it."

Nate started to object, then thought better of it. Joe did have a wealth of contacts and was the kind of man people liked to talk to. Joe was empathetic. People told him things they shouldn't, and Nate was guilty of that as well.

"That might be okay," Nate said. "As long as you don't try to *do* anything. If you did and something happened and Marybeth and those girls lost a husband and a father . . . well, that can't happen. I mean it, Joe."

Joe scoffed.

"You think I'm kidding, don't you?" Nate said. "And I don't mean that as an insult. You've got a way of getting into the middle of things and you usually come out on top. But it's a percentage game, Joe. The odds wouldn't be with you if you got too close to him. He's not like anybody you've ever run across."

Nate paused, and said, "I've always admired you, Joe, you know that."

His friend looked away, but even in the firelight Nate could see he was flushing and uncomfortable.

Nate said, "You've got a beautiful wife, great daughters, and a house with a picket fence. I know it sounds trite, but there are assholes out there who think my life is hard, but it isn't. Anybody can keep to themselves and be selfish. What you do every day is hard, Joe. Staying true and loyal, man, that's not the easy path. I admire what you've got. . . ."

Joe leaned back on the log and rolled his eyes, said, *"Enough!"* but Nate kept going.

Nate said, "I want to defend it, even if I can't ever get there myself. That's what this has always been about: admiration. So I can't let you get hurt trying to solve my problem. And this guy . . . he's something else."

"He really scares you, doesn't he?" Joe asked. "What is it about him?"

Nate thought about it as the fire died down. He didn't put any more fuel on it. "You know what I'm like," Nate said. "You know what kinds of things I've done."

"*Some* of them," Joe said, cautioning Nate again not to go beyond their conversation.

Nate said, "There's a certain kind of ruthlessness that can only be achieved by the coldest professionals or the truly deranged. The middle ground is mushy as hell, and unpredictable. Nemecek taught me professional ruthlessness. It takes a certain kind of mind-set to believe that whatever you do is correct and whoever gets hurt in the process is no more than collateral damage when it comes to achieving something greater. He has that mind-set. He's the greatest asset imaginable to his masters and to a righteous cause. Those are the circumstances I met him under. But if things get warped . . ."

Nate wasn't sure he was making sense, based on Joe's quizzical expression. Nate paused, thought about it, and said, "Nemecek is the greatest falconer I've ever seen. He's better than I will ever be, and

I'm good. But what you need to realize is that great falconers, master falconers, see the world differently than anyone else. Think about it, Joe. A falconer devotes his life to a wild raptor and develops a partnership based on killing prey. But at any time, the falcon—the wild, untamed weapon—can simply fly away. Imagine devoting years of your life to a potential lethal partnership that could dissolve in an instant. It takes a crazy devotion to a possible outcome that may never materialize. Falconry is as old as human civilization. It goes against the nature of things that a human and a killer bird should work together for a common purpose. But when it happens, man . . . it's the greatest thing in the fucking world. When it does, all the normal human social conventions seem like bat shit. And humans become just another hunk of meat compared to the rapture of wild and man when they intersect."

Joe seemed stunned and said nothing.

Nate said, "What I'm telling you is that really great falconers, like Nemecek, think they've transcended low human boundaries in regard to behavior and morals. Therefore, everything they do is on a different and higher plane."

Joe nodded.

Nate said, "So you take a person like this and you have to understand that he's worst when he's cornered. He has nothing but contempt for those who put him in that position, because they've never experienced what he's experienced, and they don't even comprehend the sacrifice that he's undergone. And something has made him feel cornered. Believe me, he's capable of *anything*."

Joe shook his head, not fully comprehending what Nate was getting at.

Nate said impatiently, "Once, in a country I won't name, I watched him saw the face off of a child with piano wire in front of her father to make the old man talk." Nate paused and said, "He talked."

*"My God,"* Joe said, as an obvious shiver ran through him.

Nate said, "I've seen him do worse than that. But what you have to understand is that when you've devoted your life to studying and worshipping birds of prey, you can lose your empathy for mere humans. When you turn yourself over to the call of the wild and understand it, things we would consider cruel are just part of the game."

Joe looked even more uncomfortable than before, the way he was shifting his seat on the log. He said, "I guess what it comes down to is values. And I'm in no position to argue that."

Nate said, "You could argue, but this isn't the time."

Minutes went by.

Joe asked, "Tell me what I can do to help. Since you don't have a phone, how can I reach you if I find anything?"

"Give me your notebook," Nate asked.

Joe handed it over, and Nate flipped it open to a fresh page and jotted down the address for a website: www.themasterfalconer.com.

"It's an old website," Nate said, handing the notebook back. "It hasn't been updated since it was put up over ten years ago. It's one of those sites where there are dozens of comment threads on it about different aspects of falconry. No one monitors the comments, and there are probably less than a few dozen people who even look at it anymore. But if you need to reach me, call it up. You'll find a recent thread with words or references in it you know are mine. Register on the site and keep your comments brief and vague. I'll understand."

Joe looked at the address. "How often will you check it out?"

"I can't say for sure. But at least every couple of days from a public computer somewhere."

Joe shook his head. "If there are dozens of threads, how will I know which one you're using?"

"Look for a recent thread with a question about flying kestrels."

"Why kestrels?" Joe asked. "Aren't they little tiny birds?"

Nate nodded. "Yes, they're the lowest and the most unreliable of the falcons. There's a royalty of falcons, starting with the eagle, who is the emperor. The gyr falcon is the king, the peregrine is the duke, and so on. On the bottom of the pecking order is the kestrel, which is considered the knave or servant. The reason I'm choosing a thread with a kestrel is because no self-respecting falconer would give a rip and look at it. Even so, don't say anything directly that could be interpreted by a lurker."

"Can't we do better than this?" Joe asked. "Can't you call me from a pay phone or something?"

"Not a chance," Nate said. "Nemecek has his tentacles everywhere. It's better to be low-key and obscure. And remember—don't write anything that could possibly be used to tie you to me."

"Nate . . ."

Nate stood and ground the last of the fire out with his boot heel. It was suddenly very dark.

"One more thing, Joe," he said. "If you get the word from me to evacuate, that means grab your family and fly away somewhere. Don't even take the time to pack—just get the hell out."

From the dark, Joe asked, "Do you think he'd come after us to get to you?"

"I told you," Nate said. "He's capable of anything."


AS THEY made their way through the downed timber back to the vehicles, Nate heard Joe clear his throat in a way that indicated he wanted to say something.

Over his shoulder, Nate asked, "What is it?"

"This thing you did," Joe asked. "How bad was it?"

Said Nate, "Worse than you can imagine."

"And Nemecek was there?"

"Yes."

"It couldn't have been that bad," Joe said. "I mean, I know you pretty well after all these years."

As Nate reached his Jeep, he said, "You just think you do, Joe."

Joe reached out and grasped Nate's hand. He said, "Be safe, my friend."

"I will."

Joe turned to leave. Nate said, "And if I don't ever see you again, I just want you to know it was an honor to know you and you're a good man and a good friend. As far as I'm concerned, there's nothing better I can say."

Joe was uncomfortable, obviously, but he met Nate's eyes and said, "Knock it off. When did you get so mushy?"

And Nate said, "When he came here after me."

# 9

JOE RETURNED HOME shortly after ten to find another Game and Fish pickup parked in his place in front of the garage. The lights were on inside the house, and Joe swung in next to his trainee's vehicle.

He got out and took a deep breath of the cold, thin air. Nate had rattled him and he didn't want to show it.

Luke Brueggemann sat on the living room sofa and looked up when Joe came in. He was wearing his uniform and cradling a can of Pepsi between his knees. He looked at him expectantly, his eyes wondering why Joe hadn't called him.

"I called your room," Joe said. "I left a message. In the future, you need to be prepared or let me know your cell phone number."

At the same time, though, Joe was grateful Brueggemann hadn't been along to see Nate Romanowski.

His trainee plucked his cell phone out of his pocket and punched numbers. Joe's own phone burred in his pocket and he leaned back to pull it out but Brueggemann said, "That's me. You have my number now."

"Okay."

"Did you find anything up there?" Brueggemann asked.

"Nope," Joe said, as he turned and hung his jacket on a peg in the mudroom and put his hat on the shelf. "Somebody's idea of a prank call, I guess."

Brueggemann shook his head. "I've heard that happens."

Joe sat down in a chair facing Brueggemann and said, "It does." Then: "Why are you here?"

The trainee grinned and his face flushed. "I got your message when I got back to my room. So I threw on my uniform and waited for you to pick me up. When you didn't, I started driving up here thinking I'd meet you here. But when I got here, you were gone."

As he talked, Marybeth came into the living room from the kitchen, shaking her head at Joe. "My husband has forgotten what being a trainee is like," she said. "Even though it should be scarred into his memory. It sure is scarred into *mine*."

"I said I left a message," Joe said, sitting back in the chair.

His wife looked casual and attractive in a pair of sweatpants and an oversized white shirt rolled up at the sleeves. Her blond hair was tied back in a ponytail, making her look young, Joe thought. She wore a pair of horn-rimmed glasses Joe referred to as her "smart glasses." It was obvious she'd taken pity on Luke Brueggemann.

She said, "I saw him sitting in his truck out on the road, so I invited him in and fed him some dinner," she said. "I told him you'd be back soon. I didn't think it would be two hours."

Joe shrugged.

"I tried to call you on the radio," Brueggemann said, looking away from Joe so as not to pile on too much, "but you must have been out of range."

"I guess so," Joe said. He'd turned his radio off when Nate had appeared in the woods.

"Anyway," Marybeth said, apparently finished with her admonishment, "Luke here helped April with her math and listened to Lucy recite some of her part from the play. So all in all, a nice evening."

She winked at Joe to show Joe she was teasing. Joe shook his head at his wife. Those items would have been on his agenda for the evening.

To Brueggemann, Marybeth said, "Remember this when you get married and move your new bride to your game warden quarters in the middle of nowhere. Advise her that you are always on call so she won't be angry when you suddenly have to leave the house at any hour. In fact, before you get married, have her give me a call."

"Don't do it," Joe said to Brueggemann. "Keep her in the dark. It's better that way."

The trainee looked from Marybeth to Joe, and to Marybeth again.

"I'm kidding," Joe said.

Brueggemann visibly relaxed and realized he'd been played by both of them. "You had me going there," he said.

"And another thing," Joe said. "Don't ever go out on a call without your trainee."

"Ha! I never would."


MARYBETH SENT Brueggemann back to his room at the TeePee Motel with leftovers, which the trainee was enthusiastic about.

"I've been eating too much fast food and microwave soup and drinking too many sodas," he said. "A home-cooked meal is pretty nice."

"Anytime," Marybeth said.

Joe told Brueggemann he'd call him in the morning.

"Are we going to check out those elk camps?" Brueggemann asked at the door.

"Maybe," Joe said. "It depends on the weather and circumstances. Everything's fluid at all times."

Brueggemann nodded earnestly and shut the door.

"I like him," Marybeth said, giving Joe a delayed hello peck on the cheek. "He's an eager beaver. He reminds me of you when you started."

Joe nodded, and realized how hungry he was. He asked, "Did you give him all of the leftovers?"

"Oops," she said.


WHILE MARYBETH cooked Joe an egg sandwich in the kitchen, he said, "Nate was out there."

He noticed how her back tensed when he said it. She looked over her shoulder from where she stood at the stove. "I had a feeling about that," she said. "In fact, I knew we could have reached you by cell phone, but I didn't suggest it to Luke. I thought if you'd hooked up with Nate, you probably wouldn't want your trainee showing up."

"You're right about that," Joe said.

"So how is he? Was he . . . involved with those men they found in the boat?"

Said Joe, "Nate's injured, but he claims he's okay. And yes, that was him who shot those men in the boat. He says they tried to ambush him and it was self-defense."

Her eyes got big and she started to ask Joe a question, when she suddenly looked around him and said, "Hello, Lucy. Time for bed?"

"Yeah," Lucy said. "I wanted to say good night."

Fourteen-year-old Lucy was in the eighth grade at Saddlestring Middle School. She was blond and green-eyed and lithe—a miniature version of her mother. She was still getting used to not having her older sister Sheridan in the house, but was using the occasion to bloom into her own personality, which was expressive and good-hearted. She was growing into an attractive and pleasant young lady, Joe thought.

Joe said, "Sorry about missing your speech tonight."

"It wasn't a speech," Lucy said. "It was the first act of the play. I've got to have it memorized by the end of the week."

"And how's it going?"

"Good," she said, and flashed a smile.

Sheridan had been an athlete, although not an elite one. Lucy had opted for speech and drama, and had recently been chosen for one of the female leads in *The Lion, the Witch and the Wardrobe*.

"My character is *Lucy* Pevensie," Lucy said, and cued Marybeth.

Marybeth said, *"'The White Witch? Who's she?'"*

Lucy's face transformed into someone younger and more agitated, and she said, *"'She is a perfectly terrible person. She calls herself the Queen of Narnia though she has no right to be queen at all, and all the fauns and dryands and naiads and dwarfs and animals—at least all the good ones—simply hate her. . . .'"*

When she finished, Joe said, "Wow."

"I always think of Grandma Missy when I say those lines," Lucy said. "She's my inspiration."

Joe laughed and Marybeth said, "Get to bed, Lucy. That was a cheap shot."

"But a good one," Joe said, after Lucy had padded down the hall-way to her room, pleased with herself for making her dad laugh.

"Don't encourage her," Marybeth said.

"Yeah," sixteen-year-old April said, as she passed her sister in the hallway. "She gets enough of that as it is."

April was wearing her tough-girl face and a long black T-shirt she slept in that had formerly belonged to Sheridan. Although the shirt was baggy, it was obvious April filled it out. Joe caught a whiff of wet paint and noted that April had painted her fingernails and toenails black as well.

April had come back after years of being passed from foster family to foster family. She'd seen and done things that couldn't be unseen or undone. Marybeth and Joe had thought they were on a path to an understanding with April, and then Marybeth had discovered April's stash of marijuana.

"Good night," April said, filling a water glass to take to bed with her. Then: "Seven more days of hell."

Joe and Marybeth exchanged glances, and Marybeth arched her eyebrows. *For a second there,* she seemed to communicate to Joe, *April forgot she was angry with us.*

"Maybe," Marybeth said, "the sentence could be reduced by a day or two for good behavior. But there will have to be some good behavior."

April turned and flashed a beaming, false smile and batted her lashes. "Good night, my wonderful parents!" she said. "How's that?"

Joe stifled a smile.

"Not buying it," Marybeth said. "But close."

"Why did you paint your nails black?" Joe asked.

April recoiled as if shocked by the stupidity of the question. "Because it matches my mood, of course," she said.

"Ah," Joe said.


MARYBETH POURED herself a glass of wine and sat down at the kitchen table while Joe ate his egg sandwich. After April's bedroom door closed, she said, "It's been tough, but in a way this grounding might turn out to be a good thing for all of us, if it doesn't kill me first."

Joe raised his eyebrows.

"In a weird way, she seems happier."

"She does?"

"Not judging by what she says, of course. But she seems to have an inner calm I haven't noticed since she's been back," Marybeth said, sipping at her glass. "Maybe it's because she finally knows where the boundaries are. Sheridan and Lucy just know, but April, I don't think, has ever been sure. She probably doesn't even realize it, and she'd *never* admit it. But I think she might be kind of like my horses: she just needs to know the pecking order and where the fences are and then she'll be more comfortable."

Joe finished his sandwich and opened the cupboard door over the refrigerator, where he kept his bottle of bourbon.

Marybeth said, "But judging by the way things usually go, something could always happen that screws things up."

"Are you thinking about Nate?" Joe asked.

She nodded.

"Me, too," he said, thinking of what Nate had said earlier. Thinking of Nate's devotion to Joe's family, his tenderness toward Sheridan, his protection of Marybeth. How much he'd miss Nate if he never saw him again.

# 10

AT THE SAME TIME, fifteen miles upriver and four and a half miles to the east, Pam Kelly slammed down the telephone receiver and cursed out loud: "Fuck you, too, Bernard!"

Bernard was her insurance agent. He didn't have any good news.

She spun around in her kitchen on the dirty floor—she'd quit scrubbing it years before when she realized Paul and Stumpy would never learn to take off their muddy boots outside—and jabbed her finger at two yellowed and curling photographs held by magnets to her refrigerator door, Paul squatting next to a dead elk with its tongue lolling, and Stumpy holding the severed head of a pronghorn antelope just above his shoulder, and shouted, "Fuck you, Paul. And fuck you, too, Stumpy! How could you do this to me?"

SHE'D MET Paul Kelly thirty-two years before at a rodeo in Kaycee, Wyoming. She was chasing a bareback rider across the mountain west named Jim "Deke" Waldrop who had charmed her and deflowered her behind the chutes at her hometown rodeo in North Platte, Nebraska, and she was convinced he'd marry her if she could only get him to slow down long enough. So she'd borrowed her father's farm pickup and stolen her mother's egg money and hit the Professional Rodeo Cowboys Association circuit that July, trying to locate Deke and nail him down. She'd missed him in Greeley, caught a glimpse of him getting bucked off in Cody but couldn't find him afterward, and had a flat tire just outside of Nampa, where she could hear the roar of the crowd in the distant arena as he rode to a 92, and Deke Waldrop, flush with cash, went off to celebrate with his buddies.

With less than ten dollars, Pam had rolled into Kaycee on fumes and a mismatched left rear tire, feeling sick to her stomach—she suspected she was pregnant with Deke's child—to find not only Deke but Mrs. Waldrop and two towheaded Waldrop boys waiting to watch their dad ride.

She was devastated and furious, and as she returned to the parking lot, she saw a handsome, laconic cowboy climbing out of his ranch pickup that he'd just parked so closely to hers she couldn't wedge in between them and open her door. It was the last straw. She set upon the stranger, pummeling his chest and shoulders with closed fists, but the man didn't strike back. Instead, he smiled and said, "Whoa, little lady," and leaned back so she couldn't connect a punch to his jaw. She wore out quickly, and he gently clasped her wrists in his hands to still them and he asked if there was anything he could do to help her out, because she was obviously upset.

She'd looked around him through tear-filled eyes and saw the rifle in his gun rack across the back window of his truck. "You can give me that rifle so I can shoot Deke Waldrop," she'd said. Then a whiff of fried meat from the concession area wafted over them and the smell turned her stomach and she got sick on the hard-packed ground.

He said, "You're a pistol, all right," and untied the silk bandanna from his neck and handed it to her to dry her face and wipe off her mouth. "Name's Paul Kelly," he said.

FOR THE NEXT thirty-two years, she'd remind him that was the first and last act of kindness he'd shown her.

But at the time, it worked. He bought her some ice cream and sat with her on the top row of the bleachers as she cried. Then he took her to his weathered old line shack in the Bighorn Mountains and offered her his bed and didn't try to jump her. He was working for a local rancher, he told her, fixing fence and rounding up cows to earn enough money to go to college to become a mechanical engineer. He was, she told her mother over the telephone, "almost dashing."

They married, and Pam convinced her father to cosign on a loan for an ancient log cabin on twenty acres in the foothills of the mountains. It was to be their starter home, and they planned to burn it down and build a real house on the property. But Paul never went to college, and they never built a house, and his stint as a ranch hand was the last steady job he'd ever hold. If it wasn't for monthly disability checks that came because that asphalt truck ran over his foot after he'd hired on that summer with the county road construction crew, they'd have no steady income during the months when Paul (and later Stumpy) weren't guiding hunting clients.

And now, she thought, the son-of-a-bitch went and got himself killed and took Stumpy—Deke's son—with him, leaving her the place and six cows and two horses no one could ride. All that was left of her life was a stack of unpaid bills.

"Fuck you, Paul," she said again at the photo on the refrigerator. Earlier that afternoon, after the game warden had left, Will Speer, the county coroner, had called to ask her what plans she had for "making arrangements." She'd asked him if she could donate Paul's body to science.

"Will they pay something for him?" she asked. "There's got to be a college somewhere that wants to see what the inside of a loser looks like."

The coroner stammered that he didn't know where to start.

"Find out," she said, and hung up the phone.

PAM KELLY was still cursing to herself in the tiny cluttered mudroom as she pulled on a pair of knee-high rubber boots. On top of everything else, the cows and horses had to be fed. She normally ragged on Paul to go out and do it, but he wasn't there to rag on. Inexplicably, she fought back tears as she buttoned up her barn coat.

Several years before, she'd begged Paul to buy some life insurance. She made the appointment for him with Bernard, the insurance salesman she'd met in Saddlestring who said they could get $100,000 in term life for less than $20 a month. Paul drove to town with the checkbook and came back with a new hunting rifle. He shook it like a war lance and said, "*This* is all the life insurance I need." Completely misunderstanding what she'd sent him to do, as usual. When she blew up, he'd promised he'd go see the insurance guy later. He never did, and Bernard had just confirmed it.

She looked at her reflection in a cracked, flyspecked mirror next to the door. She was too old, too fat, too crabby, and too used up to ever get another man in her life now.

"It just ain't *fair*," she said aloud.

THE COWS milled around in a mucky pen on the north side of the collapsing old barn, and the two horses were in a corral on the south side. When she emerged from the cabin, the horses pawed at the soft dirt and whinnied. They wanted to eat. "Calm down," she said to the mare and her colt.

The cows just looked up at her dumbly, the way they always did.

As she grasped the rusty door latch to the barn, she wondered what she could get for the stock. She'd heard beef prices were on the rise and she figured among all the cattle they weighed maybe five thousand pounds total. There should be some cash in selling the cows, and she sure didn't want to have to keep feeding them. The hay supply was low, and the bales too heavy for her to stack on her own if she ordered a couple of tons. And the horses? They weren't worth anything except to a slaughterhouse. The French could eat them, she thought. They liked eating horse meat, she'd heard.

She swung the door back and reached for the light switch, which was mounted on the inside of the doorframe, when a hand grasped her wrist and twisted her arm back. The pain was sudden and excruciating, and she collapsed to her knees, gasping for air. She heard a muffled *pop*, and fireworks burst in front of her eyes. It felt like her arm had been jerked out of the socket.

The light came on, and she looked through the tears and starbursts at the Game Changer, the man she'd seen at her kitchen table talking with Paul, Stumpy, and Ron Connelly. The man who gave her arm another wicked twist.

He said, "I believe we've met."

# 11

WHEN THEY WERE SURE the girls were in their rooms with their doors closed, Joe and Marybeth sat together on the couch and he told her about his conversation with Nate. He left out the part about the falconry website. Although it was his practice to share everything with his wife, in this case he felt the need to hold back a little for her own protection. She wouldn't agree with his decision—he was sure of it—but Nate had spooked him.

"Nemecek?" Marybeth asked.

"Nate said we wouldn't find out much about him," Joe said. "He said he was off the grid as well."

"No one is completely without identity."

Joe shrugged.

"I have my ways," she said.

He nodded. "I know you do."

Marybeth's part-time job at the library gave her access to data and networks that rivaled those of most local law enforcement, and certainly the Twelve Sleep County Sheriff's Department. She'd used that access to her advantage many times, and, through a coworker who had once worked for the police department, had obtained passwords and backdoor user names that allowed her into N-DEx, the U.S. Justice Department's National Data Exchange, and ViCAP, the FBI's Violent Criminal Apprehension Program.

"I'm curious to hear what you find," Joe said.

"Of course, we could just go to the source and *ask* him," she said.

"I'm holding that in reserve."

She shook her head. If it were up to Marybeth, Joe knew, she would have had Nate spilling everything.

They sat in silence for a while on the couch, each consumed by their own thoughts.

Finally, Marybeth asked, "Do you think we'll see Nate again?"

Joe shrugged. "I hope so."

"If he said the things you told me, he must be really worried. I've never heard him talk like that."

"Me either."

She said, "I can't help wondering what it was he did that drew him here. What was so awful that he thinks he deserves to die?"

AT 2:30 IN THE MORNING, Joe slipped out of bed and pulled on his robe and walked quietly down the hallway to his tiny and cluttered home office. He shut the door, turned on the light, and sat down at his computer.

Emails from Game and Fish headquarters flooded his inbox, but nothing looked urgent. The department was temporarily without a new director, and a search by the governor was under way. Governor Rulon, who in the past had employed Joe directly but off the books in a bureaucratic sense, had two years left in his second and last term and had seemed to have mellowed somewhat. Joe hadn't received an assignment from Rulon in more than a year, which was fine with him, although if forced to admit it, he'd come to crave the adventure and uncertainty of his missions. The respite had been healthy for his family, though, and being able to stay home was something he'd never regret.

It didn't take long to find the falconry website Nate had given him. He took a few moments to register a username and a password, and he was in. The site was rudimentary and cluttered, no more than a screen filled with topics and comment threads:

**WHAT KIND OF HOOD SHOULD I BUY**
**FOR A PRAIRIE FALCON?**                    <17 COMMENTS>

**FLYING SHORT-WINGS**                        <21 COMMENTS>

**HOW LONG WILL MY BIRD KEEP MOLTING?**    <7 COMMENTS>

**HOW DO I RECOGNIZE A STATE OF *YARAK*?**   <14 COMMENTS>

Joe clicked on that one because he was unfamiliar with the word *yarak* and recalled Nate had used it earlier. The thread had begun more than ten years before, and the last comment was eight years old. Nevertheless, he read the thread with interest. *Yarak* was a Turkish word describing the peak condition of a falcon to fly and hunt. It was described as "full of stamina, well-muscled, alert, neither too fat nor too thin, perfect condition for hunting and killing prey. This state is rarely achieved but a wonder to behold when observed." In order to achieve an optimum state of *yarak*, one commenter wrote, full-time care, exercise, diet, and training were required.

*"Don't think you can get your bird into primo* yarak *by working with*

*it at night or on weekends. This is a twenty-four/seven commitment, and there are no guarantees."*

Joe didn't expect to find a new thread with the word "kestrel" in it, and it wasn't there.

He wondered if Nate would launch the thread before he achieved his state of *yarak*.

# 12

FIFTEEN MINUTES LATER, on the Wind River Indian Reservation, Bad Bob Whiteplume had a dream in which he was hunting for pronghorn antelope. As he raised his rifle, a car horn blared from somewhere behind him and spooked the buck. He watched in vain as the pronghorn he wanted zoomed away and turned its small contingent of does and fawns, and the herd raced away trailing a dozen plumes of dust. The horn wouldn't stop, and he rolled over in bed and wrapped the pillow around his head and it helped a little. In his dream, the buck antelope he'd been after had run so far away Bob would never get a decent shot.

When Rhonda next to him elbowed him in the ribs, he opened his eyes to total darkness. But he could still hear the horn.

"Bob," she said, "get up. There's someone outside."

"Who is it?" he croaked.

"How in the hell should I know? But it's nearly three in the morning and somebody is sitting out front in their car, honking their fucking *horn*."

"Go make them stop," he said, scooting farther away from her and her elbow and her yammering. He wanted to go back to the antelope hunt. "And don't turn on the light or they'll know I'm back here and they'll keep honking."

The house had been built long before his grandfather had added the convenience store to the front of it. The two structures were joined via a metal door with several bolt locks on it he always forgot to secure.

This came in handy because if Bob and his buddies did too much alcohol or weed, Bob could crash in his own bed without having to drive anywhere. But sleeping so close to his day job came with annoyances. Like this. All the Indians were family on the reservation, which was fine, usually. There was always someone to borrow tools or bullets from. But familiarity sometimes meant neighbors didn't honor rules, like when a store was open or closed.

"No," she said, prying his hand and pillow away from his ear and leaning into him. "*I'm* not going out there. You go make them stop."

"Give it a minute," Bob grumbled. "They'll realize I'm not coming out and they'll go away."

She huffed a long stream of air into the back of his neck from her nostrils as she sighed in frustration. There was a few seconds of silence.

"See?" Bob said, closing his eyes.

Then the horn resumed: a long blast, followed by several short blasts, followed by the long blast again.

"They're not leaving," she hissed.

"Okay, okay," he growled, swinging his thick brown legs out from beneath the sheets. The floor was cold when his wide bare feet slapped it. "But I'm going to tear those knuckleheads a new one."

"Just make them stop," Rhonda said, collapsing back into bed.

Rhonda liked showing up around closing time and staying the night. She was a thick white woman with red hair and broad hips originally from Boston, who had shown up in Wyoming after a messy divorce looking for, she said, spirituality and something that would give her life meaning. Hence, she gravitated toward the folks on the res and provided free mental-health-care services at the tribal center one day a week.

She ran the only psychology practice in the little town of Winchester to the north, and she said she liked the idea of being a shrink to ranch wives and other assorted miscreants during the day and sleeping with an angry Indian at night, that somehow it gave her existence a kind of balance. She told Bob she considered herself a liaison between white problems and Indian problems, and maybe someday she'd write a book about her experiences. Bob doubted anyone would buy or read such a useless book, but he didn't tell her that.

Before he could get her into bed, Bob had to answer her questions about native culture and beliefs and practices. He made them sound more mysterious than they were, and he made up a lot of it on the spot. For example, he had shown her the mottled scars on his chest and claimed they'd come from participating in a traditional sun dance where warriors pierced their pectoral muscles with sharpened bones and let themselves be hoisted into the air on rawhide ropes until they obtained their visions or the flesh ripped. Actually, the scars were a result of a motorcycle accident when Bob was a teenager. But no matter. It got her engine running, which was the point.

She begged him to take her to a sweat lodge someday, to show her how to do a vision quest, to let her see the actual sun dance (where dancers no longer pierced themselves or hung from ropes). He told her she'd have to earn those privileges by submitting to him and "his hot-blooded ways." He suspected at times she was onto him—she was a psychologist, after all—but she didn't put up any objection or question his stories or his motives. So one or two times a week he took her to bed, where she showed dexterity and a youthful hunger that decried her appearance and profession. Afterward, she'd rise early and drive back to Winchester before he got up, so he didn't even have to feed her.

HIS MOOD was very, very dark as he stood and fished around on the chair through a pile of old clothes. He pulled on a pair of baggy gym trunks and a grease-stained hooded sweatshirt. His flip-flops were side by side under the bed, and he stepped into them.

"Come back soon," she sang from bed. "I'm wide awake now."

"Go back to sleep."

The .30-30 lever-action Winchester was propped in the corner, and he grabbed it by the barrel as he walked by and shuffled down the hallway.

Maybe, he thought, the people outside honking their horn were visitors to the res, because locals would have known by now he wasn't coming out. They'd know he meant business when they looked up and saw a big pissed-off Indian approaching the car with a hunting rifle.

He pushed through the steel door into his retail store. It was dim inside; the only lights were from the drink coolers. He paused at the front of his store and squinted, trying to see who was in the offending car. But because the bulb on the overhead pole light had been shot out recently—teenagers Darryl and Benny Edmo and their new pellet gun, he suspected—he couldn't see much more than the outline of a vehicle in the moonlight on the other side of the gas pumps. One of the pumps blocked his view of the driver, but he could see no other occupants in the car.

Bad Bob slammed back the bolt locks and threw open the front door. Without the barrier, the blaring of the horn was louder and more infuriating than before.

"Hey!" he yelled. "Knock it off!" But his voice was drowned out.

Bob strode across the loose gravel on blacktop, ignoring the sharp little stones that wedged between his bare toes and between the soles of his feet and the flip-flops.

"KNOCK IT THE FUCK OFF!" he bellowed, and worked the lever action on his rifle with a swift and metallic *clatch-clatch* sound.

The horn ceased.

Bob said, *"Thank you!"*

Overhead, the full moon hung fat and low over the western mountains. As he glanced at it, he noticed a distant hawk cross over the white/blue surface like a miller moth dancing across a porch light. The hawk gave him pause, and something inside of him stirred a little. *What?* he thought. *Does it have some kind of meaning?* The old folks still talked as if everything that happened in the natural world had meaning outside of the obvious, but Bob never paid any attention to that stuff. But something tweaked him inside now and he couldn't entirely ignore it.

He squeezed between the pumps to confront the driver, when a flashlight beam blinded him.

"Hey," he said, raising his left forearm to block the light.

"Bad Bob, right?" came a male voice. It was somewhat familiar. A white voice.

"Get that light outta my face. I can't see. Buddy," Bob said, "do you know what fucking *time* it is?"

Although the light clicked off, all Bob could see was a round green orb burned into his eyes. He heard the car door open, though, and just as quickly the rifle was wrenched out of his right hand.

"Fuckin . . ." Bob started to say, but he heard the shuffle of someone behind him and something icy and sharp bit into his throat and squeezed off any further words as well as his breath.

"I don't want to hurt you," the voice said calmly in his right ear. "But you'll need to stop struggling. Do you understand?"

Bob tried to draw air in through his nose, but the cord—or wire—around his throat restricted that, too. He reached up involuntarily with both hands to feel what was choking him, but the man slapped his hands down.

"Relax. I'm not going to hurt you. I just need some information."

Bob could feel his heart whumping, and a voice inside his head told him to stay still. He lowered his hands and rocked back slightly, which lessened the pressure of the thin wire noose—or whatever it was. His eyes had readjusted to the dark, and he glanced toward his store, hoping Rhonda would see what was happening at the front door. She wasn't there.

"Do you remember me?" the man asked, his lips inches from Bob's ear. "Do you recognize my car?"

Despite the biting pain it caused, Bob managed to shake his head. Even though he remembered the Audi Q7.

The man behind him chuckled. "Oh, we both wish it were so. Now, listen to me carefully, Bob. I'm going to ease up on you so you can talk. Like I said, all I need is information. Then, if you help me out and you don't turn around and you walk straight back into your little store, everything will be fine. You'll have an abrasion on your neck, but that's all. Do you hear me?"

Although spangles were replacing the stars in the night sky, Bob managed to nod.

"Okay," the man said, and the pressure eased, but the wire was still cutting into the soft flesh of Bob's throat. "I'm looking for a house. Seven seventeen Farm Station Street. The street numbers here on the reservation—I can't make heads or tails of them."

Bob knew that to be true, and it was something he was used to. No one ever used street or house numbers, anyway. They just said, "I'll meet you at Mary's house" or "turn west by where Jimmy Nosleep used to live."

"I don't know the numbers," Bob croaked. "Tell me who you're looking for."

"Alice Thunder," the man said. "She works at the school."

Bob felt a stab of pain in his heart. If this man would do this to him, what would he do to Alice? *Everyone loved Alice. . . .*

As if the man could read his thoughts, the wire cinched tighter, and Bob groaned.

"Where does she live?" the man asked.

Bob thought, *I'll tell him. Then I'll call Alice and tell her to run like hell and I'll call the tribal police right after that.* Then he'd call his buddies and tell them to grab their hunting rifles and meet him at Alice's place, where they'd teach this son-of-a-bitch a lesson before the cops got there. He still couldn't quite believe how quickly the man in the dark crossover—the man Nate Romanowski had asked him about—had taken his rifle and slipped the garrote over his head. He looked again at his store and wordlessly begged Rhonda to look out.

Then, when the noose eased, Bob said, "Go down this street in front of us about a mile and a half and turn right on a dirt road just past a big stack of hay. Her house is half a mile from that, on your left."

"Ah," the man said. "I was right by it earlier and didn't see it. You people need to come up with a numbering system that makes sense."

Because of the wire around his neck and the man's hands on the wire, Bob felt intimately connected to this person, and he could feel it when the man shifted his weight, as if he were digging something out of a pocket.

His keys. There was a dull *thunk* of an electronic lock releasing. In his peripheral vision, Bob saw the trunk of the vehicle lift on its own and an interior light come on inside. Until that moment, he'd thought he had a chance. No longer.

"We're going for a ride now," the man behind him said, and steered him toward the open trunk. Bob saw that thick clear plastic sheeting had been laid down inside.

"I thought you said . . ."

Bob never finished his question before the wire was cinched tight and his world went black and the last thing he saw was the after-image of the hawk flying across the surface of the moon and he wished he'd understood earlier what it foretold.

# PART THREE

*No living man can, or possibly ever will, understand the instinct of predation that we share with our raptorial servant. No man-made machine can, or ever will, synthesize that perfect coordination of eye, muscle, and pinion as he stoops to his kill.*

—Aldo Leopold

# 13

NATE ROMANOWSKI reached the outskirts of Colorado Springs as the morning sun lit up the fresh snowfall on the western slope of the mountains in a brilliant green and white palette. There had been a light snowfall during the night that was melting away in the high-altitude sun, and wisps of steam wafted up from the asphalt. His tires hissed on the wet surface. It was Tuesday, October 23.

For the last seven and a half hours, he'd driven straight through the state of Wyoming from north to south on Interstate 25 and squeezed through Denver before the morning traffic approached its apex. Because he had no cell or satellite phone and he paid cash for food and fuel and therefore created no credit card receipts, his route and movements were untraceable.

The U.S. Air Force Academy glinted like a glass-and-steel castle fortress in the foothills to the west as the highway expanded to three, then four lanes. Cars and pickups streamed onto the highway from entrance ramps, drivers sipping coffee and dressed for work. An SUV shot by him, driven by an attractive fortyish woman applying lipstick in her rearview mirror and singing along with a song on the radio.

Nate smiled to himself because he'd been away so long he'd almost forgotten what it was like to experience the morning rush of normal Americans going to work at normal jobs for normal hours. The pure dynamism and hurly-burly of the scene made him wistful.

SEEING THE ACADEMY brought back a flood of memories, several so powerful they made him wince. He recalled arriving there as a freshman just appointed by Montana senators, a tall and raw-boned middle linebacker with a buzz cut, still stinging from his goodbyes and from releasing his falcons to the wind. The upperclassman cadets jeered and confronted him, and he was paired with an older cadet named Vince Vincent who informed him that as of that moment he was his "dooley"—all freshmen were dooleys—and he had no past, no reputation, no rights, and no value as a human being. It was Nate's responsibility, Vincent said, to start his life over at zero. And he could start by shining Vince Vincent's boots. Nate gritted his teeth, said, "Yes, sir," and dropped to his knees with a brush and jar of polish. Vincent stood there in the gleaming hallway with his hands on his hips and his chin in the air while other cadets walked by and laughed.

The humiliation continued. Between classes, orientation, and football practice, Nate fetched Vincent's lunch and dinner, ironed and hung his uniform, and cleaned up after him. Nate was asked to stand at attention outside the bathroom stall while Vincent had his morning bowel movement, and to note on a pad the shape and number of excrement bits Vincent called out to him.

He spent days shadowing Vincent through the grounds so he was available do his bidding at any moment. The campus was numbered with similar relationships, and dooleys rolled their eyes at one another in shared humiliation as they passed in the hallways. But after a month, Nate observed that most of his classmates, although still designated dooleys, as they would be throughout the first year, spoke comfortably and freely with their assigned cadets. The pairs could be seen walking side by side on the campus, and the cadets became more like mentors and advisers. They even sat together in the cafeteria, where Nate was required to stand at attention beside his cadet in case Vincent dropped a napkin or fork and needed it retrieved immediately.

And Vince Vincent didn't let up.

That lasted for forty-eight days, until Nate slipped into Vincent's dorm room at three in the morning and crouched down next to the bed and hissed into the cadet's ear: "I know how the game is played and I've played it without bitching. Your role is to break me down and build me back up. But you don't know me, and you've let your power go to your head. My father is an Air Force technical sergeant who spent his life breaking me down. He's a professional. Compared to him, you're a bad joke and a fucking embarrassment to the uniform. You've had your fun, and I've taken it until now for your sake, not mine. I've been your dooley."

As Vincent started to sit up, Nate reached over and placed his fingers around Vincent's windpipe and pushed him back down. The cadet's eyes pleaded to him to stop. Nate said, "I'm a falconer. I've spent more time outside than inside. I'm a student of violent death in nature. I could rip your throat out right now and it wouldn't make me blink. You'd bleed out before you got to the door, and I'd step over your body on the way out to brush my teeth for the night."

Nate tightened his grip. "We don't have to be friends, and I don't like you, anyway. But from this minute on, you'll respect me and I'll pretend to honor your rank. No one will have to know we've had this discussion. Do you understand?"

Vincent blinked his eyes to indicate he did. Nate's life improved after that, and Vince Vincent went on living.

DISCIPLINE AND ROUTINE at the Academy was nothing new to Nate; he'd grown up that way. His father was an Air Force lifer, and they'd lived all over the country and the world on military bases: Goodfellow in San Angelo, Texas; Edwards in Rosamond, California; McChord in Tacoma, Washington; Ellsworth in Rapid City, South Dakota; Incirlik in Adana, Turkey; Mountain Home, in Idaho; and Malmstrom in Great Falls, Montana.

He'd been a dooley all his life. Friendships with kids his age were fleeting and incomplete. Schools and teachers were temporary. Nate sought some kind of permanence and an anchor outside his family and found it outside. No matter where they were located there was hunting, fishing, camping, and wildlife. Sure, the weather and terrain varied. But outside the base housing and civilization, there was a whole world out there that was harsh, beautiful, tough—and didn't judge him.

While they were still stationed in Montana, Nate's mother died from lupus and his father doubled down on Nate because he didn't know what else to do. He instilled in his son, through thought and deed, an ethos of loyalty, duty, and love of country. In his father's mind, warriors held an exalted place in society and should be honored even if they weren't in the modern world. According to Nate's father, it was more important to serve than it was to be recognized or appreciated for it by those soft and ignorant ninnies who benefited from the warrior's service. Every right the ninnies and sissies enjoyed had been protected over the years by the blood shed by American warriors, despite the contempt shown them as a result.

The message was pure and tough and noble, but Nate's father was absent for long periods of time. And when he was gone, the world-view he described fascinated Nate, who wondered how much of it was true and how much of it was self-justification for a nomadic life and a dysfunctional family. To confirm or deny his father's rationale, Nate sought out and found another ordered universe in the amoral world of nature. He found a place where the strong killed and ate the weak and the small. Nate came to realize the only difference between a warrior culture and the tooth-and-claw natural world were the values and compassion humans had but wild creatures didn't. So to better understand the former, he became a student of the latter.

That's when he got his first falcon.

When Nate was a junior in high school in Great Falls, his father was thrilled when his son was nominated by the Montana senators and accepted by the Air Force Academy, but it came with well-known caveats. As a lifer, he had very mixed feelings about college-bred officers, and he wasn't shy about expressing them. When his father found himself in a situation that was chaotic, disorganized, or wholly screwed up, he described it as "worse than following a second lieutenant with a map."

AS NATE melded into the flow of traffic toward the center of town, he recalled standing in the end zone of the football stadium in uniform during a home game. He'd been in the Academy for a year and had been assigned a dooley of his own, whom he'd released the day before without humiliating him. The Air Force Academy Falcons were playing the Colorado State Rams. Because of a knee injury the year before, Nate was no longer on the team, but he'd been chosen for a role he relished even more: falconer for the school's live mascots. It was an Academy tradition. The birds were released at the start of the game and at halftime, and they'd circle the stadium and return to fist.

It was two minutes until the half, and the Falcons were up 21–14, when an officer he'd never seen before approached him and stood a few feet away, studying him up and down with a flat, superior expression, as if he were about to bid on him in an auction. The officer looked hard, and there was a palpable sense of purpose, dark menace, and explosive action about him. Although he had the single silver bar that designated the officer as a lieutenant, he had a black patch sewn onto his uniform sleeve Nate didn't recognize. The patch was in the shape of a badge and it had no words or numerals. Just a white embroidered profile of a falcon slashing through the air with both talons outstretched. And above the lieutenant's breast pocket was a black metal pin with the roman numeral V, or five.

"This isn't your first time handling falcons, is it cadet?" the lieutenant said.

"No, sir. I've flown birds all my life."

"Name them."

"Started with a prairie falcon, sir. I've worked with three prairies. But I've flown redtails and kestrels, and a gyr."

The lieutenant cocked an eyebrow, but his mouth didn't change. "A gyr? Isn't that like flying a B-52 bomber?"

"A little. It was a challenge."

"Ever hunt a peregrine?"

"No, sir. But that's something I want to do someday."

The lieutenant nodded knowingly. "Pound for pound, it's the greatest hunter alive. Fastest, too."

"Yes, sir."

"How did you get all those birds?" the officer asked.

"Trapped them myself, sir."

"Really?"

"Yes, sir."

The officer extended his hand and Nate shook it. The man's grip was dry and hard.

"I'm in command of a small Special Forces unit, and I've been looking for a couple of fellow falconers to round it out. The reason, I can't disclose. Is that something you might be interested in?"

Nate shrugged. "I'm not sure, sir. But I'd be eager to learn more about it."

"Our official team name is Mark V," the officer said. "Informally, we're known as The Five. But within the team, we call ourselves the Peregrines."

Nate grinned.

That was the first time he met Lieutenant John Nemecek.

NATE SLID into the right-hand lane and took the exit for Cimarron Street onto State Highway 24 west toward Cascade. It wasn't long before the buzz of morning traffic was behind him. As he climbed into the foothills, he noted that the inch of snow from the night before still clung to the pine boughs of the trees and sparkled in the grass.

The gravel road he took to the right wasn't marked with a sign. Within a few minutes, the canopy of trees closed above him, and for half a mile it was like driving through a tunnel.

The place he was looking for was a squat brick home nestled into a shaded alcove with a view of a sloping mountain meadow in front and the massive jagged horizon of Pikes Peak behind. A single stringy white cloud seemed to have snagged on the top of the peak like a plastic bag caught on a tree branch.

He pulled into the circular driveway and drove around it until his Jeep was adjacent to the porch and front door. There were no signs of life, but a rolled-up Colorado Springs *Gazette* on the top stair of the porch and an American flag flapping on a pole indicated someone was there.

Nate killed the motor and swung his legs out of the Jeep. He looked at the house through squinted eyes, trying to remember the last time he'd been there. And wondering why it seemed so lifeless. He slipped off his shoulder harness and holster, and bundled it under the front seat.

Before he reached the front steps, the interior door opened and Nate's father stood behind the storm door with a scowl on his face.

All he said was, *"You."*

"Hey, Tech Sarge," Nate said, hesitating on the porch. "Are you going to let me in?"

Although his father was still tall and wide-shouldered, his body looked ravaged and sunken-in. His thin, pale hair was wispy, and his eyes looked out of deep sockets like dull chunks of basalt.

"I'm thinking," his father said.


"WHERE'S DALISAY and the girls?" Nate asked, when his father finally stepped aside and let him enter.

"Around," Technical Sergeant Gordon "Gordo" Romanowski growled.

"Is there coffee? I've been driving all night."

"In the kitchen."

Nate paused for a moment, then said, "It's okay, I'll get it myself."

"You know where the cups are."

The interior of the house hadn't changed much, Nate noted. Despite the mountain location and the three-hundred-plus days of sunshine in Colorado, it was designed to be dark inside. The shaded windows were small, and the corners were lit with dim lamps. The wall of framed photographs of Gordo Romanowski in exotic locales was as it had always been, but there had been a few changes. As Nate poured a cup of coffee, he studied the photos.

Gordo, Nate's mother, and five-year-old Nate in Turkey. Gordo with a forty-pound tuna off the coast of Baja, Mexico. Gordo in full dress in his tech sergeant's uniform.

What was missing, Nate observed, was his Academy entrance photograph. And a shot of him with his first falcon. In their place were photos of Dalisay when Gordo first met her in the Philippines, and another of Gordo, Dalisay, and their two infant daughters. The girls were striking miniatures of Dalisay: petite, dark hair, big eyes, caramel skin. Because it was Colorado Springs and therefore a military town, Nate assumed Asian wives and children weren't unusual at all in the community. But Nate had never met his stepmother or half sisters.

"You look fit," Gordo said.

"Wild game meat and clean living," Nate replied.

Gordo snorted with doubt and disapproval. "Why are you here, anyway? Why now, after all these years?"

Nate sipped the strong coffee and met the glare of his father with his own. "That's why I called. I wanted to touch base."

"What's that mean?" His father was uncomfortable, and looked away.

"I wanted to see you one last time," Nate said.

"Shit," Gordo said, and groaned.


THEY SAT in overstuffed chairs on opposite ends of the coffee table. Gordo seemed stiff and edgy. Nate put his cup down on a coaster and sat back.

"So Dalisay and your girls . . . they're still with you, right?"

Gordo nodded.

"What, they're at school? Dalisay is working?"

"Let's not talk about them."

Nate shook his head, puzzled. He swiveled his head around. A stack of children's books was on the floor by the bookcase next to a plastic milk crate of Barbie dolls and accessories. The refrigerator in the kitchen was cluttered with school photos and a Polaroid shot of a grinning seven-year-old girl labeled *"Melia's first checkup: no cavities!"* It was dated from August, two months prior. In the photo, Melia boasted a perfectly symmetric row of Chiclets-like teeth.

"Why in the hell did you come here?" Gordo asked, pain in his face.

"I told you."

His father said, "Do you know how many times men have come to this house asking if I'd heard from you? Special agents from the FBI? Pentagon brass? Even detectives from the Montana and Wyoming DCI?"

Nate hadn't thought about it, but it made sense.

"I had to tell them I hadn't heard a damned word from you in twelve years. That the last time we talked, you called me from who-the-fuck-knows-where saying you'd left the service and had decided to drop out of the world and become a fucking anarchist."

"I don't think I said that, exactly," Nate said.

"You might as well have." Gordo leaned forward in his chair and gripped his knees as if to squeeze the life out of them. "Do you have any idea what it's like to live in a patriotic military town when your only son is *a goddamned traitor to his country?*" The last words were shouted out.

Nate said, "I'm no traitor. Who told you that?"

"Nobody in so many words," Gordo said. "But I didn't just fall off the turnip truck. I looked it up: you didn't get a proper discharge back in 2001. You just fucking *left*. That's AWOL in my book, son. And when you just vanish and all I know about it is that officers and federal agents come here asking about you, it ain't too hard to figure out.

"And if there's another story," his father said, "it hasn't come to light. I just figure you're ashamed of yourself, and you ought to be. Because you brought shame on the uniform and the country. And you brought shame on *me*."

Nate let the words hang there for a minute without responding. Then he said, "There's another story. Or at least a different version."

"Well, then spill it out," Gordo croaked.

Nate stood up slowly, taking in his father. The man was exercised, and tiny beads of sweat dotted his upper lip. His eyes were haunted. Then he looked again at the children's books, the photos on the refrigerator, the small stack of unopened mail on the kitchen counter.

He said, "When was the last time you saw Dalisay and the girls? I'm guessing two or three days, judging by the mail."

Gordo's face twitched as if slapped. It wasn't a reaction Nate had seen much in his life growing up with his father.

"They've taken them, haven't they?" Nate said. "They've got them somewhere. And they told you that if I showed up, you should let them know right away or you won't see them again. Is that about right, Dad?"

His father sat as if frozen, but his tortured eyes gave Nate the answer he sought.

"Did you call them when you saw me outside? Are they on their way now?"

Gordo's eyes flashed with defiance. "No."

"To do this to a man like you," Nate said, shaking his head, feeling his stomach clench. "A man who spent his life serving his country. That should tell you all you need to know about who I'm dealing with."

Gordo Romanowski's face twitched again.

"If I told you what happened," Nate said, "it would be like putting a death sentence on you, like the one that's on me. So I'm not saying another word.

"What you need to know, Dad, is I haven't been in contact because I wanted to protect you and your new family. I don't care if you believe me right now, but I think if you dig deep, you will."

Nate took his cup to the sink, returned and gripped his father on the shoulder, and said, "Take care of Dalisay and those girls. Tell them not to be too ashamed of their older half brother. I'm out of here."

As he opened the front door, Gordo asked softly, "Where are you going?"

Nate turned. "That's what they want to know, isn't it? Tell them I wouldn't tell you. Which I won't."

Gordo blinked slowly. Nate could only imagine the torture he was in.

"Give me ten minutes to get back to the highway," Nate said. "Then do what you need to do to get them back."


NATE ROARED away from the house, eyes wide open, weapon on his lap. But when he cleared the tunnel of trees, he didn't turn left toward town and the highway. If they were on their way, they'd see his Jeep.

Instead, he cranked the wheel to the right and floored it. The movement made his wounded left shoulder pulse with pain. He headed straight west toward the wall of mountains.

Nevertheless, he had no doubt that whoever was holding Dalisay and the girls would be right behind him.

# 14

AS NATE CLIMBED the mountain toward Pikes Peak and the road began to curve upward and he approached a devilish series of switchbacks, he shot glances into his rear and side mirrors. He eased slightly on the gas as if riding a motorcycle when he leaned into the steep turns, so he could hang his head out the window to survey the bends of the two-lane far below and behind him. He'd passed a couple of small rental cars—tourists, with children in the backseats, wide-eyed mothers in the front, and fathers with death grips on the steering wheel—and grumbled "Flatlanders" when he blasted around them. The short wheelbase and all-terrain tires of the Jeep were made for this kind of driving: tight, fast, and full of sprints and sharp turns.

He didn't know the area or the road system well, but he knew the general direction he wanted to go: over the mountains and on to Rexburg, Idaho, seven hundred miles to the northwest. So like he'd done so many times in the wilds of Wyoming and Montana, he navigated not by GPS or maps but by studying the terrain and geography in the direction where he wanted to go and trusting there would be two-tracks, old logging or ranch roads, or even dry streambeds he could take to get him there. One thing he was sure of was that he needed to get off the state highway as soon as possible. If operators of The Five were coming after him, they'd by now ruled out his presence on the main road to town and to the interstate, which meant he could have only gone the opposite way from Gordon's home. Given that, it would be a matter of time and determination to pin him down. The Five was known for its determination.

The route he'd taken narrowed and went straight up the mountain. In a few miles, the pavement would end, and from there on the road climbed an additional nineteen harrowing miles to the top of 14,100-foot Pikes Peak. He'd been up there once. On top, there was a developed parking area, views of blue waves of mountains to the west and the foothills and plains of Colorado all the way to the Kansas border. But it wasn't a place to make a stand: too open, too many civilians, and only one escape route, which was back down the road he was on.

Nate was disconcerted after seeing his father. The old man had been rattled and scared. He wasn't the man Nate remembered, and it made him angry. The Gordon Romanowski he'd grown up with had been fearless and tough. He was the guy you wanted near you in a fight, a man so hard and set in his ways, so without nuance, that despite his intractability, there was comfort in his pure stubborn black-and-white worldview. Whoever had gotten to this tough old man in such a personal way . . . well, something bad should happen to them, Nate concluded.

Nate assumed Gordon had made the call he had to make and the operations team was on its way. Nate wondered about the numbers and the makeup of Nemecek's force. He doubted locals had been recruited in Colorado and had to assume the team had come with Nemecek. Trusting locals to hold a family hostage and respond with lethality when called upon was too much of a stretch. But how many operators would agree to deploy domestically, and what had Nemecek told them about their mission? Surely, Nemecek had lied, and that likelihood put Nate in a quiet rage. Operators of The Five that Nate had known and fought beside were good men: loyal, patriotic, and tough as nails. They wouldn't simply do the bidding of a superior officer without being convinced of the righteousness and morality of the mission. These men, like Nate himself back then, were well trained and efficient but not automatons. They'd do anything asked of them if they thought it would save lives and protect their country. Kidnapping Gordon's family and setting a trap for Nate would happen only if Nemecek had fed them lies, and he hated his old superior for taking such craven advantage of good men.

Good men, Nate thought, who would kill him in an instant, because that's why The Five existed. In other circumstances, these were the kind of men he'd fight beside and lay down his life for. But because of Nemecek and Nate's secret history, and Nemecek's willingness to lie to subordinates, some warriors would likely die. Nate hoped he wouldn't be among the first. Not until he did everything he could to cut the depraved head off the snake.

HE WAS a little surprised surveillance hadn't been set up near his father's home. It heartened him that whoever was in charge of this phase of the operation—surely not Nemecek himself—had allowed such a lapse. If they'd been stationed in the trees when Nate had arrived, the game would be over by now. But sloppiness or some kind of anomaly had prevented that. And he knew it wasn't unusual. Things just happened—machinery broke down, people got sick or injured, gaps appeared in surveillance because someone read their watch wrong or misheard the schedule—no matter how much time had been spent on the plan. He'd been involved in so many intricate operations, he knew that when things got hot, plans evaporated and instincts and training took over. He could only hope whoever might be after him hadn't been in the same kind of crazed and chaotic balls-to-the-wall combat he'd encountered. If not, he might have an edge on them.

NATE TOOK a sharp turn to the right onto another steep switch-back. Dark pine trees climbed up the right-hand slope of the road, but to the left there was open air all the way down to Colorado Springs, which glittered in the distance in the mid-morning sun. It was the kind of vast, achingly clear view rarely seen from anywhere except an airliner as it broke from the clouds. He swallowed hard several times to clear his ears of building pressure from the altitude of the climb. Judging by the thinness of the air and the looming snow-covered monolith of the peak to his south, he guessed he'd broken ten thousand feet.

That was another advantage, he thought. If his pursuers weren't acclimated to the altitude, they'd find their mental and physical reactions slowed down. Altitude sickness produced foggy thinking and rapid exhaustion.

Around the corner was a small gravel turnout on the other side of the road, with barely enough space for a single vehicle. The turn-out existed so descending drivers could pull over and let their brakes cool before making the rest of the drive. He whipped the Jeep across the center line of the road and into the turnout. He parked parallel to the guardrail and stomped on his emergency brake and kept his engine running.

Slowly, he looked around and took measure of the situation he was in.

The highway ahead of him continued ascending for about five hundred feet and then vanished to the right in a blind corner for what was no doubt the start of another switchback up the mountain. But from where he parked, it seemed as though the road simply disappeared from view. He looked up the side of the right-hand slope, but trees blocked him from seeing any flashes of the higher switchbacks up above him.

From the perch, he'd be able to see if a vehicle was coming. Because the road was carved along the vertical rise of the mountain itself, only a two-foot-high guardrail on the east side of each turn separated the ribbon of asphalt from a sheer drop of more than a thousand feet. It was the kind of aerie that terrified some visitors, and he could imagine—and understand—the swoon of vertigo the view could bring on. But because he'd spent so many hours rappelling down cliff faces to trap falcons, height—or being suspended in air—didn't bother him.

From his vantage point, he could see the bends of four switchbacks below him on the mountain. It was as if he were nearly on the top of a tiered wedding cake. There were glimpses of the outer edges of the tiers below him. But from those lower tiers, it would be difficult to look straight up and keep the car on the road at the same time.

Across the road from where the turnout was carved into the mountain face was a narrow clearing in the trees about the width of a vehicle. Sure enough, there appeared to be an old overgrown two-track Jeep trail coming down from high in the mountains. The entrance to the road was partially blocked by four steel T-posts that had been driven into the rocky ground. There were no fresh tracks on the trail. He didn't know where the trail came from or where it went, but it was pointed in the right direction: northwest. He nodded and turned back to the panoramic view of the switchbacks out of his driver's window.

There was the metallic flash of reflected sun off a windshield four switchbacks down. Nate narrowed his eyes and homed in, but he saw the vehicle was one of the four-door rentals he'd already passed creeping around the corner. Before he could grumble "Flatlanders" again, a white SUV with smoked windows barreled around the turn, overtook the rental as if it were standing still, and shot back out of view into the trees as it cleared the turn.

Grunting aloud from pain because he kept forgetting about his injured shoulder, he slipped the .500 revolver out of its holster and extended it out the window. He trained the scope on the widest part of the third switchback down and waited, giving the SUV a minute and thirty seconds to appear. It did, and it filled the scope.

The SUV was a new model Chevy Tahoe with green-and-white Colorado plates. No doubt a rental, Nate guessed. Whoever was driving was going too fast, barely keeping the big unit under control. Unfortunately, though, because of the fleeting glimpse of the SUV and Nate's angled view of the darkened windows, he couldn't see the faces or outlines of who was driving or how many others were inside.

His instincts told him whoever was driving the Tahoe was after him. That they were hurtling up the mountain because his father had been coerced into placing a call.

They'd appeared behind him so quickly he got another thought that sent a chill through him: Dalisay and the girls could be inside. It was possible whoever was holding them had responded quickly to the call and had brought them along for the ride.

Nate thought: *Melia's first checkup: no cavities!*

He pulled his weapon inside the cab of the Jeep and laid it across his lap. Then he weighed his options.

He could simply wait where he was, parked in the only pull-out on the fifth switchback, and take out the driver as the Tahoe roared by. But if the girls were inside and the Chevy plunged off the road . . .

Or he could drive up ahead, keeping a protective cushion between them, and hope there would be a scenario where he could somehow get the Tahoe to stop and pull over so he could see who was inside and take action. But he knew he was close to the top of the tree line. Even if he got well ahead, he'd have no cover, and the occupants of the Tahoe would see him up ahead on the road and know he had nowhere to run.

Or he could barrel across the highway, mow down the T-posts, and four-wheel it up the Jeep trail and hope his pursuers didn't notice the damage or the fresh tracks up through the grass as they blasted by. But even if he got away, he had no idea where the road went. He could be trapped in a situation where he didn't have an escape route. The road might be impassable due to downed trees or a rockslide. Or, if they saw the bent posts and followed and the road opened up, he could be overrun by the Tahoe.

Nate wasn't encouraged by his options.

He looked out his window to see the white Tahoe blast around the hairpin turn of the closest switchback. He knew at the rate the car was climbing, they'd be right on top of him in less than two minutes.

He took a deep breath. His choices of staying or trying to outrun them or outclimb them all had vicious downsides. And if Dalisay and the girls were inside the Tahoe, all the variables changed.

But he had his advantages. They didn't know he was there or that he knew they were coming. And although the driver of the Tahoe was likely well trained in evasive driving, Nate owned these mountains. They were *his* Rocky Mountains, and he knew how to use their savage beauty and extreme character to his benefit.

He'd been in a similar situation once on a mountain road in Montana. At that time, he'd recalled something he'd once learned about counterinsurgency tactics from John Nemecek himself. Nemecek had said, "When you're in the middle of a shitstorm and your back is to the wall and the only options that exist are fucking horrible, you need to think, that instant, about the last possible thing you want to see coming at *you*. Then do it to *them*."

Nate looked around him and smiled. He released the parking brake and gunned the Jeep up toward the blind corner. In the thin, still mountain air, he could hear the building roar of the Tahoe coming.

NATE KNEW that for his tactic to succeed, timing was everything. While he roared up the road and careened around the blind corner, he tried to calculate the speed and distance of the closing Tahoe, and visualize where it would be on the highway when he pulled the trigger on his plan.

There were no cars on the stretch of road up ahead of him, and he thanked Providence for a clean palette. Then, out of sight from where he'd pulled over moments before, Nate stomped on his brakes and performed a quick three-point turn so the Jeep was headed back down the mountain. He paused for a few seconds, trying to anticipate the progress of the Tahoe, then tapped on the accelerator.

He coasted around the corner just as the grille of the Tahoe appeared a quarter of a mile below him. The SUV was coming fast. Because the angle of the sun illuminated the inside of the oncoming vehicle, Nate could now make out two forms inside: a driver and a passenger. Dalisay and the girls didn't appear to be inside, but he couldn't be sure of it. They might be bound or hunkered down in the backseat.

At the rate of speed the vehicles were nearing each other, he knew he'd have only a few seconds to make this work. At that instant, he eased the Jeep over to the left so it straddled the center line of the road. He took a quick intake of breath and held it, then gripped the wheel tight and locked his arms and floored it. There was now no way the two vehicles, if they stayed on their present path, could avoid a violent head-on collision.

The distance between Nate and the Tahoe melted away. He lowered his chin to his chest and braced himself, even though he knew that if the driver of the Tahoe didn't veer away, it wouldn't matter what he did to prepare for the impact. As he hurtled toward the SUV, Nate noted that the rear end of the Tahoe was suddenly fishtailing: the driver had hit his brakes. Nate didn't slow down. He saw a pair of white palms flash up to the windshield of the Tahoe as the passenger panicked.

Nate bore down.

A second before he drove headlong into the front end of the Tahoe, it veered right. But not fast enough. The Jeep's right front bumper clipped the rear quarter panel of the SUV and shattered the taillight. The collision had enough impact to wrench the steering wheel hard, but he fought to keep the Jeep on the road and he slammed on his brakes. Behind him, he heard an even louder crash of metal on metal and the crack of broken wood.

The driver of the Tahoe had taken the only available option other than hurtling off the mountain or heading for a fiery head-on collision: he'd shot into the same gravel pull-out Nate had used a few minutes before. But he'd done so recklessly due to the situation, and had flattened the guardrail and broken the posts that held it up. The two left tires of the Tahoe hung over the lip of the road and spun lazily, suspended in air.

When his Jeep finally stopped in a haze of burned tire smoke, Nate slammed the gearshift back and reversed. The side of the Tahoe filled his back plastic rear window and grew larger. But instead of ramming the Tahoe and sending it over the side, Nate jerked the wheel so he slid in next to the SUV with only inches between them.

The two vehicles were side by side. Nate kept the motor running in his Jeep.

He bailed out of the cab and kept low. He'd stopped his Jeep so close to the Tahoe that the occupants were trapped inside. They wouldn't be able to open the passenger door because his Jeep blocked it, and outside the driver's side was nothing but thin air.

Nate crab-walked around the front of his Jeep with his .500 Wyoming Express drawn. He was still low enough that he couldn't see the people inside, and therefore they couldn't see him. The splinters from the exploded guardrail posts smelled of pine and creosote.

He squatted down by the bent rear bumper of the Tahoe. A deep male voice inside shouted, *"Keep still! Don't move or shift your weight!"* As Nate reached up toward the back door handle, he knew why they were panicking. The SUV was literally balanced on the lip of the drop-off. He could feel the big vehicle shift slightly to the left, toward the abyss. It was a miracle it was even still up there.

Even though Nate was ninety-nine percent sure the occupants were operators from The Five, and Dalisay and the girls weren't inside, he needed to make sure. He stood and threw open the back hatch and leveled his weapon.

"Raise your hands and press your palms to the roof liner!" he barked. *"Both of you. Now."*

He didn't recognize either of the men, but the sight of them jarred him, because they didn't appear to be the righteous fresh-faced warriors he'd expected. They were older than he'd thought they'd be: late twenties, although ripped with lean muscle. The driver had a shaved head and a lantern jaw and wore a single diamond earring and wrap-around sunglasses. He had scooted from behind the wheel toward the center of the Tahoe when he looked back. The passenger was dark-skinned and dark-eyed, and had a buzz cut. His shirtsleeves were rolled back to reveal a latticework of tattoos. He was pressed against the passenger door as if willing the vehicle to shift over to level. A stream of blood flowed down the side of the passenger's nose from a cut he'd received in the crash.

"You've got to let us out of here, man," the passenger said, pleading.

The bald driver didn't move or speak, but Nate could feel his glare even though he couldn't see his eyes.

"Nothing happens until you let me see your fucking *hands*."

The passenger shot his arms up and did as he was told. The driver didn't move.

"I'm not going to ask again . . ." Nate said, leveling his weapon at the driver's head.

But before Nate could say another word there was the rapid *crack-crack-crack* of gunshots and the inside of the Tahoe was suddenly filled with swirling debris from the exploded cushioning from the bench seats. The driver was trying to put bullets into Nate by firing through the two sets of seats, and Nate dropped to the gravel. But he wasn't hit. The steel framework and springs inside had stopped or diverted the rounds.

He rolled away back to his Jeep and clambered inside. He could hear the two men shouting inside the Tahoe. The passenger was screaming at the driver to stop firing, saying he'd seen the big blond man go down.

Behind the wheel of his Jeep, Nate cranked the front wheels and drove quickly out onto the road. Then he shoved the gearshift into reverse again and goosed it and T-boned the SUV. The spare tire mounted on the back of his Jeep hit the Tahoe squarely between the front and back doors on the exposed side. Nate's head snapped back from the force of the collision, but the last thing he saw before the impact and pure blue sky was the muzzle of the driver's weapon being raised toward the glass of the passenger window.

The Tahoe made an unholy racket as it rolled down the mountainside, snapping trees and breaking up in showers of glass and plastic and pine boughs until it settled upside down eight hundred feet below in a small rocky ravine.

In Nate's mind, the faces of the two men—one of his brethren raising his weapon to try and take him out before the impact—hung suspended in the air. But something about them didn't jibe. Unlike Nate's fellow operators in The Five, these guys looked less like cool and efficient warriors than well-conditioned thugs. Either The Five were recruiting a different class of special operators, or he was so far away from his days in the unit that he remembered his brothers with murky nostalgia. He shook his head sharply, trying to make their faces and his thoughts go away.

HE PARKED in the trees so his Jeep couldn't be seen from the highway or from his father's home. He kept in the timber as he skirted the clearing, getting just close enough to confirm there were fresh tracks in the drive from when the Tahoe had come and gone earlier. He suspected there was a third operator of The Five inside, possibly two, and prayed that Dalisay and the girls had been returned unharmed. The operators were no doubt waiting for the two men in the Tahoe to come back and pick them up after dispatching Nate.

He approached the house from the side, running from tree to tree, keeping low. He had to close a distance of eighty yards from the timber to the siding of the structure. The three windows on the side of the house went to the back bedrooms and the bathroom. All had curtains drawn, but as he made his last desperate sprint to the house over open lawn, he looked up and saw the curtains part on the bathroom window. Nate dropped to a squat and raised his weapon and cocked the hammer in a single move.

The crosshairs through his scope settled on the bridge of his father's nose as the old man looked out. He was using the toilet and happened to part the curtains while he stood. Nate saw his Dad's eyes widen in shock and surprise when he saw him.

Nate lowered the gun and raised a single finger to his lips to indicate "Sssshhh."

His father nodded slightly before looking over his shoulder. Then, apparently satisfied no one was watching, he turned back.

Nate mouthed, *"How many?"*

His father mouthed, *"One."*

*"Front or back?"*

*"Front."*

*"I'm going to ring the doorbell,"* Nate mouthed, and illustrated by jabbing his pointer finger. He turned his finger on his Dad. *"You answer the door."*

Gordo looked back at him blankly for a moment, then nodded that he understood.


NATE KEPT below the windows as he turned the corner from the side of the house. He approached the porch, then reached through the railing to press the doorbell. When the chime rang inside, he heard a series of sudden footfalls. Light and heavy steps. Meaning there were more inside than his father and the bad guy. Dalisay and the girls? He hoped so.

"Who the hell is that?" an unfamiliar man asked.

"I'll get it," he heard Gordon say.

"Stay where you are," the other man said.

"Who's here, Mom?" A small girl's voice. Nate smiled to himself.

Nate heard and felt the sucking sound of the front door opening out. He pressed himself against the siding of the house with his weapon cocked and pointed up at a forty-five-degree angle.

A man's head poked outside, squinting toward the circular drive. The operator was older than the two men in the Tahoe, but his features were just as hard and rough. Heavy brow, close-cropped hair, zipperlike scar on his cheek, and serious set to his mouth. Another thug. At Nate's eye level, he recognized the blunt round snout of a flash suppressor mounted on the barrel of a semiautomatic long gun.

The operator sensed something wrong and his head rotated toward the big revolver.

Nate blew it off.

As he holstered his weapon and the shot rang in his ears along with shrieks from inside, he thought: *Yarak.*

# 15

THE NEXT MORNING, Wednesday, outside Saddlestring, Wyoming, Joe Pickett backed his pickup toward the tongue of his stock trailer in the muted dawn light. The glow of his taillights painted the front of the trailer light pink as he tried to inch into position so he could lower the trailer hitch onto the ball jutting out from beneath his rear bumper.

It was a cool fall day, with enough of a wind that the last clinging leaves on the cottonwoods were releasing their grip in yellow/gold waves. It had dropped below freezing during the night and he'd had to break through an inch of ice on the horse trough. Southbound high-altitude $V$'s of Canada geese punctuated the rosy day sky, making a racket.

He'd left a message on Luke Brueggemann's cell phone that it was time to ride the circuit in the mountains and check on those elk camps they hadn't gotten to earlier. While he bridled Toby to lead him over to the open trailer, he heard a vehicle rumbling up Bighorn Road from town. Hunters, he guessed, headed up into the mountains.

Gravel crunched in front of his house and a door slammed, and he leaned around the corner of the trailer to see who it was. It wouldn't be unusual for a hunter to stop by to verify hunting area boundaries or make a complaint. But it wasn't a hunter, it was a sheriff's department vehicle. Joe caught his groan before it came out.

He stuffed his gloves into his back pocket and walked around the house to the front. Deputy Mike Reed was on his porch, fist raised, about to knock.

"Hey, Mike," Joe said.

"Joe."

"You're out and about early."

Reed sighed and crammed his hands into the pockets of his too-tight department jacket. "It seems late to me. I've been up most of the night."

Joe frowned. "What's up?"

"Hell is breaking loose. I was hoping you might offer me a cup of coffee."

"Sure," Joe said. "Just let me go inside and check around first. I've got one bathroom and three females in there getting ready for work and school in various stages of undress."

Reed nodded. "I've got daughters. I remember what that's like. I used the lilac bushes on the side of my house for eight years, I think. Maybe you could bring the coffee out here."

"That would be a better idea," Joe said, shouldering past the deputy.


THEY LEANED their arms over the top rail of the corral at the opposite sides of the corner post. Each held a steaming cup of coffee and put a single boot up on the bottom rail. When they breathed or talked, small clouds of condensation puffed out and haloed their heads before dissipating.

"Like I said, long night," Reed said.

"Seems like you want to tell me something."

"That's right, Joe." There was gravity in Reed's words.

"Then you'd best get to it," Joe said. "I've got horses to load and a trainee to pick up, and if the sheriff or one of his spies sees us out here talking, he'll think we're plotting against him."

Reed barked a laugh. "At this point, he's probably already convinced of that. At least as far as I'm concerned."

Joe sipped his coffee and waited.

"Since I've worked at the department," Reed said, "I can't remember more of a clusterfuck than we've got going right now. And the timing! Just a few weeks until the election. I should be kind of happy, I guess, but I almost feel sorry for that idiot of a sheriff right now."

"Meaning what?" Joe asked.

"Well, the triple homicide, of course," Reed said. "We're not getting anywhere on that. We've notified the FBI, but we haven't made a request for assistance. State DCI boys are bumping into each other in the office, but until something breaks, we've got nowhere to run with it. Ballistics is inconclusive, other than they were all shot with a big projectile that passed through their bodies and can't be found. No one's come forward to link them up, and nobody seems to know anything about why they were in that boat in the first place."

Joe looked into the top of his coffee cup, because he couldn't meet Reed's eyes.

Reed said, "On top of all this, we get a call from Dr. Rhonda Eisenstein. She's a psychologist from Winchester. You know her?"

Joe shook his head no.

"She's . . . interesting. Anyway, this psychologist was in a house with a man named Bad Bob Whiteplume out on the res."

"I know Bob," Joe said, looking up.

"Anyway, according to this Dr. Rhonda Eisenstein, she was staying over with Bad Bob at his place Monday night and someone started honking their horn outside about three-thirty in the morning and wouldn't stop. Bad Bob went outside to see what the problem was in his bathrobe and never came back. She thinks something might have happened to him and she's raising hell with the sheriff to start a search."

"Did she hear an argument or a fight?"

"No. She was in the back room."

"She didn't see anything?"

"No."

"Why'd she wait two days to call?" Joe asked.

"Actually, she didn't," Reed said. "She called Tuesday. But with everything we've got going on, nobody got back to her. That really hacked her off."

"I see," Joe said.

"So when Bob didn't show up later and nobody from the sheriff's department came out, this doctor went on the warpath, so to speak."

"So to speak," Joe echoed.

"She started calling everybody. The newspaper, the radio station, all the television folks in Billings and Casper. Even the governor. She accused the department of racism because we didn't respond quickly."

Joe looked up. "Well . . ."

"I know," Reed said, shaking his head. "But that sort of thing happens all the time on the res. We all know it. People just kind of come and go. We don't get too worked up about it until we know someone's really missing and the Feds give us the go-ahead since they've got primary jurisdiction."

"Was this your decision not to call her back?" Joe asked.

Reed shook his head. "No, it was McLanahan's. But it doesn't reflect very well on any of us."

"Probably shouldn't," Joe said.

"Anyway," Reed said, "what happened happened. The result was the mayor and the city council called McLanahan in yesterday to demand some answers. Nobody likes it that we've got unsolved murders like this, but it's even worse when the whole department is accused of racism. Nobody likes us making this kind of news, especially the sheriff. I almost feel sorry for him, and I didn't think that was possible."

Joe clucked his tongue. He thought he knew where this was going but didn't want to encourage it.

"That's not all," Reed said. "About eleven last night, we got a call from the FBI in Cheyenne. They wanted to see if we could confirm the fact that our person of interest in the triple homicides, Nate Romanowski, was the son of one Gordon Romanowski of Colorado Springs, Colorado."

Joe felt his throat go dry.

"Seems a body was found in the senior Romanowski's place. No ID, but a massive head wound that sounds suspiciously like our three rubes from the boat."

"No ID?" Joe asked.

"That's what they said. We don't have a lot more information on it yet, but they're investigating. You know the Feds—they don't share information. They just collect it and make their case and keep us in the dark pretty much."

"Do they think the body was Gordon Romanowski?"

"No," Reed said. "That they're sure about. But they said it looks like Gordon and his family—a second wife and two little girls—have split the scene. No one can locate them."

Joe's head spun. He'd checked the falconry website that morning and there had been no new entries.

"I got the impression there were some other unexplained things going on down there in Colorado Springs," Reed said. "They wouldn't tell us what was going on, but maybe there were other bodies found. I don't know."

"Man oh man," Joe said, and whistled.

"So because of this mess we've got," Reed said, leaning forward on the rail so he could get closer to Joe, "McLanahan is personally leading the Whiteplume investigation, so he assigned me as lead investigator on the triple homicides. He called the mayor and the editor of the newspaper last night to let them know. He hung me out to dry and set me up to fail. It was a good move on his part, I'll give that to him. This way, when the election comes around, the voters will have a choice of the racist incumbent who has been there for a while and the incompetent deputy who can't solve a triple homicide. It evens the playing field, wouldn't you say?"

"Yup."

"I need to ask you something," Reed said, his voice dropping. "I know we're friends, but I've got a job to do."

*Here it comes,* Joe thought.

"I know you're close with Romanowski," Reed said. "So I've got to ask you if you've been in contact with him the last couple of days. In any way."

Joe looked up. "I talked to him a couple of nights ago."

Reed's face hardened.

"He told me he didn't commit murder," Joe said. "I believe him."

"You knew we wanted to talk with him," Reed said.

Joe nodded. "And there wasn't—and isn't—an arrest warrant. I could have asked him to voluntarily show up at your office for questioning, but he wouldn't have done it."

Reed said softly, "I appreciate you being straight with me."

Joe looked away again.

"Now I've got to ask you if you've been in contact with him in any form the last couple of days."

Joe said, "I haven't."

"But you'll let me know, right? Now that our department and the Feds are wanting to talk to him?"

"The Feds have been wanting to talk to him for years," Joe said. "That's nothing new."

"But a dead body in his father's house is."

Joe nodded.

"Do you know where he is?"

"No."

"Do you know how we can reach him?"

"Don't ask me that."

Reed reacted as if slapped. "What are you saying?"

"I don't want to lie to you," Joe said. "So don't ask me questions like that. Nate's my friend. It's possible he may reach out to me. I won't betray him unless you can look me in the eye and say you know he's done something bad."

"It's sure looking that way, isn't it?" Reed asked. "The guy isn't exactly stepping up to clear his name. And now this thing with his dad."

"I honestly don't know anything about that," Joe said. "It does worry me, though."

"That's nice. You know, Joe, there are a few people who wonder about you. They wonder that when it comes to Nate Romanowski it's a little questionable whose side you're on."

"Gee," Joe said. "Who would those people be?"

Reed blew air out through his nose in a long sigh. "Jesus, Joe," he said. "You've got to help me out here. Or *I'll* start to wonder."

Joe thought about it. His stomach was in knots. Reed was an honest cop and a friend as well. He might just be the next sheriff. Withholding information didn't seem right.

Finally, Joe said, "Go out and talk to Pam Kelly. Sweat her if you have to."

Reed looked up. "Did you interview her? Does she know something?"

"Go find out," Joe said. He reached out for Reed's empty cup and started for the house.

"Joe," Reed said behind him.

Joe stopped.

"Tread lightly here," Reed said. "Don't get too tangled up in this. It isn't your case. If it starts to seem like you're playing games with us, well . . ."

"I know," Joe said, and walked through the backyard to his house. While he was inside rinsing the cups, he heard the deputy's vehicle start up and drive away.

MARYBETH LOOKED in on him in his office as he booted up his computer.

"If you're trying to find John Nemecek, don't waste your time," she said.

He turned in his chair and raised his eyebrows. She stood there dressed only in flesh-colored panties and a matching bra.

"Good thing I didn't invite Mike Reed in here for coffee," he said, looking her over. "He might have been kind of distracted. *I* might have been kind of distracted."

"How about you look me in the eye," she commanded. "You're not going to find what you're looking for down there."

He did so, reluctantly.

She said, "Unless you somehow got the name wrong, he doesn't exist," she said. "Nothing. Nada. He's never been born."

"I didn't get the name wrong," Joe said.

"Then he's got some pretty powerful capabilities," she said, glancing over her shoulder to make sure Lucy and April were out of earshot, "because no one can simply not exist on the Internet. It's impossible. It takes some real juice to scrub a name off every search engine. The fact that he doesn't exist at all in cyberspace says we're dealing with someone with clout."

"Interesting," Joe said. "But I wasn't actually going to look for him."

"Leave that to me," she said. "When I get to work I'm going to access the networks I'm not supposed to know about. I'll find him."

"Call me when you do," Joe said.

She agreed with a wink. When she left the room to try and hurry up their girls, he opened the falconry site.

No new entries.

# 16

LUKE BRUEGGEMANN tried not to show his obvious relief when Joe Pickett arrived at the hotel in his pickup without the horse trailer. Brueggemann tossed a small duffel bag of gear, clothing, and lunch into the bed of the vehicle and climbed in.

"Sorry I'm late," Joe said, adjusting the volume down on the universal access channel of the radio. "It's been another busy morning."

"No problem," Brueggemann said, buckling in. "What's going on? Aren't we going up to check on those elk camps?"

"Not today."

"What's going on?"

Joe chinned toward the radio. "Haven't you been listening in? I thought you did that."

Brueggemann's face flushed red. "Girlfriend problems," he said. "I've been on my phone all morning with my girl in Laramie."

"Does she go to the university?" Joe asked, pulling out of the parking lot onto the street.

"Fifth-year senior. She kind of misses me, I guess. But she doesn't have to make it so hard on me because I'm not there, you know? She's used to being in contact with me twenty-four/seven."

Joe grunted. He didn't know, but he really wasn't sure he wanted to hear the details. His mind was racing from what he'd heard from Deputy Reed that morning.

Brueggemann got the message that Joe didn't want to hear about his personal life. He said, "So what'd I miss out on?"

"A guy from the reservation is missing," Joe said, nodding toward the radio. "A well-known guy named Bad Bob Whiteplume. I know him a little, but I knew his sister very well."

"You mean like he was kidnapped?"

"No. Missing."

"Doesn't that kind of thing happen all the time?" his trainee asked.

When Joe shot him a look, Brueggemann flushed again and said, "I didn't mean anything by it. Sorry. I just meant I've heard those folks tend to come and go more than . . . others."

"You sound like the sheriff's department. Did you learn that growing up in Sundance?" Joe asked.

"You know what I mean," Brueggemann stuttered.

Joe said, "It's an odd deal. There's all kinds on the res, just like there's all kinds here in town. His sister, Alisha, was one of the best people I've ever met, God rest her soul."

"She died?"

"Not that long ago," Joe said. "It was an accident. The guys who killed her were after someone else and she was in the wrong place at the wrong time."

"This missing-persons case," Brueggemann said. "What does it have to do with us?"

Joe cruised down Main Street, nodding hello to the few shoppers out on the sidewalk. "In normal circumstances, nothing," he said. "But if you'll recall, we had a triple homicide here a few days ago. Sheriff McLanahan has his hands full with that, and he's apparently not getting anywhere finding the killer. He's got FBI and DCI people here bumping into each other, and the voters are getting pretty antsy. And in the middle of all that, this doctor sets up camp and starts demanding a full-scale investigation to locate Bad Bob."

Brueggemann shook his head, confused.

"If you haven't noticed," Joe said, "we don't have a lot of law enforcement bodies around this county. When something major happens, everybody gets pressed into the effort. Highway patrol, local cops, brand inspectors. And game wardens."

The trainee grinned. "So we're gonna be part of the investigation?"

"Bet they didn't tell you this part in game warden school," Joe said.

"There isn't any game warden school," Brueggemann said.

"I know."

IT TOOK forty minutes to get to Bad Bob's Native American Outlet. On the way there, Brueggemann peppered Joe with questions about cases, investigative methods, Game and Fish violators, and landowner relations in Twelve Sleep County. They were the kinds of questions Joe had once asked of his mentor, Vern Dunnegan, when he'd been a trainee. While Vern loved to talk and tell long stories about the characters in the district, Joe kept his answers short and clipped. He didn't have the paternalistic contempt for the locals Vern had.

While they drove, Joe noticed Brueggemann had his phone out and was furiously tapping keys. When his trainee saw Joe look with disapproval, he said as explanation: "Texting my girl."

"Ah," Joe said. "Maybe you can tell her you're working. We're at work."

"I'll do that," Brueggemann said, his face flushed from being caught. After he pressed send, he slipped the phone back into his uniform pocket.

"You remind me of my daughters with your texting," Joe said, realizing how old he sounded. And realizing how young Brueggemann was.

As they turned off the highway toward the reservation, there was a late-model black pickup off to the south in the middle of a sagebrush-covered swale. Joe instinctively pulled off the gravel road, put his truck into park, and raised his binoculars. After a full minute, he lowered them to the bench seat and pulled back on the road.

"Hunters?" Brueggemann asked.

"Yup."

"Are we going to check them out?"

"Nope."

"Can I ask why?"

"I know 'em," Joe said. "The biology teacher at the high school and his son. They've got deer licenses and habitat stamps. I talked to them a few days ago, and I know they're clean and legal. This is a general deer area, so they're not trespassing. And they haven't shot any game."

Brueggemann shook his head. "How do you know they haven't?"

"Clean truck," Joe said. "No blood on it."

"Oh," Brueggemann said, obviously not entirely convinced.

"Like every newbie," Joe said, "you want to roust somebody. I used to be like that. Most of these folks are solid citizens. They're meat hunters out to fill their freezers. Most of them have been hunting for years, sometimes for generations. They pay our salaries, and the money from licenses goes to habitat management and conservation. Even the majority of the violators are just a little stupid about rules and regulations or trying to feed their families. Times are tough. Some of these men feel bad about being unemployed. They'd rather take their chances with the game warden than stand in line for government cheese. So I don't roust 'em just to roust 'em."

"That's a question I have," Brueggemann said. "What do you do when you catch someone red-handed with a poached deer and you know he was going to take it home to his family?"

"Are you asking if I ever use discretion?"

"Yeah, I guess."

Joe thought about how he should answer the question. Then: "Yeah, I do. But I never let them off entirely if they broke the law. I'll give the guy a ticket for the poached deer, but I might look past other violations he committed at the same time. You can really build on the charges in just about every situation, and you'd be correct. Or you can make a point that one time and go a little easy on the guy. It's different, though, if the violator is after a trophy or doesn't have a starving family at home. In that situation, I lower the boom on 'em."

Brueggemann smiled. "I heard you once issued the governor a ticket for fishing without a license. Is that just an urban legend, or what?"

Joe said, "Nope."

"You really did that?"

"Of all people, he should have known better."

"I can't believe they let you keep your job."

"Is that right?"

"Yeah," his trainee said. "I think I'd have given the guy a warning or looked the other way. I mean, who cares if he pays a hundred-dollar fine? It wouldn't mean anything in the end, anyway, and maybe I'd have a friend in high places."

Joe looked over at Brueggemann for as long as he could before turning back to his driving. *"Really?"* Joe asked. "I think I should have lost my job if I *didn't* give him a ticket."

His trainee's silence became uncomfortable. Finally, Brueggemann said, "Sorry, I wasn't thinking when I said that."

"No," Joe said, "you weren't. I've got a job to do out here, and I do it." After a moment: "I know this will come across as old-school, but I hope you approach this job the right way. It's easy to be cynical. That's the way a lot of young people think about the world. I know that because I've got three kids of my own and I see glimpses of it from them at times. But I really do believe there's nothing wrong with doing your best and doing the right thing. Just because you have a badge and a gun doesn't mean you're any better than these folks. If it weren't for them, you wouldn't have a job.

"I screw up sometimes," he said, "but I'd rather screw up trying to do the right thing than looking the other way. And what good does it do you if your friend in high places knows firsthand that you'll compromise your oath? Tell me that?"

"Jeez," Brueggemann said, looking away. "You don't need to get so hot about it. I said I was sorry."


A FEW MILES LATER, after minutes of silent tension, Brueggemann said, "I don't want to get you all riled up again, but there's something I'm curious about."

"What's that?" Joe said, tight-lipped. He was surprised at himself for getting angry so quickly, and he knew exactly why it had happened. He was also surprised that the reason for his outburst was the next thing to come out of Brueggemann's mouth.

"This Nate Romanowski guy, the one the sheriff asked you about. Do you know him pretty well?"

"Well enough, I guess."

"How? I mean, from what I heard yesterday at the garage, he

doesn't seem like the kind of guy you'd want to hang out with. He seems like the kind of guy you'd want to *arrest*."

Joe knew he was boxed in. He said, "I'm not going to talk about it right now."

"Do you know where he is?"

"No."

"I'm just curious," his trainee said.

"You can stay curious for a while," Joe said so sharply that Brueggemann flinched.

A FEW MINUTES LATER, after he'd cooled down, Joe said, "It's not just you I find so annoying. I'm trying to work some things out in my own mind right now."

"I'm glad it's not just me," his trainee said, in a way that made Joe grin.

Joe nodded toward a low-slung building that emerged from the cottonwoods on the right. Two sheriff's department vehicles were parked out front. "We're here."

SHERIFF KYLE McLANAHAN looked distressed. Deputy Sollis stood next to him, his face a mask of deep feigned sympathy for his boss. Both looked up as Joe parked his truck and got out. Neither looked excited to see him.

"We're in the middle of an investigation here," Sollis called out.

"Looks like it," Joe said, strolling up. Luke Brueggemann was a few feet behind Joe, hanging back. "Looks like you've got a lot going on by the way you're standing around with purpose next to gas pumps."

McLanahan said, "Unless you've got something you can tell us to help out, I'd suggest you move on down the road, Game Warden."

"Deputy Reed filled me in on what was going on this morning," Joe said. "I know you're shorthanded until the state boys and the Feds show up."

"He did, huh?" Sollis asked, as if Joe and Mike Reed's conversation was proof of some kind of collusion.

Joe said, "Yup. You guys have a lot on your plate right now, and there's two of us available."

The sheriff snorted a response.

Joe ignored him and looked around. There was very little that stood out about the scene, Joe thought. The convenience store was still, the WE'RE CLOSED sign propped in the window. Bad Bob's blue Dodge pickup was parked on the side of the building where it always was, meaning he hadn't driven it away. Two battered Dumpsters had been turned over behind the building and the contents inside scattered across the dirt. The concrete pad housing the gas pumps was dusty but not stained with blood.

Joe said, "I was wondering if you'd talked to the folks at the school. They seem to know everything that's happening on the res." He was thinking in particular of Alice Thunder, who had her finger on the pulse of the community and was supposed to be gone, according to Nate.

"We really don't need your help with real police work," Sollis said. "Aren't there some fishermen you can go out and harass?"

"Not many," Joe said. "Most folks are hunting by now."

Joe was struck by McLanahan's demeanor. He was usually blustery and sarcastic, roiling the calm with quaint and colorful cowboy sayings. But he looked gaunt, and the dark circles under his eyes were pronounced. This whole thing—the murders, the disappearance of

Bad Bob, the upcoming election—was getting to him, Joe thought. There were many times in the past when Joe would have paid to see the sheriff in such pain. But for a reason he couldn't put his finger on, this wasn't one of them.

Joe said, "Bob is kind of a renegade. He might show up."

"You think we don't know that?" McLanahan said. "Do you think we want to . . ." But he caught himself before he finished the sentence.

"Get a move on, the both of you," Sollis said. "We're busy here, and you're interfering with a crime scene."

"A crime scene, is it?" Joe said.

"You heard him," McLanahan growled. Joe noted that when the sheriff was truly angry, the West Virginia accent he once had and now suppressed poked through.

"Hey," Luke Brueggemann said to the sheriff, gesturing toward Joe. "He's just trying to help. He spends a hell of a lot more time out here than you people do, and he's a lot more effective. Maybe you ought to listen to what he has to say."

Joe raised his eyebrows in surprise. Sollis glared and squared his feet as if bracing for a fight. McLanahan turned his attention from Joe to the trainee.

"Who in the hell are you?"

"Name's Luke Brueggemann."

McLanahan let the name sit there. After a moment, he shook his head and said to Joe, "Get him out of here. He ain't no older than my grandson, and even stupider, if possible."

Joe hooked his thumbs through his belt loops and rocked on his boot heels. He nodded and said, "I guess you're right. We've got fishermen to harass."

He turned and put his hand on Brueggemann's shoulder as he walked past. Brueggemann gave Sollis a belligerent nod and the sheriff an eye roll before turning and walking with Joe toward their truck.

"What was *that* about?" Joe whispered.

"They piss me off," Brueggemann said. "They've got no good reason to act like that."

"The county sheriff has jurisdiction in his county," Joe said. "We can assist if asked, but he can say no."

"That guy needs a lot of help, if you ask me. And I don't even know what the hell I'm talking about."

"Welcome to game warden school," Joe said, a smile tugging on the corners of his mouth.

As he opened the door to his truck, McLanahan called after him, "And you can tell your friend Nate we're going to find his ass and put him away."

JOE AND LUKE BRUEGGEMANN stood in front of the counter in the principal's office of Wyoming Indian High School, waiting for the principal, Ann Shoyo, to conclude a phone conversation. She held a slim finger in the air to indicate it would be only a few more seconds.

She was native, well dressed, and attractive, with a long mane of jet-black hair that curled over her shoulders. He noted the pin on her lapel, a horizontal piece that had a red wild rose on one side and a flag with parallel red and black bars on a field of white on the other side. The pin represented the two nations on the reservation: the rose was the symbol of the Eastern Shoshone, and the flag was the Northern Arapaho.

Ann Shoyo sat back and blew a stray strand of hair out of her face. "I'd like to talk to Alice myself," she said. "But she hasn't come in for two days. I would *really* like to talk to Alice."

Joe quickly fished a card out of his pocket and handed it to her. "Please call me if she shows up or if you hear anything," he said.

———

"NOT GOOD NEWS," Joe said to Brueggemann as they approached the pickup.

His cell phone burred and he retrieved it from his pocket. Deputy Mike Reed calling.

"Joe," Reed said, "I've hit a brick wall. Pam Kelly isn't here, and her stock is going crazy, kicking the fences all to hell and screaming at me."

Joe could hear braying and anguished bleats in the background.

Reed said, "They act like they haven't been fed for a couple of days."

"Did you look inside the house?" Joe asked.

"I looked in through the windows, is all. I've got no probable cause for going in, although I might just make something up. I wonder if she did herself in, considering she lost her husband and her son?"

Joe paused for a moment, then said, "That doesn't sound like her. She's too mean."

"I'll keep looking," Reed said. "I'll let you know if I find her. But this place gives me the creeps, and I've got a real bad feeling about it."

Joe understood. He felt the same way as they turned into the rough driveway off Black Coal Road that led to the back of Alice Thunder's home. Her GMC wasn't parked on the side, which gave him an ounce of hope.

"Give me a minute," Joe said to Brueggemann as the trainee reached for his door handle. "I'll be right back."

Brueggemann shrugged a *whatever* shrug.

Joe realized as he walked up Alice's broken concrete path that something was amiss. It was when he rapped on her back door that he realized what it was: no dogs. Every time he'd ever been there, her little dogs put up a cacophony and she'd have to push them aside to get to the door.

She wasn't home, and the dogs were silent.

He thought: *Bad Bob, Pam Kelly, and now Alice Thunder.* His chest tightened, and he took several deep breaths as he stepped back and pulled out his phone. He was surprised to see he had a message from Marybeth. Apparently, she'd called while he spoke to Mike Reed and he'd missed it.

He punched the button to retrieve it.

Her voice was tense. "I'm frustrated. I've looked everywhere—every database I have access to. John Nemecek doesn't exist," she said.

He thought: *Yes, he does.*

# 17

THE NEXT MORNING, in the long cold shadow of the sawtoothed Teton Range in the mountains outside of Victor, Idaho, Nate Romanowski smeared a tarry mixture of motor oil and road dirt below his eyes, across his forehead, and over his cheeks. The morning sun had not yet broken over the top of the mountains. Light frost coated the long grass in the meadows and the cold, thin air had a scalpel-like bite to it. Below him, through a descending march of spindly lodgepole pine trees that strung all the way to the valley floor, a single sodium pole light illuminated the center of a small complex of faded log structures. It was 7:40, Thursday, October 25.

He raised the field glasses. Below was a lodge and four smaller outbuildings in the complex: a garage, a sagging barn, a smokehouse, and what looked like a guest cabin. He focused in on the hoary metal roof of the lodge and noted several wet ovals on the surface, meaning there were sources of heat inside. That was confirmed when he shifted his view to the mouth of a galvanized chimney pipe that exhaled a thin plume of white woodsmoke.

When the wind shifted from east to west, he thought he caught the slight aroma of coffee and bacon from below. *Breakfast,* he thought. The place was occupied, but by whom?

He turned to his vehicle and slid the scoped Ruger Ranch rifle from beneath the front seat of his Jeep. It was the rifle he'd liberated from the old man in the boat. He checked the loads. The thirty-round magazine was packed full with red-tipped Hornady 6.8-millimeter SPC shells in 110 grain. Nate seated a live round in the chamber with the Garand breech bolt-action and slung the weapon over his shoulder. His .500 shoulder holster was buckled on over his hoodie and fleece for quick access. A pair of binoculars hung from a strap looped around his neck.

He was ready.


THE TRIP from Colorado Springs to the compound in Idaho had taken slightly more than nineteen hours after the killing of the third operator.

Despite initial objections from Gordon, Nate had persuaded his father to take his family away. Nate gave him half a brick of cash and apologized to his stepmother and half sisters for meeting the way they did.

Nate didn't leave the scene until 1:00 in the afternoon. No other operators arrived.

He'd debated himself how much evidence—if any—to leave behind. The body contained no legitimate identification. The man had a wallet in his pocket with $689 in it and a Colorado driver's license. No credit cards, no receipts, no other cards of any kind. And when Nate studied the license, he recognized a professional forgery right away. The license was too new, stiff, and shiny. It was the kind of identification Nate had been given to use a hundred times in the past. There wasn't a single thing wrong with it except the wrong name, Social Security number, address, and birthplace. Nate had nodded to himself in recognition. In the rare circumstance that the body of a member of The Five was left in a country they weren't supposed to be in, there would be no means of identifying him. It rarely happened—they prided themselves on bringing everyone back every time—but it was standard operating procedure. This alone would send Nemecek a message.

RATHER THAN backtrack through Colorado Springs and drive north on highly trafficked I-25, he took rural county roads for sixty miles until he merged onto I-70 west and on to Grand Junction, Colorado. The way north and west from there lost him five hours more than if he'd taken the other route, but he thought if anyone were looking for him, he'd escape their attention. It was evening when he hit the outskirts of Grand Junction and stopped to fill the tank and spare gas can before proceeding west into Utah, and then north toward Salt Lake City. He was never out of sight of the mountains, and he drove with his eyes wide open, noting every potential escape route toward those mountains if he encountered a roadblock or an enemy vehicle.

AS HE DROVE and lost his light, he replayed all the events of the morning, from meeting his father to sending his old man away from his own house with a wad of unmarked cash. He could only speculate on what faced him, based on his knowledge and experiences with John Nemecek. When he ran everything back through his mind, he concluded with more questions than answers.

Nate needed to know how many people were in the team with Nemecek. Once he knew for sure, he could tailor his strategy and defense. His mentor liked working with small strike forces of no more than eight, but it wasn't a hard-and-fast prerogative. Nemecek liked eight because the number was perfect for a small footprint but an effective infiltration. Only one large vehicle or two midsized cars were necessary to move everyone into place on the ground. Eight could be broken up into the smaller units Nemecek favored: two killing squads of four each, including the team leader, a communications operative, and a jack-of-all-trades (JOAT) operator trained in emergency medical triage and whatever other special skills the particular mission required.

Assuming eight was the number, Nate could identify five so far. This included the three dead operators, and the mystery woman who'd killed Large Merle. That meant there were three other operators out there somewhere—maybe with Nemecek, maybe on an assignment of their own. In this case, Nate guessed the JOAT would be the woman. She was attractive and aggressive enough to turn Large Merle's head and manipulate him into giving away Nate's previous location as well as cold-blooded enough to kill his colleague when he was no longer useful to her. Women were rare in the ranks of Mark V, but not unheard of.

He didn't count the three locals Nemecek had recruited to ambush him from the river.

And what if there were more? Nemecek knew Nate knew *him*. The number could be smaller, but Nate doubted that because of logistics. But it could very well be larger, maybe even double or more the size Nate anticipated. If that was the case, Nate would need help. And he knew there was only one place he could find it: Idaho.

NATE WAS still puzzled by the demeanor and physical appearance of the three dead operators in Colorado. The colleagues he had worked with years before were unique in looks and attitude in that they were fairly normal and didn't stand out from the crowd: Nate and

Large Merle being two exceptions to that rule. The Peregrines who made it through training weren't the bodybuilders, or the ex-jocks, or the street fighters and ex-bouncers who volunteered for special ops. They weren't the hard cases covered with tattoos and jewelry. The men who'd spent their young lives being ogled, brown-nosed, or feared by peers couldn't handle what Mark V training threw at them. They didn't have what it took when the mental part of the training took place, the weeks designed to humiliate and break down the recruits.

The ones who made it, like Nate, made it because of something different inside: a desire to succeed no matter what, a defined and accomplished hatred for their tormentors, and an almost pathological desire to be a member of one of the most elite special-operations units ever devised. The Peregrines who emerged had unbelievable mental toughness, what Nemecek called "high-tensile guts." They weren't necessarily the greatest physical specimens, or the tallest or biggest. The majority of them were fresh-faced and soft-spoken. Most came from places like Oklahoma, or Arkansas, or South Carolina, or Montana, or Wyoming. Many were raised on farms and ranches, and most were hunters and fishermen or mountain climbers or kayakers. Men who had grown up amid the cruelty and amorality of nature itself, where predators were predators and prey was prey.

Nate had always thought he had an advantage over the others in his class, and it was that thought that kept him going. He had since realized that perhaps it was a false advantage, but at the time it sustained him and drove him on. Nate thought at the time, during the training, that no one around him could possibly understand the single-minded dedication it took to be a falconer. The rigors and psychological suspense of logic and disbelief he'd encountered capturing and flying birds of prey had honed his disposition and dedication to a place none of his fellow operators could yet grasp. Nemecek got it, which is why he'd approached Nate in the first place.

The men who survived Peregrine training were highly intelligent, resourceful, entrepreneurial, apolitical but loyal to their country and their fellow operators—and capable of killing without second thought or remorse. Killing was considered part of living, a by-product of the job and nothing more or less. It had to be done, and there wasn't anything particularly glorious about it. And those who were killed had it coming.

So the look of all three operators Nate had encountered ran counter to his experience. The two in the Tahoe looked like hyped-up gangbangers. The older one in the house looked like a middle-management thug.

It puzzled him. Either Nemecek's standards had slipped or his current operators were harbingers of a new generation.


NOW NATE picked his way down the mountainside toward the compound below. He moved from tree to tree, and paused often to look and listen. Despite what many people thought, mountain valleys didn't awake in silence. Squirrels chattered warnings of his approach to their compadres. A single meadowlark perched on an errant strand of wire sang out its haunting chorus.

He moved within a hundred yards of the compound before he slid down to his haunches to observe. Although the outbuildings and guest cabin looked unoccupied, he could see the shadowed grille of an old Toyota Land Cruiser in the open garage. The vehicle was familiar. It was a stock SUV that had been retrofitted to accommodate a handicapped driver. But he wondered why there was only a single auto present when there should have been three or four.

Although he couldn't yet figure it out, something was awry from how he remembered the place. His only proof was a sense of unease.

Through his binoculars, he swept the tree-lined slopes on the far side of the small valley. In the early-morning sun there was the chance of a glint from glass or metal. If there were operators up there in the trees watching the compound, he couldn't pick them out.

THE LAST FOUR TIMES he'd visited the compound there were five ex-operators who used it as a base camp and headquarters. Oscar Kennedy, who'd been a paraplegic since taking a bullet in the spine in Somalia, owned the compound and managed its operations. Kennedy was a contemporary of Nate's in Mark V, and the man he knew best and trusted the most. Kennedy maintained close contacts with personnel in the Defense Department in Washington and operators within the Joint Special Operations Command, the small and secret agency that oversaw special ops for every branch of the military. When Nate needed to know what was going on, he asked Oscar Kennedy to make inquiries.

Oscar Kennedy was a man of God, and the reverend for a small wilderness church located off Highway 33 between Victor and Driggs. His congregation was small and diverse, including not only ex-military and isolated survivalists but counterculture diaspora from the resort areas over the Tetons in Jackson Hole. Nate had attended a couple of services over the years. The Reverend Kennedy preached self-reliance and self-determination, and shameless love for a tough and judgmental God. He worked in themes and lessons he'd learned in Special Forces with a twist, and spoke of the holy need for warriors, the moral authority of Christian soldiers, with special emphasis on Romans 13.

OTHER EX-SPECIAL OPERATORS who had found their way to Idaho and the compound—dubbed Camp Oscar—were Jason Sweeney, Mike McCarthy, Gabriel Cohen, and Aldo Nunez. Only two of the men, Sweeney and Kennedy, had been operators for Mark V. The others had been members of other branches. Naturally, there was a built-in rivalry between them, but they had one thing in common: all had turned their backs on the government they had once worked for but considered themselves patriotic Americans. They were well armed, well trained, and absolutely out of the mainstream. Since Idaho and Camp Oscar offered refuge and common ground, they'd found their way there. Nate had told no one of the existence of Camp Oscar, including Joe Pickett. It was important to maintain the secrecy and integrity of the camp and its occupants.

Idaho was one of the few places in the country suited so well for such a compound of ex-operatives. The state was unique and its people independent, for the most part. Nate found Wyoming and Montana to have similar traits, but he understood why Kennedy had chosen Idaho.

There was a live-and-let-live mentality, Kennedy had explained to Nate, that allowed and even encouraged diversity of politics and opinions as long as neither were imposed on others. The ex-operatives were all libertarians of different degrees, although there were mighty political arguments among them. A couple of the men, including Gabriel Cohen and Jason Sweeney, considered the country already ruined. Cohen called it "the wimpification of America." They were fully prepared to join a secessionist movement at the drop of a hat to help create a nation along the lines of what the Founders intended. Nunez and McCarthy weren't yet ready to give up completely on Washington, D.C., but they simply wanted to be left alone. And if they weren't left alone, they planned to push back. Oscar Kennedy kept his innermost feelings close to the vest, but Nate suspected Oscar would join with the secessionists if compelled to make a choice.

The one thing all the ex-operatives agreed on, though, was their solidarity. It was all for one and one for all, much like the credos of each branch of the Special Forces. But in this case, the enemy was likely to be the same government that had trained and selected them.

The year before, when Joe and Nate had found a missing woman named Diane Shober in the mountains of southern Wyoming, Joe had wanted to return her to her dysfunctional family because it was his duty to do so. After talking to her and assessing her views, Nate had disagreed and escorted her to Camp Oscar, where she'd thrived. And as far as he knew, she was inside the lodge.

But why no vehicles, except for Oscar Kennedy's?

Something was very wrong. And who was inside cooking breakfast?

AFTER WAITING for another hour and giving up on the idea that someone would come outside, Nate kept low and sprinted to the back of the lodge and leaned against the outside wall. He kept still and scanned the trees behind him for movement but saw nothing unusual. With his cheek and ear pressed against the rough surface of a log, he concentrated on trying to detect movement inside. Rapid footfalls could mean they knew he was there. But it was quiet.

Closed-circuit cameras were installed throughout the property and fed to several monitors inside, but they were mounted in trees and on poles, and they pointed away from the lodge, not back toward it. Motion detectors were set up along the approach road on the far side of the property, but Nate had come from the back, through the trees, where he assumed there were no electronics. He'd learned through experience that motion detectors in wildlife-heavy brush were virtually useless and generally ignored.

He assumed his arrival had been undetected, either by anyone watching the compound or by whoever was inside.

There was a dark door that led inside into a mudroom. The door was painted reinforced steel made to appear to be wood. Like the door, the lodge itself looked rustic, but it was a fortress. Oscar Kennedy had used family money as well as disability income to make sure of it. The windows were triple-paned and designed to be bulletproof. All the entrance doors were steel, set into steel frames. Inside, like so many spare pairs of reading glasses scattered around in a normal residence, were loaded weapons within easy grasp.

Still pressed against the outside wall and keeping his senses on full alert, he reached out and felt beneath a log on the left side of the back door until his fingertips brushed against metal buttons: the keypad.

He wondered if they'd changed the code since he was there last. If they had, his old entry numbers would signal them inside that someone was trying to gain access. And if they hadn't, punching correct numbers would alert whoever was inside that he was coming in.

But he needed answers as much as he needed allies. And if his friends had been replaced by Nemecek's men, he'd know very quickly and try to fight his way out. He was willing to take the chance. Nate slung the rifle over his shoulder and secured it. He didn't think he'd be needing a long gun inside right away: too clumsy and cumbersome in a tight space.

With his .500 out and cocked, he reached under the log and found the keypad. The code always set his teeth on edge: *9-1-1.*

The lock on the door released with a click, and he grasped the handle, threw the door open, and hurled himself inside.

# 18

NATE HIT THE FLOOR of the mudroom and rolled a full rotation with his revolver extended in front of him. The door from the mudroom into the main lodge was propped open, and he could see clearly down a shadowed hallway all the way to a brightly lit corner of the kitchen itself. A slim woman stood at the stove, and she turned in his direction at the sound of the door opening.

She was young, mid-twenties, dark-haired, and obviously frightened. She held a cast-iron skillet aloft about six inches from the top of the range. In her other hand was a spatula. Her wide-open blue eyes were split down the middle by the front sight of his .500. Her mouth made a little *O*.

"Who's there?" a male called out from inside the kitchen. Nate recognized the Reverend Oscar Kennedy's voice.

"Me," Nate said.

"Jesus," the woman said, still holding the skillet and spatula in the air as if her limbs were frozen, "It's *him*." She had a pleasant Southern accent that made everything she said seem significant and earthy.

"Is it the infamous Nate Romanowski?" Kennedy boomed, then

appeared on the threshold in his wheelchair. The woman stood motionless behind him.

"Oscar," Nate said as a greeting, and stood up.

"You can put that thing away," Kennedy said, wheeling down the hall toward him. "She's on our side."

"Maybe not *his* side," the woman huffed, pronouncing it like *sad* and throwing a vicious evil eye toward Nate, and turned on her heel and vanished out of view.

Nate grunted, holstered his weapon, and leaned forward to give his old friend a greeting hug. They slapped each other on the back—Kennedy was surprisingly strong, and the slaps stung Nate's injured shoulder—then released quickly.

"What's her problem?" Nate asked.

"Haley? She's all right. You scared her, is all."

From out of view in the kitchen, Haley called out, "He didn't scare me, and you know it. Now, make him go away."

Oscar Kennedy waved his hand as if to suggest to Nate to pay her no mind. "Let me look at you," Kennedy said, wheeling back a quarter-turn and squinting. Then: "You look not so good."

"I'm fine," Nate said, releasing the rifle sling and letting the weapon slide down his arm, where he caught it before the butt hit the floor. He crossed the room and propped it up in the corner.

"I guess the fact that you're actually here and still with us is a miracle in itself," Kennedy said.

Nate sighed. "So you know."

"Some of it, anyway."

"So where is everybody? Where's Diane Shober?"

"Gone."

"Where are the others?"

"Gone."

"*'Gone'?*"

"Nate, the purge is on. But for some reason the operators seem to have packed up and left. I've seen no sign of them since yesterday."

"I might know why," Nate said. Then: "'The purge'?"

Kennedy nodded. He was dark and fleshy, his bulk straining the pearl buttons of his patterned cowboy shirt. His condition had made him resemble an upside-down pear: pumped-up upper body, shriveled legs. His big round head was shaved, and he had no facial hair save a smudge of silver-streaked black under his lower lip. Nate noted the holstered .45 semiauto strapped to the right side of his wheelchair within easy reach. The old-school operators still loved their 1911 Colts.

Oscar Kennedy narrowed his eyes. The look, Nate thought, was almost accusatory.

"They're taking us all out," Kennedy said. "And you're the reason why."

"SO WHERE DID everybody go?" Nate asked Kennedy. He sat at the kitchen table. A bank of computer servers hummed in the next room. Somewhere above them on the top floor, Haley stomped around in a room. The reading room of the lodge, which had once been where hunters gathered after a day in the mountains, had been converted into a communications center. Large and small monitors were set up on old pine card tables. Wiring, like exposed entrails, hung down behind the electronics and pooled on the floor. Nate remembered the size of the generator in one of the outbuildings that supplied the compound with power. From this location, Oscar Kennedy could monitor events and communications across the globe via satellite Internet access. And because he didn't draw from the local grid, he could do so without raising much attention.

Kennedy wheeled his chair up to the table and sighed. "This isn't *High Noon*," he said. "They didn't desert you when you needed them most. It's a lot worse than that."

Nate cocked his eyebrows, waiting for more.

Kennedy said, "Sweeney and McCarthy were killed in a car accident two weeks ago. On that steep hill into Victor. The Idaho Highway Patrol said they lost control of their vehicle, but I think they were forced off the road."

"Any proof of that?"

"None," Kennedy said. "Other than they'd negotiated that stretch of highway hundreds of times. Yes, it can get treacherous in the snow and ice, but they were used to that. We had our first winter storm that morning, and they were going into town to get groceries. They never came back."

Nate felt cold dread spreading through him. Jason Sweeney and Mike McCarthy were serious men. Sweeney was paranoid at times and scary when he got angry, but he was capable of locking his emotions down when the going got tough. McCarthy was an ex–Navy SEAL who was so silent it was easy to forget he was in the room.

"Two weeks," Nate said. "That's about the same time things started happening in Wyoming. You heard about Large Merle?"

Kennedy nodded and gestured toward the communications center.

"Any chatter about McCarthy and Sweeney from official channels?" Nate asked.

"None. Which told me everything I needed to know." Kennedy smiled sadly. "Whenever one of our brothers passes on, there's chatter. Guys email and post stories about the fallen warrior and let others in his unit know where to send flowers and donations and such. But in this case, there was *nothing*. Not a word. Not even a link to the write-up in the local paper. And when I sent a few emails out to their old unit, there were no replies. That means somebody put a lid on it."

"How can that be?" Nate asked. "Nobody has the juice to tell ex-operators not to grieve. No one can tell them *anything*."

"It's not that," Kennedy said. "The emails I sent never got there. And if anything was posted on the secure blogs and websites, it got deleted just as fast. Our guys in high places have that ability: to scrub digital communications. They've had it for years, but I've never encountered it personally. Somebody somewhere put out the word that there would be no mention of Sweeney and McCarthy. And because all communications go through conduits that we—our government, I mean—own, they can squelch anything they want to. They even have the ability to go back and 'disappear' items that were posted years ago. That's a new capability, I think, but I've heard them talk about it unofficially."

Nate shook his head. "You mean they can delete history?"

"Digital history, at least," Kennedy said. "They have the ability, if they wanted, to scrub every story, article, post, or reference to the moon landing. They could make it appear that the event never took place. Or change the narrative."

*"Christ."*

"It's a tremendous tool for counterinsurgency," Kennedy said. "Think about it. The terrorists use email, websites, and social media to connect. If our guys can alter or delete their communications and history, they're fucked."

"But someone is doing it to us," Nate said.

"I'm afraid so, yes."

"Official or unofficial?"

"You tell me."

As Oscar Kennedy talked, Haley reentered the room and studiously avoided eye contact with Nate. She padded over to the sink.

"Mind if I do the dishes now?" she asked Kennedy.

"It can wait," he said.

She turned on him, and her eyes flared. "How about you do them when you feel the time is right, then? I'm not your maid."

"Fine, then," Kennedy said with a sigh. She did a shoulder roll away from him and turned on the taps.

She said, "Let me know when he's gone, okay?"

Nate looked to Kennedy for an explanation.

"She came with Cohen," Kennedy said. "They were an item."

"*Were*?"

Gabriel Cohen had been tall and rangy, with black curly hair. He was a talker and a charmer, and women fell for him. He was charismatic, passionate, and he drew people in. He'd looked Middle Eastern enough to be dropped inside the region into the hottest spots. Since he spoke Arabic and a smattering of Urdu, he could operate in several countries, including Pakistan.

Kennedy nodded. "He's gone, too."

"Jesus. What happened?"

"*You* happened," Haley spat. She scrubbed the pots so violently, water splashed across the countertop.

"The cops said it was a bar fight," Kennedy said, ignoring her. He chinned toward Haley. "Those two got in a big argument. It had to do with her staying here. Nunez didn't like the idea of anyone bringing a stranger inside, and she overheard him telling Cohen. When Cohen didn't defend her, she ripped into him. This place," Kennedy said, "isn't as big as you might think. There are lots of spats and arguments when you've got a bunch of people cooped up in here. Plus, there was the stress of Sweeney and McCarthy dying."

"Anyway . . ." Nate prompted.

"Cohen left pissed-off ten days ago. It wasn't the first time. I knew he'd likely just go down to Victor or over to Tetonia to get drunk and hash it out in his own mind. They found him beaten to death outside a bar in Tetonia. Blunt-force trauma. No suspects at all."

"So they were waiting for him," Nate said.

"That's my theory."

"They probably jumped him from behind," Nate said. "Cohen was a tough guy, and you wouldn't want to take him on from the front."

"He was tough," Kennedy said, shaking his head sadly. "But we're all just flesh and blood. We're all mortal. Even *you*."

Haley reacted by throwing the dishrag into the sink with obvious disgust. When she turned on them, her eyes were filled with tears and her chin trembled. "You talk about Gabriel like I'm not in the room, Oscar."

"Your choice."

"But I'm not here by choice," she said. Her Southern accent was honey-laced, Nate thought. But her voice built as she said, "I'm a prisoner. My man is gone, and the wolves are right outside the door. I'm doing my best, but I don't have much left. So at least extend me the courtesy of not talking about him as if I wasn't in the room, okay?"

Then she faked a slap at Kennedy's head—he ducked—and again left the room. Nate watched her leave and was surprised to find his insides stir. She was fit and fiery, with that mane of jet-black hair and large blue eyes. She filled her tight jeans nicely and had a graceful way of moving—even when she was throwing a wet rag or stomping around—he found surprisingly attractive. He stanched the feeling. Alisha was still there with him—a braid of her hair on his weapon—and he instantly felt guilty about it.

When she was gone, Nate asked, "How long has she been here?"

"Three months, July," he said. "We're like an old married couple the way we fight all the time. She's got a good heart, though. I'm fond of her, and it's tough on her Cohen is gone. Really tough."

Nate did a quick calculation in his head. She couldn't be the vixen who lured Large Merle to his death if she'd been in Idaho for three months. But who was to say there was only one vixen?

"Have you checked her out?" Nate asked Kennedy softly.

The man nodded. "Of course, or I wouldn't have let her in the door with Cohen. In a nutshell, she's a North Carolina girl, born and raised in Charlotte. Old Southern family. Went to the University of Montana, then moved to New York. She was some kind of prodigy at a big public-relations firm for a while, got married to a sharpie, then divorced. No kids. She wanted to move back home, and she bounced around for a while until she ran into Cohen at Sun Valley and he brought her back here. No gaps in her history, no likely interactions with bad guys. Most of all, no incentive to infiltrate our compound. She was crazy about Cohen, even though they fought all the time."

Nate nodded. "Are you two . . . ?"

"No," Kennedy said flatly. "Not that I haven't suggested it. But no."

"And Nunez?" Nate asked.

Aldo Nunez was a wiry man of Hispanic origins with a cherubic face and the ability to insinuate himself into any group. Nate had met him only once but liked him immediately.

Kennedy said, "He went down to talk to the local cops to find out what they knew about Cohen's beating a week ago. That's the last we've seen of him. He just never came back. You didn't know Nunez very well, but believe me, he's not the type to bug out."

Nate rubbed his face with his hands.

"Diane Shober went with him," Kennedy said flatly.

"So she's gone, too."

"I'm afraid so. Collateral damage."

"It's worse than I could have guessed," Nate said.

Kennedy simply nodded as he kept his eyes on Nate.

"She's right," Kennedy said, referring to what Haley had exclaimed. "We've been virtual prisoners here. Honestly, I'm not afraid to go out, but I understand the odds. So we haven't left this place since Nunez vanished. I haven't been able to go to the church to preach."

He chinned toward the window above the sink. "We haven't opened the curtains until just this morning. We're locked down and I'd like to say we're ready for anything, but it depends what they throw at us. As you know, this is a tough place to get into if you don't know the keypad code. I can't see them trying an all-out assault. Instead, they've been patient and they picked us off one by one."

Nate said, "Why do you think they're gone now?"

Kennedy shrugged. "Because we're still alive, and God has a plan for me. He wants me to continue to do what I'm doing here."

AFTER A FEW MOMENTS, the Reverend Oscar Kennedy said, "You came here for help and information, Nate. I'm not sure I can provide information, and the men who could help you have been taken from us."

"I understand," Nate said. "I'm sorry."

"It is what it is."

"Do you know how many men Nemecek has on his team?" Nate asked. "Has there been any chatter about changes in tactics?"

"A little," Kennedy said. "Obscure references. Some serious complaints. But I can't recall seeing a number, and certainly not a list of operatives."

"Damn."

"Everything is locked down tight. Tighter than you can believe."

"What do you mean when you say 'serious complaints'?" Nate asked. "About what?"

"The quality of Nemecek's team. There is some grumbling from ex–Five operators still in the business that quality control isn't what it used to be when he'd been selecting men. I get the impression," Kennedy said, "there is a feeling Nemecek has surrounded himself with a close group of men without strong character. Not that they aren't well trained like we all were, but that he'd let the intangibles slip. There's been some chatter that Nemecek prefers yes-men to patriots these days. That at least *some* of the Peregrines are there to serve John Nemecek instead of their country. He's ambitious—we both know that. He likes power, and he always thinks he's the smartest man in the room."

Nate nodded. "So he's surrounded himself with thugs."

"That sums it up pretty well. But you know how it is. Ex–Five operators always think they had it tougher than the new recruits. It's part of the game."

"But in this case they may have a point," Nate said. "The three men I saw in Colorado wouldn't have been in Mark V ten years ago. They would have washed out, believe me."

"Because you defeated them?" Kennedy asked.

"Because they weren't that good," Nate said. He looked around the small kitchen, at the thick window and the steel window frames. At the dishes undone in the sink.

"Maybe we should all get out of here," Nate said.

Kennedy quickly shot that down. "Never. This is my home, and my church needs me. I owe them. I can't just leave. My work has just started here, Nate. The word is starting to get out that people like us have a place to come and find fellowship and worship God."

Nate didn't argue. Kennedy was adamant.

"Can you print out some of the chatter you found?" Nate asked. "I might be able to decipher some of it. I need anything I can get."

"I'll find what I can," Kennedy said, wheeling back from the table. "I'll check to see if there's anything new. Maybe we can find out what happened to our friends out there."

"Thank you."

Kennedy spun in his chair and propelled it toward the next room, where his computers hummed. But in the doorway he stopped suddenly, and turned a half turn so he could look at Nate.

"Are you finally going to tell me what this is all about? A lot of blood has been shed, and we've lost some really good men. I'd like to know why directly from you, because I'm not sure I can believe what I read on the Net anymore. I'm sure Nemecek has changed history."

Nate said, "You know why."

Kennedy's face flushed with anger. "I know John Nemecek is your mortal enemy. But what I don't know—and I deserve to know—is exactly what happened back in 1998 in the desert."

"Nineteen ninety-nine," Nate corrected.

"So be it," Kennedy said. But his face was set and he wasn't moving.

"Print out what you can," Nate said, "and I'll tell you if you really want to know."

The Reverend Oscar Kennedy glared at Nate for a while until his expression finally softened. "Okay, then," he said.


WHILE KENNEDY was in the computer room, Haley reentered and strode purposefully toward Nate and sat down at the table. There was no avoiding eye contact this time. She was all business.

"I want you to find the men who did it," she said. "You owe it to me and to Gabriel. Not to mention the others."

He stared back at her and again felt the little tug inside him as he looked into her wide blue eyes. He had always been a sucker for long black hair and blue eyes, especially if they belonged to intelligent women.

"I've heard a lot about you," she said. "At one point I really wanted to finally meet you and hear if what they said was true. But not under these circumstances. Now I just want you to go and find them."

He remained quiet.

She said, "I've heard about the falcons and a little about what you were involved in years ago. Gabriel talked about that big gun you carry. He said you'd just show up from time to time without any notice. He also said if it came to a fight, he'd want you in his corner more than anyone else he knew. That's saying something, you know."

Nate had to look away because it seemed her eyes were reaching inside him.

"Diane Shober told me how you brought her here. She said you were good to her, but she couldn't figure you out. She said she got the impression you were carrying a very heavy weight around with you, but you wouldn't talk about it. I liked her, although she was very intense. We got along, and it was nice to have another woman in the place. I never had a sister, and she was like a sister to me. To think that they would hurt her, too . . . it makes me sick."

Nate nodded.

"Oscar is a wonderful, gentle soul," she said, her eyes shifting toward the computer room. "He really does want to help people, and he's a true believer. I can't really say I buy everything he says, but I know in my heart he's sincere and kind. He almost makes me believe in God, to be around a man like that. If a man as tough and practical as Oscar becomes an evangelical, I almost have to concede that there *is* something out there bigger than what we see, you know? And after what's happened to us here, I have no doubt there is true evil in the world. So doesn't it make sense there would be true good? If nothing else, you need to do what you can to protect *him*. You need to eliminate the people depraved enough to try and hurt him."

Before Nate could reply, she said, "I'm going to go pack. You can take us both out of here. Maybe someday Oscar can come back when it's safe."

With that, she reached out and patted the back of Nate's hand and left the table to go upstairs and pack.


NATE TOOK a chair next to Kennedy and opened a laptop.

"Do you mind?" Nate asked, gesturing to the computer.

"Feel free."

"Is it a secure IP address?"

Kennedy said, "As secure as I can make it. But that's no guarantee of anything with the capability they have."

"Got it," Nate said while the laptop booted up. If Nemecek had gotten to Gordon in Colorado and sent a team to the compound in Idaho, there was only one other target close to Nate: Joe Pickett. And his family. He prayed they weren't under surveillance, or worse.

He called up the old falconry site and started a new thread:

**TRAINING AND FLYING MY NEW KESTREL**     **<0 COMMENTS>**

Under it, he wrote:

> TRAINING MY NEW FALCON IS TURNING OUT TO BE A VERY BAD EXPERIENCE. NOTHING I TRY WILL WORK, AND I'M GETTING FRUSTRATED AND CONCERNED. IT'S A DISASTER ON EVERY FRONT. I JUST WANT TO SAY TO THAT BIRD, "FLY AWAY NOW AND DON'T LOOK BACK."

"Thank you," Nate said to Kennedy, closing the laptop.

"I'm finding some stuff," his friend said. "I'll be back with you in a minute."

WHEN OSCAR KENNEDY rolled back into the kitchen with a sheaf of printouts, he eyed Nate with suspicion.

"I hope Haley didn't unload on you," he said.

"She didn't."

"She can come on pretty strong."

"I like that in her," Nate said.

"Uh-oh, you're smitten," Kennedy said simply, shaking his head.

"She agrees with me that we should all leave now."

"I'm not surprised," Kennedy said. "But I'm not going anywhere. You can take her, though. Get her on a plane somewhere so she can fly back to her family."

"Are you sure you won't go?"

"I'm sure, and that's that," Kennedy said.

He handed the printouts to Nate. "I was able to locate most of the blog posts. But a few have been scrubbed since the last time I saw them."

Nate took the stack and put it aside on the table for later. Upstairs, he could hear Haley shuffling around in her room, no doubt throwing clothing into a suitcase.

"Unburden yourself," Kennedy said.

"We don't have much time," Nate said, gesturing toward the upstairs room.

"We have enough."

Nate sat back, putting himself back in that place again. Recalling the heat and hot wind and dust, the smells of desert and cooking food. The elaborate tents and fifty four-by-four vehicles flown in just for the occasion. The flowing robes of the guests. And the dozens of falcons, hooded and still, roosting on their poles.

"Have you ever heard of the houbara bustard?" Nate asked Kennedy.

"No."

IT TOOK NATE ten minutes to tell the story. As he did, Kennedy's reaction changed from intense interest to seething outrage. Red bloomed on his cheeks, and beads of perspiration appeared across his forehead.

"Holy Mother of God," Kennedy said, when Nate was done. "It's worse than I imagined."

"That's who I'm dealing with," Nate said. "And *what* I've been dealing with for all these years. I hate that all of you've been dragged into it."

"Nate," Kennedy asked, his tone softening. "How have you kept this to yourself?"

"No choice, because I'm responsible for what happened, too. And the result."

Nate heard Haley descending the stairs heavily, likely with her suitcase. He rose to go help her, but Kennedy pushed his chair back and blocked his path.

"You can't blame yourself, Nate."

"I do," he said, attempting to step around the chair. Kennedy was quick and rotated the wheels sharply and pushed back into the doorway. Mid-morning sun lit up his face from the window above the sink.

"Oscar, let me by."

"We need to talk about this. No one can shoulder the burden of what you've just confessed."

"I'm just going to give her a hand with her suitcase."

"We need to talk—"

Oscar Kennedy didn't finish his sentence because his head snapped back violently and his hands fell limply to his sides and there was a simultaneous *crack-pock* sound inside the kitchen. Blood and matter flecked the wall behind Kennedy from floor to ceiling, and Kennedy slumped in his chair.

Nate instinctively dropped into a squat and fought an urge to cover his head as he did so. He wheeled and saw the neat dime-sized hole in the glass of the window above the sink, then dived toward the chair to push his friend out of the view of the window.

From the stairwell, Haley called out, "Hey? What was that?"

Nate shouted, *"Sniper! Get down now!"*

On his hands and knees, he scrambled into the computer room, pushing Kennedy's chair in front of him. Nate hoped to God the injury to his friend wasn't as bad as he thought it might be.

But it was. When Nate rose to look he saw how much damage a .50 caliber armor-piercing sniper round could do to a man. Then he looked up and saw Haley in the stairwell, almost to the bottom of the threshold, clutching the handle of her suitcase with both hands. When Haley saw Kennedy's splayed-out body in the chair, she dropped the suitcase and screamed, covering her face. The suitcase tumbled down the last four steps.

"I said, *Get down!*"

Still shrieking, she sat straight back on the stairs, her face still hidden by her hands.

NATE RETRIEVED his rifle as he ran through the mudroom to the back door and then pressed the lock-release mechanism. Once he heard the click and the door was free, he kicked it open rather than fly through it into the grass.

Wondering if the shooter would anticipate his exit from the house and fire again. But there were no shots. Did the shooter even know he was in the house?

He kicked the door wide open a second time—no reaction—and followed it out on the third, hitting the ground and rolling until he could find cover behind a tree trunk.

When he raised the rifle to where he thought the shot had come from—a *V* in the brush on the northern horizon—he clearly heard a motor start up and a car roar away. Forty-five seconds later, it was gone.

He stood up, bracing himself against the tree. Only then did he realize he'd landed on his injured shoulder, and the pain screamed through him. But not as loud as the screaming from Haley inside the house.

Nate thought of Oscar Kennedy and spun around with pure rage and cried out: *"Goddammit!"*

Then: "Come on, Haley. We're going after them."

# PART FOUR

*The true falconer must at all times be patient.
He must realize that he is under an immense
obligation to his hawk. Whatever he wants to
do, his hawk must be his first consideration,
the ruling factor of his life.*

—Sam Barnes in *Bird of Jove* by David Bruce

# 19

DUSK CAME QUICKLY on Teton Pass as Nate crossed the border from Idaho east into Wyoming. He had ruthlessly scoured Victor, Swan Valley, Driggs, and Tetonia for any sign of the assassins throughout the afternoon and into the evening. His only lead had come from the manager of the Rendezvous Motel in Driggs, a spindly old tattooed galoot openly wearing a shoulder holster, who said two men had checked out early that morning after a ten-day stay.

Their descriptions fit: mid-twenties, hard, businesslike, no small talk about the weather. The manager said he pegged them for mountain climbers or hunters based on the number of gear bags they possessed, but they'd claimed they were in the area to look for work in construction. Apparently, several multimillion-dollar resorts were being built on the Idaho side of the Tetons. The manager said the men were unusual in that they kept odd hours and were often gone the entire night. Also, they requested their rooms not be entered and made up during the day. The owner said they shared a late-model white Chevy Tahoe with Colorado plates. Their names on the register were Bill Wood and Tom James, and they paid seven days in advance with cash and daily after, as if they knew they might have to leave at any time.

Nate peeled off several twenties and gave them to the manager for the information and made him promise he wouldn't clean the vacated rooms right away. The manager agreed with astonishing speed.

"WHERE ARE WE GOING?" Haley asked, as they climbed the mountain. A heavy horizontal curtain of storm front reached across the sky from north to south, devouring the jagged range of mountain peaks as it came. From their elevation, they could see it coming, and it had no end in sight.

"Jackson Hole," he said.

"Why?" she asked. She was apparently cried out and slowly coming back into the here and now. Throughout the day, while Nate drove from small town to small town and crept around mom-and-pop motels, she'd sat in the passenger seat of his vehicle and wept. He'd offered water and food, but she refused both. As with Alisha in the past, he marveled how her tears seemed to slowly expunge the tragedy from inside her, how it seemed to help her recover. He envied the phenomenon but could not imagine replicating it himself. His release, he knew, would come another way.

"Jackson is a choke point," he said. "I don't know which road they took to get back into Wyoming, but they'll have to go through Jackson to get to the Bighorns. They may stop, or they might drive right through. But my guess is they think they're home free. Their mission is accomplished, and it's time to take a breather before they reconnoiter with their team leader. So they might not be looking over their shoulders right now."

"Why not?" she asked. "Don't they know we might be chasing them?"

He shook his head. "I don't think so. I don't think they knew I was there, and I'm the primary target. If they knew I was in the house, they would have held off for a shot at me, or stuck around to hit me when I came out of the house."

He explained that by approaching the compound from the back through the timber that morning, he likely couldn't be seen from where the assassins had set up a mile away, facing the front of the house.

"A mile away?" she asked. "I don't know much about guns, but isn't that a little far?"

"No," Nate said. "Not with the kind of weapon they used. You saw that hole in the window, didn't you?"

She nodded.

"It was a perfectly round hole. It didn't even shatter the glass. That round passed through the so-called bulletproof glass and through Oscar's head and through the other side of the house. I'm pretty sure it was a fifty caliber round and the shooter has a specialized sniper rifle. We used them overseas. It's accurate at two thousand yards. The shot that killed Oscar wasn't even that far."

"This is just so unbelievable," she said. "All of it. I can't believe this is happening."

Nate said, "It is."

"Why did they kill them all? It's so cold-blooded."

"Two reasons," Nate said. "They thought our friends knew my secret, and if they were allowed to live, they'd leak it. Especially Oscar, since he had the contacts and his computer network. If Oscar decided to broadcast the information it would be around the world and back within a few minutes and it would destroy Nemecek and The Five.

"The second reason was to eliminate anyone who might help me out. War is still just a numbers game. It *is* cold-blooded, but that's what it is. Kill more of them than they can kill of yours. And if possible, kill them all."

"What are you going to do to them if we find them?"

"What do you think? Revenge is something I'm good at. I enjoy it for its purity."

She shrunk away from him, shocked.

"And to further reduce their numbers," he said. "Two can play at this game."

ONCE THEY started climbing the mountains and Idaho was in his rearview mirror, he borrowed Haley's cell phone and called the Teton County, Idaho, Sheriff's Department.

"I need to report a murder," he said to the dispatcher.

"Come again?" she said. He heard a slight click and knew the dispatcher had engaged the recording device.

"Two men using the names Bill Wood and Tom James murdered the Reverend Oscar Kennedy in his own home this morning with a sniper rifle. They're also responsible for the deaths of Gabriel Cohen, Jason Sweeney, Mike McCarthy, and Aldo Nunez, all former Special Forces vets. And an innocent named Diane Shober. You know the names from the case files in your department, but these weren't accidents. Wood and James stayed the last week at the Rendezvous Motel in Driggs, room eight. Make sure you get a forensics team there to collect hair, fiber, and DNA samples to help determine the true identities of the killers—"

"Please slow down," she said. "Where are you calling from?"

"That's not important," Nate said. "You can listen to the tape afterward. What is important is that Reverend Kennedy's body is taken care of and his family notified. He was a good man."

"What is the name of the reporting party?" she asked.

"That is all," Nate said, and closed the phone.

Haley shook her head. "That's why you told the guy not to clean their rooms. So there would be DNA samples."

"Right," he said. "If they were there for ten nights, the room is crawling with their residue. The cops will find enough to positively ID the killers—provided their DNA is on file somewhere. Which may be a long shot. I don't expect them to ID our bad guys right away, but they'll send a car out to Oscar's compound. I can't stand the thought of his body unattended all night."

"Neither can I," she said, and her eyes again filled with tears.

After a few minutes, she reached toward Nate to retrieve her cell phone.

"No, sorry," he said, and rolled down his window. He extended the phone outside and flipped it down and back under the back tires. The crunch sounded like a car door being closed.

"Hey!"

He said, "They can track us from the call I just made or at least figure out what cell towers sent it."

"How am I supposed to function without my phone?"

He grinned wolfishly. "Welcome to life off the grid."

They summited the mountain, and the lights of Jackson Hole splayed out beneath them in the valley.


JACKSON IN OCTOBER was predictably empty. The throngs that packed the wood sidewalks in the summer were gone, and those wearing skiwear and fashionable snow boots were yet to come. It was the time of the year when the Mercedes, Lexuses, and BMWs of tourists and seasonal residents gave way to the muddy four-wheel-drive pickups of elk hunters, but in much smaller numbers. The town seemed to be resting and recovering, and many of the retail stores downtown were closed until winter and skiing resumed.

But not the bars. Nate located the white Tahoe parked at an angle on the side of the Wort Hotel. He drove past it, with Haley pointing out the Colorado plates, and kept on going.

"Aren't you going after them?" she asked, confused.

"Yes."

"Then where are we going now?"

"I'm taking you to the airport so you can fly back to North Carolina, or wherever."

She sat back hard in her seat as if slapped, and crossed her arms over her breasts. "I'm not going *anywhere,*" she said.

"Sure you are," he said. "Do you need money for the ticket?"

"I need you to shut up and turn around. I was there when these guys destroyed my world. I've got to see this through."

He took a long look at her. In response, she set her jaw and tipped her head back. Her eyes caught and reflected passing lights. *Lovely,* he thought.

He said, "If you stay with me you'll either get killed or wind up in prison. This isn't a lighthearted choice."

She waved his words away and clamped her hand back under her arm. "But I've made it. I'm sticking with you and seeing this through. I want to see the men who did this. I want to see them go down."

He slowed the Jeep but kept it rolling down the highway. They were clear of the southern town limits, but the lights of the town sparkled in his rearview mirror. The National Elk Refuge was on his right, and he could see the first of the arrivals out on the moonlit pasture.

"If you stay," he said, "you have to do whatever I tell you. This is my operation, and I'm good at these things. I don't want or need your advice or your questions."

She didn't respond immediately. After a beat, she said, "Okay. But you have to understand I've never done anything like this before. Never. Cohen was trying to teach me how to use a handgun, but I didn't like it."

"I'm not letting you near a weapon," Nate said. "And remember to fight against your first instinct."

"My first instinct?"

"To talk," he said. "When things get hot, I need you to listen to me and do what I tell you, and not yammer on. Repress that first instinct. Can you do that?"

"Of course," she said, obviously insulted.

"Good," he said, slowing down to begin a U-turn back to town, "because I think I like your company."

As they drove, she shot her arms out and settled back in her seat. "I thought for a brief moment I liked yours," she said, "then I found out what an asshole you can be."


THE WORT HOTEL stood on the corner of Glenwood and Broadway in the heart of Jackson, and it stretched the length of the short block. Constructed of rough stone with eaves and gabled windows, it looked like a regal 1940s matriarchal ghost amidst the gussied-up faux-western storefronts. The Silver Dollar Bar had its entrance on Main, and as Nate and Haley cruised by, they could see men with cowboy hats at the bar and smaller groups of hunters sitting at tables. They didn't slow down as they drove by.

"Did you see our boys?" she asked.

"No."

Nate turned on Glenwood and passed the Tahoe and continued on across Deloney and backed into a dark alleyway and turned off his motor. From there, they could look out the front window and see the back bumper of the Tahoe jutting out into the street. There were fewer than ten other cars parked, and plenty of spaces. It was an entirely different feel from the busy summer and winter months.

"How can you be positive it's the right car, or that the bad guys are inside?"

Nate shrugged. "I can't."

"Do you want me to go in the bar and look around?"

"No. They might recognize you. Those bastards were up there in the trees for days looking down at the compound through binoculars or a spotting scope. They might have seen you."

"Oh," she said, then hugged herself. "It creeps me out to think they were up there all that time. Just waiting for us to finally open the curtains."

"Lots of patience," Nate said. "But no surveillance is perfect. The longer it goes on, the more there's a chance for a mistake. Like not seeing me come down to the house this morning."

After ten wordless minutes, he could tell it was killing her not to talk. She squirmed in her seat, and took deep breaths that ended in long sighs.

Finally, she asked, "Have you thought about calling the sheriff again? Telling them you might have found the killers?"

He shook his head.

"Why not?"

"Because I don't want them arrested. I want them dead. But not before I get some intel."

AFTER TEN MORE MINUTES, she said, "So are you going to tell me what this is all about? Why those . . . men . . . are after everyone?"

"Maybe later," Nate said, opening his door and swinging out. "One thing at a time."

"I deserve to know," she said. "Gabriel and all my friends . . ."

He looked up sharply. "Remember what I said about talking? I meant it."

She sat back quickly as if he'd threatened her with a knife.

He said, "Stay here, be quiet, and keep your eyes open. If you see anything hinky, flash the headlights once."

"Hinky?"

"You'll know it when you see it."

Nate rattled around through gear in the small back floor well and came out with an eighteen-inch crowbar and a two-foot length of stiff wire.

"Back in a minute," he said, and walked across Deloney with the tool pressed to his thigh so it couldn't be seen in silhouette. Dime-sized snowflakes sifted down through the orbs of streetlights and began to gather like goosedown in the cracks of the wooden walk.

HE DIDN'T NEED the crowbar to get into the Tahoe, and he was grateful, because he feared setting off an alarm. A car alarm blasting in the quiet night would be a small disaster. He kept low as he cased the vehicle, looking in all the windows but not standing tall enough to be seen over the roof.

The front seat was uncluttered except for a sheaf of folded maps and documents crammed down between the driver's seat and the console. The backseat was loaded with duffel bags and gear bags. Not unusual in a mountain location if the occupants were mountain climbers or trekkers.

The back compartment had a couple of suitcases, plastic tubs with lids, and a heavy blanket spread across the carpeting from one wheel well to another. The blanket didn't lie flat, but was rounded down in the center. It was obviously covering something long and bulky.

Nate held the wire up to the light and bent the tip into an L shape. He made another bend about eighteen inches from the *L*. After checking the walks for passersby—there were none—he glanced down the street to where his Jeep was parked. He couldn't see Haley in the passenger side because of the shadows, but she was not flashing the lights. Quickly, he stood and jammed the pointed tip of the wire through the rubber seal on the back window. He had to work the wire up and down until the pointed tip found the edge of the glass in the channel. With a shove and twist, the wire poked through the seal on the inside and he could see it on the other side of the glass.

The rubber seal squeaked as he raised the butt end of the wire and shoved it farther into the back compartment. No alarms went off. He pushed it until it reached the rear bend, then farther raised the back end. The L-tip bit down into the fabric, and he pulled the wire from left to right, drawing back the blanket, revealing the black heavy barrel of a rifle. He pulled it back far enough to see the bipod, legs folded, mounted to the undercarriage of the front stock and the blunt snout of the scope.

A Barrett M82A1M .50 sniper rifle, all thirty pounds' worth. It shot 690- to 750-grain .50 caliber Browning machine-gun cartridges, each nearly five inches long. The murder weapon. Just as he'd guessed.

NATE TOSSED the crowbar and the wire back into the rear floor well and brushed snowflakes from his coat and sleeves before he climbed inside and shut the door.

"It's them," he said, describing the find.

"What if they're staying for the night?" she asked. "I mean, it's a hotel."

"Then we wait until morning," he said.

"I'm getting cold. It's *snowing*."

"Haley . . ."

"I know, I know."

AFTER TWENTY MINUTES, he noticed she was hugging herself and trembling from the cold. She'd obviously chosen not to complain, and he appreciated it, and he reached forward and started the motor. It took a while before dust-smelling heat—it was the first time he'd had to turn on the heat since winter—poured through the vents.

"Thank you," she said.

The snow came straight down and had coated the streets and cars with a clean white inch. Falling snow haloed around the lampposts and turned pink in the neon red light from the Silver Dollar Bar sign. Nate checked the time and was surprised to see it was only 8:15. The tragic day they'd had, the stillness, the dark streets, and the smothering snowfall made it seem much later.

Haley said, "Maybe we could stay inside? Separate rooms, of course."

Nate grunted. He liked the soft, husky tone of her voice. Despite what he'd told her earlier about talking, he found her voice attractive. Although she'd been sitting next to him nearly all day, he could feel her presence very strongly at that moment. He was tuned in to her every movement, every breath. Her dark hair shined blue with diffused ambient light from outside, like Superman in the comics. In the warm air of the heater, he could also catch a light whiff of her scent.

As the cab warmed up she had her eyes fixed on the windshield but said, "Gabriel told me about your loss. About your girlfriend getting killed."

"She was more than that," he said.

"You know what I mean. It must have been horrible."

"It was. It is."

"You don't want to talk about it, right?"

"Right."

After a moment, she said, "So we've both lost the people closest to us. What are the chances of that?"

He didn't reply. But he found it more than interesting that she was thinking of the two of them that way. He'd been thinking the same thing but keeping it at bay because he was frightened of the possibilities.

"I'd like to get some sleep," she said softly, "but I'm afraid if I close my eyes I'll see Oscar's body again. I'll never be able to get that image out of my mind for the rest of my life."

He nodded. "I've seen a lot of violent death. If you spend a lot of time in the natural world, there's little else. I know there are wild animals that die of old age, but I've rarely seen one. There's a point where you get like a hunter or a farmer—or a doctor—and you look at it almost clinically. Bullets are just chunks of metal thrown really fast through the air, and when they hit soft flesh they do terrible damage. You get used to it. But when it happens to a friend who was talking to you just a minute before—he's there and then he isn't, and all that's left is meat—you *never* get used to that."

He felt her eyes on him and almost didn't want to look over.

"Your secret," she asked. "You told Oscar, didn't you?"

"Yes."

"But no one else?"

"No, although a friend named Large Merle figured it out. He's no longer with us. I tried to tell a good man I know, a game warden in Wyoming, but he didn't want to hear it."

She said, "Maybe I do."

"Maybe you don't," he said, turning on the wipers to clear the windshield of snow that melted on contact.

"Not that it seems to matter," she said. "Everybody you come in contact with seems to wind up '*no longer with* us.'"

Nate grimaced and closed his eyes for a moment. "You don't need to remind me," he said, thinking of Joc and Marybeth. Hoping they'd see and understand his message to them to get away fast. Hoping they were in the process of packing bags that very minute. Wondering if he shouldn't step out from his self-imposed communications blackout and make an unsecured phone call to emphasize his concern.

"I'm sorry," she said. "That came out wrong. I didn't mean . . ."

He grunted again and waved her words away with his hand.

She said, "I meant you might as well tell me, because the bad guys will think you did, anyway, and they'll try to kill me, too."

He looked over at her as if seeing her for the first time. God, she was lovely. She didn't deserve to know him, he thought. She didn't deserve to get hurt.

He said, "If I do—"

She cut him off. "Like I said, it doesn't matter. So you might as well. Lord knows, we seem to have the time." He liked the way she pronounced *time* as "*tahm.*"

After pausing for a minute, he said, "It's very close to me right now. Telling Oscar opened it all up like it was yesterday. All these years, I've struggled to keep it somewhere in the back of my brain, in the reptile part. But I spent too many years alone, with too much time to fight it back constantly. So at times, it crawled over the wall and haunted me, and after I'd chased it back I'd sit around for days and consider all the implications. In a strange way, I think Nemecek has the same problem. I dealt with it by staying out of the world and doing what good I could do. Trying to make up for what I did in a very small way, although I know it isn't possible. I kind of adopted this family named the Picketts, and I swore I'd protect them. I have, up until now. But I'm afraid of what could happen to them. Their only crime is trusting me."

She shook her head sadly, and asked, "How does Nemecek deal with it?"

"By making me go away," Nate said. "And everybody who knows or *might* know. That's one of the tragedies about what happened to Cohen and the rest back in Idaho. They didn't know, but he thought they might."

She said, "Could you go to someone? Maybe someone in the government who would be sympathetic? Or maybe a reporter?"

"No," Nate said. "I've given it a lot of thought over the years, but I don't know who I can trust. Something has happened to make Nemecek double down, to want to take care of his problem: me. Until I know what caused him to come out from under his rock, I don't know who I can trust."

"You can trust me," she said.

"Can I?"

"Your arrogance is off-putting," she said, an edge creeping into her voice. "You ask that question but you assume I should trust *you* with my life. Maybe you've spent too much damn time alone."

He turned to her, amazed. "Maybe I have."

Then he noted movement in his peripheral vision and sat up straight.

"What?" she asked.

Through the wet-streaked windshield undulating with moisture, he could see two men emerge from the side entrance of the Wort. Even without seeing their features clearly, he could tell by their bearing and presence they were heading for the Tahoe. They were both tall and without paunches, and they moved with an athletic grace not entirely affected by alcohol. One wore a battered straw cowboy hat and the other a ubiquitous billed trucker cap, as if they'd gone to a western store and said, "I want to look like a local yokel." Cowboy Hat loped down the wood sidewalk and extended his hand toward the car. At that moment, the interior lights of the SUV came on as he keyed a remote.

"Buckle up," he said.

"Oh my God," she whispered. "We're gonna do this, aren't we?"

Nate reached over and grasped her hand. "Last chance to get out. This could get ugly."

"Like I haven't seen ugly," she said.

# 20

NATE SAT STILL in the running Jeep in the alleyway while the Tahoe backed out onto Glenwood. When he realized the SUV would be coming in his direction, he slipped the gearshift into reverse and backed as fast as he could without losing control and clipping the outside walls of the brick buildings on both sides. At the far end of the alley, he stopped.

"Get down," he said urgently, as the Tahoe swung into the street and its headlights flashed on.

She hesitated for a half second until he reached over toward her, then obeyed. Their heads touched each other in the space between the two seats, and a wash of light from the headlamps of the Tahoe flashed through the cab.

He waited for a beat and said, "Okay."

When he looked up, the Tahoe was gone.

He kept his lights off as he backed the rest of the way down the alley, and when his tires hit the pavement of the next cross-street he cranked on the wheel so they were pointed left.

Assuming the Tahoe driven by Cowboy Hat was going north on Cache Street, he turned right onto Millward, which ran parallel to

Cache through a residential neighborhood. As he crossed Gill Avenue, Nate gestured up the empty street to Haley, who looked out her passenger window.

"We should see them now," he said.

And they did. The white Tahoe cruised through the intersection headed north and disappeared from view.

Nate gunned his Jeep, keeping up with the Tahoe a block to his right. He turned right again on Mercill and paused until the Tahoe crossed their path and continued north.

He gave it a count of fifteen before nosing the Jeep up Mercill to turn left and give chase.

She said, "Nate—your lights?"

Thinking he didn't realize they were off.

"Haley," he hissed, "the thing about *talking.*"

She blew out an angry stream of air.

"But if the cops see us without our lights on . . ."

"There are no cops," he said impatiently. "They're all over the pass in Idaho, helping out the sheriff over there with a murder. That's how these small towns work."

"Oh. Clever on your part."

"Now, *please*, no more fucking help or advice."

She reached up and drew her closed fingers over her mouth in a zipping motion.


NATE AND HALEY retraced their earlier route toward the airport, although this time there was a single pair of distant taillights a half mile ahead of them on the road. Nate still drove with his lights out, faster than he should.

The heavy snowfall blanked out the stars and moon and made the night landscape two-tone: black above and dark purple below. He used the faint double set of tire tracks ahead to follow, as well as the distant taillights. He could see nothing in between.

"Watch for wildlife on the road," Nate said to Haley. "Warn me if you see anything."

The route from Jackson toward Grand Teton National Park was famous for grazing bison and elk alongside the two-lane highway.

"Okay," she said, tentative. He knew she was frightened. He didn't blame her. He gently pressed harder on the accelerator, beginning a long process of closing the gap between the Tahoe and the Jeep in the dark.

JACKSON HOLE AIRPORT was on their left. It was low-slung and obscured by the darkness and the storm, but several red warning lights shone through the snowfall. After they passed it, the darkness descended on them further. There were no houses and no lights. They were officially in Grand Teton National Park, headed north.

He'd been on the road many times before and tried to recall the landscape, the features, and the turns. The Gros Ventre Range was to his right, the Snake River Valley to his left, and beyond the river the jagged sawtooths of the Teton Range. The highway was on a flat bench skirting the river valley.

Nate guessed the Tahoe would continue to Moran Junction, then take U.S. 26/287 over Togwotee Pass via Dubois and on to the Big-horn Mountains.

Before the road crossed the river and wound through pockets of timber, there was a long straightaway of three to five miles. Long enough to make sure there was no one coming, or behind them. Long enough, if he gunned it, to make his move. He didn't want them to leave the park and get as far as the junction, where the route over the mountains became narrow and heavily wooded. Plus, it would likely be snowing harder.

Nate pried the fingers of his right hand from the wheel and reached across his body for the grip of his .500. He drew it out of the shoulder holster and laid it across his lap.

He said to Haley: "Hold on, roll down your window, keep your eyes open, and duck when I tell you."

He could tell she wanted to question him, but she swallowed her pride and cranked down the window. Cold air and whirling snow filled the cab.

"Here we go," he said, flooring it. His rear tires fishtailed slightly, then gripped through the snow to the asphalt, and they shot forward.


THE TAILLIGHTS ahead of them started to widen. His engine howled, but he doubted Cowboy Hat and Trucker Cap would hear him coming before he was on top of them. In his peripheral vision, he saw Haley dig back in her seat and grasp the handhold on the dashboard as if it would cushion an impact.

But just twenty feet before he plowed into the back of the Tahoe— he could suddenly see the smudge of white from its back hatch— Nate hit his headlights, clicked them to bright, and swung his Jeep to the left into the oncoming lane.

The brake lights on the Tahoe flashed quickly—no doubt Cowboy Hat was temporarily blinded—and Nate roared up beside the SUV so they were rolling down the road side by side.

"Duck!" he yelled to Haley.

She went down.

He extended his revolver straight out away from his body, aimed at the Tahoe, and looked over.

Cowboy Hat turned his face to him as well. He was blinking from the unexpected blast of light and his mouth was slightly open, as if he was about to say something. Nate saw a face that was chiseled by bone and fashionably stubbled. His view within the scope trembled crazily, but when the crosshairs paused for a half second on a spot between the brim of the cowboy hat and the man's left eye, he squeezed the trigger. The roar of the gunshot was deafening inside the cab of the Jeep, and a four-foot ball of orange flame leapt between the two vehicles.

And just as suddenly, the Tahoe dropped away.

"Oh my God!" Haley screamed into her arms.

*"Stay down."*

Nate pumped his brakes to slow the Jeep and prevent an icy skid in the snow, while at the same time noting the sweep of errant headlights in his rearview mirror as the Tahoe left the road.

After a three-point turn, Nate sped back to the scene. He found the Tahoe on its side in the sloped bottom of a sagebrush-covered swale, the top tires spinning in the air and the moist ground churned up behind it. Nate switched the Jeep into four-wheel drive and drove through the fresh gaping hole in the right-of-way fence, his headlights on the underside of the Tahoe. There was no movement from inside. The rear hatch had popped open in the rollover, and the gear bags, the suitcases, the plastic tubs, and the unsheathed Barrett rifle were slung across the snow.

He drove around the vehicle until his lights framed the dented hood. The inside of the front windshield of the Tahoe gleamed bright red, as if it had been painted with a large bucket of blood. He hoped the slug hadn't taken off Trucker Hat's head as well.

Keeping his lights on the Tahoe, Nate stomped on his emergency brake and leapt outside the Jeep with his weapon in front of him.

Snow stung his eyes and gathered on his coat and hair. He could smell the sharp odor of leaking gasoline mixed with the sweet smell of crushed sagebrush.

As he approached the Tahoe, he heard a thump from inside, and suddenly there was a heavy-soled footprint in the blood on the inside of the windshield. Then another thump, and another footprint. A football-sized star of cracks appeared on the glass. He waited.

It took two minutes for Trucker Cap to kick his way outside.

Trucker Cap crawled out into the snow on his hands and knees. His face and clothing were covered in blood, and it took him a few seconds to realize headlights were on him, and that Nate stood between the headlights of the Jeep with his gun out.

"Oh, fuck me," Trucker Cap said. "I didn't think I'd ever get out of there. His head just . . . *blew up.*"

Nate kept his eyes on Trucker Cap as he called over his shoulder, "Stay down, Haley."

From behind him, he heard her say indignantly, "I'm *not* a dog."

He ignored her and gestured with the muzzle of his gun toward Trucker Cap. "Don't move."

"Are you the guy?" Trucker Cap asked. His voice was thick with shock as he stumbled to his feet. "Are you the guy who did this?"

Nate could see his bright teeth through the gore on his face.

"I told you not to move," Nate said, and lowered his revolver and blew Trucker Cap's right knee away. The man shrieked and fell straight down in a heap, moaning and writhing in the snow.

"You're going to answer a couple of questions," Nate said, approaching the wounded man, hoping Haley had obeyed and wasn't watching what was going to happen from the Jeep behind him. "I'm not asking you to answer questions," he said. "I'm telling you what's going to happen."

Trucker Cap groaned from pain and rolled to his back. He grasped his shattered knee with both hands, and blood pulsed out from between his fingers.

"You should have known this was coming when you went after my friends," Nate said.

Nate thought of what Haley had said earlier: *Like I haven't seen ugly.*

He quickly closed the gap to the man and rolled him over with his boot. As he did, Trucker Cap's jacket hiked up and Nate saw the grip of a .45 Heckler & Koch semiauto tucked into this belt. He snatched it out and tossed it over the top of the Tahoe.

"Any more weapons?"

"God, no," Trucker Cap moaned. His eyes were closed tightly.

Nate dropped to one knee next to Trucker Cap and patted the man down with his free hand through his clothes. His hand came away sticky with blood, and he wiped it clean in the snow before reaching back and gripping Trucker Cap's left ear. He gave it a vicious twist, and the man's eyes shot open.

"I'm going to bleed out," the man said.

"And what's the downside?" Nate asked. Then: "Three things, or I rip your ear off."

Trucker Cap's eyes narrowed on Nate's face.

"One: how many operatives were on your team? Two: why is Nemecek coming after me now?"

Trucker Cap's mouth twisted into a defiant leer. "Why should I tell you? I heard what you did over there, you fucking traitor. When he gave us a chance to come after you, we jumped on it, you son-of-a-bitch."

Nate ripped his ear off and tossed it over his shoulder like an apple core. Trucker Cap howled, and Nate waited for the man to catch his breath. While he did, he reached across the man's face and grasped his other ear.

Nate said, "Everything Nemecek told you is wrong, but it doesn't surprise me, and I don't have the time or inclination to convince you otherwise. But now I know how he convinced good men to go rogue with him. Now back to the three things. . . ."

Trucker Cap said, "But you only asked two."

"Oh," Nate said, "the third. I want you to make a call when we're done here. If you do *exactly* what I say, you might survive this. If you don't, I'm going to pull you apart with my bare hands until you're begging me to kill you. Got that?"

Nate became aware that Haley must have watched, because behind him he could hear her sobbing.

# 21

AT THE SAME TIME, 360 miles to the east, Marybeth Pickett left her counter at the library, walked back behind the new acquisitions display to the business office, and picked up the hand microphone and made an announcement: "The library will close in ten minutes."

As she cradled the mic, her own voice echoed through the near-empty building and sounded severe and tinny. The acoustics in the old building were awful. To complete the protocol for closing the building, she doused the lights and quickly turned them back on so patrons who were wrapped up in whatever they were doing—or wearing earbuds—would get the word. It was 8:50 p.m.

She didn't like closing the building at night and wished she hadn't made a deal with the other senior librarian to switch shifts. Part of the negotiations for coming back to work was her insistence that her shift conclude by three so she could be home when the girls got out of school. But once a month or so, she traded shifts for the sole reason of maintaining a good working relationship with her colleagues.

Both Lucy and April were at home—they'd sent texts asking if they could heat up some frozen pizza—and Joe was still out in the field and hadn't communicated his whereabouts or when he'd be getting back to their house on Bighorn Road. She was anxious to hear from him how the multiple investigations were going. Three homicides and three missing-persons cases within the span of a week had unnerved every local she'd talked with. Things like that didn't happen here, she knew, and never all at once. Although someone driving through the town of Saddlestring would see a sleepy community hugging the banks of the Twelve Sleep River as winter approached, they would have no idea that the people who lived there were filled with anxiety and it felt on the streets and in the shops like the wheels were coming off the place. The weekly Saddlestring *Roundup* had a story in it just that day featuring residents who said they were openly carrying weapons and locking their doors at night for the first time in their lives.

The pressure growing on Sheriff Kyle McLanahan to restore order was immense and more than a little unreasonable, she thought. Locals directed a hefty part of their fear and frustration toward him, and talked about the incompetence of the department. Several of the small business leaders who gathered for morning coffee at the Burg-O-Pardner—Marybeth's former clients who were struggling in the down economy and barely holding on as it was—discussed circulating a recall petition for McLanahan if he somehow won reelection. Although she'd never liked McLanahan and wanted him to lose, Marybeth thought most of the criticism recently to be over the top and unfair. Though, she thought, it couldn't happen to a more deserving guy.

THE OLD COUNTY LIBRARY was a wholly different place at night, Marybeth thought. It was an original Carnegie library built in the

1920s, and added on to. Outside, the classical Greek architecture, columns, and scrollwork were impressive in the floodlights that shone back on it. But inside, the high ceilings and corners weren't lit well, and sounds carried in odd ways, like her announcement had. It was too cool in the winter and too warm in the summer, and the ancient boiler sometimes shuddered with enough force to rattle the windows and scare children in the children's section. At night, the original hardwood floor produced moans and squeaks she never heard in the daytime. The layout of the building was outmoded and crowded, with high shelving that prevented her from seeing who was at the study tables or reading area in the back of the building from her counter.

Outside, clouds had been drawn over the moon and stars. She could see from the wet windows it was spitting snow. The valley was due for the first serious winter storm of the season, and she hoped it didn't roll in until later that night, after she was home safely. After Joe was home safely. The closeness outside and the water-streaked windows added to the overall gloom of the building—and her mood.

She listened for the sounds of books being snapped shut or patrons gathering up their possessions on their way out, but it was quiet inside. Marybeth walked over to a side window and looked at the parking lot. There was only one car besides her own—a dark new-model crossover she didn't recognize. So there was at least one person still in the building, maybe more.

Marybeth usually noted and greeted each patron as they entered, but she'd been busy all night with library work as well as her own project. At the time the patron entered, she guessed, she'd been entranced in reading accounts of the murder in Colorado Springs on the Internet on the website of the Colorado Springs *Gazette*. About the unidentified victim found in Nate Romanowski's father's home. According to the sheriff, there were no suspects yet, but they were hoping the analysis on the forensic evidence obtained might shed light on the identity of the victim or the killer. Neighbors were quoted saying what neighbors always said, that Gordon Romanowski was a friendly man who kept to himself and would never be capable of such an act, as far as they knew.

She was curious about Nate's father. She wondered what he looked like and how he'd raised such a son. Nate himself had rarely mentioned his family, and had made only one passing reference to his father years ago that she could recall. He'd said, after observing Joe with his daughters, "So that's how it's done."

She was also drawn to a separate story on the newspaper website that appeared unrelated to the body found in the Romanowski home but that set off alarm bells within her: two unidentified male victims had been found as the result of a rollover on Pikes Peak Road. Unrelated but similar in Marybeth's mind to the "accident" in Montana years before involving a vehicle remarkably similar to Nate's Jeep.

She checked the clock behind her and went back, once again, into the business office. "The library will close in five minutes," she said, and again blinked the lights.

She hoped the driver of the crossover would appear and go out into the lot for his car. Marybeth didn't enjoy going back into the library to roust patrons, because she never knew what she'd find. Once, it was a couple of teenagers she knew making out under a study table, partially undressed. Sometimes it was a homeless old man sleeping in one of the lounge chairs in the reading area and she'd had to wake him up. Once, she'd found an ancient sleeping ranch hand with his sweat-stained cowboy hat lowered over his face.

When she awakened him, he jumped up wild-eyed and hollered: "Close the damned gate, Charlie! The fucking horses are getting out!"

THERE WAS a *creak* from the shadows beyond the stacks, and she looked up but could see no one.

"Hello?" she asked.

There was no response.

"Oh, please," she whispered, "it's time to go."

There were myths that the old library building was haunted, but she didn't believe in ghosts. Lucy told her the library was now a stop on the Halloween night "Ghosts of Saddlestring" tour the chamber of commerce sponsored. According to Lucy, the story recounted on the tour by Stovepipe—the county court bailiff who volunteered to lead the ghost tours—was about a workman who'd died from an accident while the building was under construction. Because the man who died was an ornery Swede and the foreman a resentful Norwegian, the body was left where it lay and the walls were built up around it. Now, according to Lucy via Stovepipe, passersby sometimes heard Swedish wailing from inside the library late at night. Marybeth had laughed off the story at the time and said, "*Swedish* wailing? How would they know?"

But now she thought about it. And felt foolish for doing so.

Then she heard another creak from the stacks of books.

She took a deep breath and walked out from behind the counter. She'd need to find whoever was still inside the building.

Several times over the last year, Joe had driven into town and waited for her to come outside after the late shift. She'd told him it wasn't necessary. Tonight, though, she wished he was out there.

Before leaving the desk, she retrieved her purse from under the counter. Clutching her cell phone in one hand and a small container of pepper spray Joe had pressed on her years before in the other, she went to find the last remaining patron. Joe had once tried to talk her into carrying a gun in her purse and she'd disagreed with him, saying it was dangerous and unnecessary. Now, though . . .

SHE ASSUMED the last remaining patron would be at the tables. But there was no one in the study area or reading lounge. On the way to the back she'd glanced down the aisles between shelves of books and hadn't seen anyone loitering. She pushed open the door to the women's restroom and called, "Hello?" No response. She leaned in, glanced for shoes beneath the stalls, shut the lights out, and did the same with the men's. Both were empty.

Marybeth took a deep breath and walked from one side of the building to the other, methodically checking each aisle of shelves for the owner of the vehicle outside. She speculated that perhaps the driver wasn't even in the library—that he or she had simply parked his or her car in a public lot and walked elsewhere or was picked up. It seemed unlikely, though, since there were no retail stores open in the neighborhood and the Stockman's Bar was four blocks away, with plenty of parking available on the street.

There was no one in the aisles.

As she walked back up to the front counter, she defied her inner librarian and called out, "Is anybody still in the library? I'm ready to turn out the lights and lock up." Her voice sounded weak to her. "Hello? Is anyone here?"

From the front of the building, she heard a man clear his throat.

She froze for a moment, squeezing hard on both the phone and the pepper spray. At least she *thought* she'd heard a man. But it might be that damned boiler. . . .

HE STOOD at the checkout counter with his back to her as she approached. The man was tall, with light hair, wide shoulders, and long legs. He wore a heavy brown suede leather jacket that looked expensive.

"May I help you?" she asked. "We need to close up the building."

The man swiveled his head toward her, and she instantly felt a chill. He was pale, with sharp, close-set blue eyes and high cheekbones that looked sculpted. What was striking about him were his full red lips. His mouth was set in a slight, bemused smile.

"I think you can," he said softly. There was a twinge of a Southern accent. He held up a stack of three or four books.

She bustled around the end of the counter, putting it between them. She felt his eyes on her as she casually moved the hand with the pepper spray behind her back. As she bent over to sit in her chair and slid close to the counter, she placed the phone on her desk and the spray can on her lap where he wouldn't be able to see it. She tried not to appear rattled.

"I'd like to check these out," he said. "But I can't seem to find my library card."

"I can't issue you a new one right now," she said, "but we can have it done tomorrow for a five-dollar replacement fee."

"Five dollars?" he asked, amused. "That's just highway robbery."

She looked up at him. He seemed to be playing with her, and she tried to make him know she wasn't entertained. "You can check out the books with a temporary voucher, provided you're a county resident. But you'll need to find your card or get a new one as soon as possible."

"Or what happens to me?" he asked, smiling with his mouth.

"What happens to you?" she repeated.

"Yeah. Do I get thrown in jail? Does the sheriff come to my house and lock me up?"

She felt the hairs prick up on the back of her neck and her forearms as she said, "No. You can't check out any more books."

"What if these are the only books I'll ever need? Then what?"

She looked back at him, exasperated. "I really don't have time for this," she said. "We need to close the library."

She reached out for the three books, and he handed them to her. As she took them, he kept a grip on them for a second, then released. His smile never wavered.

"Please," she said.

She quickly scanned them. *The Art of War* by Sun Tzu, *The Looming Tower* by Lawrence Wright, and *Falconry and Hawking* by Phillip Glasier. She paused before she scanned the last book.

"Something wrong?" he asked.

"No."

She'd seen a copy of the book before. Nate had given it to her daughter Sheridan when she first showed interest in becoming an apprentice.

"It's kind of dated," he said, "but the basic foundation hasn't changed for thousands of years. So how dated can it really be?"

"I have no idea," she said, scanning the book. She had trouble meeting his eyes again. How could that book be a coincidence? She turned to the side to face her computer monitor.

"What's your name, please?" she asked, calling up the database of county residents who had library cards.

"Bob White," he said, chuckling. "Just like the bird."

She entered the name. "There's a Randall White and an Irene White but no Bob. Do you go by Randall?"

"I'm surprised," he said, but his tone wasn't. He said, "There must be some kind of mistake."

She turned back to him and shrugged.

"Maybe you can try again," he said. "Maybe you entered the wrong name."

"I don't think I did."

"Try it again," he said. "Just for grins."

She didn't want to but had no good reason to refuse other than reluctance to turn her back on him again. But if it would move things along and get him out of there . . .

While she tapped the keys he said, "So where is your husband these days? Still out *investigating*?" The last word simmered with sarcasm and she mistyped "W-h-i-t-e" and had to delete and rekey. It wasn't unusual for patrons to ask about Joe. The location of the game warden was valuable information in a hunting and fishing community. But the question was tinged with malice, and was too familiar from someone she'd never met.

"No, he's on his way here now," she lied.

"He is, is he?" he chuckled. He obviously didn't believe her, and she felt her neck flush.

Then: "What about your kids? Are they home?"

A chill rolled through her. She couldn't type. She swiveled in her chair and stared at him.

"Why are you asking about my family?" she whispered.

"I guess I'm just neighborly. I'm a neighborly guy."

"You need to leave," she said, dropping her right hand below the counter and gripping the pepper spray. "You have no idea who you're talking to. You do *not* talk about my family," she said, her eyes flashing.

"Who are you?" she asked, terrified that she already knew.

"Bob White. Like the bird. I already told you that."

"I could call nine-one-one right now," she said.

He nodded. "Yes, you could, Marybeth. And we could both wait here in embarrassed silence until they arrived."

She opened her mouth, but nothing came out. When he used her name, she felt as if she'd been slapped.

"Your name tag," he said, gesturing toward her breast.

She felt her face flush.

"What I'm really interested in," he said, leaning forward on the counter so his face was two feet away, "is falconry. They call it the sport of kings, you know. It's an ancient art with almost religious overtones." He tapped the book as he talked. "I understand you're acquainted with a master falconer. I'd love to talk with him and, you know, *pick his brain*."

"I don't know what you're talking about," she said.

He shook his head slightly, as if disappointed.

"Please," she said, her mouth trembling. "Just leave."

A low hum suddenly came from the breast pocket of his leather jacket, and she saw a split-second look of irritation in his eyes. He rose off the counter and pulled his phone out of his pocket and checked the caller ID.

He stepped back away from the counter until he was in an aisle of shelving. Close enough to keep an eye on her but far enough not to be overheard. Or so he thought. Due to the strange acoustics in the building, she could clearly hear him when he raised the phone to his mouth and said, "Yes?"

Beneath the counter, out of his view, Marybeth reached down and opened her own phone. She kept her chin and eyes up, though, so he couldn't sense what she was doing. Opening her phone, she opened up her "favorites" screen. Joe's number was at the top, and she pressed send. Quickly, and without looking down, she keyed the speaker button and turned down the volume of his voice message. It was good to hear his recorded voice, even briefly, before she dialed it down. When the prompt came to leave a message—she had the cadence memorized and knew without hearing it—she increased the volume all the way. She was now recording on his phone, wherever it was. And he'd hear what happened in the library if anything did.

The man who called himself Bob White listened to his phone without responding. But even at that distance and in the poor light, she could see him stiffen.

"But not our target?" His voice was clipped and angry.

Then: "I don't care. We can talk about it when you get here."

After a minute more of holding the phone up to his ear, the man closed it without another word and dropped it into his pocket. He hesitated for a moment, then strode back toward her out of the shadows. His head was tilted slightly forward, and his eyes pierced into her from under his brow. She felt her heart beat faster.

He turned sharply toward the door to the parking lot, as if changing his mind from his original intention. Over his shoulder, he said, "You can keep the books. I've already read them."

He walked toward the doors swiftly, retrieving his phone and raising it to his face. Before he pushed his way out, he covered the speaker and looked back over his shoulder.

"It was a real pleasure to meet you, Marybeth Pickett," he said through clenched teeth. "I look forward to the next time."

And he was gone.


SHE WAITED until he was clear of the vestibule before running to the doors herself and throwing the locks. Even though she was sure she'd attended to all of them, she double-checked each. Through the glass, she could see him backing out of his space and turning toward the exit onto Main Street.

She was shaking so badly she had to concentrate to punch the three numbers on the handset back at her desk. When Wendy, the dispatcher, answered, Marybeth said, "This is Marybeth at the library. A man was just here. . . ."

And after she hung up, she picked up her cell phone and said, "Joe, I hope you heard that. It was *him*. *Get home now.* I'm calling the girls to tell them to lock everything up and stay inside. Joe, he knows too much about us."

# 22

JOE PICKETT didn't receive the message, because at 9:30 he was miles away from the highway, on the side of a mountain, grinding his departmental pickup down a brutal and narrow two-track in the falling snow. He was looking for an abandoned line shack deep in the timber that might or might not contain the remains of Alice Thunder. By the time he neared the shack, he was quietly fuming.

Heavy wet snowflakes shot through the beams of his headlights like meteors. Luckily, the road was knuckled with protruding rocks so the traction on his tires was sound, but they made for painfully slow progress and a ride similar to being caught inside a tumbling clothes dryer.

"We're getting closer," Luke Brueggemann said, the GPS unit glowing in his lap. "That is, if those hunters who found the body gave the sheriff the right coordinates."

Joe leaned forward and tried to see the sky through the top of the windshield. "I don't like this snow right now," he said. "We've got to get in, check out that line shack, and get out. I don't want to get stuck back here on the dark side of the moon."

"I think I've heard that story," Brueggemann said, grinning.

"There's not much funny about it."

"It's kind of a legend among the trainers," Brueggemann said, referring to the time Joe had been handcuffed to his steering wheel by a violator, who escaped during a blizzard. "In fact, there's probably more case studies of things you've gotten into than any other game warden."

"Is that so?" Joe said, not knowing whether to be angry or impressed.

"Seems that way."

"How far until we reach the line shack?"

Brueggemann held the GPS up and traced the contours on the screen. "A mile, maybe."

"Good. I've got a lot of patience, but I'm just about ready to call Cheyenne and ask them to cut us loose from this investigation. I've never done that before, but we're doing nothing out here except burning fuel and calories."

"So you don't think we'll find her body?"

"Look around us," Joe said. "We're forty miles from the res. Do you really think a nice middle-aged lady like Alice Thunder would end up here?"

"I don't know her."

"I do," Joe said. "This is a wild-goose chase."

"But we're gonna check out the shack first, right?" Brueggemann asked.

"Of course. But first thing tomorrow morning—provided we can get out of here tonight—I'm calling Cheyenne."

"Does that mean we're going to get to do real game-warden stuff?" the trainee asked. "Like checking out hunters and finally visiting all those elk camps?"

FOR THE PAST day and a half, they'd been assigned to Sheriff Mc-Lanahan through an agreement reached between the governor's office and the Twelve Sleep County Sheriff's Department. To both Joe Pickett's and Sheriff McLanahan's chagrin, County Attorney Dulcie Schalk had gone over the sheriff's head and pulled together a multi-agency effort that involved local, county, state, and federal law enforcement personnel. In addition to the state DCI and the Bureau of Indian Affairs investigators, Schalk had also commandeered state troopers and had borrowed deputies and investigators from adjoining counties, over the sheriff's objections. But characteristically, McLanahan claimed credit for the effort to the Saddlestring *Roundup* and described it as "a show of force not seen since the Johnson County Range War." Despite McLanahan's frequent interviews with radio journalists and television stations from Billings to Casper and the impressive coordination effort spearheaded by Schalk, no progress had been made on either the three missing-persons cases or the triple homicide.

Because of Joe's familiarity with the vast and empty corners of the county—and to keep him out of the way—McLanahan had assigned him the job of following up on far-flung anonymous tips and unsubstantiated sightings of Bad Bob Whiteplume, Alice Thunder, or Pam Kelly. All the leads had gone nowhere. Bad Bob was reportedly seen in Las Vegas and in the crowd of a Denver Nuggets basketball game. The Feds got those to follow up on. But when someone called in that they'd witnessed Bad Bob rappelling down the steep walls of Savage Run Canyon, it fell into Joe's bailiwick. Joe and his trainee had driven as close to the rim of the canyon as they could and hiked the rest of the way, to find no evidence of Bad Bob or anybody else.

Pam Kelly had been reported lurking around the corrals of a

neighboring ranch, but when Joe and Brueggemann got there, the mysterious person turned out to be a barmaid from the Stockman's Bar. She explained haltingly that she was "moonlighting"—performing an erotic dance routine for three Mexican cowhands in the bunkhouse for money. They drove her back to her car.

The anonymous report from hunters said that they'd seen a body matching Alice Thunder's description at a remote line shack on the other side of the Bighorn Mountains—for which they'd provided GPS coordinates—but it looked to be another dry hole.

For the past two nights, Joe hadn't returned home until after ten. He'd barely seen Lucy or April. Each night, despite his exhaustion, he'd booted up his computer and checked the falconry website. There wasn't a single entry on the kestrel thread. Nate seemed to have vanished from the face of the earth. And for the first time he could recall, Marybeth hadn't been able to provide any information from her legal and extralegal research into John Nemecek.

On the way up the mountain to check out the line shack, Luke Brueggemann tried to hide the fact that he was trading text messages with his girlfriend. He'd turn his shoulder to Joe to keep his phone out of view while pretending to be enthralled by something outside his passenger window while he tapped messages by feel.

"You're not fooling me," Joe had said as they neared the summit. Storm clouds from the north had marched across the sky and blacked out the stars and moon. "I can see the glow of your phone."

"Sorry."

"Luke, I've got teenage daughters. I know every texting trick in the book. I even know the one where you look right at me with a vacant expression on your face while you text under the table."

Brueggemann looked away, obviously embarrassed. He said, "I told you, this is tough on her."

"It's going to get tougher," Joe said, slowing the pickup, "because once we leave the highway you'll lose your cell signal. We won't even be able to use the radio for a while."

"Okay," he said.

"Consider it tough love," Joe said. "For the both of you."

JOE DIDN'T KNOW the area well, because he rarely patrolled it. The mountainside had burned in a forest fire twenty-five years before, and the surface of the ground between the new six- to eight-foot pine trees was still littered with an almost impenetrable tangle of burned logs and upturned root pans. The slope was so crosshatched with debris even the elk steered clear of it, thus there were few elk hunters for Joe to check. And although the topo map he'd consulted showed several ancient logging trails through the mountainside, the first two trails they'd found were blocked by dozens of fallen trees.

The third, which of course was the most roundabout route to the abandoned line shack, was passable only because the hunters who'd reported the body had cleared it painstakingly with chainsaws.

"Less than a half mile," Brueggemann said.

It was snowing hard enough that it stuck to the hood of the pickup and topped outstretched pine boughs like icing.

Joe said to Brueggemann, "The chance of there being a body way in here, and that body belonging to Alice, is slim to none. But that's not the way we approach it. We approach this like a crime scene. We're professionals, and we take our job seriously. Don't touch or move anything. Be cautious, and keep your eyes open and your ears on."

Brueggemann sat up straight and looked over at Joe, wide-eyed.

"When we get there, grab my gear bag from the back," Joe said. "Find the camera. We may need to take some shots."

After a beat Brueggemann said, "I gotta ask. What's a line shack, anyway?"

Joe was surprised. "You really don't know?"

"I guess not."

Joe said, "Cowboys built them back when all of this was open range. It's a shelter against sudden bad weather, or if the ranch hands got caught in the middle of nowhere toward dark. None of them are very fancy, and most of them are in bad shape these days. But they saved some lives back in the day, and we've found more than a few lost hunters in remote line shacks."

"Ever find any bodies?" Brueggemann asked.

"Nope."

THEY ALMOST missed it. Joe was taking a slow rocky turn to the left through the trees when his headlights swept quickly across a dark box twenty yards into the timber.

"Any time now," Brueggemann said, his eyes glued to the GPS.

"You're a little late," Joe said, reversing until the beams lit up the old structure.

The heavily falling snow didn't obscure the fact that the line shack was a wreck. It was tiny—barely ten by ten feet—and made of ancient logs stained black with melting snow. The roof sagged, and there was no glass in the two rough-cut windows on either side of the gaping door. A dented black metal stovepipe jutted out of the roof at a haphazard angle.

"What a dump," Brueggemann said.

"Yup," Joe said, swinging out of the cab. He dug his green Game and Fish parka out from behind the bench seat. It had been back there, unused, for the last five months, and he shook the dust off. His twelve-gauge Remington WingMaster shotgun was behind the seat as well, but he decided to leave it. He reached inside the cab for the long black Maglite flashlight, which was jammed between the seats. He clicked it on and shined it toward the line shack. He choked the beam down so it peered into the open windows, but all he could see were interior log walls.

"I've got the camera," Brueggemann said, tossing the evidence bag into the cab of the truck.

Joe took a step toward the line shack, then stopped. He turned and got his shotgun.

"You think you're going to need that?" Brueggemann asked.

"Probably not."

The snow crunched under their boots as they approached the line shack. Joe held the flashlight with his left hand and carried the shotgun in his right.

"Why a shotgun?" Brueggemann asked. "What's wrong with your service pistol?"

"Nothing," Joe said, "except I can't hit a damned thing with it."

Brueggemann chuckled. He said, "I knew that. I just wanted to hear you say it."

"You're starting to get on my nerves," Joe said. "Now, get behind me."

THE HEAVY SNOW hushed the rumbling of the running motor of Joe's pickup as he neared the front of the line shack. He swept the beam left to right and back again, covering the front of the structure as well as the roof and several feet to each side. Because of the snowfall, any boot prints that might have been there were hidden.

"Anybody home?" Joe asked, feeling more than a little silly.

He heard Brueggemann's breath behind him, and was grateful he didn't giggle.

As he got close to the line shack, still sweeping the light across the windows, he saw something that surprised him: a glimpse of brightly colored cloth on the cluttered dirt floor inside.

"There might be something," he said over his shoulder.

"*Really?*" Brueggemann asked, surprised.

Rather than enter the sagging open door, Joe moved to the left to the broken-out window.

Joe took a deep breath of cold air and inhaled several large snow-flakes that melted in the back of his sinus cavities. Then he stepped forward and thrust the Maglite through the window frame toward the floor, slowly moving it up and down the length of the body wrapped in a blanket. The beam swept across the partially exposed skull, the matted hair, the gaping eye sockets where the flesh had been eaten away by rodents and insects.

"Want to look?" Joe asked Brueggemann.

"Is it her?"

"Not exactly," Joe said, stepping aside and handing his trainee the flashlight.

ON THE WAY OUT of the forest toward the highway, Luke Bruegge-mann said, "Jesus, who would do something like that? Wrap a dead deer in a blanket and leave it in a line shack? What in the hell could they have been thinking?"

Joe shrugged.

"That's just sick, man," the trainee said.

"It happens," Joe said. "My guess is some hunter shot an extra deer than he had permits for, and decided to dump it. Why he'd wrap it in a fake Navajo blanket—I don't know. I hate it when hunters waste a life and all that meat. It makes me furious. Luckily, it doesn't happen very often."

"I wish we could have found the bullet," Brueggemann said. He'd watched Joe perform the necropsy with equal measures of curiosity and disgust. But because of the deteriorated condition of the carcass, the fatal wound couldn't be determined. "I'd like to figure out who did that and ticket their ass."

"We'll never know unless someone fesses up," Joe said. "Sometimes it takes years to solve a crime like that. But we've got the photos, and we'll write up an incident report for the file. One of these days we may solve it. Someone talking in a bar, or telling the right person about it—that's when we can cite them. And you'd be surprised how many of these miscreants show up and confess. Crimes against nature eat on some of these guys the way nothing else does."

"It's a puzzle," Brueggemann said, withdrawing his cell phone and glancing at the screen.

"What's even more of a puzzle," Joe said, "is how those hunters saw a deer carcass in a blanket and thought it was Alice Thunder. There seems to be something strange in the air right now. The missing people and that triple homicide have everyone looking over their shoulders and seeing things that aren't there, I think."

When his trainee didn't respond because he was concentrating on his phone, Joe said, "We're still a few miles away from getting a signal."

"I can wait."

"You'll have to."


THE SNOW had accumulated so quickly they couldn't see their entry tracks in the rough two-track on the way out. The big rocks in the road made them pitch back and forth inside the cab like rag dolls.

"I'll be glad to get back on asphalt," Brueggemann said.

"Uh-oh," Joe said, as his headlights lit up a dead tree that had fallen across the road in front of them, blocking their progress. Luckily, the tree didn't look too large to push aside.

"When did *that* happen?" Brueggemann asked.

Joe said, "Heavy snow brings down those old dead trees. Try and push it out of the way. If that won't work, I'll get the saw out of the back."

The trainee hesitated for a moment, as if preparing to argue, but apparently thought better of it. "It'll just take a minute," he said, pulling on leather gloves.

While Brueggemann walked toward the fallen tree, his back bathed in white headlights, Joe withdrew his own cell phone to check messages. No bars. He glanced to the bench seat and realized Brueggemann had absently left his there. Joe wondered if Brueggemann's smart phone picked up a signal yet, and picked it up to check.

There was no signal yet, but the darkened screen hinted at the text thread underneath. Joe glanced up to make sure Brueggemann's back was still to him—it was, as his trainee lifted the tree and walked it stiffly to the side—before tapping a key to light up the screen. Although Joe had no business looking at the extended text thread, he was curious. But the phone was locked and a password was required for access. He lowered the phone back to the seat, ashamed of his attempted spying.

Out on the road, Brueggemann stepped aside and brushed snow from his sleeves and signaled for Joe to drive forward. When he drew up alongside, Joe stopped for his trainee to crawl in. He noted that the first thing Brueggemann did when he swung inside was to immediately retrieve his cell phone from the seat and drop it in his breast pocket.

"Thank you," Joe said.

"The pleasure is mine," Brueggemann said sarcastically. "It's snowing like a motherfu—" He caught himself before the curse came out. "Like crazy," he said instead.

"It is," Joe said. "But we're not that far from the highway now, and we should be fine."

"Late, though," his trainee said, looking at his wristwatch. He seemed to be in a hurry to get back to his motel. Probably to talk to his girl. Joe wondered what her name was.

AFTER BEING TUMBLED about the cab on the two-track, it felt like heaven to drive onto the snow-covered highway again, Joe thought. He turned right and began to climb toward the summit.

After shifting out of four-wheel-drive low, he snatched the mic from its cradle. They were now back in radio range. Since they were participating in the task force, the under-dash radio unit was still tuned to the mutual aid channel that included all the law enforcement agencies.

"This is GF-48," Joe said. "We investigated the lead and it's negative. We're heading back to the barn now."

"Roger that, GF-48," the dispatcher said. The signal—and her voice—crackled with static. "I'll inform the county sheriff's department."

"It was a dead mule deer wrapped in a blanket," Joe said, and glanced to Brueggemann, who smiled.

"Roger that. A dead deer."

"GF-48 out," Joe said. As he leaned forward to cradle the mic, the dispatcher came back. "Joe, have you been in touch with your wife yet?"

Concerned, Joe said, "Negative. We just regained radio contact."

"Better call her," the dispatcher said.

"Right away."

To Brueggemann, Joe asked, "Do we have cell service yet?"

The trainee looked at his phone and shook his head and said, "Must be the snow."


THERE WAS an untracked foot of it on the summit of the mountain, and Joe used the reflections of the delineator posts to make sure he kept the pickup on the road. As they finally began to descend, he felt the vibration of an incoming message on his cell phone in his pocket. At the same time, Brueggemann's cell phone chirped with received text messages.

As both men reached for their phones, the radio chatter increased in volume and was filled with distant voices.

Brueggemann reached forward to turn down the volume when Joe recognized the fast-clipped exchange of officers somewhere involved in a tense situation.

"Hold it," Joe said to Brueggemann. "Something's going on, and I want to hear what it is."

They listened as Joe drove. One of the speakers identified himself as a Teton County sheriff's deputy. The other was a Wyoming highway trooper. The third was the local dispatcher in Jackson Hole. Snatches of the conversation popped and crackled through the speakers of Joe's pickup radio.

. . . *One dead at the scene of the rollover* . . .

. . . *transporting a second victim now to Saint John's* . . .

. . . *the vehicle is a Chevy Tahoe, Colorado plates, VIN number* . . .

"Where's Saint John's?" Brueggemann asked Joe.

"Jackson," Joe answered quickly, imploring his trainee to be quiet.

. . . *need to alert the emergency room doctors that the victim is in bad shape* . . . *claims he was tortured and it sure as hell looks like it* . . .

"Tortured!" Brueggemann yelped.

"Please," Joe said, "I can't hear."

*. . . The dead one at the scene appears to be male, late twenties to early thirties, no identification . . . massive head wound . . .*

*. . . The staff at Saint John's has been informed. . . .*

*. . . snowing like hell here . . . not sure if there are other victims around . . . can see tire tracks but no other vehicles . . .*

*. . . cannot send additional units because our personnel is currently across the border in Idaho . . .*

*. . . Idaho! We need them here. . . .*

*. . . Teton Pass is closed because of the storm. . . .*

*. . . We need an evidence tech on the scene ASAP. The snow is covering the tracks and we're gonna lose the chance of figuring out what happened. . . .*

*. . . Requesting once again any possible backup or assistance on the scene . . .*

"Jesus," Brueggemann said. "What do you think happened?"

Joe shook his head as if he didn't have any idea, and raised his phone to listen to Marybeth's message that had been left two hours before.

When he heard it, he felt his insides go ice cold. Despite the road conditions, he punched the accelerator.

"Jesus!" Brueggemann said. "What are you doing?"

"I've got to get home," Joe said through clenched teeth.

# 23

NINE MILES WEST of Dubois, after summiting and descending the Absaroka Mountains, Nate slowed his Jeep and turned right on an untracked dirt road that led to a wide ribbon of ink that serpentined through the snow. The inside of the cab smelled of burned dust from the heating vents, hot tears from Haley, and the musky congealing blood that covered his flesh and clothing. The grille of his Jeep was packed with wind-driven snow from the drive over, and melting rivulets coursed down his headlights.

He wheeled parallel to the bank of the Wind River and parked behind a thick stand of willows, concealing the location of the Jeep from anyone behind them on the highway. He cut the headlights before opening his door and swinging his legs out.

"Do you want me to keep the motor running and the heat on?" he asked Haley.

He couldn't see her face well in the soft glow from the dome light. It had been nearly two hours since she'd spoken to or even looked at him. She'd spent the whole of the trip over Togwotee Pass staring out the front windows in unsettled silence, her head tilted slightly forward, her hair hanging down over her face. Her cheeks were wet with tears, but she'd rarely sobbed, as if she'd been too proud to make a sound and reveal herself. Instead, she gripped the safety bar across the dashboard as if holding on for dear life.

He'd spent the whole of the trip deconstructing what he'd done to Trucker Cap, and analyzing the information he'd tortured out of him.

"Haley . . ."

She mumbled something that was snatched away by the muscular flow of the river behind him.

"What?"

*"I said I don't give a fuck what you do, you fucking monster!"* she shrieked, her mouth twisted into rage, her eyes wide and rimmed with red.

Nate leaned back on his heels and waited a full minute before walking to the back of the Jeep for his duffel bag. He left the engine running and said, "I told you not to watch."


FALLING SNOWFLAKES disappeared on contact with the icy surface of the river, leaving tiny one-ring disturbances. Curls of steam rose from the flow into the even colder air and vanished like ghosts. As Nate shed his shoulder holster and hung it over a willow branch, he heard a beaver slap its tail on the surface upriver and the *gloop* sound of the creature diving deep. What little filtered moonlight there was marked the sides of the current with accents of light blue.

His clothing crackled as he peeled it off, because blood had dried through to his skin. He tossed each item into the middle of the river so it would float downstream, undulating in the current and over rocks, ending up who knew where: the Fitzpatrick Wilderness Area, Crowheart, or back home on the Wind River Reservation. Maybe his wretched clothing would be trapped beneath the heavy ice for the winter, washing the blood away, diluting the dissolving blood and fluids with startlingly clean and cold mountain water.

Snowflakes landed on his bare skin like icy fly bites.

The river itself was so cold it burned his skin and made him gasp. He waded in above his knees until the current upset his balance and his feet slipped on the smooth tops of the river rocks and he sat backward and went under. The tumbled silence underneath was awesome.

For twenty long and silent seconds, he bounced along the riverbed on his back and butt, naked feet out ahead of him, arms out to the side, eyes closed. As the river cleansed his flesh and the cold numbed all feeling, he briefly forgot about the blood that flowed from ripping a man's ears off, the muffled pop from twisting his victim's nose sidewise until the nostrils looked up at his cheek, the dull, dry cracking sounds of fingers being snapped back one by one, the undignified screaming, the unholy crunch of shinbones being stove in.

And when he emerged from the Wind River howling and trembling and thirty yards from where he'd left his duffel bag of clean dry clothes upstream, he fought back the depraved and exhilarating sense of *yarak* that had engorged him until he'd have to summon it back again.

SHE WAS STILL staring at the snow-covered windshield when he climbed back into the Jeep. He'd found an old pair of jeans in his duffel as well as a dark green wool tactical sweater from the old days to wear. He closed the car door and sat in silence for a few minutes, letting the heat from the vents warm his body until his muscles stopped quivering.

Then he turned to her and swiftly reached out and with his right hand grasped her ear through her dark hair. At his touch, her hands fluttered briefly in her lap like wounded birds. He drew out his .500

with his left hand and pressed the gaping muzzle against the white flesh of her neck just below her jawbone.

"This is how it starts," he said.

She still wouldn't look at him, but her eyes welled with tears. She said, "Do whatever you have to do, Nate. Torture me like you tortured that man back there. I'm sure once you get started you'll get me to say whatever you want me to say, but it won't be true."

"How did you hook up with Cohen?" he asked.

"You should believe me when I tell you he hooked up with *me*," she said. "The man was relentless. Why would I throw my life away to go off in the middle of the mountains in Idaho and live like a hillbilly with a bunch of other men? There's only one reason people do such things. It's called love, Nate. Maybe you've read about it."

He gripped her ear with more pressure and said, "Haley, the man back there told me there was a young and beautiful operator on the team. He didn't know her name except by code. I'm thinking she was the one that got to Merle a month ago. I didn't ask him to identify you in person, but now I want you to tell me something. Did you ever leave Camp Oscar?"

"I can't believe you're asking me this," she said. He could tell she was trying hard not to let her lips tremble and betray her emotions. "If he said it was me, he was lying. He couldn't even see me in the Jeep. The headlights were on him, and we never made eye contact."

"Did you ever leave Camp Oscar?"

After a beat, she said, "Yes. And yes, it was two weeks ago."

He increased the pressure but didn't twist.

"My father is dying back in North Carolina," she said. "I flew home to see him. Then I flew back."

Nate said softly, "That would have been the third week of September?"

"Yes," she said. "Right now I can't think straight. Cohen took me to the airport on a Monday night. . . ."

"September seventeenth," Nate said.

"Okay. I got back Friday."

"The twenty-first."

"If you say so."

"Merle was gutted on September twentieth," Nate said. "So you had time to find him, get close, and murder him. Or did you just set him up so one of the operators could get to him?"

She blew out a quick, frustrated breath. More tears. "That whole week I was either at my parents' house in Rocky Mount or at Nash General Hospital seeing my dad."

She laughed bitterly. "I assured my dying father I knew what I was doing out here. That I'd found a good man and I was safe. That gave him some comfort, and I didn't know I was lying at the time."

She tried to turn her head toward Nate, but the grip on her ear prevented it.

She said, "I wasn't in Wyoming. In fact, this is the first time I've ever even been here. If this is what it's like, I never want to come back."

"I never said Merle died in Wyoming."

"Oscar told me. He knew because you contacted him. Think about it, Nate."

Nate said, "I can check on that story pretty easily."

"Do it," she said, pleading. "Please do it. I flew from Idaho Falls to Salt Lake City and on to Raleigh, where my mom picked me up."

"What airline?"

"Delta."

"What flight number?"

"I have no fucking idea."

"Why didn't you tell me this sooner?" he asked.

"Why should I?" she asked. "I guess I didn't realize you planned to torture me. That you didn't trust me."

"Oscar told me you'd been there the whole time."

"Oscar . . . must have forgotten," she said. "It was before everything started to happen. Or maybe," she said, a lick of flame reentering her tone, "maybe Oscar was in on it, too. Maybe you should drive back to Idaho and break his fingers and pull his goddamn ears off if you can find what's left of his head."

He released her ear and slipped his weapon back into the shoulder holster.

"I had to be sure," he said, and turned back and put the Jeep into gear.

"Are you sure *now*?" she asked, then followed it with a sharp slap across his face. He flinched but didn't retaliate.

"I think so," he said.

Her words reminded him of his own father, and how he'd left him in Colorado Springs. Nate wondered where Gordo had taken his new family, his stepmother and two half sisters he barely knew. The thought flooded him with remorse for uprooting them, and he hoped someday he'd be able to make things right. Gordo had made him what he was, for better and worse. Nate no longer resented him for that, and he hoped to tell Gordo all was forgiven. Then Nate shook his head to clear the thought away. The task ahead of him left no room for sentimentality.

THE LIGHTS of Dubois emerged through the snowfall ahead. It was a small, sleepy mountain town of barely a thousand people surrounded by closed guest ranches, hunting lodges, and working ranches, and rimmed by the Absaroka and Wind River Mountains.

Nate slowed before he reached the town limits, looking for activity ahead, a roadblock or law enforcement presence. He saw nothing unusual.

Finally, she said, "What else did you learn from that man back there in Jackson?"

"Enough," Nate said. "The playing field isn't close to even, but at least it's not as stacked against us as it was before. Now I know there are more operators where Nemecek set up his headquarters."

"How do you know he wasn't lying?" she asked. "How do you know he wasn't just telling you what you wanted to hear, or making something up you'd believe?"

"I know the difference," Nate said. "He lied at first. He lied through all of his fingers being broken back. He was a tough guy."

"What you did to him," she said angrily, "it was *awful*. Savage."

"I let him live," Nate said. "I called the hospital with his phone when I could have let him bleed out or freeze. I could have finished him off. Now I've got a broken Special Forces operator out there who may someday come back at me."

"But what you did to him . . ."

"Means to an end," Nate said. "Torture works. It always has. That's why they call it torture."

"You looked like you were enjoying yourself."

"I told you not to watch."

"I finally turned away," she said, "but by then I'd seen too much. In ten minutes I went from kind of trying to like you to hating your fucking miserable guts."

He shrugged.

"That's all you're going to say?" she said, eyes flashing. *"Means to an end'?"*

"Look," he said, "that guy back there was a Peregrine. I went through the same training. He's been waterboarded, sprayed in his open eyes with pepper spray, and dropped off in both jungles and deserts with no weapons or food. He wasn't going to just tell me what I wanted to know unless he was *convinced* I wanted to kill him slowly. If there was a shadow of a doubt in his mind, he wouldn't have talked."

She thought about that for a moment, then said, "But he talked."

"It took a while," Nate said. "A lot longer than I'd hoped. Not until I started on his second hand, and even then he held back. For a while."

"It's just so inhuman," she said. "I always knew Gabriel had seen things and even done things overseas, but he never talked about them. Now I think I hate him, too."

"Don't," Nate said. "Cohen was like that poor son-of-a-bitch back there in the trucker cap. He was doing what he was hardwired to do and what he thought was right. It's been going on for thousands of years, but you've had the wealth and comfort to go soft. Our whole country has. If it weren't for men like those two, you'd see a lot more savagery, but you'd see it in the streets."

He said, "They protect you from knowing what's out there, and there's no appreciation for them. No gratitude."

"Don't paint me like that," she said defensively. "I know there's violence in the world. I know there are people who want to kill us. I'm from a military family," she said. "But I don't have to enjoy what you did."

"And I hope you never do," Nate said, "or your world would turn into mine."

They passed under a huge retro neon trout struggling on a fishing line that marked a closed sporting-goods store.

"I'm looking for a pay phone," Nate said.

"They still have those?" she asked.

He ignored her. "I need to call a buddy of mine. He's in big trouble, but he doesn't know it."

AS THEY backtracked through town and Nate located a public phone mounted on the side of a sleeping grocery store, she said, "For a while there, it seemed like something was happening between us, didn't it?"

He looked over, not sure how to respond.

"I'd like to say it ended back there," she said, looking away.

"But it didn't," Nate said.

"I'm not so sure now."

"Bad timing, I guess."

"It always is," she said, and sighed.

# 24

JOE FELT A PUNCH OF PANIC in his gut when he saw the strange vehicle parked in front of his house through the cascading snow. It was a half hour from midnight: no one should be visiting. Worst-case scenarios corkscrewed through his mind, and he instinctively reached over and touched the shotgun—propped muzzle-down on the bench seat—to make sure it was there.

His anxiety level had climbed each time he'd tried to call Mary-beth's cell phone as he roared down the mountain, only to get her voice-mail message. She was either on her phone or the phone was turned off. The message he'd left was: "I'm on the way." While he'd dropped off Luke Brueggemann at the hotel, he'd speed-dialed the house phone, but all he got was a tinny recording announcing that the number he'd called wasn't "in service at this time."

As he neared his home, he recognized the SUV as belonging to Deputy Mike Reed, and breathed a sigh of relief. Not until that moment did he realize how tightly he'd been gripping the wheel.

Nevertheless, he carried the shotgun with him as he skipped up the snow-covered porch steps and threw open the front door.

"Whoa, there, buckaroo," Reed said when he looked up from a

cup of coffee and saw the weapon. "Just us friendlies here." He was seated on the couch in full uniform.

Joe lowered the weapon and propped it in the corner of the mud-room before entering the living room. He could hear Marybeth talk-ing in the kitchen on her cell phone—the reason he couldn't reach her earlier. He shook snow off his parka and hung it on a peg.

"It doesn't look like it's letting up much outside," Reed said to Joe.

"Nope."

"Road okay?"

"Hasn't seen a plow, if that's what you're asking," Joe said.

"I'm not surprised," Reed said. "I don't think the county road and bridge guys were ready for an October blizzard. No one was. The heavy snow knocked down some tree limbs south of town and took out the phone lines, too. They're just now getting them fixed. The phone company didn't have crews ready. You'd think they'd all just moved to Wyoming or something."

Joe nodded, relieved by the explanation for not being able to reach his wife.

"So you found a dead deer in a cabin instead of a missing Indian woman?" Reed asked. When Joe looked up, Reed patted his handheld radio, from which he'd obviously been monitoring the transmissions.

"Yup."

"What a waste of time," Reed said, chuckling bitterly.

"That's how it goes these days," Joe said in the same tone. Then: "Have you heard anything more about that situation in Jackson with the rollover?"

"Not for a while," Reed said. "I think we had a window there in the storm where we could hear them. But it's closed now. I haven't heard anything but static in that direction."

Joe nodded, then said, "Be right back."

He walked down the hallway and cracked open Lucy's door. She was in bed. Her blond hair shimmered in the bar of light from the open door, and she turned over with her back to him and moaned in her sleep. Joe eased the door shut and went across the hall to April's room. It was locked. He rapped on it with a knuckle.

"*What?*" she asked, her voice shot through with outrage.

"You okay?"

"Why shouldn't I be?"

"No reason," Joe said, turning back down the hall. Behind him, he could hear her voice trail off. Something about being grounded without a cell phone, practically a prisoner in her own home . . .

*Situation normal,* he said to himself.

He returned to the front room. Tube yawned and padded down the hall on his heels.

Joe stopped inside the threshold and squinted at Reed.

"Mike, why are you here?"

Reed chuckled, lowered his coffee cup, and said, "Your wife called and told me what happened at the library when the lines went down. I thought I might just come up here and check on her and kind of hang out until you got home. Just to make sure this Bob White guy—or whoever he is—didn't decide to come by for another visit."

"Thank you," Joe said. He was touched.

"Don't mention it," Reed said. "To be honest, it feels kind of nice to get out of the office for a while. McLanahan is going crazy. He's lashing out at everyone like Hitler in his bunker during the last days of Berlin. I don't mind getting away from *that.*"

Marybeth peeked out at Joe from the kitchen. She held her cell phone to her ear and gestured with a "just a minute" finger in the air.

"Did you locate the guy who spooked Marybeth?" Joe asked Reed.

The deputy shook his head. "He was long gone, unfortunately. We're circulating his description and the make of the vehicle she saw in the parking lot, though. If we get an identification I'll let you know right away. This town isn't big enough to hide in very long."

"I know," Joe said. "But it's a hell of a big county."

"Joe," Reed said, "let us handle it if we find him. I don't think it would be a good idea for you to be there. I've seen that look in your eye before."

"Hmph."

"Do you have any idea who it was?" Reed asked, shooting Joe his sidelong cop stare.

"Not for sure," Joe said.

"Marybeth told me it might be a guy named"—he glanced at his notebook—"John Nemecek. We ran the name and came up with absolutely nothing. No priors, no record of any kind. We don't even know where he's from."

"That sounds about right," Joe said.

Reed said, "There's something you're not telling me."

Joe thought about it for a few seconds and came clean. "Nate told me this John Nemecek might be after him. Apparently, they served together in Special Forces. I don't know much more than that, but it's possible Nemecek had something to do with all that's been going on around here."

Reed didn't blink, and continued to deadeye Joe. "So you're all but admitting Romanowski offed the Kellys and Ron Connelly."

Joe said, "I don't want to go there. But this Nemecek might be the key to everything."

"How long have you suspected this?"

"From the start. But I've got no proof at all. I've never seen the guy, and I don't know anything more about him than what Nate told me before he flew the coop. I'm not about to take my suspicions to McLanahan or Dulcie until I've got some kind of solid proof."

"Still, you should have said something before now," Reed said. "We might have found this guy sooner."

Joe shook his head. "I don't have any evidence, Mike. I've only got a suspicion. And I don't want McLanahan to botch it by overplaying his hand."

Reed put his coffee down and looked away, a thoughtful expression on his face. "I understand," he said. "I could see the sheriff announcing this guy's name in the press as our suspect so it looks like we've made some progress in the investigation, and drive this Nemecek underground. And if we didn't find him right away, McLanahan would hang you out to dry and say you've been withholding evidence. He desperately needs a scapegoat."

"I've played that role before," Joe said.

"I know."

Joe turned, walked past Marybeth in the kitchen, and found a six-pack of Coors in the refrigerator. He twisted the cap off a bottle.

"Want one?" he asked Reed when he returned.

"I want one so bad I could die," Reed said. "But I'll have to pass."

"Sorry," Joe said, recalling Reed's problems with alcohol a few years before. "I forgot."

"So what's next?" Reed asked, gesturing with both hands to include the whole of it all.

"I might go over their heads," Joe said.

"You mean McLanahan and Dulcie Schalk?"

"Yup."

"To who? The governor?"

Joe shook his head. "He can't help me. But there's a guy named Chuck Coon in the FBI in Cheyenne. I've worked with him a few times. He's by the book all the way, but he might be interested in this, and he'll have better resources to find out something about Nemecek—or rule him out."

"McLanahan's not going to like that," Reed said, obviously savoring the prospect.

"Too bad," Joe said. "When this guy—whether he's Nemecek or Bob White or both—approached my wife, he made it personal. I'm going after him with both barrels."

"And you think the Feds might know about him?"

Joe took a long drink and lowered the bottle. "Feds can find out about other Feds easier than we can."

Reed sat back. "'Other Feds'? Nemecek is a government guy?"

"Used to be," Joe said. "I don't know his status right now. He used to be in Special Forces with Nate."

"And you think the FBI can find something on him? You might be giving them too much credit," Reed said.

"Maybe."

Reed nodded toward the kitchen and lowered his voice. "You're married to a tough lady, you know. My wife would have fallen apart if that guy showed up at her office."

"She's tough, all right," Joe said. "Do you know what she's doing in there right now?"

"I gather she's calling airlines and hotels," Reed said. "I think you're all going on a little vacation. And I think it's a damned good plan, myself."

"Vacation?" Joe said. "How are we going to afford that?"

AFTER REFILLING Reed's cup and asking him to stay around a little longer, Joe ducked into his office and booted up the computer. Marybeth was still occupied, although when he heard her read her credit card number to the agent on the other end of the line, he assumed she was about done.

He was pleased to find out the phone company had restored service and he could both use the house phone and access the Internet. He sat down and opened the browser and scrolled through the bookmarks and clicked on the falconry website. His scalp crawled when he saw there was a single new entry:

NOTHING I TRY WILL WORK, AND I'M GETTING FRUSTRATED AND CONCERNED. IT'S A DISASTER ON EVERY FRONT. I JUST WANT TO SAY TO THAT BIRD, "FLY AWAY NOW AND DON'T LOOK BACK."

JOE PUSHED his chair away from the monitor and rubbed his eyes. Nate was often obscure when he spoke, and there were times after they talked when Joe wondered what his friend was trying to say. But this seemed extremely clear.

In the other room, he heard Marybeth close her phone. She was in his office within fifteen seconds. She eased the door shut behind her and leaned back against it.

"Thank God you're home," she said. "I hate it when I can't reach you."

"Likewise," he said, then told her what they'd found at the line shack.

"You got my message, though?" she asked.

He stood up and closed the gap and wrapped his arms around her. She was stiff at first, but then welcomed the embrace and burrowed her face into his shoulder. Her hair smelled good. She said, "He scared me, Joe. And what bothered me the most was how *confident* he was. He didn't really threaten me, or say anything that we could use against him. There was no mistaking his intent, and who knows what would have happened if he hadn't gotten that call."

"Any idea who called him?"

"No. But it made him change his plans."

"I'm sorry I couldn't be reached," Joe said, stroking her back. "I wish I could have been there. But I'm very glad Mike came here."

"Me, too. He's a good man."

Then: "Joe, he knew us. And he seemed to know you wouldn't show up even when I told him you were on the way."

Joe stopped stroking her and asked, "Really? He knew my location?"

"I don't know about that for sure, but he knew you were in the field and wouldn't show up to interrupt him."

"That's no good," he said. "He must be keeping close tabs on the sheriff's office." His mind leapt. And he couldn't help but suspect Mike Reed in the other room, even though Reed had never given Joe a reason not to trust him. But he instantly wished he hadn't told Reed so much.

Marybeth stepped back and looked up at Joe. "This man, Bob White or John Nemecek, whoever he is, just oozed creepiness. I honestly had no doubt he would have hurt me if he didn't get that call. I don't have any doubt he will go after our girls if it would help him get what he wants."

"Which is Nate," Joe said.

Her eyes flashed as she said, "Which is why we're leaving this place for a while. I can't put my girls at risk any more than they are now. Or you, Joe. I refuse to let a member of our family get hurt."

She said it with such vehemence that there was no point in arguing, Joe knew.

"Nate agrees with you," he said, handing her the printout.

She read it and handed it back.

"You didn't tell me you were in touch with him," she said, hurt.

"I haven't been," Joe said. "This is the first communication he's sent since he left."

"I thought we didn't keep secrets from each other," she said.

"We don't, and I'm sorry. But I didn't want you to get any more involved than necessary."

She glared at him, and he eventually looked away.

"We can talk about this later," she said. "Right now, Nate and I are on the same page. I booked us on the first flight out tomorrow morning."

"To where?" Joe asked with no enthusiasm.

"Saddlestring to Denver to Los Angeles," she said.

"Los Angeles?" Joe said incredulously. He'd never been there and didn't have any desire to see it. But Marybeth had lived there for a few years while growing up, and she was somewhat familiar with the city.

She said, "I can't think of a better place to get lost, can you? I don't know anyone there anymore, and no one knows us. Maybe we can take the girls to Disneyland."

"Disneyland . . ." Joe repeated, shaking his head.

"Do you have a better idea?"

Joe thought, *Find Nemecek and take him down.* But he said, "Nope."

"Then let's start packing. I've booked us into a Holiday Inn in Anaheim. It's one of those places with a package deal that gives discounts to Disneyland and caters to young families. It's so boring, no one will even want to try and find us."

Joe cringed.

She said, "I'll wake the girls up. Tomorrow, as we're boarding that plane and not before, I'll call the schools and let them know Lucy and April will be missing some classes. And I'll tell Sheridan what's going on. I've got some sick leave built up at the library I can take, and I know you've got plenty of time coming because you never take any days off."

Joe screwed up his face and crossed his arms over his chest.

*"What?"* she asked, her voice rising.

"How are we going to afford this?" he asked.

"We'll figure something out," she said, and started to leave the room. "Don't forget, my mother left us money for the girls."

Joe groaned at the mention of Marybeth's mother. "That's for their college," he said. After all, he'd negotiated the deal with Missy several weeks before, as her price for leaving without him revealing what he knew about her. Money had shown up in their college funds via wire transfer. It had been an act of pure extortion, and Joe was proud of it.

Marybeth said, "They've got to get to college first, Joe."

He didn't argue with that logic.

"I'm going now," she said. "I've got to get the girls up and help them pack."

When he didn't follow, she turned back to him and locked his eyes with hers. "Joe, I know what you're thinking."

He didn't say yes or no but let her continue.

"What I'm telling you is we need to leave," she said. "All of us. I looked into that man's eyes and I saw no empathy at all. Not even a spark. It was like looking into the eyes of one of Nate's falcons. He's capable of anything, and he'll do anything to get to Nate. Our family means nothing to him except as bargaining chips. We can't let him use us as bait to lure Nate here to his death. Do you understand me?"

Joe didn't respond. It made perfect twisted sense, he thought. The man at the library had set the trap.

"I bought four tickets," she said, opening the door. "Your name is on one of them."

She started to reach for the door handle but stopped short. Turning, she gestured to a stack of books on Joe's desk. He followed her finger. He hadn't noticed them previously.

She said, "I don't know if it means anything at all, but those are the library books he brought to check out. They could have been chosen at random for an excuse to engage me, but my intuition tells me they mean something to him."

Joe picked the books up one at a time and frowned. *The Art of War* by Sun Tzu. *Falconry and Hawking* by Phillip Glasier. And *The Looming Tower: Al-Qaeda and the Road to 9/11* by Lawrence Wright. Joe felt his neck get hot.

"What?" she asked. "Do they mean something to you?"

"I've seen them all before," he said. "At Nate's place. They read the same books. It was our man, all right."

JOE SAT DOWN heavily at his desk and reread the message from Nate on the screen. There was no other way to take it than Nate wanted them to hit the road.

He looked through the three books again. Both *The Art of War* and *Falconry and Hawking* seemed too specialized and unrelated to provide much insight. But *The Looming Tower*? Joe opened it and turned straight to the index, looking for the names Nemecek or Romanowski. He found neither. But he agreed with Marybeth: something in the book had meaning to them. But where to start?

He rubbed his face and tried to think of alternatives to leaving— some kind of action he could take to try to help Nate and protect his family—but there were simply too many unknown variables. He felt impotent, useless, and cowardly.

When Joe tried to figure out how White/Nemecek knew so much about his family, his whereabouts, and the investigation, there were few people he could rule out. There were dozens of people privy to the proceedings: deputies, dispatchers, reporters, administration, maintenance, visiting state and federal agents, even McLanahan's coffee group that met every morning at the Burg-O-Pardner. He could rule out only the sheriff himself, because without solving either the murders or the missing-persons cases, the man was circling the drain of his own career. He'd do whatever he could to stop the spiral by making arrests, Joe knew.

He leaned back in his chair and sneaked a long look at Mike Reed in the other room. Reed thumbed through a hunting magazine and sipped the last of his coffee on the couch. The man was affable and good-natured. By all rights, he should be the next sheriff. And although he certainly wanted to win the election, could he possibly be predatory enough to assist a killer so his opponent would go down in flames? Joe couldn't conceive it.

Who else would know?

Then he thought about the password-protected text thread on Brueggemann's phone.


WHEN LUCY entered his office rubbing her face from sleep, she said, "Mom said we're going on a trip." She didn't sound happy about it.

"That's the plan."

"What about my play?" she asked. "I can't let everybody down. I'm the *lead*. This really means a lot to me, and Mom doesn't even want to talk about it. I mean, I could stay with Heather until you got back."

Joe didn't have a good answer. "Maybe we'll all be back in time."

"But I'm the *lead*," she said again. "If I'm not here they'll give the part to Erin Vonn or somebody else."

"I'm sure they'll take you back," Joe said, not sure about it at all.

"Mom won't even tell me why we're leaving."

"For your safety," Joe said. Lucy rolled her eyes in response.

"I have a life of my own, you know," she said, folding her arms in front of her and striking a pose very much like Marybeth had a few minutes before. "You and Mom treat me like your property."

Joe said with some sympathy, "You've got to get a few more years on you before it's otherwise."

"You sound just like *her*," she said, meaning Marybeth.

"We're a team."

"Yes," she said, her eyes flashing. "An *evil* team trying to destroy my life."

"That's a little dramatic, isn't it?" he asked, stifling a smile.

"I'm in *drama*!" she cried. "That's the *point*!" But her anger was diffusing.

Joe said, "Before you pack, I need your help. I don't understand how Facebook works, and I know you're an expert. You spend more time on it than you do sleeping or eating."

She rolled her eyes again, and said, "*Thanks*, Dad."

"Everybody around your age is on it, right?"

"Yes. Everybody."

"Everybody in college, right?"

"Yeah."

He said, "What I'd like you to do is use your laptop to find the page or the profile or whatever it is for Luke Brueggemann, my trainee. See if there are any comments from his girlfriend, if he has one. See if he's sharing things about his new assignment."

She asked him how to spell the name, and he did.

"I may not find much," she said. "It depends on how much he's got his profile set up to share. I'm not his friend or anything."

"Just find whatever you can," Joe said. "Let me know what you find."

She sighed, and said, "At least we're going to Disneyland. I can't believe it."

"Neither can I," Joe said.


IT WAS MIDNIGHT when the house phone rang. As always, Joe ignored it. He was talking with Mike Reed and waiting for Lucy to come back and tell him what she'd dug up on Brueggemann and his girlfriend.

Marybeth came into the living room holding the handset, and the moment he saw her face he knew something momentous had happened.

She handed him the phone with concern in her eyes. "You'll want to take this," she said.

As he reached for it, she said, "In your office."

She followed him back in and again closed the door behind them. "It's Nate," she whispered.


"WHERE ARE YOU?" Joe asked immediately, careful not to use his name.

"We can't talk long," Nate said. The connection was clear, but from the airy tone of it, Joe assumed Nate was speaking from somewhere outdoors. Maybe a pay phone, he thought.

"Gotcha," Joe said. "Where . . ."

"No," Nate said. "We can't go there right now. Our friends might be listening."

"Right."

"It's time to fly," Nate said. "Take the entire nest. Don't think about it, and don't play hero. Just go."

"I understand," Joe said, glancing up at Marybeth, who nodded.

"The threat is on top of you right now."

Joe hoped he didn't have to respond to Nate in falconry terminology. Instead, he said, "Yup."

"At least three of the Peregrines are still out there," Nate said. "One may be a young female."

"Only three?" Joe asked, wondering how many men Nate had taken out of the game.

"At least," Nate said. "But there could be more I don't know about. Leave them to me."

"Are you sure about that?"

Nate laughed bitterly. "So far, so good. But the cost has been too high and the collateral damage has been heavy."

Joe thought, *So many questions.* He said, "Is there any way we can talk more?"

"No," Nate said, no doubt measuring the time of the call and trying to end it quickly. Joe wanted to tell him it didn't matter: *If the call was being traced, it was already too late.* But he didn't dare say it.

"Just remember," Nate said, "these creatures won't return to the fist no matter how much you've done for them. They kill, they eat, and they move on. Do you understand me?"

"Yes."

"They might be right next to you, but you can't trust them. Just get away now."

And he hung up. Joe listened to the dial tone for a moment, then cradled the phone and picked it back up and dialed star sixty-nine. The phone rang on the other end, but no one picked it up.

"He's gone," Joe said.

"Is he okay?" Marybeth asked.

"I guess he is."

"What did he say?"

Joe tried to recall the conversation verbatim, and repeated it.

She frowned. "The only thing I understand is he wants us to go. That I got. What was the rest about?"

Joe said, "He thinks Nemecek has someone inside. And so do I."

He stood and said, "I've got to go out for a while." Marybeth stepped aside, puzzled. "Where are you going?"

"Out," he said. "I'll ask Mike to hang around until I get back."

HE TOLD HER his suspicions and her eyes widened and she raised her balled fist up to her mouth.

She said, "I won't even tell you to be careful," she said. "Because if you don't, *I'll* kill you."

He handed her the copy of *The Looming Tower*. "You might want to look through this," he said. "You're a much faster reader than I am. See if you can find anything that might relate to Nate, or Nemecek. Maybe you can find something about their old unit, or something they might have been involved in."

She took the book and eyed him warily. "You mean when I take a break from packing and organizing the girls?"

He nodded. "Yup."

"I'll see what I can find," she said.

AS JOE REACHED for his coat, he noticed Lucy standing in the mudroom, a look of annoyance on her face.

"Did you forget something?" she asked.

He paused as he pulled on his parka, and it came to him. "Oh, Brueggemann on Facebook. I did forget."

"Just as well," she said. "He doesn't have a page. There was nothing to find."

Joe paused while he took it in.

"It's weird," she said. "*Everybody* has a Facebook page. But not him."

"I don't," Joe said, reaching for his shotgun.

"I mean everybody *young*," Lucy said.

"Oh, thanks."

# 25

SEVEN MILES NORTH of Crowheart on U.S. 287, past midnight, Nate Romanowski broke the long silence and said to Haley, "There's an airport in Riverton with a commuter flight to Denver in the morning, where you can connect to wherever you want to go. I'll give you money for a ticket."

"Keep your money," she said. "I don't need it, and I'm not going anywhere."

He shook his head and sighed.

"You're stuck with me, dooley," she said, her jaw set defiantly.

When he didn't respond, she turned her head and looked out at the darkness and falling snow. "Where are we?"

"Out of the mountains," he said. "If you could see anything, you'd see the Wind River Mountains to the west."

"Okay."

Nate gestured to the left. "Crowheart Butte is out there. On the other side is Bald Mountain. The road goes between them."

They'd not encountered a single oncoming car for two hours.

"How do you know?" she asked. "I can't see a thing anywhere."

"I can feel it," he said.

She snorted. "And how does one acquire this skill?"

He shrugged. "It comes from experience. Climbing trees, burrowing into the dirt, watching clouds go over. You've just got to open yourself up and not clutter your mind with thinking. Have you ever skied with your eyes closed?"

"Of course not."

"Try it," he said. "All of your senses open up. You can feel the terrain through your feet, and smell how close you are to the trees. You don't have to go fast. Just try it sometime. The contours of the slope and the surroundings become clear even though you can't see them with your eyes. It's like being in a dark room. As you walk around it, you discover how big it is, where the tables are, how thick the carpet is. Sometimes, you can hear your own breath and your beating heart."

"You sound kind of nuts," she said.

"My friend Joe Pickett says the same thing."

"Maybe we're right," she said.

"Maybe. But test it out," he said softly. "Close your eyes. Crowheart Butte will come to you. You'll know where it is. . . ."

After a few minutes, she opened her eyes. "I've got nothing," she confessed.

"Practice," he whispered.


THE HIGHWAY cut through a vast carpet of foot-high sagebrush that gathered clumps of snow in the palms of its upturned, clawlike branches. But it wasn't yet cold enough on the valley floor for the road to ice up.

"You said you wanted to ride this out until we found the guys who killed Cohen and the others," he said. "We found them and put them down. Now you can go home and spend some time with your dad."

"I already did that," she said. "I said goodbye. Now I'm committed to riding this out."

"You're sure?" he asked.

"You don't sound that disappointed," she said.

"Remember the rules," he said. "I can't guarantee your safety. And I can't promise you won't see something much worse than what you saw back there."

She hesitated, and for a moment he thought she might reconsider. Instead, she said, "Just drive. You said you know where this Nemecek is located, right?"

"Yes." He nodded. "Unless that guy back there was lying or somehow tipped off Nemecek. But I don't think so, given the circumstances."

She cringed at the word *circumstances* and said, "You made that poor man back there make a call on his cell. What was that about?"

"I told him to call his team leader and tell him they'd lost Oscar and you. That you broke out of the cabin sometime during the night and they didn't know where you went. That you were on the loose and they were coming back to reconnoiter."

Haley looked over, puzzled. "Why?"

"So it would throw a huge kink in Nemecek's operation. The idea was to eliminate all the operators in Camp Oscar so they wouldn't be able to help me. But if two of you got away, Nemecek would need to figure out how to track you down before you went to the cops or the media. It throws his timetable off and threatens the entire operation."

"Did Nemecek buy it?"

Nate said, "It appears so. He got real quiet and told our operators to meet him at his command post."

"Is it possible Trucker Cap told him something in code? That Nemecek will be expecting you?"

Nate shrugged, "Unlikely, but possible. I was right there with him, and I could hear both sides of the conversation. Nemecek got very calm and cold. That's how he reacts to pressure. He doesn't scream or threaten, he just goes dead. That's when he's the most dangerous."

"So why tip him off that his plan went screwy?" she asked. "Why not just let him think everything is sailing along?"

Said Nate, "It's a diversion. I want him to coil up for a while and stew in his own juices. If he's trying to figure out what his next move will be, that family in Saddlestring might have a chance to get out of there before he turns on them. And it could give me the opportunity to get close enough to him to do some damage."

"Then let's go get him."

Nate snorted.

"What?"

"If only it was that easy."

"What do you mean?"

Nate took a few moments, then turned to her.

"He's got me right where he wants me, but he doesn't know it yet. He doesn't need to send operators to flush me out or set up traps. I'm delivering myself straight to *him*."

She gestured that she didn't quite understand. "If we surprise him, won't you have the advantage?"

"Yes," Nate said.

"But what?" she prompted.

"I'm very good at this," he said. "But John Nemecek is better. He's my master falconer, and I'm his apprentice. I don't expect to get out of this alive."

Haley slowly covered her mouth with her hand in alarm.

HE SLOWED the Jeep and edged it to the shoulder of the highway. A double reflector emerged from the dark, indicating the mouth of a two-track road that exited onto the highway. He turned on it and drove over a cattle guard and continued over a hill. On the way down the other side, the headlights illuminated an ancient wooden barn that stood alone on the edge of an overgrown field. The roof of the barn had fallen in years before, and the open windows gaped wide and hollow like eye sockets on either side of the rotting half-open barn door.

Haley sat in silence, but he could feel her eyes probe the side of his face, obviously wondering what his intentions were.

He stopped in front of the barn and kept his headlights on. Light snow sifted through the air.

"You've fired a gun," he said, killing the motor but keeping the lights on.

"Yes," she said, hesitating. "I used to go grouse hunting with my dad, but I didn't like shooting them. And Cohen took me out to the range a couple of times, but I'd rather read a book than shoot."

"Can you hit anything?"

She shrugged.

"Okay, then," he said. "Get out."


NATE FOUND an aluminum beer can in the opening of the barn—there were dozens more inside, and he guessed the structure was a meeting place for wayward ranch hands—and speared it aloft on a nail that stuck out from the weathered wood on the barn door. It was eye level, fifty yards from the Jeep.

While Haley stood in front of the vehicle shuffling her feet and hugging herself against the cold, Nate drew out the Ruger Mini-14 Ranch rifle and handed it to her. He showed her how to load a round into the chamber by pulling back on the breech-bolt feeder, where the safety was located underneath, and how to raise it to her shoulder so the stock rested against her cheek.

"It's called a peep sight," he said, touching the small steel ring near the back of the action. "Look through it until you can see the front sight, which is a single blade."

"Okay, I see it," she said.

"Find the front sight in the middle of the circle. Exactly halfway up, and centered in the circle from side to side."

"Okay."

"When you aim, think of a pumpkin sitting on a post. The post is the top of the front sight. Put that beer can right on top of the front sight, remembering to make sure it's in the center of the back circle. Make sense?"

It took her a few seconds, then she grunted.

"Keep both eyes open and squeeze the trigger."

He stepped back. He was impressed that she held the rifle firmly and the barrel didn't quiver.

The boom was sharp and loud, and the muzzle spit a tongue of orange flame.

"Wow," she said.

"You missed," Nate said. "High and to the right of the can by an inch. That means you flinched just as you pulled the trigger. Now breathe normally, don't hold your breath, and do it right this time."

"I was close."

"You don't get extra credit for trying and missing," he said. "Instead, you get killed."

"You can be an asshole sometimes," she said as she raised the rifle again.

"Relax," he assured her. "Pumpkin on a post."

The second shot ripped the bottom of the can away.

"Do it again," he said.

She fired until she'd emptied the thirty-round magazine and

the air smelled sharply of gunpowder. Hot spent shells sizzled in the snow at their feet.

Nate said, "Twelve direct hits, nine near-misses, seven bad shots because you flinched. Overall, not so bad. Just remember: breathe, relax, both eyes open."

She grinned and handed the rifle back to him. "Pumpkin on a post," she said.

He nodded while he loaded fresh cartridges into the magazine and rammed it home. "Haley," he said, "you're a very good beer-can shooter. In fact, you're a natural, as long as you remember all the steps. But I want to tell you something important, and I need you to listen carefully."

His tone made her smile vanish, and she looked up at him openly.

"Knowing how to shoot is a small part of killing a man. Too many of these damned gun nuts think it's all about their hardware, but it isn't. It's about keeping things simple."

She nodded, urging him on.

"Don't shoot unless you have a fat target. Aim for the thickest part of the target. Don't try a head or neck shot—aim for the mass of his body. That way, if you flinch a little you still hit something vital. And don't assume one shot will do it. That only works in movies or unless I'm shooting. Keep pulling the trigger until the target goes down. Then shoot him a few *more* times and run like hell. Got it?"

"Got it," she said. "I just hope I won't have to put all this advice into action."

"Me, too," Nate said, sliding the rifle back beneath the seat.

When he turned she was there, right in front of him. She reached up with both hands and pulled his head down and kissed him softly. He could taste her warm lips along with melting flakes of snow. His hands rested on her hips, and he could feel her fingers weave through his hair.

As he reached around her to pull her closer, she gently pushed him away.

"Thank you for teaching me that," she said.

"Thanks for the kiss."

They held each other in their eyes for a long tense moment. He could feel his heart beat.

"I don't know why I did that," she said, grinning and turning away.

"I do," he said, and turned her around so she was facing him. He reached down and grabbed her hips again and launched her up onto the hood of the Jeep. She collapsed back on the hood until her head was propped up against the windshield, and she looked at him with heavy-lidded eyes. Snowflakes landed on the warm sheet metal on both sides of her and dissolved into beads of moisture and he stepped up on the front bumper next to her.

"Let me get a blanket from the back," he said.

*"Hurry,"* she begged, and he felt her fingers trail off his shoulders as he rolled away.


"I DON'T KNOW what I was thinking," she said, looking down at her shoes while she cinched her belt. Fresh snow—larger flakes now but more infrequent—tufted her hair and shoulders.

"Whatever it was, I hope you think it again," Nate said, folding the blanket.

"Too much has happened," she said, still not looking up. "My nerve endings are exposed, I guess. My force field is worn out. My reserve has been blown away. I've never . . ."

"Stop talking," he said.

"It's different for you," Haley said. "In one day you kill a guy, torture another guy, and get the girl. This must seem like fucking Christmas to you."

"Only the get-the-girl part," he said.

She finally looked up and smiled. "Well, I guess that's kind of a nice thing to hear."


THEY WERE back on the highway and no more had been said since they left.

"Since it's very unlikely we'll be around much longer," Nate said, "you should know something about me. And when I'm done telling you, there won't be any hard feelings on my part if you want to get dropped off at the airport. In fact, I wouldn't blame you."

She reached over and touched his arm and turned to him, waiting.

Nate couldn't meet her eyes. He said, "Because of me, thousands of people are dead. Maybe tens of thousands."

She gasped, and her fingertips left his sleeve for a moment as she recoiled. Then, surprisingly, she touched him again.

"Tell me," she said.


AFTER THEY crossed the border of the Wind River Indian Reservation, Nate told Haley about growing up, moving around, discovering his interest in falconry, and meeting Lieutenant John Nemecek at the Air Force Academy. And the six brutal months of training to become a full-fledged member of Mark V, a secret and off-the-books Special Forces unit comprising the best special operators from the Army, Navy, Air Force, and Marines. As with the other members of the Peregrines, Nate didn't know how many men were involved, or most of their real names. Eight-man teams were assembled for specific tasks based on their skills, sent overseas to kill, cripple, and destroy targets, then broken up when they returned. Although all the operators assumed Nemecek reported directly to superiors high in the government, it was never clear who gave the orders or even which branch or federal agency had ultimate authority. It wasn't their business to know.

Peregrines operated under false identities in foreign countries, and got in and got out. Their assignments were highly choreographed and impeccably planned, and rarely failed. Nate was sent to South America, Eastern Europe, Africa, island fiefdoms in the Pacific, and the Middle East. None of his teams ever lost or left a man. There were only two missions that weren't completed successfully. Once, when their target—a Central African warlord—was tipped to their presence and the team immediately evacuated, and another instance where a team member got too intimate with locals and inadvertently blew their cover. None of the other Peregrines from that mission ever saw or heard from the operative again.

The one constant in all the operations and planning for all the Peregrines was the man who'd recruited and trained them: Lieutenant John Nemecek.

"He is the greatest falconer I've ever seen," Nate said to Haley. "He's flown every species of raptor imaginable, from kestrels to golden eagles."

Haley said, "I'm confused. What does falconry have to do with thousands of people getting killed?"

Nate drove on for a full minute before he said, "Everything."

# PART FIVE

*Falconry is not a hobby or an amusement; it is a rage. You eat and drink it, sleep it and think it. You tremble to write of it, even in recollection.*

—T. H. White, *The Godstone and the Blackymor*

# 26

THERE WAS STILL a sifting of powdered-sugar snow that held in the cold night air as Joe slid his shotgun into the cab of his pickup and pulled himself in. He shut the door and started the motor and sat for a few seconds with the engine idling, sorting out his route and hoping his suspicions about Luke Brueggemann were wrong. Lord knows, he thought, he'd been wrong before.

As he backed out of the drive onto Bighorn Road, he recalled the first time he'd heard that he'd be getting a trainee. It had been less than a month before and in the form of a departmental email sent by the assistant director of the Game and Fish Department in Cheyenne. It wasn't a request as much as an order. Joe hated orders, balked at them simply for being orders, but in this case he swallowed his consternation and remembered his own days as a trainee, and how the experience—for better and for worse—had set him on the path he had taken. Pay it forward, he had thought.

But Joe recalled that the initial email was typically terse: the trainee's name, origin, and date of arrival. No other information, and Joe didn't have additional reason to ask for more at the time. Joe knew the state system well enough to doubt whether Brueggemann had somehow infiltrated it with this end in mind. He doubted it. More likely, he thought, Brueggemann had been recruited by someone— probably his girlfriend.

Brueggemann was of the age and station in life—single, barely twenty-two, and practically penniless—that he'd likely be vulnerable to an approach, Joe thought. If sex, a future, or money were offered, few boys that age would refuse. So maybe they got to Brueggemann once it was known he'd be assigned to Joe Pickett in Twelve Sleep County.

Or maybe, Joe thought, she'd replaced the real Luke Brueggemann with a Luke Brueggemann of her own? If so, what happened to the real kid? Joe shivered at the possibilities.

Or maybe, Joe thought, he should stop letting his imagination run wild until he knew more and could actually base his speculation on a foundation of facts.

As he drove away from his home, he watched it recede in his rearview mirror. The house was lit up like Christmas, which was all the more striking because of the utter darkness all around. It looked like a beacon, every room lit up as Marybeth and Lucy and April packed for their early morning flight. The place looked so . . . inviting.

He took his foot off the gas and coasted for a moment, thinking about turning around. It wouldn't be that many hours before they'd need to gather up and go to the airport. If something happened while he was away, he'd never forgive himself.

But . . .

Mike Reed had agreed to stay until he got back. Reed could be trusted, couldn't he?

Joe swatted away his paranoia and drove on.

AS HE LET the threads of speculation hang there, one item jolted him in another direction: Brueggemann's girlfriend. All he knew about her, or thought he knew about her from Brueggemann, was that she lived in Laramie because she was a student at the University of Wyoming. And he thought about what Nate had said: *a young female*.

Which made his mind leap and his scalp contract. Joe drew his cell phone out of his breast pocket and opened it and scrolled down the speed dial until he found Sheridan's cell phone number.

The call went straight to voice mail.

"Call me the second you get this," Joe growled, "and don't turn your phone off at night."

He cursed aloud. One of the problems with every person having a cell phone instead of a landline was that if they turned their phone off, there was no way to contact them in an emergency. Sheridan was a serial offender, and like most girls her age, she was casual about keeping her phone on or properly charged up. To her, the phone was for her personal convenience—for calling or texting *out*. She needed her sleep, after all, and rarely considered the possibility of a worried father trying to call her in the middle of the night.

Joe considered letting Marybeth know of his concern but decided to let it lie for now. Marybeth had enough on her plate that very moment. He'd tell her after he'd come up with some kind of plan. Meanwhile, he sent a CALL ME text to Sheridan's phone.

Then he scrolled further down and found the name CHUCK COON and pressed send.

Coon was the special agent in charge of the FBI office in Cheyenne in southeastern Wyoming, which was only forty-five miles from

Laramie. Coon was approaching middle age but looked surprisingly youthful. He was upright, tightly coiled, and crisply professional. In a perfect world, Joe thought, Coon would be on track to move up in the Bureau to the top echelon. But in the bureaucratic and political world of the federal government, there was no assurance of his advancement. Coon, like Joe, didn't do politics well.

Luckily, Coon seemed to like the unique and sometimes bizarre challenges of living and working in a state with dozens of overlapping state and federal law enforcement agencies despite its tiny population of barely a half million residents. Joe had worked with—and against—Coon on several cases over the past few years. They respected each other. Joe had happily become a thorn in Coon's side more than once, and Coon used Joe for background and as a sounding board for all things Wyoming. Since both were family men with young daughters, they had a common bond. Coon had asked Joe never to call him at home on his private number unless it was an emergency.

Coon's phone rang four times. Joe imagined the special agent plucking it from a nightstand, reading the caller ID, and groggily making a decision whether to take it or not.

Then: "Joe, what do you want?"

"Sorry to wake you up," Joe said.

"What makes you think I was sleeping in the middle of the night?"

"You don't sound very excited to talk to me."

"It's"—Coon was likely fumbling around for his glasses before he said—"*twelve thirty-five in the morning.*"

Before Joe could speak, Coon said, "Hold on a minute."

Joe waited, assuming the special agent was padding out of the bedroom and shutting the door behind him so his wife could go back to sleep.

"Okay, what?" he asked.

"I'm sure you're tracking all the troubles up here," Joe said. "The triple homicide, the missing residents, all that."

"Of *course*," Coon said, instantly irritated. "Your sheriff asked for some technical help, but he won't let me send in the cavalry."

"I know," Joe said. "He's funny that way. Anyway, I'm starting to believe everything is connected to one man. And I'm narrowing down his motives and location. I wish I could say he's lying low, but I think he's just taking a breather until the next shoe drops."

Coon didn't speak for a moment. Finally, "You think one bad guy is responsible for all that?"

"One guy and his team. He has others," Joe said. "I don't think I have enough time to lay it all out right now. But the bad guy I'm talking about has federal connections. He's one of *you*—only on the special-operations side instead of the Homeland Security side."

"One of us?" Coon asked, doubt in his voice. "What's his name? No, let me guess: Nate Romanowski."

Joe snorted. "Not this time."

"Then who?"

Joe told him, and spelled out N-E-M-E-C-E-K so Coon could jot it down.

"Never heard of him," Coon said.

"I'm not surprised. And you likely won't find much on him, is my guess. But if you dig deep enough into the Defense Department or talk to some secret spooks, you might find out more."

"This is crazy," Coon said. "This is too much for the middle of the night. Why are you calling me with this now?"

"So you can start the process," Joe said. "And I know you've got no reason to believe me yet. But just start the process, get things going in the morning with your guys. It's Friday and you wouldn't want to wait over the weekend to get started because it may be too late. I'm thinking if official inquiries are made it might get back to the bad guy that he's got trouble. It might make him back off and we can save some lives up here."

Coon moaned the moan of a frustrated federal bureaucrat. Joe had heard it before.

"I know," Joe said. "But some of those lives might belong to my family."

*"What?"*

Joe told him about the visit to Marybeth in the library.

Coon was flummoxed. "But why would he do that? Was he trying to intimidate her?"

"I guess," Joe said. "Of course, he didn't know who he was dealing with. But it did put the fear of God in her when she considered our daughters. We're leaving for a few days in the morning."

Coon sounded genuinely concerned when he said, "You're taking your family out of the state? Jesus—this is serious."

"I wouldn't have called you otherwise," Joe said. "But I need something else."

Coon's concern turned quickly back to agitation. "What?"

"It's a personal request," Joe said, "but it may connect with everything else. Do you remember I have a daughter going to school in Laramie? Named Sheridan?"

"Yes," Coon said. "I remember her."

"I'm asking you to drive over the summit tomorrow and wake her up in her dorm room. I'll give you the hall and the room."

"Wake her up? *Why?*"

"Ask her about a new friend of hers from Maryland. A female. I'm sure Sheridan will give you her name and location. When you find this Maryland girl, check her out. Look into her background, then go see her. It should be you in your official capacity. You in your suit and tie and that FBI ID. If this girl from Maryland is who I think she is, you'll get a whole different response than I would. And be careful—she might surprise you. And find out if she's acquainted with a boy who just graduated named Luke Brueggemann. I'll spell that . . ."

"You can't just throw this crap out there and expect me to jump," Coon said. "Did you forget who I work for?"

"Look," Joe said, "trust me on this. Chuck, I wouldn't call if I didn't think it was important. This is my family and my daughter I'm talking about, plus who knows how many other innocent people will go down before this is over. I can't prove a darned thing, but we can sort it all out later. I'm not asking you to do anything unethical or illegal. I'm just asking you to rearrange your morning and get your guys in the office to start an investigation of John Nemecek. If it all pans out, you and your office will be heroes. If it doesn't, I'll be the jackass."

"Won't be the first time," Coon chuckled.

"Or the last. And as soon as I know more from my end, I'll call you. I think the pieces will start to fall into place if we force it."

Another sigh.

"I'd do it for you," Joe said. "If you ask me a favor to help your family, you know I'd do it."

"I was waiting for you to play that card," Coon said, defeated.

"I would," Joe said.

"I know you would," Coon said. "Now what was the name of this Luke kid?"


AFTER JOE closed his phone and dropped it into his pocket, he looked up and the road was suddenly filled with mule deer. He weaved around a doe and two fawns—barely missing them—and stomped on his brakes inches away from hitting a five-point buck.

Then something hit him.

Over the last week, Brueggemann had made several references Joe found discordant, but he hadn't placed any significance to them at the time. But now, in retrospect, they were odd things to hear from a Wyoming boy who claimed to have grown up in Sundance.

First, Brueggemann had asked Marybeth for another soda, instead of a soft drink or pop. More significantly, now that Joe thought about it, was when Luke said he'd done a full head mount of an "eight-point buck" and that he liked his venison bloody. In the west, hunters classified deer by the number of antler points on one side, not both. Hence a buck with a set of four-point antlers was called a "four-point," not an eight-point, like they said in the east. And no one used the term "venison." Everybody simply called it "deer meat."

He sat motionless in his pickup, breathing hard, while dozens of deer flowed around him. They were moving from the mountains toward the valley floor in a thick, shadowy stream.

JOE DROVE down dark and silent Main Street, noting that even the Stockman's Bar had closed early, and turned left on First. A single set of tire tracks marked the asphalt. Light snow hung like suspended sequins from the streetlights.

As he drove up the hill toward Brueggemann's motel, he took a side street and turned up an alley toward the building. As if he were approaching potential poachers in the field after dark, he slowed down and turned off his headlights and taillights and clicked on his sneak lights. He crept his pickup up the alley and slowed to a stop at the egress where he could see the front of the TeePee Motel parking lot but remain hidden in the shadows.

It didn't take long.

There was a sweep of headlights from the street that licked across the windshields of parked guests' cars followed by the sight of a dark crossover Audi Q7. The vehicle paused near the front doors of the motel and the brake lights flashed. Because of the darkness, Joe couldn't see the driver or any other passengers in the car.

He dug for his spotting scope and screwed the base into a mini-tripod and spread the legs out on his dashboard. He leaned into the eyepiece just as a silhouette framed the left-front door.

Brueggemann was looking out from the TeePee Motel alcove into the parking lot with a strained expression on his face. He'd changed from his uniform shirt into a dark bulky fatigue sweater, and he clutched his cell phone in his hand as if it were a grenade he was about the throw. Joe pivoted the scope until he could see Luke Brueggemann's shadowed face in full frame. He adjusted the focus ring to make the image sharp.

Then, apparently confirming who was out there, he pushed his way through the doorway.

Joe sat back away from the scope and watched his trainee stride across the wet pavement toward the Audi. As Brueggemann neared the vehicle, he did a halfhearted wave, then paused at the passenger door. Apparently getting a signal from inside, Brueggemann opened the door without hesitation and swung in.

The crossover sat there for a few moments, and Joe removed the spotting scope and folded the legs and tossed it on the passenger seat. He assumed Nemecek and Brueggemann were having a conversation, or outlining plans. After fifteen minutes, Brueggemann climbed out and went back into the building. The brake lights flashed on the Audi, and the vehicle pulled away and turned left on the street and was quickly out of view.

Left was the way to get to the mountains.

"Oh, Luke . . ." Joe whispered, shaking his head.

JOE NOSED his pickup out of the alley and turned left and hugged the building he'd been hiding behind. He slowed to a crawl before turning onto the street to make sure the Audi hadn't stopped or pulled over, but he saw no activity.

With his sneak lights still on, he drove out onto the street to give chase. The TeePee was on a rise and the road ahead dropped out of view. At the crest, he slowed again before proceeding and saw the taillights of the crossover about a quarter of a mile away. He checked the cross-streets on both sides to make sure there were no other cars, then eased his pickup down the hill. Up ahead, the vehicle he was following turned right on Main Street. When it was out of view, Joe accelerated to close the gap, then slowed again as he drove through town, over the bridge, and onto the highway. At the entrance ramp he checked both directions, assuming Nemecek would drive toward the mountains but not positive of it, and waited until he could see the single set of red lights heading west. Then he gunned it so he could keep the vehicle in view.

Because of the absolute dearth of traffic in either direction, Joe dared not turn on his headlights again. Instead, he used the faint reflections of his sneak lights from delineator posts along the sides of the road to keep himself in the center of it. He wished the snow had stuck to the pavement so he could simply use the tracks to follow, and as the elevation rose he began to get his wish. One set of tire tracks marked the snow, and far up ahead—so far he prayed the driver couldn't detect him back there—the Audi continued toward the Bighorns.

Elk and deer hunters longed for heavy snow in the mountains and foothills during hunting season. Joe knew that when local hunters saw what had happened during the night, they'd start gearing up in the morning. No doubt there were a few dozen men looking out their windows at that moment, planning to call in sick the next morning so they could get into the mountains and get their meat. As a game warden, Joe often did exactly the same thing and planned the next day accordingly. In this case, the elk and the deer and the hunters were off his radar. But he'd take advantage of the snow for tracking.

He wondered what Nemecek and Brueggemann had discussed. After all, as far as his trainee knew, Joe would pick him up early in the morning. Brueggemann had no idea Marybeth had planned the Pickett family exit.

As he drove, Joe wondered how many more operatives Nemecek had in the area besides his trainee.


THE FALLING SNOW increased in volume as he rose in elevation. Joe ran his heater and windshield wipers, and the snow made it harder to see the reflector posts as he coursed along the highway in the dark. Luckily, the tires of the Audi had crushed the fluffy snow into the asphalt and the result was two dark ribbons. Easy to follow.

He simply hoped Nemecek had no inkling he was being followed. If he did, he could simply slow down and pull over in a blind spot and wait. Joe could only hope that—as usual in his career—he was being underestimated. That Nemecek's strategy and thinking was all about finding Nate Romanowski, and determining his whereabouts. That he'd never really consider that the local game warden was tailing them with his lights out.

Joe weighed grabbing his mic and requesting backup from the highway patrol or sheriff's office, but quickly dismissed the idea. The lone highway patrol officer stationed in Saddlestring would be asleep in bed, and wouldn't be able to join in pursuit in time to provide assistance. McLanahan might have a man available on patrol, but because it was Joe making the request the call would be routed to the sheriff himself for approval. The delay and subsequent radio chatter could prove disastrous and tip off Nemecek. Brueggemann, after all, had a department-issued handheld radio and could follow the conversation.

Besides, Joe thought, he had nothing on Nemecek except his odd visit to the library and the suspicious behavior involving Brueggemann. By following them and maintaining radio silence, he thought, there might be a chance to determine the location of Nemecek's headquarters. Then, if there was probable cause, he could alert the cavalry. . . .

AS THE AUDI neared the turnoff to Bighorn Road and his house, Joe could feel his stomach clench and his scalp crawl—two sensations that always kicked in just before a fight. Instinctively, he reached down with his right hand and touched the stock of his shotgun, which was muzzle down on the floorboards.

"You take that road, mister," Joe said aloud, "and things are going to get real western real fast."

The crossover continued on without slowing down for the exit. Joe exhaled.

Twenty miles out of town, Joe got an inkling where the crossover might be headed.

So much so, in fact, that he decided he could slow down and allow the cushion to lengthen, reducing the risk that he'd be spotted. Since dark timber now formed walls on both sides of the road and he couldn't see his quarry ahead, he decided to simply stay in the tracks to see if his speculation proved correct.

If so, he'd located the headquarters of John Nemecek.

And now that he was sure of Luke Brueggemann's involvement— or whoever his trainee really was—he smacked the steering wheel with the heel of his hand.

It made perfect sense.


JOE HAD no intention of following the Audi all the way to its destination. He just wanted to make sure it was going where he thought it was. When he confirmed it, he'd return to his house and have a lot of thinking and sorting and worrying to do—while he packed.

The road narrowed, and the tracks he was following went straight down the center. The trees were so thick and close on both sides that if the crossover stopped suddenly and Joe came upon the vehicle it would be nearly impossible to turn around quickly. It wasn't much farther until the old road he guessed Nemecek was aiming for intersected the pavement.

He envisioned rounding a corner to find the Audi blocking his path, Nemecek straddling the tracks, rifle ready. Joe slowed down around the next turn, eyes straining through the darkness beyond his sneak lights, hoping to see the vehicle before the occupants of the vehicle saw him.


THE TRACKS made an abrupt turn off the old highway onto South Fork Trail, and Joe stopped his pickup. He would pursue no farther, because he now had no doubt where the Audi was headed. He was both relieved and anxious at the same time.

He backed slowly up the road he had come on, careful to keep his tires in the same tracks. If it kept snowing, the tracks would be covered and Nemecek would have no idea he'd been followed. But if the snow stopped suddenly, Joe's pursuit would be revealed as plainly as if he'd left a note.

So he ground backward in reverse, keeping his tires in the tracks, until his neck hurt from craning it over his shoulder. When he thought he'd retreated far enough from the logging road that the evidence of a three-point turn in the snow could be explained away as a wandering elk hunter, he headed back toward Bighorn Road.

HIS CELL PHONE burred a few minutes after he cleared the timber, and he snatched it out of his pocket. Joe wasn't surprised to see who was calling.

"Hi, darling," he said.

"Are you okay?" Marybeth asked.

"Okay enough," he said. "Luke is working with Nemecek. I followed Nemecek as far as the road to his camp."

"My God," Marybeth said, and he heard sincere disappointment in her voice. "He seemed like such a good kid."

"He might be," Joe said. "I'm about forty-five minutes out. Is everything okay there?"

"Everything's fine," she said. "Mike is sticking around until you get back. Every fifteen minutes or so, he goes outside and looks around. He said nobody is out and about yet."

"Good," Joe said.

"You sound distracted," she said. He didn't realize he was, but she was good at pulling things out of him.

He said, "I was thinking about something."

As briefly as he could, and with a real effort not to color the theory or worry her any more than necessary, he told her about what Nate had said about the female operative on Nemecek's team.

"Since we haven't encountered any young women that would fit that profile," Joe said, "something came to mind. . . ."

She didn't let him finish his thought. Her voice quickly rose through the scales: "A young woman, probably from the east. Sheridan's new friend is from Maryland. She doesn't know much more about her, I don't think. *The girl who wants Sheridan to go to the East Coast for Thanksgiving.* It might be her. Nemecek may know Sheridan is Nate's apprentice, and this girl might be in Laramie to keep an eye on her—*or do something to our daughter to lure Nate.*"

"Calm down," Joe said. "We don't know anything yet."

"And she won't answer her phone!" Marybeth said, clearly alarmed.

"She never does," Joe pointed out. "Really, we can't do any good getting worked up."

*"I'm not worked up!"* Marybeth shouted.

The juxtaposition of her statement with her tone gave them both pause. He waited until she came back, this time more calmly. "I could try to call a couple of her friends to go wake her up, if only I knew they'd have their phones on," she said. "Or better yet, we could call the dorm front desk or the Laramie police department."

He told her about his conversation with Chuck Coon, and she agreed that was the best way to go.

"I'm going to keep trying to get in touch with her, though," Marybeth said. "She'll have to wake up and turn on her phone eventually, won't she?"

"Yup."

"Hurry back," Marybeth said. "We'll need to leave for the airport in three hours, and you haven't packed anything."

Joe shrugged, even though he knew she couldn't see it.

"Oh," she said, "I had something to tell you when I called."

"Go ahead," he said. The road was covered with an inch of slush as he descended from the mountains into the valley, where it was a few degrees warmer.

"I looked at that book I brought home."

"Yes," he said, prompting her.

"It's a lot to digest. Did you know the idea for al-Qaeda got started in Greeley, Colorado, of all places?"

"Greeley?" Joe said, thinking of the northern Colorado city that smelled of feedlots and cattle. "Is that our connection?"

"Hardly," she said. "That was 1949. It's interesting and sick at the same time. The Egyptian named Sayyid Qutb was at the college there as a visiting professor, and he became disgusted with Western morality because he went to a barn dance! I'll tell you all about it on our plane trip."

"Okay," Joe said.

"But that's not what I found that makes me think we're onto something. I think we might know the secret of Nate: why he is how he is and how he got that way. And maybe why they're after him. The timing is perfect as far as Nate goes, and we know he was involved in some bad stuff. Listen closely. . . ."

Joe strained to hear, as she obviously found her place in the book and began to read aloud:

*"In early February 1999 . . ."*

# 27

NATE AND HALEY DROVE through Riverton without seeing a single person awake or out on the streets. It was 2:30 in the morning and the bars were closed and not even a Riverton town cop was about. For the past hour he'd filled her in on assignments he had undertaken on behalf of Mark V, and some of the things he'd seen and done. He said he used to have several passports, issued to him under different names. In fact, he said, he'd used the last clean one a month before to fly to Chicago and back under a false identity.

Before they cleared town, Nate stopped at a twenty-four-hour convenience store and filled the gas tank as well as his reserve tank. Inside the Kum & Go, he awoke the Indian night-shift clerk. He bought two large cups of coffee, granola bars, and energy drinks, and handed over five twenty-dollar bills. Although it hadn't occurred to him yet that he hadn't slept for nearly twenty hours, he wanted to stave off exhaustion when it came for him.

He climbed back in the Jeep to find Haley sitting up, wide awake. She rubbed her eyes and thanked him for the coffee, and said, "You left off in 1998."

"Do you really want me to go on?" he said, easing out onto the street. He turned north until it merged onto U.S. Highway 16. One hundred eighty miles until they hit Saddlestring.

"Yes."

"Are you sure?"

"Yes," she said. "You said Nemecek came to you with a special assignment."

IN MARCH OF 1998, John Nemecek called Nate Romanowski into his office. The building itself was a small, single-level brick residential bungalow. There was no plaque or sign out front to indicate it was anything other than one home of many at Warren Air Force Base in Cheyenne. Airmen and their families occupied the houses on either side of the bungalow. There were bicycles and wading pools in the yards up and down the street.

"HE STARTED OUT as he usually did," Nate said to Haley, "with a history lesson. In this case, it was about how important the sport of falconry was to the Arab emirs through time. How falconry was literally the sport of kings in the Arab world, and how it had almost mythical and religious significance. Unlike here, where anyone can become a falconer if they have the time, patience, and desire, in the Arab world only the royals and elite are allowed to participate. Think of it like fox hunting in England in the past—very elitist.

"The pinnacle of falconry in the Arab world is to hunt a rare and endangered bird called the houbara bustard," Nate said. "These are large birds that mainly stay on the ground, but they're capable of short flights. Some weigh up to forty-five pounds. They remind me of prairie chickens but bigger and faster. When a falcon takes them on, it's a wild and violent fight. Bustards live in high, dry country, and they're all but impossible to get close to because they live where there are no trees. Bustards can see for miles if anyone is coming. The Arabs like to watch the kill through binoculars hundreds of yards away, like generals watching a battle far from the front line. They don't eat the dead bustard or use it for any purpose. It's all about the kill.

"To me, their philosophy of falconry is perverse. They hunt their birds for the sake of killing, and it's done in big social gatherings of the upper crust. They buy raptors from around the world as if they're racehorses, and the royals gain status by having the most exotic and deadly birds."

Haley said, "How is that different from your experience?"

"Every falconer I know hunts his birds as a means of getting closer to the primitive world," Nate said. "It's a way to become a relevant part of the wild. There's nothing sweet or Bambi-like about it. It's not about status or elitism. Most of the falconers I know are barely getting by, because it takes so much time to get good at it. You can choose a family and a career or you can devote your life to falconry. They don't mix well. The only exception to that I can think of was Nemecek himself. He was able to maintain his falconry while running Mark V. He thought of himself as a royal falconer because of this strange connection he had with his birds, and I really can't blame him for it."

WHILE NEMECEK detailed the Arab obsession with falcons and falconry, Nate listened patiently and waited for the general outline of the mission ahead. Instead, Nemecek asked him about obtaining young peregrine falcons from the nest.

"AT THE TIME," Nate told Haley, "peregrines were hard to find. They were on the endangered species list, and even though there were plenty in zoos and aviaries, it was illegal to capture the wild birds. Wild birds are what falconers want, not birds raised in captivity. They're considered to be a much higher prize.

"I knew of a nest—maybe two—in Montana where I grew up, and I told Nemecek about them. He asked me if there were young birds up there, and of course I didn't know at the time, but I assumed so. Right then, without telling me anything more about the operation or explaining why there were no other team members present, he signed a travel authorization for me to fly up to Great Falls. He told me to go as a civilian, take my climbing gear, and operate under my real name."

ON A THIRTY-DEGREE spring day under leaden skies, Nate snapped on his climbing harness, threaded the rope, and backed off the edge of a five-hundred-foot cliff overlooking the Missouri River. Beneath him, car-sized plates of ice floated sluggishly with the current of the water and occasionally piled up at river bends. The northern wind was sharp and cold and teared his eyes as he descended.

He rappelled down, feeding rope through the carabiners of his harness, bouncing away from the sheer rock with the balls of his feet. Tightly coiled netting hung from his belt.

It was fifty feet down to the first nest, which filled a large fissure in the cliff face. The next was a huge crosshatching of branches and twigs and dried brush, cemented together by mud, sun, and years. It was well hidden and virtually inaccessible from below, but he'd located it years before by the whitewash of excrement that extended down the granite from the nest, looking like the results of an over-turned paint bucket.

As he approached it from above, he noted the layers of building material, from the white and brittle branches on the bottom to the still-green fronds on the top. The nest had been built over genera-tions, and had hosted falcons for forty years. Nate couldn't determine if all of the inhabitants had been peregrines, but he doubted it. The original nest, he thought, had been built by eagles.

The nest came into view, and Nate prepared for anything. Once he had surprised a female raptor in the act of tearing a rabbit apart for her fledglings and the bird had launched herself into his face, shred-ding his cheeks with her talons. But there were no mature adults in the nest. Only four downy and awkward fledglings. When they saw him, they screeched and opened their mouths wide, expecting him to give them food.

He guessed by their size that they were two months old, and would be considered eyas, too young to fly. Four young birds in a nest was unusual, he knew, since usually there were just two or three. If taken now, they would need to be immediately hooded and hand-fed until their feathers fully developed, and kept sightless in the dark so they didn't know who gave them their food. If the birds saw their falconer too early in their fledgling maturity, the falconer would be imprinted for life as the food provider and the birds would never hunt properly or maintain their wild edge. Nate didn't like taking birds this young, not only because of the work involved but because of the moral question. He no longer wanted to own his birds, preferring instead to partner up with them.

But here they were. So where was Mom? He almost wished she would show up and drive him away. He could claim to Nemecek that the trip had been unsuccessful. But Nate was in a stage of his life where he refused to fail.

He spun himself around, and the landscape opened up as far as he could see. The sun was emerging from a bank of clouds on the eastern horizon and lighting the skeleton cottonwoods below while darkening the S-curves of the river. There were no birds in the sky.

He spun back around, pulled the net from his web belt, and reached inside the nest.

FARTHER DOWNRIVER, on another cliff face, he found the second nest. He was surprised to find out it held three more birds. The seven eyas were carefully crated, and Nate drove them to Colorado, where Nemecek maintained his elaborate falconry camp in Poudre Valley near Fort Collins. For the next eleven months, the birds were slowly and carefully brought along by Nemecek and Nate. All seven turned out to be healthy, strong, and wild. All seven turned out to be exquisite killers.

When Nate finally asked what the fate of the birds would be, Nemecek was vague, except to say their presence had a national security purpose, and that Nate would soon learn what it was.

When Nate asked why no other operators had been involved in the mission thus far, Nemecek was contemptuous. He told Nate the answer to his question should have been obvious: there were very few competent master falconers in the entire country, much less Mark V. Nemecek and Nate were the only men capable of capturing, nurturing, feeding, and training the young peregrine falcons. So *of course* no others were brought in.

Nate didn't know whether to be flattered or suspicious.

"ONE YEAR LATER, in February," Nate said, "I found out. When the falcons were a year old and in prime flying condition, Nemecek and I took the seven birds with us to Kandahar in Afghanistan. We were met at the airport by a driver in a brand-new GMC Suburban and taken a hundred miles south in the desert. The driver seemed to know Nemecek by sight, and never asked for ID. There was barely a road, and the guy driving us didn't speak a word of English."

"By then," Haley asked, "did you know what your operation was about?"

"Barely," Nate said. "All Nemecek told me was we were to meet some important people who would buy the falcons from us for a minimum of two hundred and fifty thousand dollars each."

"Good Lord."

"That's what I thought, but I didn't say it. You didn't say much around Nemecek, or question his planning. You simply did what you were told. But when I saw where the driver was taking us, I was blown away."

SEVEN LARGE jetliners and two cargo planes were parked on the desert floor on a huge flat expanse of hard rubble. Arabic writing marked the tails of the aircraft. As they passed through the make-shift airport, Nate could tell from the lettering and the green, red, white, and black flags painted on the sides that they originated in the United Arab Emirates. One had a slogan painted in English on the side that read VISIT DUBAI—THE JEWEL OF THE DESERT. They continued on the poor road but the driver never slowed down. Uniformed men with automatic weapons waved them through two checkpoints and the driver didn't even acknowledge them.

This operation continued to be unlike any other Nate had partici-pated in. There were only the two of them—his superior and him. If others had been embedded, that fact was kept secret. They were trav-eling under their own names, with their personal passports. And they had no weapons. Only the birds in their special darkened crates, their personal luggage, and a single satellite phone Nemecek kept turned off in his carry-on bag.

The predominant color in all directions was beige, Nate noted. There was little green vegetation except in shadowed pockets on the sides of rock formations, and everything looked sun-bleached and windswept and bone dry. As they drove on, the terrain rose and got rougher and wind-sculpted rock escarpments stood like monuments. Nate could see the distant outline of mountains, and he was reminded of the bleak badlands of eastern Montana or western Wyoming. That impression went away, however, when the driver topped a small hill and below him he could see an elaborate desert camp.

As they approached, he was astonished by the size and number of Bedouin-style tents. Parked next to the tents were dozens of late-model American SUVs, Land Rovers, and Mercedes luxury crossovers. Uniformed men with submachine guns strapped across their chests wandered through the tents. But what struck him most were the dozens of tall wooden poles mounted in the desert next to the tents. On each of the poles was a small platform. And perched on top of each platform was a hooded falcon.


"IT WAS a bustard hunting camp," Nate explained. "The emirs flew their falcons and handlers from the UAE to Afghanistan for a hunting trip. The cargo planes brought the tents, soldiers, and vehicles. I found out later that when they struck the camp and left, the emirs left the SUVs and tents for the Taliban as payment. And they did this kind of thing two or three times a year."

"Let me get this straight," Haley said. "These rich Arabs flew private jets to Afghanistan just to hunt forty-pound birds? That must have cost them millions to stage a thing like that."

"Absolutely," Nate said. "And it's why Nemecek schooled me. So I'd have an idea what we were getting into."

"But why were you there?"

"I was there to be the bird handler," Nate said. "I assumed when we saw the camp that our mission was to gift the peregrines to some king. As tribute, since the UAE were allies and things are done different over there. I could imagine some genius in the State Department finding out an influential emir was crazy for falcons, and having the brilliant idea of delivering rare North American peregrine falcons to him as a gift. Remember, this was a year and a half before 9/11 happened. This was after the Khobar Towers bombing but before the attack on the USS *Cole* in Yemen. Al-Qaeda was at war with us, but very few of us knew it. All I knew at the time was that in the Arab world we had both friends and enemies, but that nothing was clean-cut or predictable. Some of our friends bred future enemies, paid protection money to terrorists, and killed their own people. But it wasn't my job to know which from which, or why we were over there delivering peregrine falcons to emirs. My job was to take care of the birds and show them when Nemecek gave the word."

THEY WERE housed in an amazingly well-appointed tent on the edge of the camp. Servants appeared to bring them food and drink and to help secure the bird crates.

While they waited, Nemecek left the tent with the satellite phone and didn't return for a half an hour. Nate fed the birds—they were hungry and disoriented and now of age to fly and hunt once they were released—and wondered who his boss was checking in with.

But he didn't ask, and Nemecek didn't volunteer any information when he returned.

"WE WERE invited to the largest tent that night for dinner," Nate said. "We ate roasted goat and lobsters flown in from Maine. Our host was the prime minister of Dubai, named Mohammed bin Rashid Al Khartoum, and he was fat and jolly and a wonderful host. He spoke perfect UK English because he'd gone to school at the London School of Economics and later MIT. But his interest was in the peregrines, and Nemecek deferred to me on all the questions. It didn't take long to figure out Nemecek knew this guy pretty well, and he was our contact. There were about twenty-five other guests that night. No women. After dinner they told hunting stories and laughed about things that had gone on during the day, how one of the emir's falcons missed a bustard and smashed into the ground, that sort of thing. I could understand bits and pieces of the conversation, but it wasn't unlike any hunting camp I've ever been to. They broke out the single-malt Scotch, although technically as devout Muslims they weren't supposed to drink, and it went on late into the night. I know now it was a *Who's Who* of UAE royals and underlings. Plus, there were some visiting guests in addition to us. All I remember about the guests was that several of the emirs really groveled around them, and I assumed they were locals. I guessed they were emissaries from the Taliban government, but it was only a guess."

Nate said, "One of them was tall and handsome and the other older and very intense. Both had long beards in the Taliban style— one black, one gray. The older man wore glasses and talked a lot. He kept looking at us in a way that gave me the impression he was suspicious of our being there. The tall one just smiled the whole time, as if he was enduring the stories in a good-hearted way. He seemed serenely calm. They were never introduced to us. The storytelling went on for hours, and I was bushed. It was obvious Nemecek wanted to stay, and I didn't care. I needed to feed the birds. As I said good night, the two other visitors got up and made all kinds of apologies about leaving as well. From what I could understand, they had a camp of their own a few miles away and it would take them a while to get back."

NATE THANKED his hosts and paused while two soldiers threw back the tent flap and let him out. The night was cool and dry and the stars brilliant. He paused outside and looked up, marveling at the upside-down constellations.

The two other visitors followed, and Nate stepped aside to let them pass. He nodded at them as they strode toward their car and driver. The driver, Nate noticed, eyed him coolly and thumbed the receiver of the AK-47 he had strapped across his chest. The older, intense man removed his steel-framed glasses and cleaned the lenses with his robe while the tall cool one paused next to Nate. Surprisingly, the tall man spoke in English for the first time that night.

"You're from America," the man said. "Do you watch the cowboy shows?"

Nate was confused. "The cowboy shows?"

"You know, what you call *westerns*. Cowboys and Indians."

His tone was soothing, whispery, almost hard to hear. His eyes were dark and soulful, his features thin and angular.

"Like *Gunsmoke*?" Nate asked.

The man grinned and gently clapped his hands together. Nate thought the display oddly effeminate. "*Gunsmoke*," the man said. "Marshal Matt Dillon. Miss Kitty. Doc. And that Festus, he makes me laugh. Do you remember the one where Festus went to San Francisco and thought they were trying to feed him a mermaid?"

Nate was flummoxed. He vaguely remembered it from when he was a boy. "I think so," he said.

"That one makes me laugh," the man said. "And the one where Marshal Dillon is trapped in the mine with the outlaw? Do you know that one?"

"I'm sorry. I don't."

"Did you ever watch *The Rifleman*?" To illustrate his question, the tall man pretended he had a Winchester lever-action rifle and fanned his right hand as if firing and ejecting spent shells.

"I remember that one," Nate said.

"Good show," the tall man said, and grinned. "His son was named Mark."

In the dark, the older man with glasses had reached their car. He coughed politely and insincerely. The tall man talking to Nate waved in his friend's direction.

He said, "Maybe we can talk about westerns later. Before you go back to America."

"Sure," said Nate.

The tall man bowed with a nod and turned toward his car.

"SO DID you sell the falcons to this Mohammed guy?" Haley asked.

"I'll get to that. Plus, half of them were named Mohammed. Our guy was Al Khartoum."

"Sorry," she said. "I just think of all those innocent birds from Montana sitting there in a crate halfway across the world. It kind of breaks my heart."

Nate snorted. "I wasn't crazy about the deal, either. I don't mind killing bad guys I've never met. I didn't lose a minute of sleep afterward. But those birds . . . it bothered me to leave them there, to be honest."

"Anyway," she said, a lilt in her voice to prompt him to continue.

"Anyway," he said, "you're focused on the falcons. That is the least significant part of this story."

FOR THE NEXT two days, Nate took out each of the seven peregrines one by one to demonstrate their ability. The Arabs would gather on an escarpment under a temporary cover with binoculars and long-lens video cameras as Nate drove out farther into the desert. Nemecek stayed behind with the emirs to detail the strengths and abilities of each young bird, as well as the attributes and characteristics of peregrine falcons in general.

"THE BIRDS were magnificent," Nate said wistfully. "It was almost as if they'd been born there, the way they took to the sky. There was no hesitation, and no lack of confidence in any of them. All of them were perfect aces—they performed as if they'd been bustard-hunting all their lives. Those little falcons would drop out of the sky at two hundred miles an hour and take out a bustard running full-bore across the desert that weighed four times as much. I could hear the approval of the Arabs even without using the radio.

"It was more like an air show than falconry," Nate said. "As if we were defense contractors showing our new equipment in front of rich generals who wanted to buy."

NATE NOTED that late at night, after the inevitable long dinner in the tent of their hosts, after he'd fed and secured the falcons on their stoops and tightened their hoods and gone to bed, Nemecek would gather his pack and slip outside without a word. He'd be gone for an hour or more and return silently and slip back into his blankets. Nate never asked Nemecek where he went, and Nemecek never explained.

But Nate knew that along with personal items and clothing, the satellite phone was located within the small pack he took along with him.

ON THE MORNING of the fourth day, as the wind picked up and sandblasted the fabric of the tents with the sound of angry rattlesnakes, Nemecek appeared and said, "Let's go."

They left the peregrine falcons, and the drive back to the airport through the makeshift camp and parked jetliners seemed strangely hollow to Nate. Nemecek, however, was buoyant.

When they were seated together in first class on the commercial airplane on the way home, Nemecek said, "Establishing and nurturing relationships with these people is more important than anything else. We've got billions of dollars of hardware and technology, but what we don't have is on-the-ground human intel. It's like the Jetsons versus the Flintstones, and we're the Jetsons. But that doesn't mean the Flintstones might not win in the end if we don't figure out a way to relate to them on a human level."

Nate nodded, not sure where the conversation was going.

Nemecek said, "Now all those men back there know us and respect us on a basic level. We can sell them planes and rockets and technology, but that doesn't mean they like us. But appealing to their actual wants and needs, like we did back there, puts us on a different level. We can now call on them if we need something, even if it's personal. They'll receive us in their homes and palaces. If the diplomats and the politicians can't get them to do what we want, they'll ask *us* to help out."

His commander grinned at Nate, an expression Nate had rarely seen before.

"If you think you were valuable to our government as an operator," he said, "imagine how valuable you are now. Imagine how valuable *we* are. Suddenly, Mark V is the tip of the spear in Special Forces because we know these people personally. And the Middle East is where everything will happen when the shit hits the fan."

Then he turned, still smiling, and closed his eyes. Nemecek slept for the remainder of the flight. Nate spent his time wondering what he'd just been told.

Nate's incomprehension grew deeper the next time he was called into Nemecek's bungalow.

"THAT'S WHEN he handed over two million dollars in cash to me," Nate said. "A full military duffel bag filled with bricks of hundred-dollar bills. He said it was my share."

Haley gasped.

"The peregrines performed so well there was a bidding war between the emirs," Nate said. "The final price was a half million each. Or so Nemecek said. It might even have been more."

Nate paused and said, "I've been living on it ever since."

HE TOOK the duffel bag of cash back to his quarters. He sat next to it on the bed for the entire night, thinking. How many other operations was Nemecek involved in that provided such huge payoffs? How many other Peregrines were tethered to Nemecek because of off-the-books operations that resulted in personal wealth?

*Of course* it wasn't right. Operators didn't become operators for the money. But if by doing good and valuable things for their country and risking their lives every time they went out resulted in rewards that would provide for them (if they lived) and their families for years, where was the harm? After all, the only other logical recipient of cash would be the U.S. Treasury. Might as well feed the bricks of cash, one by one, into the garbage disposal, right?

The next day, he drove back to Nemecek's bungalow to return it. Nemecek was gone, cleared out. Nate guessed he'd moved—as he often did—to one of his other small offices throughout the world.

He went back to his quarters, expecting a secure set of orders for his next operation or at least a communication from his commander. But there was nothing.

Over the next year, Nate spent a good deal of his time deconstructing the mission and analyzing everything that had occurred both at home and in Afghanistan. Because of the vertical and decentralized design of Mark V, he never saw or heard from Nemecek. That in itself wasn't unusual, except for the special circumstances of Nate's relationship with his superior officer. Nate had questions and concerns. And later, guilt.

"THE WEEK after 9/11," Nate said in a whisper, "I walked away. I didn't say goodbye to anyone, and I didn't file any papers. I didn't submit to debriefing, which was in my contract. I just threw that duffel bag in the back of my Jeep and started driving. I ended up in Montana.

"All along the way," he said, "I saw American flags on every store-front and in every yard. I remember looking out once over the prairie near Billings, way out in the distance, and seeing a single flag flying above a ranch house. The world had changed, good people had been killed and damaged, and I was partially responsible for it. And when they needed me most, I quit."

Haley had wrapped her arms around herself, and she shook her head from side to side. She seemed deeply troubled.

"I don't get it," she said. "I don't see why you just left them when they probably needed you the most. It doesn't seem like you."

Nate snorted.

"Why did you do it?" she asked. "Why did you desert our country and your service?"

Nate took a deep intake of breath. "I was young. I was stupid. I was devastated."

He turned away. "I believed in Mark V and John Nemecek. I devoted my life to the cause, and I killed human beings all over the world on their behalf. I knew what we were doing was questionable in terms of laws and treaties, but I thought it was for the greater good. But when I found out Nemecek was using the Peregrines for his own benefit, and that much of what we'd been doing was all a game, I lost faith in the entire system. I just wanted out. I couldn't look at myself in the mirror anymore, and I sure as hell couldn't go on another operation. So I went to Montana to leave Mark V and the rest of the world behind."

She asked, "And why do you say you were responsible for innocent lives lost?"

"I told you the story," Nate said, "except for the most important parts. It all became clear that week after September eleventh. I watched those buildings go down in New York and the speculation on who was responsible. Then they showed the old video of who had masterminded the attack. Until then, I didn't know."

"Know what?" she demanded, her tone shrill and accusatory.

He took a deep breath and held it. Then: "The visitor to the camp that night, the lover of westerns, was Osama bin Laden. His friend was Dr. Ayman al-Zawahiri. Together they were the heart and brains of al-Qaeda, and at the time they were putting the final touches on the 9/11 attacks."

"But how could you know that?" she asked.

"I didn't, and nobody did at the time," Nate said. "But our government wanted to kill bin Laden for things he'd done already—the USS *Cole* bombing, the embassy bombings. They were watching that camp with satellites while we were there, ready to launch cruise missiles and take him out. In the end, the reason they didn't pull the trigger was because they were afraid of collateral damage—they didn't want to be responsible for a bunch of dead princes in the desert as well."

Haley shook her head. "But you said the visitors had a camp a few miles away. They could have hit *that* camp and everybody else would have been fine."

"Exactly," Nate said.

"So how are you responsible for that bad decision?"

Nate turned his head, his eyes slitted. "Because our government man on the ground called them up each night on his satellite phone to tell them bin Laden was staying in *our* camp. So we wouldn't risk our lives and so we'd personally get rich with blood and oil money."

Haley recoiled. "Oh my God."

"Now, apparently," Nate said, "Nemecek has gone semi-private, like a lot of the old spooks have with all the defense cuts. His company is up for a massive contract to do clandestine counterintelligence, and he looks like a shoo-in, at least according to that poor bastard I got the information from back in Jackson. The skids are greased for him to make millions more and do what he's best at. His reputation in Washington is stellar because of the great work of the Mark V Peregrines. But if the staffers and senators awarding the contract knew that he did his damnedest to save bin Laden's life before 9/11 . . ."

"He'd lose the contract and his reputation and probably go to jail," Haley said, finishing Nate's sentence.

"And there's one guy who could blow it for him if this ever got public," Nate said.

"Now I understand," she said. "So your friend Large Merle? He knew?"

Nate nodded.

"What about Oscar and Gabriel and the rest back in Idaho?"

"No. But Nemecek thought they might. So he had to take them out."

"What about your friends in Saddlestring? The ones you called and told to leave?"

"No," Nate said. "But it doesn't matter."

"I don't understand something," she said. "I don't understand why you never went to the government or to the press with your story? You could have put Nemecek out of business."

"It wouldn't have worked," Nate said. "Nemecek is inside of the inside. He would have found me before I even made contact with anyone. He used every resource the government has to try to find me, which is why I went low-tech and completely dropped out of society. No credit cards, no phone, no address. But if I'd stepped forward and tried to contact someone, it would have been like signing a death warrant on us both. Very few people in the bureaucracy can operate with complete impunity. They've got to report to people and write summaries. Nemecek would have intercepted the communications within minutes and cut everything off and eliminated anyone involved.

"Believe me," Nate said, "I've spent years agonizing over this. I could never figure out a way to take him down without taking down innocents as well. I don't mind killing people who deserve it, but not those just doing their jobs. So I dropped out. I did what I could to help out a friend. I carefully made contact with a few others, like Oscar and Cohen. And look what happened to *them*."

Haley squirmed in her seat. He could guess what she was thinking.

"And now *I* know," she said.

"I tried to get you to leave," he said.

"We don't have a choice, do we? We've got to kill him and stop this."

"It's our only option," Nate said. "But an old saying keeps coming to mind: *If you're going to try to kill the king, you'd better kill the king*."

AFTER THEY'D driven a few more miles in silence, Nate looked over at Haley. He said, "It's a different version of events than you heard from Nemecek, isn't it?"

The question froze her in her seat. Even in the dark, he could see her face drain of color and her eyes fix on the windshield in involuntary terror. She looked like a frightened ghost with dark, hollow eyes.

"He told you it was me who was in business with bin Laden, didn't he? And that there was a score to settle? That's what he told all the other operators, wasn't it?"

She didn't react other than to continue staring ahead. But the fact that she didn't lash back told him everything he needed to know.

"You don't have to explain," he said. "I can figure it out. He recruited you for this operation with the story about letting bin Laden get away. Only he reversed the players and the motivation. You don't know how many others are on the team, and you don't know who they are or what they've been told. And you've spent the last few hours trying to reconcile what he told you against what you've seen and heard yourself."

He said, "I think you've got a good heart, Haley. I think your reaction to what happened to Cohen and Oscar was genuine. And I sure as hell know your passion back there with me felt real."

Her mouth trembled, and her eyes blinked too fast.

"You'll have plenty of opportunities ahead to take me out," Nate said. "And if you choose, you can probably find a way to warn Nemecek I'm coming for him. I'm not going to stop you or kill you now. I'll let fate take its course."

In a barely audible whisper, she asked, *"Why?"*

"Because I think you'll do the right thing."

She said, *"If you're going to try to kill the king, you'd better kill the king."*

He didn't ask which king.

# 28

THE PICKETT FAMILY sat in a line on uncomfortable red plastic scoop chairs in the predawn at Saddlestring Municipal Airport as the tiny cinder-block structure staggered to life. Their luggage, an assortment of mismatched suitcases and duffel bags, had been checked through by the lone ticket agent, a pierced dark-haired stocky woman of indeterminate age who had communicated via a series of grunts, and who had gone outside the double doors for a cigarette the minute she'd completed grunting as she tossed the bags on a cart.

Joe turned in his chair and watched her out there, the tiny red cherry of her cigarette bobbing in the darkness, until she returned and sulked back to her counter to check the manifest. He'd caught a glimpse of it as they checked in: only five passengers were listed. The Picketts and a local rancher named Donald M. Jones, also known as Rowdy. Rowdy Jones hadn't checked in yet.

Joe wore civilian gear and his battered hat. No uniform shirt, holster, or equipment belt. He felt lighter than air and vulnerable without his weapons and gear and sense of purpose.

Joe hadn't slept since he'd returned from following Nemecek into the mountains, and his sleep deprivation heightened his sense of despair. His thoughts were like too many large fish in a small tank—writhing and intertwining over one another, depleting the oxygen available, in search of some kind of blue-water relief.

Three locals dead. Bad Bob and Pam Kelly—missing. Nate gone, his only communication a cryptic warning to get his family out. Nemecek, planning his next move. Brueggemann's betrayal. Snow, elk hunters, *The Looming Tower*.

He thought about the community he was leaving, the residents bunkered in their homes. And he felt like a coward.

Marybeth looked over to Joe and smiled in a worried way. He knew she wouldn't be comfortable until they were all on the airplane and Sheridan had checked in with them. It was still an hour or two before Chuck Coon could get over the summit from Cheyenne to Laramie, and likely longer before Sheridan would awake and turn on her phone. Nevertheless, Joe reached out and patted his wife on her knee to reassure her, then stood up and paced behind the row of chairs. He couldn't sit still until they were all on the plane, either, he thought. His stomach churned and he had the sour taste of acid in his mouth.

They'd left Marybeth's van in long-term parking on the side of the terminal. There were only two other vehicles there, both dusted with snow—travelers who'd not yet returned. He wondered about asking Mike Reed to move the van somewhere after they'd departed, so Nemecek or one of his crew wouldn't spot it and know they'd flown away.

"Are you going to sit down?" Marybeth asked him.

"Can't," he said, wandering toward a display case on the wall that boasted faded photos of famous people who had once used the local airport, including Queen Elizabeth twenty years before to visit relatives and buy locally made saddles, and former vice president Dick Cheney en route to a wilderness fly-fishing trip. He returned to the counter and waited for the agent to look up from her magazine.

"What do you need?" she asked. He felt his anger rise from her manner.

"Just wondering who has access to the passenger lists," he said.

She shook her head, confused.

"Who keeps track of who flies in and out?"

"I do."

"I mean generally," he said, letting impatience creep into his voice. "Can anyone walk up and ask who flew out this morning?"

"Nobody ever has," she said.

He took a deep breath. "What I'm asking, ma'am, is what if someone did?"

"Nobody ever has. I just told you that."

"But if they did," he said, his voice rising, "what would you do?"

She shrugged. She looked over at his family, assessing them. He followed her gaze. Marybeth sat primly with her hands in her lap. Lucy was slumped to the side, her chin in her hand. April slouched back with earbuds plugged into her iPod.

She said, "I don't think it's public information, sir. It's nobody's business."

He glared at her. "Let's keep it that way."

She flinched and rolled her eyes in a *whatever* gesture. Then she looked over his shoulder and said, "I'll need to get you to step away from the counter, sir. The other passenger has arrived."

Joe looked over his shoulder to see Rowdy Jones enter the terminal in full western dress: boots, pressed Wranglers, massive silver rodeo buckle, string tie, fine 30X gray Stetson. He pulled a large rolling leather suitcase behind him that had been personalized with his brand burned into both sides.

"Rowdy," Joe said as a greeting, stepping aside.

"Morning, Joe," the rancher said, looking over the Picketts. "Taking everyone on a family vacation?"

"Kind of," Joe said.

"Game warden leaving during elk season," Rowdy said, grinning. "That'll get around."

JOE CONTINUED to pace. The eastern sky was lighting up into early-dawn cream. Snow crystals hung sparkling in the air. The sky looked as if it would clear soon. He looked at his watch, then his phone.

Joe listened halfheartedly as April mocked Lucy by saying, *"I'll miss my precious play rehearsal, boo-hoo."*

"April, please," Marybeth said.

Joe looked out onto the road, looking for a dark Audi crossover.

ROWDY JONES lowered himself in a chair that faced Marybeth. Rowdy commented—loudly—as white-clad Transportation Security Administration employees filed in through the doors, headed for their screening station set up in front of a small departure area.

"Five of the knuckleheads!" Rowdy said, evincing a scowl from two of the agents as they passed by. "Count 'em. Five of 'em. One per passenger. Boy, I sure feel safe now, don't you? And to think it's my tax money that's paying them. And from what I hear, they've never caught a damned terrorist. Not one!"

One of the TSA agents paused to glare menacingly at Rowdy.

Marybeth looked to Joe like she'd rather be anywhere than where she was.

Another dark fish was added to Joe's small tank. This one represented *what might have been*, back in 1999, if cruise missiles would have been launched to take out the targets who later planned and approved 9/11. Would the world be better? Would those five TSA agents even exist? Would TSA exist? Would the country still be somewhat safe and innocent and intact?

Rowdy turned back to Joe and Marybeth and said, "Make sure you don't have any tweezers on you or any liquids more than four ounces. Think about our safety!"

To change the subject, Joe asked Rowdy where he was headed.

"Europe!"

"Really," Joe said.

"Craziest thing," Rowdy said, shaking his head, "I used to have to beg folks to come and help us out on the ranch during spring and fall, when we moved cattle to and from the mountains. Literally *beg* them. Bribe 'em with a big steak dinner afterward and hope they'd show up when they said they would. Then I started *charging* tourists for the privilege. Got my son to throw up a website advertising 'Rowdy's Authentic Cowboy Cattle Drives,' and it was Katie-bar-the-door," he said.

"Fifteen hundred a person," he said, grinning, as if Joe and Marybeth were coconspirators in a scam. "And all these Easterners and Europeans are paying *me* to do what nobody around here will do anymore. Now I spend the summer ranching and taking care of these dudes, and I spend the winter visiting them in Europe. England, France, Holland, Germany . . . staying in the homes of former guests. They tell me my money isn't any good over there."

"That's quite a story," Marybeth said. Joe knew it was true.

"Saved the ranch," Rowdy said. "I don't know why I didn't think of it fifteen years ago. Hell, I finally figured out how to make that place pay, and it sure as hell isn't horses and cows. It's rich folks playing cowboy! I'm thinking about building some more cabins at the place so I can charge 'em to stay there. I used to *pay* Mexicans and provide beans and a bed, and now I can *charge* folks for the same privilege."

Rowdy looked up as the front door opened. Joe wheeled around in his chair, tense. But instead of John Nemecek, it was the two pilots, each pulling along a battered wheeled bag. They were very young, and their uniforms helped only a little, Joe thought.

"They look like they're Sheridan's age," Marybeth whispered to Joe.

Or military age, Joe thought, feeling his insides clench. But the pilots nodded to a couple of the TSA agents and addressed them by name. They were familiar with one another, and this was obviously a daily event. Joe sighed in relief but couldn't sit any longer and listen to Rowdy. Rowdy was a fine man and a good guy, but Joe was too nervous and guilty and paranoid to relax.

"I'll be back," he said to Marybeth.

"Man looks like he's got ants in his pants," Rowdy said as Joe walked to the far end of the terminal to look at the old photos.


AGAIN, Joe checked the road out front. No Audi. He checked his phone. No call or text from Sheridan. He tried her number again and it went straight to voice mail.

There was a high whine outside. He went to the window that overlooked the tarmac to see that the pilots were bringing the airplane around from its hangar on the other side of the field. It was a small Beechcraft 1900D turboprop that held nineteen passengers. All over Wyoming, like angry bees, the little planes delivered people to Denver International Airport, where they could board large jets for other places.

The aircraft swung around and parked, and the pilots killed the spinning propellers but kept the engines running. In a moment, the door opened and a spindly staircase accordioned out. Joe watched as the surly counter girl, now in an overlarge parka, tugged the luggage cart out toward the plane. The copilot stood near the back of the aircraft to help her toss the luggage inside. He could see Lucy's colorful suitcase and April's bulging duffel bag. It seemed to Joe the girls had packed everything they owned.

Beyond the small airplane, the serrated profile of the Bighorn Mountains, fresh with snow, dominated the horizon. Up in those mountains was Nemecek's headquarters. And Joe was flying away. As he stared, his stomach churning, he saw a lone falcon soaring high in the cirrus clouds, moving so slowly as to almost be motionless.

He wished he could talk to Nate, tell him what he'd found out.

Because of the whine of the aircraft, he didn't hear Marybeth approach, and he jumped when she placed her hand on his shoulder.

He turned.

"Joe, are you all right?" she asked, tilting her head slightly back, probing his face with her eyes.

He paused for a moment. "No, I'm not."

She couldn't hide the disappointment but tried. "I know how you feel about these little planes."

"It's not that," Joe said. "Think of how many times he helped me. How many times he helped *us*," he said, nodding toward Lucy and April. "Now, when he's the one in trouble, I'm flying away."

"But he wants you to," she said. "He said it himself."

"Nate doesn't always know what's good for him," Joe said.

She shook her head and said, "This is a different level they're playing at. These are different kinds of men. You said it yourself, Joe."

"Doesn't mean I can't help," he said. Her inference stung.

"But he doesn't want your help," she said, frustration showing.

"He wants you to go with us and watch over this family. That's what he admires about you, Joe. You're not like him."

Joe smiled bitterly. "I've got to see this through," he said.

Marybeth reached out to him and cupped her hands around his face and took a long moment. Then she said, "It won't do me any good to argue, will it?"

"Nope."

"If you get yourself hurt or killed . . ." She didn't finish the thought. There was no point.

Joe said, "I'll see you in California in a day or so. We can use a vacation we can't afford."

She smiled, but there were tears in her eyes.

He said, "Go into the bathroom and compose yourself, honey. We don't want the girls to see you crying. I'll go say goodbye to them and tell them something came up."

She nodded, then kissed him on the cheek.

"I'll be careful," he said. But he wasn't sure what he meant.


FROM INSIDE Marybeth's van, Joe watched his wife and daughters troop across the tarmac toward the waiting plane. Rowdy Jones followed them. At the base of the accordion stairs, Marybeth turned and gave him a little wave.

He waved back but wasn't sure she could see him.

When the airplane was in the sky and its wings tipped and it banked to the south toward Denver, he started up the van. Now that they were safe, the fish tank of his mind got bigger. He could see the individual fish, the individual problems. He began to make a plan.

He had no idea if it was a good one.

# 29

ALTHOUGH NATE ROMANOWSKI had been gone only a week from Twelve Sleep County, it seemed to him as he cruised the untracked morning roads of the Wind River Indian Reservation that he'd been gone forever. He drove by Bad Bob's, noting that although it was too early to have opened, there was a troubling and vacant feeling about the place, indicating no one was there. Bob's pickup was parked as always on the side of the building, but it was covered with snow. There was no sign of life from inside the store or Bob's house behind it.

Same with Alice Thunder's place. No woodsmoke from the chimney or exhaust fan on the roof. Newspapers, both the Saddlestring *Roundup* and the even smaller reservation weekly, gathered on the front porch sheathed in translucent orange tubes.

"She's gone, and she's been for a week or so," Nate said. "Good."

"Who's gone?" Haley asked, following his gaze toward the small frame house.

"Someone I care about," Nate said. "Everybody I was in contact with is in danger. That's why I warned them to get away."

Haley didn't respond but seemed to be looking inward, thinking. He didn't ask about what.


NATE CRUISED up Bighorn Road fifteen minutes later. As he did he checked his mirrors repeatedly and slowed down on the crest of each hill before descending. His weapon was on his lap.

He nodded as he drove by Joe Pickett's house. Joe's Game and Fish pickup was parked on the side of the garage, also blanketed with a thin coat of snow. A set of tracks emerged from beneath the garage door: Marybeth's van. They were gone.

"For once," Nate said, "Joe seems to have listened to me when I told him something."

"He's gone?" Haley asked.

"Looks like it. They've got kids, and the place would have been a beehive this time in the morning before school."

He stopped at Joe's mailbox a quarter-mile from the house and placed an object inside. When Haley gave him a quizzical look, he said simply, "I want him to know I was here."


"OKAY," HE SAID, swinging off the pavement onto a rough two-track directly away from the Pickett house, "the field has been cleared and the operation is under way."

He could feel Haley's eyes on him as he drove toward the base of Wolf Mountain. They crashed through a thick set of willows where the branches scraped both doors and emerged in a small white alcove. There was brush on all four sides of them, no way to see out, and no way to see in from the road.

He looked sternly at her and killed the engine. "Come on," he said.

Unexpected fear flashed in her eyes. She hesitated for a moment, then climbed out.

He chinned for her to move to the front of the Jeep, and when she did he raised the .500, then spun it with his index finger through the trigger guard and rotated it so the muzzle was pointed at his chest and the grip was offered to her.

"Take it," he said.

"Why?"

"Just take it," he said more gently.

She did. He stepped back three steps, his boots crunching in the light snow.

He said, "If you're going to kill me, I want you to do it now."

She stood there, uncomprehending, her eyes puzzled.

"In an hour or so, I'm going after John Nemecek," Nate said. "I'm going to hit him hard and fast and right in his face. The tactic is speed, surprise, and overwhelming violence. You don't have to participate, and I may not want you involved. But Haley, if you're going to bushwhack me, or try to warn him, I want you to do it now. Aim and fire. Blow a hole in me no one could recover from. Do it and get it over with now, not later."

She held the gun out away from her, pointed vaguely at his waist. But not yet raising it. Their eyes bored into each other's.

"Why are you testing me like this?" she asked. "Why are you doing this?"

"I'm giving you your chance to be a hero. Do it now, if you're so inclined. I have no other weapons, and I couldn't get to you in time to stop a shot. This is your chance."

"Why, Nate?"

He paused. "I can handle the enemy, and I salute him if he can get the better of me in a fair fight. But I hate betrayal. I need to know one way or the other with you."

After a few beats, she shook her head and let the weapon drop to her side.

"You know what," he said, as he took the .500 from her and fed it back into his holster, "I've never done that before. Given my weapon to someone."

He noticed her hands were trembling and he covered them with his own.

"This might work out," he said.


"IT'S TOUGH when the foundation for your loyalty and beliefs crumbles away while you're in the building, isn't it?" he said, as they drove back out through the wall of willows toward the road.

"Yes," she said.

She told him how Nemecek had found her after she'd enlisted in the Army and had gone through basic. How he'd selected her for the Peregrines and tested her character and strength. He knew her father was a lifer in the military, and that she understood the culture and the sacrifice necessary to ascend to Special Forces. She'd participated in two overseas operations—one in Bosnia, one in Iraq—before Nemecek came to her and explained that he was creating the strike team on the outside and that he had a very special role for her to play.

"He told me that same story about Afghanistan," she said, "but he reversed the blame, just like you said. There wasn't a single operator, once they heard what happened, who didn't want your head. Me included."

"He's persuasive," Nate agreed.

"And he's evil and cynical," she spat, "because he uses our patriotism and loyalty for his own benefit. Now that I know, I question both those missions I went on. Were they to help defend our country or to settle a score or eliminate competition for Nemecek? I just don't know."

"So it was you who found Merle," Nate said. It wasn't a question.

"Yes, but I didn't kill him. I'd already flown back to Idaho."

"Merle was my friend."

"And I'm sorry. I had no idea what they were going to do to him, and I was sick when I found out what happened."

WHEN THEY hit the highway, Nate turned back toward town instead of toward the mountains. It took her a second to realize what had just happened.

"Aren't we going the wrong way?" she asked.

"Yes."

"Why? You aren't going to get rid of me somewhere, are you?" she asked angrily.

"We need a new car," he said, and didn't explain any more.

AS THEY neared the town limits, he asked, "Do you know how many are on the team besides you?"

"No," she said. "He never told me. You know how it is. You get your assignment and maybe see or meet one or two other operatives, but no one knows the entire plan or all the players. I only knew my job, which was to seduce Gabriel and Merle and infiltrate that compound in Idaho. Nemecek said you'd be in contact with them, and when you were, I was to tip him off. I never knew he planned to use me to kill Oscar and Cohen and the rest. I didn't have a clue. All I knew was that when you showed up, I was to alert him."

"You didn't?" Nate asked.

"I never got a chance," she said. "And by that time I was having doubts about everything he told me, to be honest. I came to really like and admire Gabriel and Oscar and the rest. They weren't anti-government, like Nemecek had led me to believe. They were pro–American individualism. They were patriotic and honest, and they were straight shooters. I kept waiting to hear someone go on a rant about revolution or something, but it never happened. They just wanted to be left alone. I can empathize with that."

Nate said, "You never knew where Nemecek's headquarters was?"

"No," she said. "I had only one assignment. I didn't know they were going to *kill* everybody."

She looked away sharply but not before he caught a glimpse of tears in her eyes. "Damn it," she said, "I don't want to cry. *Goddammit.*"


NATE PULLED into Hinderaker's Used Cars on the south end of Main Street just a few blocks from the Burg-O-Pardner. As he entered the lot, Hinderaker—the bespectacled proprietor who had his official third-generation GM dealership dissolved when the government took over the company—emerged from a single-wide trailer that now served as his office. He shot his sleeves out so his cuffs emerged from his jacket, worked up a friendly grin, and ambled out into the drive so Nate couldn't help but see him.

Haley stayed inside the Jeep while Nate strode through the rows of used vehicles, Hinderaker on his heels.

Nate paused at a white five-year-old SUV.

"You won't be able to beat that deal," Hinderaker said. "Plenty of miles but all highway miles. Are you thinking of trading in the Jeep?"

Nate fixed his icy blue eyes on Hinderaker and noted how the man took an involuntary step back.

"Maybe," Nate said. "How's the four-wheel drive?"

"Great!" Hinderaker said. "Probably never been used."

Nate paused, not blinking. He knew he was making Hinderaker uncomfortable.

"Mind if I try it out?" Nate asked in a whisper.

Hinderaker started to object. *No problem taking it for a test drive,* he said. *No problem at all.* But company rules required a salesman to go along, and Hinderaker was on the lot all alone until his salesmen showed up at eight. . . .

Nate said, "There's my Jeep. I'll leave it here as collateral with the keys in it. Registration and pink slip are in the glove box."

Hinderaker sighed.

By the time Nate walked to the Tahoe, out of Hinderaker's sight, Haley had transferred the gear and weapons from the Jeep.

AS THEY cleared Saddlestring once again en route to Crazy Woman Creek in the Bighorns, Haley said, "White Tahoe. Got it. That's what they all drive."

TWO MILES past the Bighorn National Forest sign, Nate gritted his teeth and spoke through them.

"There's this condition elite falcons get when all they can think about is to fly, fuck, and fight. It's called *yarak.* . . ."

# 30

WHILE JOE pulled on his uniform in the darkened bedroom, he fought the growing feeling of dread that seemed to fill his empty house. It was odd being there without Marybeth and the girls, and he questioned his decision to stay, although not the reason for it. But there were so many loose threads, so many possible scenarios. . . .

He retrieved his weapons from his gun safe—two long rifles, his shotgun, and his holster—and went back outside to brush the snow off his green Ford Game and Fish Department pickup.

He swung out onto Bighorn Road—noting several sets of tire tracks already there—and did a mental inventory of his gear. Everything he might need was locked in the equipment boxes in the bed of his truck. Or at least he hoped so.

For the hundredth time that morning, he checked his cell phone for messages from Sheridan, Nate, Brueggemann, or Chuck Coon. Nothing.

He speed-dialed Coon, and after four rings the special agent picked up. "What now, Joe?" He sounded irritated.

"Is everything under way?" Joe asked.

*"Yes, sir!"* Coon said with sarcasm. "I've left urgent instructions in

my office for them to start researching this Nemecek guy and rattling cages to find him, and I myself am in my comfortable government sedan just about to leave the city limits en route to Laramie to scare your daughter's friend."

"Great," Joe said. "Thank you. Will you call me the minute you can?"

"Probably," Coon said.

"There's something else," Joe said, ignoring the epic sigh from Coon's end when he said it.

"Of course there is," Coon said.

"I got more information last night after I talked to you. Something big is about to happen up here, I think—a major break in the case. I'll know within a couple of hours if we've located the bad guy. So in the meanwhile, can you get a team together and have them ready to fly up here on your chopper? We'll need lots of firepower."

Coon moaned and said, "At least it's just a small favor you're asking."

"Yeah, I know."

"Look," Coon said, his voice rising, "I can't put together a request for that kind of operation without probable cause, and you haven't given me any. I need an official request for assistance from your sheriff or police chief. You know that, Joe. I can't just send my jackbooted *federales* on raids all over the state of Wyoming."

"I didn't say send them," Joe said. "I asked you to get them *ready*."

"We need an official request, Joe. You know how this works."

"Okay," he said, frustrated. "I'll work on that."


THE USUAL VEHICLES were parked outside in the lot of the Burg-O-Pardner, and Joe turned in beside them. This was the every-morning coffee gathering of the movers and shakers of the city and county. Discussions were off the record, and the public was never informed of what business was transacted. It had been going on since Joe first moved to the area, and he'd never been invited to coffee and wouldn't have shown up if he was.

He strode past the line of vehicles—the chief of police's SUV, the mayor's Lincoln Town Car, the one-ton diesel pickup belonging to the county commissioner, and Sheriff Kyle McLanahan's stupid old beater truck, which he tapped on as he walked past.

Inside, it was warm and close, and the small restaurant smelled of coffee, bacon, and burned toast. Five beefy faces all swung in his direction when he entered, and the conversation stopped. The sheriff had come with Deputy Sollis, who smirked at Joe with his pig-like eyes.

Joe said to Sheriff McLanahan, "Got a minute?"

McLanahan looked tired and worn-out, despite the early-morning hour. There were dark rings under his eyes, and his skin seemed sallow and gray.

"I'm eating my breakfast," McLanahan said. "Can't you see that?"

Joe nodded. "Yup."

"Hold your horses and I'll be with you when I'm done," McLanahan said, dismissing Joe and stabbing the point of a piece of toast into his egg yolk.

Joe asked no one in particular, "How many days until the election?"

McLanahan looked up, scowling. The others looked from Joe to the sheriff and back again.

After a beat, McLanahan made a show of tossing his toast down on his plate and pushing away from the table. Sollis pushed back from the table as well.

"Not you," Joe said to him.

The deputy looked to McLanahan and was hurt when the sheriff nodded for him to sit back down.

"Just a few minutes of your valuable time," Joe said, stepping aside so the sheriff could walk past him toward the door.

OUTSIDE, McLanahan turned around and put his hands on his hips and glared at Joe like a bull about to charge.

Joe said, "You know I support Mike Reed for your job, right?"

McLanahan nodded slightly.

"So you know it would be better for Mike if you continued to screw up all these investigations and nobody got caught or arrested, right?"

McLanahan's face flushed and he looked like he was about to take a swing, but he growled, "Get to your point, Pickett."

"Appreciated," Joe said. "I need you to do three things this morning, and I mean this morning. If you do them all, we might just crack this thing and get the guy responsible for all the crimes around here. If you don't, we can be pretty much assured of Sheriff Mike Reed and your unemployment."

McLanahan didn't move, but he didn't object.

"First," Joe said, "you need to assemble your SWAT team as fast as you can. Make sure Mike Reed is on it."

McLanahan did a little head bob—not an overt agreement but more of an *I-acknowledge-that-you-just-said-something-but-I'm-waiting-for-more* gesture.

Joe said, "Do you want to get out your notebook and write these things down?"

"I think I can remember them, goddammit," McLanahan spat.

"Okay, second, get the SWAT team over to the TeePee Motel, room 138. The target is my trainee Luke Brueggemann."

The sheriff arched his eyebrows at the name.

"You remember him," Joe said. "He was with me when you called me down to identify the murder victims."

"I remember," McLanahan said. "A young pup—a little wet behind the ears."

"That's him," Joe said. "But he isn't who he seems. You need to get him in custody and start sweating him. Find out who he's working for. Confiscate his phone and turn it over to your best tech people to find out who he's been calling and texting. But most important, get him behind bars for the rest of the day so he can't warn anyone or muck anything up."

McLanahan shook his head. "I can't just arrest a guy and hold him without charges."

"You forget who you're talking to," Joe said, and laughed. "You do it all the time. And besides, I'm sure I'll be the one to press charges against him."

The sheriff looked away for a moment, then back to Joe with a squint in his eyes.

"Why do we need a SWAT team to bring him in? He don't look like much."

"Because he's not who he says he is, I told you that," Joe said. "He's got weapons and he may be highly trained. You don't want anyone to get hurt, do you? Hit him fast and hard, and assume he's dangerous."

McLanahan shook his head as if he couldn't believe how ridiculous Joe was acting.

"Plus," Joe said, "you might need that assembled SWAT team later this morning. I think I know where our bad guy is located. Once it's confirmed, I'll give you the word."

"Bullshit," McLanahan said. "Tell me what you know."

Joe shook his head. "Not until I'm sure."

"Damn you, this is my county. You can't be running your own deal here. I've got jurisdiction and you know it."

Joe took a step toward McLanahan, which surprised the sheriff.

"What I know," Joe said, nodding toward the restaurant where Sollis stood watching them from inside the window, "is you've surrounded yourself with thugs and idiots. That's why I want your assurance that Reed will be on the team this morning, so there's at least one competent officer. And make sure you tell them all to stay off the radio. Brueggemann and others are likely monitoring your frequency. He'll know you're coming, and we don't want that.

"And if you send your goons out there before I pinpoint our bad guy, you could tip him off or get your goons killed. Or get my friend killed. Or get me killed."

"Your friend?" McLanahan said, perking up. "Romanowski's involved?"

"I'm not sure yet," Joe said. "But if he is, I don't want you risking his life."

"You're really pissing me off," McLanahan said. "I don't need to do anything if I don't want to. This is my county and my investigation."

"Understood," Joe said. "But imagine what people will say about you if everything explodes today and you decided to sit it out. I can't imagine that would help your reelection chances much."

McLanahan glared at Joe and then surprised him with a long, slow grin.

"You think you've got it all figured out, don't you?" he asked.

"Nope," Joe said, "not at all. I just know that being sheriff is the only thing you know how to do because you'd get eaten up in the real world. You want to keep this job as if your life depended on it, which in some ways it probably does."

The smile vanished.

"You said there were three things," McLanahan said, his tone flat.

"That's right. Call the FBI in Cheyenne and request assistance immediately. Tell them you might have a firefight up here and you need a federal strike team."

McLanahan turned away and stomped his foot in the slush.

"I'll take that as a yes," Joe said.

After a few smoldering moments, the sheriff said, "If this doesn't all work out, I'm holding you personally responsible. You better understand that. I'll hold a press conference and name names, and the governor and your director will hear from me."

Joe shrugged. "If it *does* work out, you might have a chance of being sheriff again, as miserable as *that* will be for everybody."

As McLanahan fumed, Joe walked back toward his pickup. "Keep your cell phone on and stay close to the radio," Joe said over his shoulder. "I'll call you as soon as I know if you need to send your goons in."

"Don't tell me what to do," McLanahan growled.

Joe said, "I just did."


JOE CLICKED his radio over to the county frequency while he drove through town toward the mountains. He wanted to monitor traffic as well as he could, and hoped the arrest of Brueggemann would go down as smoothly and safely as possible. And that he wouldn't hear a word about it until the arrest was made.

Then he called Mike Reed on his cell phone and woke Reed up.

"You're supposed to be on a plane," Reed said sleepily.

"Maybe tomorrow," Joe said. "But in the meanwhile, I need to let you know what's going on and apologize to you in advance."

"Apologize for what?" Reed asked.

Joe sighed and told him the story. There was silence on the other end.

Finally, Reed said, "Don't apologize, Joe. If we get the bad guys, it's all worth it, whether I win or not. McLanahan's still a fool, no matter what happens."

"Thanks, Mike."

"Well," he said, "it sounds like I better get dressed and drag my butt into the office."

HE SAW a few elk hunters road-hunting on his way up Bighorn Road. When they saw his green truck, they pulled over to be checked, but he waved and kept going.

His plan was under way, but he didn't trust McLanahan not to figure out a way to screw it up.

He looked at his watch and guessed Marybeth and the girls would be able to see the tentlike architecture of Denver International out the window of their Beechcraft.

And he wondered where Nate Romanowski was, and hoped his friend would call. Immediately.

For the second time since he'd left the airport, he drove past his house. Unlike the last time, though, Joe noted a set of tire tracks that veered off the road in the snow near the mailbox, and large boot prints going to and from his box.

Since it was much too early for mail, Joe stopped, left his pickup running, and got out. The boot prints looked familiar, and a rush of excitement shot through him.

Joe opened the door of the mailbox and saw the glint of bronze inside. He reached in and grasped the thick, heavy cartridge between his fingers, and read the stamp on the back: .500 WYOMING EXPRESS FA. The FA stood for Freedom Arms, where the revolver and the cartridge were manufactured.

He slid the cartridge in the front pocket of his Wranglers as he strode back to his pickup.

*This is it*, he thought.

# PART SIX

*The quality of decision is like the well-timed
swoop of a falcon which enables it to strike
and destroy its victim.*

—Sun Tzu

# 31

JOE DROVE through Crazy Woman Campground, where he'd first encountered Luke Brueggemann. There were a few hard-side camper trailers in tucked-away campsites. As he passed one, several hunters were lashing camo packs onto the backs of ATVs with bungee cords. The hunters looked up, saw the green pickup with the game warden inside, and stopped what they were doing. One large man with a full beard and a coffee mug in his paw instinctively reached for his wallet to pull out his elk license and ID. Joe tipped the brim of his hat to them as he drove slowly by.

*Catch you next time,* he thought.

The morning sun had yet to soften or melt the snowfall from the night before in the deep timber. There were three to four inches of it covering the two-track that exited out the back of the campground. At least one ATV was ahead of him, marked by wide tracks and knobby impressions in the snow.

The road got rougher less than a half mile from the campground as it rose up into the trees. Joe reached down below the dashboard and clicked the toggle switch to four-wheel-high. The old road was overgrown and little used since the Forest Service had placed a moratorium on cattle grazing on federal leases high in the mountains, and it no longer appeared on topo maps of the area. But local hunters and poachers knew of it, as did Joe, because it was a back route along the side of the mountain that eventually emptied onto a plateau overlooking the South Fork of the Twelve Sleep River. Below the plateau was the location of the eleven outfitter camps. They were strung out along the river, each three to four miles from the next. The camps were accessed by the South Fork Trail, which loosely followed the bends and contours of the serpentine river.

The logging road Joe was on paralleled the South Fork Trail but on the other side of the mountain, and the two roads never crossed the water and intersected.

Joe thought of the conversation he'd had with Luke Brueggemann that first day when he showed the trainee the locations for the camps. Ten were occupied by familiar local outfitter names, he told Brueggemann. One was unfamiliar.

Because the permits for the camps were issued through the local office of the U.S. Forest Service and not Joe's agency, there was no way for Joe to look up the names of the permittees. Although the USFS was supposed to forward the list of outfitters every year, a combination of bureaucracy, other priorities, and general malaise that formed between state and federal agencies usually delayed the arrival of the list until well after hunting season, when it did Joe no good. But he wished he could see the list now. Especially the new permittee who had obtained Camp Five.

Joe realized he'd misread Brueggemann's reticent reaction to inspecting the camps that morning, assuming it had to do with riding horses up to them. But now Joe understood, or thought he did. Because it had to do with who had set up in Camp Five. Brueggemann, Joe guessed, was wary because he was taken by surprise by the plan and wanted to alert the occupant, but it would be difficult to do on horseback with Joe there, not to mention they'd be in and out of cell phone coverage. How relieved Brueggemann had been that morning when the ride got called off, Joe recalled. Now it made sense, and it had nothing to do with his horses.

THE TREES closed in on the old road the higher Joe climbed his pickup. Boughs heavy with snow dumped their loads on the cab of his pickup as he brushed under them. He picked his way slowly and cautiously up the road to avoid getting stuck or hitting a fallen tree obscured by the snow, but also to keep the engine whine of his pickup as low as possible.

He had no radio or cell phone reception so deep in the timber, and he checked both periodically. On top, he knew, he would break through the thick trees and emerge above the timberline, where he might catch a signal before plunging back down the other side.

He took a slow blind corner to the left through the trees and was surprised to see four massive bull elk barreling straight toward him down the road, their antlers catching glints of morning sun, their nostrils firing spouts of condensation, their eyes white and wild. He stomped on his brake pedal as one of the bulls nearly crashed into his grille but spun to the right at the last second and crashed headlong through the brush and timber on the side of the old road. The three others—a magnificent six-by-six, a five-by-five, and a young spike— all followed. Even with his windows closed to prevent snow from coming inside the cab, Joe could hear the sharp cracking of branches as the bulls barreled down the mountainside, kicking up pine needles and clumps of dark mulch in their wake.

Just as suddenly as the appearance of the elk, a red ATV—the vehicle that had gone up the road before him—and two hunters roared around a blind corner ahead in pursuit of the elk. The driver was bent over the handlebars and the passenger behind him had his rifle out and pointed forward as if his plan had been to shoot from the moving vehicle. When the driver looked up and saw the green pickup, his mouth dropped open, but he stopped quickly and started a long skid in the mud and snow that came to a halt a few feet from Joe's front bumper.

For a moment, Joe glared through his windshield at the driver and the shooter. The driver, a thick and wide dark-haired man with a weeklong hunting beard, flushed red with anger and trepidation. The shooter, who looked to be a younger and hairier version of the driver, was simply peeved.

Because the trees on each side of the road were so thick and close, neither vehicle could proceed without the other getting out of the way.

Joe sighed and opened his door and climbed out. He clamped his Stetson tight on his head and indicated for the driver to kill his motor, which burbled loudly like a Harley-Davidson wannabe.

The driver reached down and turned the key, and suddenly the forest was still, except for the distant sound of branches snapping and breaking as the elk thundered farther and farther away down the hillside.

He could hear the shooter growl a colorful stream of curses.

"How's it going, guys?" Joe asked.

"Just great," the driver sighed, "until you showed up. We've been up here busting our ass looking for elk for seven days without seeing a goddamn one, and then last night it snows and we ride right into them."

"Yup, I saw 'em," Joe said, indicating the churned-up path in the snow where the elk bolted into the timber.

"Then you showed up and fucked it up," the shooter said, sitting back and propping the rifle on his thigh, the barrel in the air.

Joe nodded. He'd found over the years that his silence often produced confessions and was more effective than talking.

After a few beats of Joe simply looking at them, the driver said, "I guess we were acting kind of stupid chasing them like that."

Joe nodded.

"And I guess my son here shouldn't be trying to pop them from the back of a four-wheeler."

"Nope."

"And I *think* we're still in our hunting area," the driver said, raising his palms in an exaggerated way. "At least I hope so. It's harder than hell to tell sometimes. I mean, it ain't like you guys mark where one area ends and the other one starts."

The shooter got quiet when he finally realized they might be in trouble.

Joe said, "Chasing wildlife is a violation; so is hunting them from a moving vehicle. And if you think you're still in Area Thirty-four, well, you left it about a mile back."

The driver took a deep breath as if to challenge Joe, then thought better of it and said, "Well, we're damned sorry if we fucked up." He thought better of his language and said, "I mean, *screwed* up."

Joe said, "Yup."

The father sighed. "You gonna write us up?"

Joe didn't answer directly. He asked, "How far did you two go up the road this morning?"

The father looked worried, as if he was trying to figure out if they'd committed additional violations that morning. Finally, he said, "Just a couple miles. That's where we jumped the elk. They took off running down this road and we followed their tracks."

Joe nodded. "You didn't go up far enough to get to the top? To see over into the river valley on the other side of the mountain? Where the outfitter camps are located?"

"Not today," the shooter said quickly.

Joe thought he said it in a way that implied there was more to the story. "But you've been up that far this week?"

The father and son exchanged glances.

"What aren't you telling me?" Joe asked amiably.

After a beat, the father turned back around and said, "Up until yesterday, we was hunting with my brother-in-law Richie. He said he had to go back last night to do some stuff at home. Richie is kind of a pain in the ass, but he knows this country up here like nobody else."

"Anyway . . ." Joe prompted.

"Richie likes to hunt alone," the father said. "He knows of some old miner cabin up there, and he likes to go up there by it and sit and glass the meadows with binoculars to see elk. He sits for hours up there, just looking around. He usually gets a nice bull that way. But something happened the last time he went up there. When he came back down, he looked fucking spooked. We asked him what happened or what he saw, but he just made up some bullshit about having to get home. He just packed up his gear and left us up here. We never could get him to tell us what happened."

Joe felt a twinge in his scalp. "When was this?" he asked.

"Yesterday afternoon," the father said. "He left last night before it started to snow. I'd normally say he'll be back up soon because of this snow, but the way he left, I kind of wonder. It was just weird. Richie's an elk-hunting fool, and I've never seen him just want to up and leave like that."

Joe withdrew the notebook from his breast pocket and asked the father for Richie's full name, address, and contact numbers. Neither the father nor the son knew much more than Richie's last name and the part of Powell, Wyoming, he lived in, but the driver said his wife had those details. Joe closed the notebook. He knew that, if necessary, it was enough information to find Richie in a state with as few people in it as Wyoming.

"You gonna call him?" the son asked Joe.

"Maybe."

"Tell him he still owes me for that case and a half of Coors he drank up here."

"I'll try to remember that," Joe said, sliding the notebook back into his uniform shirt.

He left the father and son wondering what was going to happen next and went back to his pickup. No cell signal. No radio reception. Joe dug a card out of the holder in his glove box and walked back to the hunters and handed it to the father.

He said, "If you'll promise me something, you can consider this your lucky day, because I don't have time to write you up right now and you're both in clear violation. Tonight, if you haven't seen me come back down the mountain, call nine-one-one. Tell the dispatcher we met and which road we're on. Let her take it from there."

The father asked, "That's it? Just that we met you?"

"Yup."

Joe said, "Get your vehicle out of the road and take it back into your designated hunting area and make that call tonight, and for now I'll look the other way."

After thanking him profusely and reversing the ATV into the brush so Joe could get by, the driver looked at the card and said, "So you're Joe Pickett?"

Joe nodded.

"I've always heard you wouldn't give a guy a break."

"Like I said, it's your lucky day."

---

AS HE LEFT THEM, he glanced into his rearview mirror to see them talking excitedly to each other and gesturing toward where the elk had run. He had an inkling that once he was gone they'd ignore him and go after the elk and probably get stuck somewhere in pursuit.

He shook his head, vowed to look out for them and give them a ticket if he ran into them again, and ground up the road until they were out of view.

He hated not doing his job properly, even given the circumstances. But if they made the call to dispatch as they'd agreed, at least someone would know where he was last seen.

And he thought about something Nate had said.

*Recruit local tribesmen.*

ALTHOUGH he'd been to the top of this road only once many years ago, he thought he remembered where he could find the old miner's cabin. What he didn't know was what was up there that might spook a dedicated elk hunter off the mountain hours before the tracking snow had arrived.

# 32

"GOD, THE MOUNTAINS are beautiful," Haley said as Nate drove the white Tahoe toward the Bighorns, which were lit up with a full blast of morning sun that contrasted the fresh snow on the meadows and peaks against miles of dark timber. She said it as she reloaded the magazine, one by one, with 6.8-millimeter cartridges for the Mini-14.

Nate grunted. He noted that now that the mask was off, she showed a confident proficiency with weapons that she'd kept under wraps before.

"So this is where you live?" she asked, meaning the general area.

"Most of the time," Nate said. "When I'm not living in a cave."

"Do you realize how pathetic that just sounded?" she asked with a shy smile.

"Yes."

"Maybe after this you won't have to run anymore."

Nate let that hang for a moment, then turned toward her. "There's a difference between running and dropping out."

"Sorry."

———

HE WASN'T SURE how he wanted to play it, but the more he thought it through and ran different scenarios through his mind, he kept coming back to his original inclination. It had worked with the two operatives on the mountain in Colorado, on the highway outside of Jackson, and countless times over the years on special operations.

Nate said, "We're going to go right at him."

"Pardon?" she said.

"There are lots of ways to do this," he said. "We could find a position and observe him—make sure he's there and try to figure out how many guys he has with him, then make a plan. Strike at night, flank him, that sort of thing."

She nodded.

"For all we know, though," he said, "Nemecek has set up his usual electronic perimeter. He's likely got sensors, cameras, and motion detectors at all the key points around his camp. He'll know if someone is moving in on him, and he's a master at dealing with those kinds of situations. Hell, he taught *me*. And in the worst-case scenario, he just drives away and we never get a crack at him. In that case, this could go on forever."

Haley shook her head. "I can't imagine trying to live a normal life and knowing he's out there," she said.

"Welcome to my world," Nate said.

"So how are you going to confront him?" she asked. "We don't know how many we're up against or who they are."

"We have an advantage, though," Nate said. "We know how he thinks. He *trained* us. We know that anybody we encounter could be one of his. The only man in this valley I can absolutely trust just flew away on an airplane. Everyone else is a potential threat."

The gravity of what he said seemed to make her withdraw from him as she considered the possibilities.

"But the longer we wait and plan, the longer he has to devise a countermove," Nate said. "I'm thinking right now he's confused. He doesn't know we're out here and he doesn't know what exactly happened to the two operatives in Idaho. He thinks they're coming to meet up with him—that's what I made that guy back there tell him—but he's been out of cell or radio contact with them since then. No doubt Nemecek is waiting to hear from them when they arrive, and he's probably trying to raise them over the phone."

"Will he be suspicious?" Haley asked.

"He's always suspicious," Nate said. "He's probably even figured I got the upper hand on his boys somehow. But what he can't know is that you're with me. So when he sees you, he'll be confused, at least momentarily."

"I see," Haley said. "I'm bait."

Nate smiled a cruel smile. "You can still get out," he said. "It isn't too late."

"No, that's not what I meant," she said. "I just want to know what you're thinking, so I can do my job right."

He thought that over for a moment, then methodically laid out his plan of attack.


YARAK meant a condition of being hyperalert, he told her.

"Engage all your senses and push them out to their limits," he said. "Don't think—*react*. Don't consider consequences or collateral damage. If you see me go down, don't hesitate. If you hesitate, you're dead."

She shook her head, obviously doubting her ability to do it.

Then she asked, "And if I go down first?"

"I'll miss the hell out of you," Nate said. "But that's after I've blown Nemecek's head off."

"God, you can be so romantic," she said.

"Shut up, Haley," he said sharply, shocking her. "*Concentrate.* Remember what I just told you about being hyperalert until this is over."

"Why are you yelling at me?"

He gritted his teeth, and said, "I'm trying to keep you alive. I'm trying to show you, but I don't think you're listening. For example, what do you know about our situation right now that is different than a few minutes ago?"

She started to say something flippant by her gesture, but stopped herself. Instead, she looked around the Tahoe and out through all the windows at the lodgepole pines that zipped by on both sides.

"What?" she asked. "We're in a forest?"

"No," he said. "We're being followed."

# 33

JOE CLEARED the tree line of the summit in his pickup to find a barren field of blinding white punctuated by sharp blades of volcanic black scree. The sharp shards pierced upward through the thick scrim of snow, which was untracked and polished to a high-gloss sheen by wind and high-altitude sun. As he emerged from the trees, his radio came to life with a screech of static, and he checked his phone to find two messages: Chuck Coon and Sheriff Kyle McLanahan. Each had called within the past twenty minutes.

He slowed for a moment and reached for the mic, but as he did so he could feel the tires begin to sink into the snow. Since he couldn't tell how deep it was and couldn't risk getting stuck on top fully exposed, he grabbed the wheel again and goosed the accelerator. The snow was deeper than he would have guessed, but he knew if he maintained his forward momentum across the top of it he had a chance of getting across it to a windswept bank of gravel on the horizon of the mountain. If he made it to the other side, he could return the calls and call in his position.

Although he couldn't see clearly through the snow-covered windshield, he searched ahead for knobs of rock to steer toward so his tires could grab them and propel him forward. He saw a rock and cranked the wheel toward it, but the back end swung around again and his progress stopped cold. He cursed as the pickup settled in, sinking a few more inches, snow crunching and the exhaust pipe suddenly burbling as it descended into the snow, and he knew he was stuck fast almost exactly in the center of the snowfield.

JOE SAT BACK and gritted his teeth. Just a few more feet and he might have been able to gain purchase and maintain momentum enough to get to the gravel. But there was no point now but to reassess. It would take hours of digging to try and find the solid rock bottom of the snowfield. And even if he did, the only way he could safely get out was to reverse in his own tracks and end up back where he came from. He knew from being stuck many times and helping others that he needed a winch-truck to get the pickup out.

He cursed and slammed the top of the wheel with the heel of his hand. Wind buffeted the driver's-side window. Out ahead of him, on the snowfield, small waves of gritty snow moved along the surface like sidewinder snakes.

The view was magnificent. As far as he could see ahead were the snowcapped ridges of wave upon wave of mountains. Stringy cirrus clouds unfurled like battered flags through the brilliant blue sky. There wasn't an airplane or a power pole or a cell tower to be seen anywhere.

He felt incredibly lonely and frustrated, and when he caught a sharp whiff of carbon monoxide through his heating vents he reached down and killed the motor. The exhaust pipe was now buried deep in the snow and leaking back through the undercarriage. If he kept the pickup running, he risked asphyxiation.

Joe briefly closed his eyes and calmed himself, then checked his phone. He had a weak signal.

He called Chuck Coon first, and the agent came on after the second ring.

"We found her, this Maryland student," Coon said. "Woke her up at her little off-campus apartment. After I swung by your daughter's dormitory and woke her up. She's fine, Joe."

Joe felt a wave of relief. "Thank God."

"But we have a problem," Coon said, and Joe could hear the anger in his voice. "Or I should say *you* have a problem. In fact, a couple of them."

"Yes?"

"This Maryland girl checks out, Joe. Her name is Jennifer Wellington—a blue-blood name if I ever heard one—and from what we can tell, she's exactly who she says she is: an out-of-state student. Her record shows a straight line from high school to college. No gaps. No military service. Her parents check out, and right now they're very angry with the FBI, and her old man threatened legal action unless we cut her loose, which we did."

Joe said, "You let her go?"

"No reason to keep her, Joe. That's what I'm telling you. She was upset and blubbering, and she had no idea why we were there. This whole trip over the mountain was a snafu of the highest order, thanks to you."

"You're sure?" Joe asked, feeling his stomach clench. "You're absolutely positive she's clean and her identity is solid?"

"As absolutely sure as I've ever been in my life," Coon said, his voice rising. "You've wasted my time and used up your last favor."

Joe sat back and looked at the phone in his hand. He was relieved his suspicions were incorrect and Sheridan was safe but disconcerted about how he'd been so wrong and so paranoid.

"Oh," Coon said, "your daughter isn't real happy with you right now, either. In fact, I'd call her, um, *hopping mad.*"

Joe could hear someone, another agent in Coon's vehicle, laughing at that.

"Man, I'm sorry," Joe said. "But it means there is someone still out there. Another female operator."

"At this point," Coon sighed, "it means this conversation is over."

"Hold it," Joe said, sitting forward again. "Did McLanahan request assistance from you? Is your team on the way?"

"Just a second," Coon said, and Joe could envision Agent Coon covering the speaker while he asked somebody. When he came back, he said, "No word from your sheriff. Nothing. Nada."

Joe let the words sink in.

"Where are you right now?" Coon asked. "The reception is terrible."

Joe slumped to the side. It was getting colder inside the cab, and he could feel a tiny tongue of icy wind lick his earlobe from a gap in the doorframe.

"I'm stuck on top of a mountain with no backup and no plan," Joe said sullenly. "And in the valley below is John Nemecek."

# 34

NATE HAD CAUGHT two quick glimpses of a vehicle coming up the mountain behind them in his side mirrors. Each look was fleeting: a dark pickup rounding a switchback turn maybe a mile away, a glint of reflected sunlight on glass and chrome. But he'd seen enough to know the pursuing vehicle wasn't just driving up the mountain—but *flying*.

"Who is it?" Haley asked, placing her hand on the rifle next to her on the seat.

"Don't know."

"Could it be just a local? A hunter or something like that?"

"Maybe," Nate said, increasing the speed of the Tahoe. "But he's in a hell of a hurry."

"Do you think local law enforcement? Maybe that car dealer called on us?"

"I said I don't know," Nate said.

He made a switchback turn to the right that leaned into a quarter-mile straightaway climb. He roared up the stretch, noting that Haley was instinctively bracing herself by clutching the handhold above her shoulder in a white-knuckle grip. He appreciated that she wasn't a backseat driver.

There was another switchback turn to the left, and he slowed to take it. He hoped he'd put a few more seconds of distance between them and the oncoming vehicle. He'd need them. There were a few old roads leading off the asphalt, but they were few and far between on the climb up the mountain. The campgrounds and logging roads didn't appear until they crested the top.

Three-quarters of the way up the second straightaway, he said, "Is that an opening in the trees up ahead?"

"Looks like it, but I can't tell what it is."

"It'll have to be good enough," he said, slowing down.

As they passed it, he took its measure: it *had* been a road into the timber at one time, likely a Forest Service road, but a hundred feet in they'd used an earthmover to create a berm that would be impassable. It was one of the more annoying Forest Service tricks of the last few decades: blocking access roads to the public while purportedly serving the public. But it was good enough for what he was looking for.

"Hold on," he said, hitting the brakes.

When the Tahoe was stopped, he quickly reversed and backed into the opening and kept going until his rear bumper rested against the berm. Ahead of them was a narrow opening slot through the trees where they could see fifty feet of the road and the rock wall beyond it.

He turned to her and said urgently, "If he sees our tracks, he might stop and block us in, but I'm hoping he'll drive right by. Jump out with that rifle so you're clear to fire if necessary. If he makes any moves that seem hinky, don't overthink it. Just aim and fire."

"Pumpkin on a post," she said with a wink.

"Go," he said, and bailed out the driver's-side door.

He could hear the vehicle coming, tires sizzling through the slushy snow on the roadway. The vehicle was coming fast.

Nate looked through the Tahoe windows for Haley. She was leaning back on the SUV and raising the rifle. She had a calm and determined look on her face. That look made him want to run around the back of the Tahoe and kiss her.

Then he shook his head to clear it; thought, *Yarak*; and drew his heavy weapon from its shoulder holster.

The vehicle—a dark green pickup with an emblem on the door and a single occupant inside—flashed by the opening in the trees without slowing down. Nate listened as it sluiced up the mountain without slowing. The driver hadn't so much as looked their way. His profile indicated he was leaning over the steering wheel, watching the road in front of him without a sideways glance, and very determined to get to where he was going.

"Whew," Haley said, uncoiling. "False alarm, I guess."

Nate squinted, a sour look on his face.

"What?" she said. "Did you know him?"

He shook his head. "I thought for a second it was my friend Joe, that he'd decided to stay. That would be like him: dumb and loyal. But it wasn't him."

"So who was it?"

Nate shrugged. "Game and Fish pickup, driver wearing a red uniform. But it wasn't Joe. He's the only game warden in this district, so I have no idea who it was."

"I'm confused," she said, climbing back into the Tahoe.

"You're not the only one," Nate said.

"Are you disappointed your friend didn't stay to help you?" she asked.

"Of course not," he snapped.

# 35

JOE'S HAND was trembling when he returned McLanahan's call. Even before the sheriff answered, he wished he could reach through his phone and throttle him.

"Yeah?" McLanahan answered.

Joe took a deep breath and tried to keep his anger in check. "Sheriff," Joe said, *"I just talked to the FBI. They said you haven't called for their help."*

There was a beat of silence, then: "Dang it, that plumb slipped my mind."

"How could it slip your mind? Tell me how it could slip your mind? Tell me how that could happen?"

"Whoa, there," McLanahan said, annoyed. "Change your tone or I'm hanging up. I'm up to my ass in alligators right now and I don't have time for your attitude."

Joe closed his eyes.

"You heard the bad news, right?" McLanahan asked.

"No."

"Oh."

"What happened, sheriff?" Joe finally asked.

"We had an incident this morning."

Joe's left hand was balled up into a fist, and his nails were cutting into the palm of his hand just to keep from shouting.

"And what would that be?" Joe asked.

"I sent Mike Reed and Deputy Sollis over to roust your trainee, just like you asked. But the son-of-a-bitch came out *shooting*. Sollis was killed in the line of duty, and Reed's in critical condition in the hospital. Doctors say it's touch-and-go at this point."

*"What?"*

"This Luke Brueggemann character—your trainee—got away. We issued an APB for him, and as soon as I get you off the phone I'm calling the Feds for help."

"I told you to send a SWAT team," Joe said, struck dumb by the turn of events. Mike Reed in critical condition?

"I don't like being told what to do, pardner," McLanahan said.

"Is Mike going to make it?"

"Shot in the neck and the shoulder, from what we know. Might have paralyzed him. But those doctors, they can do all kinds of miracles these days."

"You are such an idiot," Joe said. "You sent those men to their death." Thinking: *He sent his opponent.*

"Whoa, there, buckaroo. There's no call for that kind of talk."

"I asked you to do *three things*," Joe said, shouting into the phone, "*Three things*. You agreed. And you couldn't even do the first thing right."

"This call is over," McLanahan said, feigning outrage, but it came across to Joe like naked fear.

"When I get down from here, you and I are going to have it out."

McLanahan didn't respond.

"Where was he last seen?" Joe shouted.

"Who?"

"Luke Brueggemann, you idiot!"

"Headed west in his pickup," McLanahan said.

"Toward the mountains?" Joe asked, looking up through the windshield, remembering where he was again.

"Your guess is as good as mine," McLanahan said. "But he should be easy to find in that Guts and Feathers rig you boys drive." And with that he terminated the call.

JOE HAD to throw his shoulder against the driver's-side door to open it against the snow. It took four tries before there was enough space for him to crawl out. Strong icy wind blew into the vacant cab.

In the equipment box in the bed of his pickup, he pulled out his cold-weather gear. It didn't seem like it'd been that long since he'd packed it, he thought. He sat on the bed wall and kicked off his cowboy boots and pulled on thermal knee-high Bogs. His hooded Carhartt parka cut the chilling wind, and he was grateful he'd left a pair of gloves in the pockets.

He filled a daypack with binoculars, his spotting scope, the handheld radio, a GPS unit, digital camera, Maglite, coiled rope, a hunting knife, and boxes of ammunition. It was heavy when he cinched it down on his back and climbed down into the snow.

He checked the cartridges in his scoped .270 Winchester and slung it over his shoulder, and loaded his twelve-gauge with five three-inch shells: two magnum slugs on each end and three double-ought magnum buckshots in between. A handful of extra twelve-gauge shells went into his right coat pocket along with a crumpled bandanna to keep them from rattling when he walked.

It was tough getting the door shut because snow had drifted in, but when he heard the click he turned and started trudging for the gravel bank.

JOE WAS breathing hard by the time he reached it, and he wiped melted snow and perspiration from his face with his sleeve. The gravel bank was on the edge of the summit, and from where he stood he could look down into the steep timbered valley below. The pitch was such that he couldn't quite see the valley floor or any of the camps established along the branch of the river.

Before picking his way through the loose scree on the other side of the mountain toward the timber below, he looked up and caught a tiny series of sun glints twenty-five miles in the distance. Saddlestring, he thought, where Sheriff Kyle McLanahan preened and made incompetent decisions and poor Mike Reed fought for his life.

THE OLD miner's cabin had been built into the mountain slope itself on a spit of level ground twenty yards from the start of the timber. Whoever built it had burrowed back into the rocky ground to hollow out a single room and had fashioned eaves and a corrugated tin roof, now discolored, that extended out of the mountainside. It looked out on the valley floor and Joe caught a glimpse of a bend of the river far below as he approached the cabin from above. He could see why Richie had chosen the shelter of the cabin to look for elk. It was protected from the wind that howled over the summit and afforded unimpeded views of several meadows where wildlife likely would graze.

As he approached the cabin from the back, Joe thumbed the safety off his shotgun and tucked the stock under his arm. He tried to stay quiet and not dislodge small rocks from the scree that might tumble downhill, clicking along with the sound of pool balls striking one another.

When he was close enough to see the entire side of the small structure, he dropped to his haunches and simply listened. There was no sign of life from the old log shelter, and two of the four small panes of glass from the side window were broken out. In the rocks near the closed front door were dozens of filtered cigarette butts. Richie, Joe thought, must be a smoker. But what had he seen from this perch that spooked him off the mountain?

"Hello!" Joe shouted. "Anybody home?"

Silence from the cabin. But below in the trees, squirrels chattered to one another in their unique form of telegraph-pole gossip. They'd soon all know he was there, he thought.

He called out again, louder. If someone was inside, perhaps he'd see an eye looking out from one of the broken panes. But there was no movement.

For the first time, he noted a rough trail that emerged from the line of timber to the front door of the cabin. The trail was scarred on top, meaning it had been used recently. Maybe Richie had seen someone coming up on it? But why would that scare him?

Joe stood and slipped along the side wall of the cabin until he was underneath the window. He pressed his ear against a rough log and closed his eyes, trying to detect sounds of any movement inside. It was still.

He popped up quickly to the window and then dropped back down. No reaction, and all he'd seen inside was a shaft of light from a hole in the roof cutting through the gloom, illuminating what looked like three stout black logs on the packed-dirt floor.

Stout black logs?

THE HEAVY front door wasn't bolted, and it moaned as it swung inward on old leather hinges. Joe stood to the side, shotgun ready, waiting for his eyes to adjust to the darkness. Nothing moved in re-action to the wide-open door.

He stepped inside. It was still and musty, but he caught a whiff of a sour metallic smell. The odor seemed to hang just above the floor.

The logs weren't logs at all but three dark green plastic bundles placed next to one another on the floor. Joe stepped closer and prod-ded the nearest one with the toe of his boot. There was something heavy inside, but there was a little give, like poking a sausage casing. A chill rolled down his back.

He bent over to look closely at a line of beige-colored print on the plastic. It read HUMAN REMAINS POUCH in military stencil font.

"Oh, no," he whispered, as he dug the flashlight out of his daypack and snapped it on.

He stood quickly and took a deep breath of fresh cold air before bending back down to unzip the first body bag. Now he knew why Richie had run off. But he'd neglected to report what he'd found, the coward.

A middle-aged woman, her skin waxy, eyes open and dull, hair matted to the side. And a dark deep cut across her throat.

Joe felt his insides gurgle as he unzipped the second bag to find a familiar dark round fleshy face looking out. The body also had a deep slash around its neck, only partially hidden by a fold of fat.

The third body Joe didn't recognize. It had been a young man with sharp cheekbones and a thin, long nose. Short spiky hair. Same wound.

Joe thought, *The real Luke Brueggemann.*


AFTER HEAVING what little was in his stomach into the scree, Joe fished the radio out. No signal.

He tried his cell phone. Reception was faint; one bar lapsed into roaming and back again. He climbed back up the mountain to where the signal was stronger. He called Sheriff McLanahan.

"What now?" McLanahan asked, obviously agitated. "Is all forgiven?"

Joe ignored the question. He was shaking as he said, "I found the bodies of Pam Kelly, Bad Bob Whiteplume, and an unknown male. All murdered and stashed in an old cabin overlooking the South Fork. Here, I'll give you the coordinates. . . ."

After telling McLanahan the name of the suspect and his possible location in Camp Five, Joe said, "I don't know how many bad guys are down there, but I do know they're armed and dangerous."

Then, shouting into the phone: "Listen to me this time, Sheriff. Make that call to the FBI and tell them to send everybody they can up here. *Now.* And gather what's left of your department and gear them up and storm Camp Five. I'll try to get into position so I can be a spotter. Stay off the radio, and keep your phone on."

The phone popped hard with static, and when it quieted back down Joe no longer had the connection. He wasn't sure how much the sheriff had heard or understood.

He could only hope that enough got through that the vise was finally beginning to close on John Nemecek.

# 36

HALEY DROVE THE TAHOE through the thick lodgepole pine trees on South Fork Trail, and Nate craned forward in the passenger seat, looking ahead. The river, no more than cold crooked fingers of water probing around boulders, was on their left. He caught glimpses of it through the timber.

"There are tracks on the road ahead of us," Nate said, "but nothing fresh from this morning."

Haley didn't respond. Her face was grim and her mouth set. She obviously didn't understand the significance of his comment.

"That means that Game and Fish truck went somewhere else," Nate said. "So maybe we can forget about it."

"Okay," she said.

She looked small behind the wheel, he thought. But determined.

Nate looked over as they passed by an outfitter camp tucked up into the trees on a shelf on their right. The camp had a large framed canvas tent, but there were no vehicles around and the door of the tent was tied up. A headless elk carcass hung from a cross-pole behind the tent.

"That's the fourth camp," she said.

Nate nodded and ducked down on the seat. Anyone observing the vehicle would see only the driver.

"Talk to me," he said calmly. "Tell me what you see as you see it."

In a moment, she said, "The trees are opening. I think we're getting close to Camp Five."

OVER THE LAST half hour, Joe had worked his way down the mountain carefully, avoiding loose rock and downed branches, and he'd set up behind a granite outcropping laced through the seams with army-green lichen. From the outcrop he could clearly see the layout of Camp Five two hundred feet below.

There were two hard-side trailers parked nose-to-tail in a flat on the other side of the river. The camp was remarkably clean: no debris, coolers, folding chairs, or other usual elk camp indicators. The fire pit, a ring of colorful round river rocks, looked cold and unused. There were no skinned elk or deer carcasses hanging from a cross-pole in clear view of the trailers.

There were two vehicles he could see parked on the other side of the trailers: a late-model white Tahoe with green-and-white Colorado plates behind the second trailer and a dark SUV crossover parked on the side of the first. The second trailer, Joe thought, was a curiosity. Antennae and small satellite dishes bristled from the roof. Then he noticed something blocky covered with a blue tarp on the front of that trailer; no doubt an electric generator. The generator operated so quietly he could barely hear it hum.

The second trailer was obviously the communications center.

He was grateful his handheld radio hadn't worked earlier. No doubt, they were monitoring air traffic. He hoped McLanahan listened this time and stayed off the police bands.

A few feet from the tongue of the first trailer, Joe noted, were two five-foot pole-mounted platforms. On the top of each platform was a hooded falcon: a peregrine and a prairie.

Joe was pretty sure he'd found Nemecek.

He'd set up his spotting scope on the tripod and trained it on the white sheet-metal door of the first trailer. His shotgun was braced against the rock on his right, and next to it was his .270 Winchester.

The rock had sharp edges, and it was difficult to find a comfortable position to lie in wait. He shifted his weight from the left to the right and propped up on his daypack to see. When he heard the tick of a loose rock strike another, he assumed he'd rustled it loose with the toe of his boot.

Then he sensed a presence behind him, and before he could roll over he felt a cold nose of steel press into the flesh behind his right ear. He jumped with alarm and a palm pressed square into the middle of his back, keeping him prone.

"Put your arms out ahead of you, Joe, hands up. Don't even think about reaching for your gun." It was the voice of his trainee.

Joe did as told without saying a word, and felt his trainee pluck the Glock from his holster. His pepper spray was removed next. Then he heard the clatter of his shotgun and rifle as they were kicked off the outcropping into the brush below.

"Now slowly pull your arms down and place them behind your back."

Joe said, "You don't have to do this."

"Just cooperate, Joe. You seem like a nice guy, and I don't want to have to hurt you, but I guess you've figured some things out on your own."

"Surprising, huh?" Joe said.

"Your hands," his trainee said firmly.

Joe felt the handcuffs encircle both wrists. He balled his hands into fists and bent them inward toward his spine while the cuffs were snapped into place and ratcheted snug. It was a trick he'd learned from a poacher he'd once arrested. Now, when he relaxed his fists and straightened his wrists, the cuffs weren't tight and didn't bite into his flesh.

"Okay, now stand up. And don't turn around or do any dumb shit."

"That's kind of a hard maneuver with my hands cuffed behind my back," Joe said.

"Try," his trainee said, stepping back.

Joe got his knees under him and rose clumsily. Despite what he'd been told, he turned a quarter of the way around. His trainee wore his red uniform shirt and held a .40 Glock in each hand—his and Joe's. Both were pointed at Joe's face.

"You're a disgrace to the uniform," Joe said.

"Stop talking."

"I found Luke Brueggemann," Joe said, noting a wince of confusion from his trainee in reaction.

"Up there," Joe said, chinning toward the top of the mountain. "In an old miner's cabin. You might have seen it on your way down."

"I saw the cabin. Right after I found your truck stuck in the snow."

"But you must not have looked inside," Joe said. "The real Luke Brueggemann's body is in it. Throat cut by a garrote. Same with Bad Bob and Pam Kelly. All of them dead, but I guess you know that."

"I don't know anything about that," his trainee said.

"You know," Joe said, "I'm getting pretty hacked off the way you people operate. This is a good place, and you've turned it upside down."

His trainee simply shook his head, unbelieving.

"Did you kill them?" Joe asked. "Like you did Deputy Sollis this morning? Mike Reed might not make it, either, and you know he's a friend of mine."

"That was self-defense! That big one didn't identify himself—he smashed through the door of my room."

Joe didn't know enough about the incident to argue. But knowing Sollis, he sensed a grain of truth in the explanation.

"You're leaving bodies all over this county," Joe said. "You need to stop. You've lost sight of your mission."

"This is bullshit. There are no bodies. You're just trying to get the drop on me."

"I'm not that clever," Joe said. And his trainee seemed to take that into consideration.

"So what's your real name?" Joe asked.

"Hinkle," he said. "Lieutenant Dan Hinkle when I was still in."

The fact that he gave up his real name so easily, Joe thought, meant Hinkle had no intention of cutting him loose.

"Well, Lieutenant Dan Hinkle," Joe said, "your boss is a killer. He's gone rogue. And he's taken a lot of you good men along with him and he's murdered innocent people all over my county and terrorized my wife and family. Is that really what you signed up for?"

Hinkle's confusion hardened into a kind of desperate anger. "Shut up, Joe. And turn around. We're gonna march down there and see what my boss wants to do with you."

"I'm not done," Joe said. "The cavalry is coming. They're on their way as we speak."

"I said shut up with your lies."

"I don't lie," Joe said. "You know that."

"Turn around," Hinkle barked.

And Joe did. But not simply because he'd been ordered. He wanted to see what was happening in the camp below, because he'd heard the sound of a vehicle coming, headed straight for Camp Five.

———

HALEY SAID to Nate on the seat beside her, "There are two trailers and two vehicles."

"Anybody outside?"

"No."

"Keep going," he said. "Drive up there with confidence like you were coming home after work. Like you just can't wait to tell your boss some good news he'll want to hear."

He felt her reach down and touch his neck as if for reassurance.

"How far are they?"

"I don't know," she said. "Maybe five hundred feet?"

"You're doing great," he said.

"Oh, Jesus," she said after a beat. "Someone's coming outside."

"Which trailer?"

"The second one. Now two men. Nate, one of them has a long rifle or a shotgun. They're standing there looking our way."

"Is he aiming the weapon?"

"Sorta."

*"Is he aiming it at you or not?"*

"He's kind of holding it at port arms," she said, an edge of panic in her voice.

"Good," Nate said. "Keep going. Don't flinch. They recognize the vehicle. They think we're on their team."

"Oh my God," she said, her voice tight. "There's John Nemecek. He just came out of the first trailer."

"Keep going," Nate said. "Smile at them if you can."

JOE AND DAN HINKLE were twenty yards from the bank of the river. There was so little current this high up in the mountains it barely made a sound, just a muffled gurgle as it muscled around exposed river rocks.

The muzzles of both guns were pressed into him, one at the base of his skull and the other in the small of his back. Joe felt dead inside and his feet seemed to propel him forward of their own accord. He thought, *There is no way they'll let me go.*

He thought about what he could do to get away. If he were in a movie, he'd spin and drop-kick the weapons away and head-butt Hinkle into submission. Or simply break and run, juking and jiving, while Hinkle fired and missed. But this was real and there were two guns pressed against him. He didn't know how to drop-kick. And Hinkle was trained and skillful and wouldn't miss.

Ahead of him, across the river, three men had emerged from the two trailers. All three were facing the oncoming white SUV and apparently hadn't seen Joe and Hinkle yet. One of them, tall and fit and commanding in looks and presence, looked like the person Marybeth had described meeting in the library. Nemecek stood ramrod-straight, hands on hips, his head bowed slightly forward as if he was peering ahead from beneath his brow. The other two men, both young and hard, one in all-black clothing and the other wearing a desert camo vest over a Henley shirt, flanked Nemecek. The man in all black carried a semiautomatic rifle.

The three stood expectant, waiting for the arrival of the white SUV.

"THEY'RE JUST standing there," Haley said to Nate. "Nemecek turned and said something to the man with the gun and he lowered it. I think Nemecek recognizes me."

"How close are they?"

"A hundred feet, maybe less."

"He's confused for a second," Nate said. "He wasn't expecting *you*."

"Now he's turning back around toward me, staring. *Nate . . .*" The fear in her voice was palpable.

Nate said, "Floor it."

THE SUV came fast, Joe thought. Too fast. But then the motor roared and the Tahoe rocked and accelerated and he heard Hinkle gasp behind him.

It happened in an instant. The man in black with the rifle shouted and leaped to the side, in Joe and Hinkle's direction. Nemecek jumped back the other way and flattened himself against the first trailer. But the man in the desert camo was caught in the middle and hit solid and tossed over the hood and roof of the Tahoe with a sickening thump.

Hinkle said, *"What the fuck just happened?"*

"GOT ONE!" Haley shouted, hitting the brakes before she crashed head-on into the front of the second trailer.

Before they'd completely stopped, Nate reached up for the passenger door handle and launched himself outside. He hit the turf hard on his injured shoulder, rolled, and staggered to his feet.

*Yarak.*

The man in black who'd dived away scrambled to his feet a few yards away, his face and hands muddy, the rifle in his grip. Nate shot him in the neck, practically decapitating the body before it hit the ground.

Nate wheeled on his heels, cocking the hammer back with his left thumb in the same movement, and finished off the injured operative in the grass.

Then he turned on Nemecek, who was still against his trailer but was reaching behind his back—likely for his .45 Colt semiauto. Nate could see the impression of body armor under Nemecek's sweater, but it didn't matter. The .500 exploded twice. The first shot shattered Nemecek's right shoulder and painted the trailer behind him with a crazy starburst of blood, and the second bullet hit Nemecek square in his upper-left thigh, annihilating the bones and dropping him like a bag of sand.

Nate caught a glimpse of Haley as she bailed out of the Tahoe with her rifle. He was proud of her, and his blood was up. He loped across the grass, found Nemecek's .45 in the tall grass, and tossed it away behind him. He reached down and grasped Nemecek's collar and pulled him away from the trailer so he was prevented from rolling under it, then dropped both of his knees on Nemecek's chest and shoved the muzzle of his revolver under his old commander's chin.

*"Before you die,"* Nate seethed, bending down so his eyes were six inches from Nemecek's, *"I need some answers."*

JOE HAD SEEN it all, and was stunned by the speed and violence of what had taken place in front of him. He stumbled and nearly lost his footing in the shallow river as Hinkle shoved him across, running now, but maintaining contact with the two weapons as they splashed across.

The woman who'd emerged from the Tahoe, the woman who'd run over the man in desert camo and scattered the others, stood with her back to them, cradling a carbine, looking at Nate hunched over Nemecek near the trailer. She was young but clearly capable, and she looked over her shoulder as Hinkle cleared one of the Glocks and aimed it over Joe's shoulder at her—the gun inches from Joe's ear—and shouted, "Hey!"

She hesitated when she saw the two red uniform shirts, didn't raise her rifle, and Hinkle's Glock snapped three concussive shots and she went down. Joe instantly lost hearing in his right ear, and it was replaced by a dull roar.

At the sound of the shout and the shots, Nate looked up from where he'd pinned Nemecek to the ground. His eyes darted to the woman on the ground and then up to Joe and Hinkle. Joe had never seen such a murderous look in any man's face in his life.

"Get off of him!" Hinkle shouted to Nate. "I've got your buddy here."

Nate didn't move. His expression was ferocious and fixed on Joe.

*No,* Joe thought. Not at him. But at Hinkle behind him, who peered out at Nate over Joe's right shoulder. Hinkle aimed the Glock at Nate down his extended right arm, which rested on Joe's shoulder. The other weapon was still in the small of Joe's back.

Joe found himself straining hard against the cuffs, as if trying to pull them apart. Because Hinkle hadn't closed them hard, there was some play. The cuff on his right hand had slipped free almost to mid-thumb, and the steel bit hard. But he didn't know how he could possibly shed one without breaking bones in his hand. The pain was searing.

Joe willed Nate to look at him, to look into his eyes. . . .


NATE SHIFTED his glare from the shooter holding Joe—the man who'd shot Haley—to Joe. His friend's face was white with pain. Had he been hit?

Then he saw Joe relax slightly. He was trying to get his attention and tell him something without speaking. There was blood on his right ear.

Joe deliberately looked down at the top of his boots. Then slowly back up again.

Nate understood. Joe was going *down*.


JOE SAW the look of recognition in Nate's face and suddenly buckled his knees. As he dived forward, he bent his head down and set his shoulders for the fall.

There were three nearly simultaneous explosions, and Joe hit the ground so hard he was able to use the force of his body weight to wrench his hands apart.

Behind him, Hinkle's body was thrown into the river from the impact of a .50 caliber round plowing through his chest and out his back. But his last reaction was to fire both pistols. The one aimed at Joe had hit somewhere in the mud. Nate was hit, and it rolled him off Nemecek.


JOE WRITHED in the grass and dirt. White spangles exploded in front of his eyes from pain. Although he'd been trying to free his right hand, it was his left that had somehow been wrenched through the steel claw of the cuffs from the fall, breaking bones along the way. The pain in his left hand was sharp and awful and made him gasp for air. His injured hand felt like a boiling needle-filled balloon on the end of his arm.

He wasn't sure if he blacked out for a moment, but when he opened his eyes he could see, at ground level, John Nemecek crawling through the grass, using his left hand and right leg. Nemecek's face was a mask of anger and pain.

Joe raised his head slightly. Nemecek was going for the semiautomatic rifle dropped by the man in all black before Nate killed him.

Behind Nemecek, Nate lay on his side, his eyes open. He looked conscious.

Joe grunted and rolled to his hands and knees. His left hand was white and strangely elongated. The slightest pressure on it hurt like nothing Joe could recall. He looked around for a weapon. Hinkle had dropped two somewhere.

But when he looked over his shoulder, Nemecek was a few feet away from the rifle.

With his good ear, Joe heard Nemecek say, "Five shots, Romanowski. I counted."

There was a dull black glint in the grass, and Joe closed his right hand around the grip of one of the Glocks. He rose up on his knees, swung around, and aimed it at Nemecek as he crawled.

Joe was a notoriously bad shot with a handgun. He qualified annually by the grace of God and a forgiving firearms instructor. He wished he had his shotgun, but he didn't, and he croaked, "Freeze where you are, Nemecek." His own voice sounded hollow and tinny to him.

Nemecek paused and looked up with contempt. His shoulder and leg were a bloody mess, and his face was pale and white. He was bleeding out and knew it. And Joe apparently didn't scare him.

Like a wounded animal, Nemecek grimaced and crawled toward the rifle. As he reached for it, Joe started firing. Every third or fourth shot, it seemed, hit home. The impact rolled Nemecek to the side and when he tried to scramble back to his knees, he'd go down again. Joe didn't stop squeezing the trigger until the slide kicked back and locked. Fourteen rounds. He'd emptied the magazine. Spent shells littered the ground near his knees.

As Joe lowered the Glock, he saw, to his terror and amazement, that Nemecek was crawling again toward the rifle.

Joe heard someone speak but couldn't make out the words. He looked over to see Nate standing, bracing himself against the trailer. He was shaky. His empty revolver hung down along his thigh. Joe could see blood on the side of Nate's coat.

"I said, *He's wearing a vest.*"

In response, Joe held up his empty handgun.

The two exchanged looks for a second. Neither, it seemed, was capable of stopping Nemecek before he grasped the rifle.

Then Joe remembered. He tossed the Glock aside and reached down into the front pocket of his Wranglers with his good hand. His fingers closed around the heavy .500 round Nate had left in his mailbox.

"Nate," Joe said, and tossed the cartridge through the air. Nate reached up and speared it.

Nemecek had made it to the rifle now, and was pulling it toward him with his left hand. He gripped it and swung the muzzle up.

Joe watched as Nate ejected a spent cartridge, fed the fresh one into the wheel, and slammed the cylinder home.

With a single movement and a sweep of Alisha's black hair, Nate swung the weapon up.

Although the concussion was probably loud, Joe only heard a muffled *pop.*

Nemecek's head snapped back, and the rifle fell away.

# 37

THE SNOW CAME unexpectedly, as it did in the mountains, but the pale blue behind the storm clouds indicated it wouldn't sock in, wouldn't last all day. Large, soft flakes filtered down through the sky, clumping like cotton in the high grass. The snow muted the chirping of the squirrels and threw a hush over the river valley and Camp Five, but Joe didn't know it. He could barely hear anything.

They sat near the cold fire pit. Nate had carried Haley's body over to be with them, as if to separate her from the other bodies that littered the campsite. Her head was on his lap, eyes closed, and Nate stroked her hair.

Joe held his left hand by the wrist with his right as if it were a foreign object. It was swelling and looked like he was wearing a heavy glove. He'd drifted in and out of shock and consciousness for the hour since it had ended.

Finally, Nate said, "You should have flown away."

Joe shrugged. He could not yet wrap his mind around what had happened in the camp. Every time he glanced over at one of the bodies—Hinkle, the two operatives, or Nemecek—he half expected them to come back from the dead and attack. Snow fell on Nemecek's face and turned pink beneath his head in the pool of black blood.

Nate stroked Haley's hair and said, "Everybody. *Everybody.*"

Joe didn't ask him to explain.

Nate looked up. "Except you."

"Dumb luck," Joe said.

"WHY DIDN'T you just kill him outright?" Joe asked after a few minutes. "It would have saved us a lot of trouble."

Nate continued to run his fingers through Haley's hair. He quit and gently touched her cheek with the back of his hand.

"I wanted some answers," Nate said. "Why he did what he did. I wanted to know if he was operating alone or for somebody else. I wanted to know if he felt any guilt, like I have."

"Did you expect him to confess?"

"I don't know what I expected. But now I'll never know. He'll be a complete enigma to me forever, just like he's always been."

JOE DIDN'T hear the sound of a motor but noted that Nate had. He looked at Nate expectantly.

"They're coming," Nate said.

"Helicopter or convoy?"

"Chopper," Nate said.

The snow had stopped, and the storm clouds had moved to the west. The sky was clear and blue, and the sun lit up the remaining snow that had gathered in the pine branches.

Joe said, "You're staying around for them?"

"Are you going to stop me if I go?"

Joe thought about it and shook his head.

Nate rubbed his eyes. He said, "I'm tired, Joe. And I'm hit. I can't just walk away into the mountains."

"You could take one of those vehicles," Joe said, nodding toward Nemecek's crossover and the two white SUVs. "I can't drive you out of here in my pickup because it's stuck on top of the mountain."

Nate smiled at that.

"So what are you going to do?" Joe asked.

Nate took a long intake of breath and expelled it with his eyes closed.

"You're in a lot of pain," Joe said, thinking of the shoulder wound in addition to the gunshot.

"Yes," Nate said. "She was something, wasn't she?"

Joe felt a lump in his throat when he said, "She was."

Nate gently moved her head from his lap and struggled to stand up.

"I think I'm going to take her home," Nate said. "She's got a dad who would probably like to see her one last time."

"Go, then," Joe said.

AS THEY loaded her body into the back of the white Tahoe they'd arrived in, Nate turned to Joe and put his hand on his shoulder.

"Joe . . ."

"Just go. Get out of the camp before they see you."

Nate gestured as if to say *One more thing.* Then he walked stiffly and slowly to each of the falcon platforms, untied their hoods and jesses, and released them to the sky.

He turned back to Joe. "It might be a while before I come back."

"Get to a doctor to get that gunshot fixed up."

Nate waved the advice away. He said, "It's been a wild ride."

Joe heard the helicopter now. He said, "Better get out of here."

# AFTERWORD

THREE DAYS LATER, Joe Pickett stood in the lobby of the Twelve Sleep County Municipal Airport, waiting for the passengers of the incoming flight to disembark. In his breast pocket were his ID and boarding pass; Saddlestring to Denver, Denver to LAX, departing at 11:14 a.m.

The surly gate agent had not been as surly this time. Apparently she, like everyone else in the county and the state, had heard and read about what had happened at Camp Five on the South Fork. When she checked him in, she said, "I'll bet you can't wait to get out of this place right now."

He'd grunted a non-response response.

"Going to meet up with your wife and kids?"

"Yup. The hotel is booked for three more days."

"That doesn't give you much time at Disneyland."

"Fine with me."

"What happened to your hand?" she asked, nodding at the thick white club of a cast on the end of his right arm. The tips of his fingers and thumb poked out, but all the joints were encased and his hand was useless.

"Broke it," he said.

"Security is going to want a close look at that," she warned.

Joe sighed.

THE INTERVIEWS, affidavits, and debriefings had begun before he had even been released from the hospital. Marybeth had said she was coming back with the girls, but Joe told her to stay until he got there because there wasn't anything she could do.

FBI Special Agent Chuck Coon was leading the inquiry, assisted by County Attorney Dulcie Schalk. Joe told his version of the events and the firefight at least four times. He left out nothing. Coon winced when Joe said he'd watched Nate Romanowski drive away, but there was no hint at charges to be filed against Joe.

Speculation was rampant concerning the motivations of John Nemecek and his team. Forensics tied Nemecek to the murders of Pam Kelly, Bad Bob Whiteplume, and Luke Brueggemann. Law enforcement in Colorado and Idaho were in contact with Coon to try and fill in the whole story and clear up the multiple homicides in both states. The Teton County Sheriff's Department had a liaison on site, and he reported that the tortured man in the hospital refused to talk.

Even Agent Coon was wondering about the reason for the arrival of a three-man team being sent out from the Department of Defense in Washington.

As per Wyoming Game and Fish Department procedure, Joe had been placed on paid administrative leave because he'd discharged his firearm during the course of his duty. Another problem was his pickup, which was still stuck on top of the mountain. So far, two winch-trucks had failed to make it to the top to pull it out. Joe hoped he'd see it before the heavy winter snows buried it until spring.

Joe welcomed the respite, although in the back of his mind he hated the fact that no one was patrolling his district during the height of hunting season. The agency had been roiled by the death of one of its most promising trainees.

THE SHERIFF'S election was two days away. Mike Reed had been upgraded from critical condition but was still in the hospital. Joe had seen him while they were both there, but Reed wasn't conscious. A nurse at the duty station said Reed would likely live, but whether he would walk again was uncertain. It all depended, she said, on future surgery that may or may not repair what she called an "incomplete spinal injury" due to damages caused by a bullet to the neck.

Joe couldn't guess what the voters would decide. McLanahan was spinning the events at the South Fork as solving the crimes once and for all, and he modestly took credit for the raid and the outcome. An interview given to the Saddlestring *Roundup* by Agent Coon indicated otherwise. The stories ran side by side in the newspaper—the only edition between weekly publication and the election. The official investigation and report by County Attorney Dulcie Schalk would not be completed for weeks.

Voters were being asked either to reelect Sheriff Kyle McLanahan, hero of South Fork, or a possibly paraplegic challenger who couldn't yet speak for himself.

But he'd cast an absentee ballot for Mike Reed.

HE'D HEARD nothing from Nate, and hadn't expected he would.

A DOZEN PEOPLE emerged from the twin-prop and made their way down the aluminum staircase. Joe recognized most of them, but one in particular made his jaw drop. A dangling thread in the case would now be tied up.

Alice Thunder was in no hurry to enter the airport. She paused on the tarmac walkway and let the other passengers go around her. Joe watched as she closed her eyes, breathed in and out deeply several times, and nodded.

He met her at the door.

"You're okay," he said, relieved.

"Of course I'm okay," she said, slightly offended. Then: "It's nice to breathe clean mountain air again. I've had my fill of Texas and humidity for a while. I didn't realize how much I'd miss it."

She stopped when she realized he wanted to say more, and then looked at him with her unique stoic lack of expression.

He said, "Do you have any idea what's happened here since you left?"

"No."

Joe filled her in. She listened quietly, and her only reaction was to shake her head when she heard about Bad Bob.

"Nobody knew where you were," Joe said.

"Nate did," she said. "I told him I wanted to go see the bats. I saw them every night except one." Then: "Why are you smiling?"

"Because you're okay," Joe said.

"Of course I am."


HE HELPED HER pull her big duffel bag off the single clattering luggage carousel.

"I can take it from here," she said. "You better go get on that plane."

He nodded and turned. The other passengers were lining up at security, and the TSA agents, who outnumbered them, were shooting their cuffs so they could pull on blue latex gloves.

"Joe," she called out.

He turned.

"What about Nate?" she asked.

Joe said, "I'm not sure."

"He'll be back," she said simply. "This is his place."

"We'll see," Joe said. "He's got a lot to sort out." He thought, *And a lot to answer for.*

She nodded. He couldn't tell if she agreed with him or was simply ending the conversation.

"Go see your family," she said, and headed for the outside doors.

Joe took off his boots, removed his belt, wristwatch, jacket, and hat, fished out his phone and a ballpoint pen, and emptied his pockets of loose change and a Leatherman tool with a knife blade accessory that would soon be confiscated by one of the TSA agents.

The line moved slowly. A sixty-seven-year-old retired high school teacher had been flagged for a pat-down and asked to step aside. Already, a ruddy-faced TSA agent was eyeing his cast.

A female TSA agent with tight white curls and steel-rimmed glasses rooted through his carry-on and handed two bottles of pain pills prescribed for his recovery to a supervisor to inspect.

She reached into his bag and pulled out a hardcover book. She looked at the cover and scrunched up her face.

"What's this?"

*"The Looming Tower,"* Joe said.

"What's it about?" she asked Joe.

"This," he said.

She glared back at him, puzzled, as if trying to make up her mind whether to be angry at him.

# ACKNOWLEDGMENTS

The author would like to acknowledge several works referenced in writing this book, including *Falconry and Hawking* by Phillip Glasier, the *9/11 Commission Report*, and especially *The Looming Tower* by Lawrence Wright.

Thanks as well to Judge Jeff Donnell, the Martin and Mason Hotel in Deadwood, South Dakota, Don Hajicek, Jennifer Fonnesbeck, Laurie Box, and Molly Box.

Kudos to the wonderful team of professionals at Putnam, including Ivan Held, Kate Stark, Michael Barson, and the legendary Neil Nyren.

And of course Ann Rittenberg, the greatest.